THE TRADE-OFF

"Call me Jaimie," he said, his hand resting on Helena's shoulder. "I want to teach you about the business. I want you to learn to recognize the users and the con artists, and I want you to learn to protect yourself against them."

"Jaimie," Helena answered, beginning to feel very nervous and uncomfortable. "I think it's wonderful that you believe in me and want to help me. But you'll have to spell things out for me. What exactly do you want from me in return?"

Instead of answering, he pulled her to him and covered her mouth with his, kissing her passionately. The effect was electric, but Helena pushed him away in shock.

"Helena," he said, his hand caressing her shoulder. "I want your head, your heart, and your body."

Humiliated, she mustered all the panache she could. "Well, Mr. Cramer, you can have my head, and my heart, but as for my body, I'll keep that for myself. I'm sorry," she added, "I have to go. I've had about all the instruction I can handle for one day. And," she said, trying to control her anger, "I don't believe in mixing business with my personal life. I think a person should get a job based on her own merit, not because of her talents in bed!"

Satin Smiles, Silken Lies

Kae McCullough

PINNACLE BOOKS
WINDSOR PUBLISHING CORP.

PINNACLE BOOKS

are published by

Windsor Publishing Corp.
475 Park Avenue South
New York, NY 10016

First printing: January, 1989

Printed in the United States of America

To Richard K. Rosenberg, the supportive force from beginning to end, always positive . . . always encouraging . . . and always there for me. . . .

Special thanks to Sherry Robb, my agent, for her hard work and many efforts on my behalf; to Lydia E. Paglio, my editor, for her support beyond the call of duty from beginning to end; and finally to the runway models of Los Angeles, whose lives and dreams encompass much, much more than this small slice of their lives.

Prologue

The International Ballroom at the Beverly Hilton Hotel was already filled to overflowing as no one wanted to miss this night of viewing the latest designer fashions. Outside the huge carved double doors, the paparazzi paced, ready to snap a glimpse of anyone who looked vaguely important. And inside the mammoth ballroom, with soft lighting illuminating the sumptuous beige moiré, padded walls and gilt ceiling, a lawn of thick patterned carpeting muffled the sounds of the crowd. The floor-to-ceiling bronze velvet drapes that usually separated the cocktail area from the main ballroom were pulled back and caught with golden, tasseled cords, which almost doubled the capacity of the ballroom.

The wealthiest and most important of the guests were seated at the tables nearest the front of the ballroom and runway, while the "bargain" tables spilled out into the cocktail area. But regardless of where they were seated, *everyone* was important.

The press had predicted that there would be more glitter in the audience than on the runway, and they were probably right. Spotlights cut through the dark room as they would at a Hollywood premiere, lighting up the bejeweled audience like stars in a summer sky. This wasn't just an A-list event; this was an A+-list event. Not even money could buy an invitation to this party, as everyone present was a celebrity in his or her own right. They posed and preened for the press and gushed over each other as a current of electric anticipation ran through the crowd. This was the place to be and they had come from all over to be there: New York, Los Angeles, Miami, Dallas. For weeks afterward, this night would be the topic of gossip among the jaded Beverly Hills socialites.

The backstage area was a complete contrast to the ballroom. If the ballroom looked like a palace, then the dressing room was truly the dungeon, with its peeling cement walls and a chronic leak that left the threadbare carpeting soggy and spongy. Extra chairs and tables were stacked and folded into every available corner, and rack upon rack of clothes lined the room. The models and their dressers were squeezed together like sardines in a can, and once the show began there would be a flurry of bumping elbows and bruised knees. Here, too, the air was charged with anticipation, but of a different kind, that of the controlled professionals.

Some models were going over their lineup of clothes with their dressers, explaining how they wanted their clothes handed to them. They selected jewelry and shoes for each costume, and in some cases, hosiery changes. Others sat before the wall of makeup mirrors, putting the finishing touches on their stage makeup. Still others were running through their routines for the runway. In one corner of the room, two hairdressers worked frantically to create outrageous looks for the opening sequence.

Helena Sinclair sat before a well-lit makeup mirror, applying her eye makeup. Statuesque and graceful, the thirty-three-year-old with long, dark, chestnut brown hair and creamy, translucent English skin created, like every model, her own special look for shows—her own trademark. To bring out the green in her luminous hazel eyes, she worked with smoky purples and highlighted with iridescent yellow and orange next to her brow. As she studied the effect in the mirror, Misha, another model, sat down next to her.

"Do I have enough blush on?" Misha asked, turning her face at various angles to the mirror.

Helena studied the young woman's reflection in the mirror. Dark blond hair fringed her face, and her skin tone was golden from the California sun.

"Yes," Helena answered. "I think you have the same amount on as I do."

"You," Misha snorted. "If I had a face like yours, I wouldn't have to wear makeup!"

"Sure," Helena laughed, embarrassed by the compliment.

"It's true," Misha said, touching up her mascara. "Say," she continued, lowering her voice. "Have you seen Kabrina or Laura Ann?"

"No, but I'm sure they'll be here any moment," Helena replied as she lined her lips and applied a red lipstick to the edges, filling in the middle with orange, then blending the two colors together.

"I hope Laura Ann turns up soon. We're in the opening segment together. They're already ten minutes late," Misha said anxiously. "I'm surprised no one's asked about them."

"I'm surprised too," Helena said. "Kabrina and I are opening the show! I talked to her this morning and she said she'd see me tonight. They're probably having a hard time finding a place to park. You know how that lot is," she added.

"You're probably right."

Hearing a slight commotion, Helena glanced at the dressing room reflected in the mirror and saw Kabrina stride into the room carrying a model's bag on each shoulder. Helena could see that the beautiful black woman was highly agitated, and her copper-colored eyes were swollen as if she had been crying. Kabrina stopped, glanced wildly around the room, then spotted

9

the fashion coordinator and her assistant in a corner and hurried up to them.

Kabrina interrupted them and quickly led the coordinator to the side of the room. She threw her bags to the floor and began talking animatedly to Mrs. Kreshland, the coordinator. Helena stopped what she was doing and curiously watched Kabrina's conversation. She saw the coordinator's hand fly to her mouth as if to stifle a cry; then she turned to the rest of the room.

"Girls, girls! Listen up," Mrs. Kreshland shouted. Fifteen models in various stages of preparation immediately quieted. The room, which only moments before had been filled with lighthearted banter and anticipation, was silent.

"Laura Ann will not be in the show. I'm going to divide up her changes between Pam, Linda and Anita. Those of you who were doubling and tripling with her on the runway," she continued, "figure out your new routines. . . . Now!"

"Where's Laura Ann?" Gayanne asked.

"She's not going to make it. We'll discuss it after the show," Mrs. Kreshland replied tightly, shooting everyone a look that warned off any further questions.

"Now," she continued, "I want lots of attitude. These people came to be entertained and we're going to give them the best show they've ever seen.

"Helena, Kabrina," she said. "I want you behind the gauze scrims, posing. When the lights and music come up, the audience will see only two black shadows behind the white screens. I'll cue you and the two of you step out. Hit a beat and work the runway together. Questions, anyone?"

No one said anything.

"All right. First change, and remember, *attitude!*"

Kabrina made her way over to where Helena was sitting, and up close, Helena knew Kabrina had definitely been crying.

Kabrina shuddered and took a deep breath. "Helena," she said quietly, her voice breaking, "I've got to talk to you." She pulled Helena behind a rack of clothes.

"What is it?" Helena whispered, grasping Kabrina by the arm.

"It's—it's Laura Ann." Kabrina could barely get the words out. She choked back a sob and ran her fingers through her short, curly hair, trying to think of some way to tell Helena the news.

"What happened?" Helena asked.

"Five minutes, everyone," the coordinator called behind them.

"Kabrina! Helena! First change, *now,*" the coordinator shouted from the door. "Line up, everyone!"

Helena and Kabrina threw on their first changes, bead-encrusted gowns with high necks and graceful, billowing sleeves, without talking. Unable to ask Kabrina anything more, Helena was worried and anxious. Kabrina, however, needed the moments of silence to regain her composure.

Within seconds, the two of them were dressed and were racing down the narrow, dark corridor behind the stage, clipping on earrings as they ran. The other models were already lined up, ready to go. The Master of Ceremonies was onstage making his opening introductions. Helena and Kabrina slipped into their positions behind the gauze screen, and each took a dramatic pose. Helena leaned against the archway of her scrim. Across the way, she heard a muffled little gasp.

"Kabrina," she whispered. "Are you okay?"

"I don't think I can go through with the show," Kabrina sobbed.

"Yes, you can. I don't know what happened and we can't talk now, but we have to go on," Helena

11

whispered, holding her pose. "It's too late to stop now!"

"But you didn't see her . . . so pale—"

"The show, Kabrina. Think about the show. You're paid to be a professional model; you have to do it." Helena's voice was firm, but she took a deep breath and concentrated on controlling her own anxiety. What had happened to Laura Ann, and where was she?

The music started, soft at first, and grew, building louder and louder, stopping Helena from thinking about Laura Ann. At the same time, the lights in front of the scrim gradually brightened, illuminating the two shadows behind the screens. Mrs. Kreshland, with her earphones on, communicated with the light man and music director. Helena silently counted the beats of the music.

"Go!" Mrs. Kreshland whispered loudly, as the music reached a crescendo.

The two women simultaneously stepped from behind the screen and struck a pose. Helena saw Kabrina falter a moment. "Attitude," she said under her breath, "attitude!" as she grabbed Kabrina's hand and squeezed it.

The two stunning creatures surveyed their audience, haughtily, as the spotlights hit them. They were dressed in identical jeweled gowns, one gold and one silver, like fire and ice. Helena was a winter queen in silver, while Kabrina smoldered in the heat of gold. Each bead picked up the clear white spotlight and radiated it back over the audience in a hundred different directions. Diamond earrings cascaded almost to their shoulders, and diamond cuff bracelets adorned each wrist. Diamonds of tears sparkled in their eyes and each tear caught the spotlight, just as the jewels did.

Then they started down the runway, shoulder to shoulder, hand in hand, one black and one white, each one breathtakingly beautiful in her own distinctive way. When they reached the end of the runway, they paused before turning to start their walk back. The audience applauded wildly. The two women looked at each other and knew that they must somehow acknowledge the audience with a smile; but they also remembered a day not so long ago, when a sweet, young woman named Laura Ann first stepped onto the runway and into their lives.

Chapter One

A brown haze hung over the promised land as the sticky, late afternoon sun filtered through the heavy air. A line of cars moved at a snail's pace to leave Los Angeles, and downtown was almost empty when only an hour before the street had teemed with "rag" workers ferrying racks of clothes back and forth through the garment district.

The remaining merchants were closing for the day, like the East Indian concessionaire in the 719 Building who pulled the rusty iron gate across the front of his snack bar and snapped the lock into place, and a Mexican parking attendant who impatiently jiggled the keys of the last car left in the lot as the six o'clock closing time approached.

One half block down from the parking lot, Laura Ann Gilmore appeared at the revolving doors of the gray-and-silver Greyhound Bus Terminal, which stood out in the waning afternoon sun as buses monotonously poured in and out of the cool, dark opening. With her pale blond hair cascading down her back, there was a childlike innocence about her as she dragged two cheap, worn suitcases through the automatic doors. The dark circles under her eyes stood out against the translucency of her pale skin, and her ankles were swollen from sitting so long on the bus.

Dressed in a conservative red pleated suit and matching shoes, attire more appropriate for a church service than a cross-country bus ride, Laura Ann teetered on her heels. Pulling at the suitcases, she didn't notice that her imitation leather purse, hanging over her shoulder, was dangling open.

A tall blond in his mid-twenties, with pale, gold-flecked green eyes, stared disinterestedly at the front of the terminal through the dirt-streaked plate glass window of the lounge across the street. Handsome in a slick way, with his hair blow-dried back on the sides and longer in the back, he was dressed in Armani black-and-gray tweed slacks and a gray sweater. A buttery, soft leather jacket was flung down in the booth next to him.

As he sipped his Jack Daniels, the smoky overhead light caught the dull, warm gleam of gold from the Cartier Panther watch on his tanned wrist and bounced off the blood red garnet ring on his pinkie. The bar to his right was beginning to fill up with workers, hustlers and drifters, each one ready to leave the remains of the day at the bottom of a glass. Under the gray fog of cigarette and hash smoke, two black youths silently played a halfhearted game of pool.

As he gazed through the dingy window, a bright flash of red from the entrance of the bus terminal caught his eye. He focused on the young woman staggering through the doorway under the weight of her two suitcases, then watched as she put them down. When she bent to retrieve her cases, the wind caught her skirt, revealing the curve of her long white thigh. He watched her closely, taking in the whole picture, a scene he'd witnessed so many times before. She, like the other young girls who had come through that terminal door, carried worn, cheap bags, and was overdressed for the Los Angeles casual look. The way she walked and held her head displayed her insecurity, her youth, her vulnerability.

16

A crafty look came over his face, and without removing his eyes from the beautiful girl, he called behind him. "Snake, get over here!"

The taller of the two pool players propped his cue against the table, sauntered over to the booth, and slouched down opposite the man with the golden eyes.

"What's happenin', Marcus?" Snake asked casually.

The man pulled his eyes from the girl, and slowly took in the boy opposite him. The cheap faddish clothes, the practiced bored look on his face, the yearning for approval in his eyes. No words were necessary. Marcus knew the strength of silence and how to use it.

The bored look crumbled from the teenager's face. "Sorry," he mumbled. "I mean, Mr. Fent."

Marcus murmured something in a low voice to the kid, and he looked over his shoulder through the murky window. "Yeah," Snake said, smiling as he rose, then glided through the doorway.

Laura Ann pulled her suitcases across the sidewalk to the curb and sat down on one to catch her breath and to survey her new world. There was a lump in her throat as she looked up Los Angeles Street and felt the city pulsating around her. She didn't notice the coating of soot layering Los Angeles nor the smell of a thousand workers. Even the drunken, homeless man in the gutter didn't catch her eye.

She was finally here in this beautiful city that was so different from her native Iowa, where even the air smelled bland. There, things never changed, and the open spaces had begun to close in on her. She used to think she was like the pet gerbil she had had as a child. Around and around in her wheel she went, but the scenery never changed, no matter how fast or long she ran. She was running as fast as she could on that wheel, but life was passing her by. She could feel it. And now, sitting here on Los Angeles Street, Laura Ann knew she'd made the right choice. This city was her destiny.

17

Here, nothing was bland about the air that was alive with the perfume of auto exhaust, frying tortillas, stale bodies, and pipe dreams.

Suddenly she saw a shadow behind her and felt a soft tug on her purse. Glancing backward, she saw a black kid running around the corner. For a moment she didn't connect the two incidents, but then suddenly she realized he'd taken her wallet.

At that moment, a blond, suntanned figure raced across the street after the disappearing figure, yelling to her, "Don't worry, sugar, I saw everything! I'll get him!"

He dashed past her and disappeared around the same corner.

Oh, God, she thought as she sat miserably hunched over, holding her stomach. Her wallet was gone—and with it almost every dollar she had in the world. For two years she had hoarded and saved her nest egg, working nights and weekends, hustling hamburgers at Jack-in-the-Box while her friends went to parties, changing diapers when she had baby-sat while they were changing dance partners. It had taken two years for her to save enough money to escape Iowa and less than an hour in Los Angeles for her to lose it.

Hot tears, first angry, then frustrated and hopeless, overflowed and spilled down her cheeks as she checked all her pockets and her coin purse. All together she had exactly $5.34 in change. Now what was she going to do?

Three, maybe four minutes had gone by as she sat on her suitcases and stared. Passersby eyed her curiously, but none of them said anything. A taxi slowed as it passed, but she didn't look up.

"Sorry. The son of a bitch got away! I chased him for three blocks, but he ran down an alley and jumped a fence before I could get him."

The voice jarred her out of her misery, and Laura Ann looked up into the handsome, smiling face of the young man who had chased after the thief. He was, she

18

thought as she studied her would-be hero, in his mid-twenties, tall with broad shoulders and narrow hips. His sun-bleached hair tumbled over his tan forehead, and his angular face held that wide, engaging smile. She was entranced by the pale eyes that echoed the early evening dusk.

"Jeez, you look like you just lost your last friend," he quipped. "Things can't be that bad."

The sound of his friendly voice brought new tears which she tried to hold back, but without much success. "I haven't a friend to lose," she stammered, "and yes, things can get worse. I just got into town and already someone has stolen my wallet, and I only have a few dollars left, and it was all the money I had, and I've no place to go, and . . ."

"Hold it, hold everything. Now you do have a friend. I'm Marcus. Glad to know ya. I got an idea. Let's go get a cup of coffee and sit down and figure this whole thing out." He picked up her two battered suitcases and strode across the street to a seedy-looking cocktail lounge, as Laura Ann trailed after him.

"So as I see it, Laura Ann, you need a place to crash for a few days while you go around to the modeling agencies," Marcus said, as he sat across from her in a booth in the lounge. "I don't see a problem, princess. You'll sleep on the couch in my living room for as long as you want."

Laura Ann smiled tentatively at the handsome man. She was feeling much better now. He had ordered a shot of something sweet and almondy for her coffee. For medicinal purposes, he had said jokingly, and it made her insides glow and her head a little heavy. Yet, her mother's warning to be wary of strangers invaded her lethargy. But she was alone, almost penniless, and she needed help. Besides, he was so handsome, almost beautiful, she thought, and he seemed so confident and helpful. He made her feel secure, and she was sure he was a good person. Besides, she would stay with him

19

for only a couple of days until she was on her feet again. And anyway, what choice did she have?

After they finished their coffees, Marcus escorted Laura Ann to his car, a Cadillac Seville—an older model, but a Cadillac just the same. Not many people in Laura Ann's hometown drove Cadillacs, and she was impressed.

They drove to the crowded bowels of downtown Los Angeles and stopped in front of a run-down stucco building. The tiny yard in front of the building was littered with garbage, and Laura Ann tried not to notice the graffiti that was written across the building walls. The shabby surroundings were so different from the neatly groomed suburbs in Iowa, but Laura Ann squelched her apprehensions as she followed Marcus into the building and into his apartment by telling herself that she was in a "real" city now.

The next morning the sun streamed through the crack in the living room draperies as Laura Ann, curled up in a ball on the couch, opened first one eye, then the other. It took her a moment to remember where she was. At first she thought she was back in her own bedroom in Iowa, but as her eyes focused, she began to remember the previous day's events. After dinner, when she could hardly keep her eyes open, they had returned to Marcus's apartment and he had made up the couch for her. Laura Ann had expected him to make a pass at her like some of the boys back home had, but instead he just tucked her in and kissed her on her forehead. And as she'd settled in for the night she had thought about Marcus's strong face and warm manner. He seemed so concerned, asking all sorts of questions about her. He didn't talk a lot about himself, but rather seemed to devote all his attention to her. He was so easy to talk to that she found herself trusting him, telling him of her deepest dream and most secret desire—to become a model and be famous.

"You're like a jewel in the rough, princess," Marcus

had said when she had finished talking.

A jewel in the rough, she had thought. I wonder what he'd meant by that? I wonder if that meant he thought I had modeling potential? She had felt warm at the thought and had fallen asleep.

"Hey, princess, you awake?" Marcus walked through the doorway from the kitchen with a cup of coffee in his hand. "It's almost noon. Let's hurry. Today I'm going to give you the grand tour of your new city."

Hollywood Boulevard was a kaleidoscope of Laura Ann's dreams. The star-studded sidewalks, the Mann Chinese theatre with its walkway of stars' prints, the flashy purple walls of Frederick's of Hollywood . . . Everywhere Laura Ann looked, she saw landmarks she'd only read about in the gossip magazines.

Marcus took her to lunch at the oldest restaurant in Hollywood, Musso and Frank's, its cool, dark interior the product of a bygone era. Sitting in one of the cozy wooden booths, Laura Ann imagined she was lunching with Clark Gable and Carole Lombard, while Marcus pointed out such celebrities as Stephanie Zimbalist and James Garner.

After lunch they headed for Beverly Hills, the playground of the rich. Rolls Royces, Mercedes, and Jaguars were as numerous as Fords and Chevies in Iowa. They strolled Rodeo Drive, stopping to window shop at Fred's and Giorgio's. Outside under one of the striped umbrellas at Pastel's they stopped to sip some wine. The Rodeo collection of designers' stores sparkled like rare jewels—Louis Vuitton, Nina Ricci, Fendi.

As they walked, the air seemed permeated with wealth. Even the salespeople in the boutiques looked as if they had just stepped out of the pages of a fashion magazine. At Lina Lee's, two exotic models, one slender and black with incredible bone structure and almond-shaped eyes and the other one Oriental and as perfect as a china doll, mannequined in the window. Both were dressed all in white, the uniform color of Beverly Hills. Laura Ann stood watching them for a moment, struck by their beauty, and fantasized that she stood in the window with them.

The afternoon faded into dusk, and they returned to the apartment to rest and dress for dinner. Marcus had a special restaurant in mind, and Laura Ann dressed with care, putting on the one dressy dress she had brought with her, a bright, multiflowered sundress she had made herself. When she stepped into the living room, Marcus told her she looked like a beautiful flower garden and she blushed with pleasure at his words.

After driving for a few minutes, Marcus turned right on a tiny street that wound upward and ended at the summit of a hill. There before them was a beautiful Japanese temple. Yamashiro's, a small sign announced. Laura Ann looked out at the spectacular view. Far below them the lights of Los Angeles twinkled as far as Laura Ann could see, illuminating the skyline like a field of wildflowers in an alpine meadow. This was her city now, her new home. Los Angeles was as addictive as a drug, attracting her to its power, its wealth. She wanted to become a famous model, and soon everyone would know her name. She was sure of it.

They walked up the rustic wood stairs and through two gigantic carved doors. The restaurant was built around a tranquil Japanese garden, complete with miniature bridges and still ponds in which Japanese carp glided back and forth. Candlelit tables circled the edges of the delicate garden, and rice paper panels formed the roof overhead.

"Oh, Marcus, I've never been anyplace as beautiful as this, ever. I wish this night could go on forever," Laura Ann said, awed by the surroundings.

"Maybe it can. Nothing is too good for you," Marcus

answered, his pale golden green eyes glittering in the candlelight.

She shyly smiled at him, surprised by his compliment but she didn't want to break the spell of the moment, so she brushed aside her concern.

Laura Ann floated through the evening as they drank warm sake, ate sushi and shrimp tempura, and drank more and more sake. Marcus held her hand and whispered softly in her ear. They toasted their meeting and her new career. During the drive home Laura Ann, warm and mellow, leaned her head on Marcus's shoulder and hummed along with the radio.

Back at the apartment, Marcus drew Laura Ann gently to his side, caressed her cheeks, then kissed her eyes and her mouth, gently at first, then passionately. Laura Ann felt a fire ignite inside her and clung to him. Slowly, he undressed her and kissed every part of her body.

"My precious little jewel," he whispered as he picked her up and carried her to the bedroom.

His lovemaking was nothing like the frenzied gropings of the boys back in Iowa who awkwardly touched her with their hands rough and callused from hard work. Marcus was smooth and confident, not desperate or hurried, and she had never felt such tender hands on her body. They were everywhere, stroking, feeling, and as smooth as a baby's skin. She felt his penis, hard against her, and pushed to get closer to him. She felt the heat of their naked bodies as they pressed together, and her head swirled from the sake. She rubbed herself against him and the wiry hairs on his chest brushed against the skin of her breasts, arousing her as never before. Her excitement mounted higher and higher and Marcus pulled her on top of him, directing her movements with his hands. It was all so different from the standard missionary position she was used to, but Marcus's every nuance of movement and the practiced way he orchestrated them brought

23

gasps of pleasure from Laura Ann. Finally, fully sated, she drifted off into an exhausted sleep.

The next day, full of confidence, Laura Ann began her quest for a modeling agency. She had curled her long blond hair, donned her familiar red suit, and wore her highest pumps to look taller. Marcus had helped boost her morale by loaning her his car. She had hoped he would come along for moral support, but he said he had other business.

"You'll be just fine, precious," he added.

With a Thomas Guide in one hand and a list of modeling agencies from the telephone book in the other, Laura Ann started her career hunt.

Her first stop was the Looks Agency in Hollywood. While she waited for the elevator and wondered what the next few days would bring, the elevator doors opened and two girls about her age stepped out. They were a study in perfection, with an air of casual indifference about them, in their leggings, oversize belted shirts (one bright purple, and one a black-and-white animal print), and white socks and sneakers. Their shiny hair and scrubbed faces gave them a healthy glow. As they talked animatedly to each other, Laura Ann smiled and caught one girl's eyes. The girl seemed to look through her as if she weren't there.

As Laura Ann stepped into the elevator she felt overdressed and clumsy, and when she got off and opened the door to the agency she was greeted by a waiting room lined with beautiful young men and women. She felt all eyes on her when she entered and walked to the receptionist's desk.

"Excuse me," she said.

The receptionist barely looked up from her desk.

"I'd like to see someone about signing with the agency."

"Open interviews are on Tuesdays and Thursdays," the receptionist answered in a monotone.

"Should I—"

24

"Open interviews are on Tuesdays and Thursdays," the receptionist repeated, dismissing her.

"Oh, ah, thank you," Laura Ann stammered. Intimidated, she hung her head and retreated out the door.

The second agency she pulled up in front of was the Catherine Beck Agency. This time she hesitated and took a deep breath before going into the black, somber building. The agency was dimly lit, musty smelling, and filled with carved antique furniture. It had an almost reverent air about it. Laura Ann made her way to the counter and stood there quietly, hoping to attract someone's attention.

A tiny, wizened woman finally looked up from one of the desks. She had a telephone in one hand and was chain-smoking with the other. "May we help you?" she said in a gravelly voice.

"I'd like to speak to Catherine Beck," Laura Ann said timidly.

"I'm Catherine Beck." The woman stood up and slowly walked to the counter, her cigarette still dangling from her fingers. She was a frail woman, in her mid-seventies. Her face, crisscrossed with a network of thin lines, underscored her age, while her strawberry blond hair tried to downplay it.

"What can I do for you?" she asked in clipped, stern, businesslike tones.

"I'm interested in signing with your agency," Laura Ann said, faltering a bit before Catherine's brusque attitude.

"Do you have pictures?" Catherine asked, openly looking Laura Ann up and down.

"No, I just got into town," Laura Ann answered, hanging her head and avoiding direct eye contact.

"Well, dear, let me give you some advice. I've been in this business forty-seven years," Catherine began, warming to her favorite subject. "You should go home, marry the boy next door and settle down. Los Angeles is a tough town. There isn't a lot of fashion work here and the competition is stiff.

"You seem like a bright girl, so I'm going to be honest with you," she continued. "Models aren't all that glamorous. They're freaks. They just happen to be born with a look that the camera loves and a body you can hang clothes on. You'll be much happier if you go back home." She took a drag off her cigarette for emphasis.

"But, but—" Laura Ann stuttered.

"No," she interrupted Laura Ann. "You go home and think about what I've said. You'll see that I'm right." She took another puff of the cigarette.

Laura Ann turned and walked dejectedly out the door. She held her head high to keep the tears from spilling down her cheeks and almost collided with a young brunette going into the Beck Agency. Gorgeous, very tall, slender, and polished, her skin was flawless and the color of fresh cream. She was dressed in a long sea green cape that flowed behind her. Laura Ann immediately recognized her from numerous cosmetic ads on television. The beautiful woman gave Laura Ann a friendly smile and went through the agency door.

"Hi, Catherine!" Laura Ann heard her call as she turned to close the door.

"Hello, Helena," Catherine Beck called back to her as the door shut.

Freaks, huh, Laura Ann thought miserably to herself as she walked to the car. She slid behind the wheel and picked up her list of agencies and their addresses. She fought back her tears and with a pencil crossed out the Catherine Beck Agency.

"I've got to find an agency that will take me," she said desperately to herself. "I've just got to." Then she shifted the car into gear and started out for the Hallowell Agency a short distance away.

The sign read, William Halsey Hallowell and Associates. This time, Laura Ann sat in the car a full half hour before going in. Contrary to what Catherine Beck said, she didn't need to think any more about what she wanted to be. She'd had plenty of time to think about it on the bus from Iowa to New York. Back home everyone had told her she was pretty and should be a model. She had assumed the people in Los Angeles would think so, too. She thought that she would walk into an agency, be discovered, and start on her way to the top, just like it always happened in the fan magazines. But everyone here was much prettier than she and her special red suit didn't look so special anymore. All the other girls were so chic.

Finally, she forced herself to leave the car, push through the building's door and climb the stairs. The agency was bright and inviting with glass walls and skylights and plants everywhere.

"May I help you?" the receptionist at the door said.

"Yes," Laura Ann mumbled. By now her confidence was dragging on the ground. "I'd like to talk with someone about signing with the agency."

"Do you have an appointment?" the receptionist asked.

"No," Laura Ann replied meekly.

"Open interviews are on Fridays. But let me check, maybe Carol has a free moment." She pressed a button and spoke into the telephone.

"If you'll have a seat, Carol will talk with you in a few minutes."

Laura Ann sat down on the beige couch, thumbed through a magazine, fidgeted with her suit, and tried to bolster her sagging confidence. But she wasn't successful when she saw several beautiful young women coming and going through the door at the end of the corridor. As sleek as racehorses, they moved gracefully and with complete assurance. She recognized the exotic black model she had seen in the window of Lina Lee on Rodeo Drive and overheard snippets of two of

27

the women's conversation. They casually bandied about the names of legendary designers and places like Paris and Milan, people and places she had only dreamed about. She couldn't help but compare herself to these stunning women and wonder how she could ever compete with the likes of them. They were worlds away from her.

Her confidence slipping a notch lower, Laura Ann had started to get up to leave when the receptionist motioned to the door at the end of the corridor. "You can go in. Carol will see you now."

Laura Ann stood up and walked woodenly to the door. She would have turned and fled, but she was too afraid to pass the receptionist. So instead, she slowly turned the handle and walked into the office.

"Hi, I'm Carol McMahon." The young woman smiled at her from behind the desk. In her late twenties, she had a turned-up nose and sparkling brown eyes.

"I—I'm Laura Ann Gilmore," she answered timidly. "I'm interested in becoming a model with your agency."

"Do you have a portfolio?" Carol asked, sizing Laura Ann up.

"No, I'm just starting out," Laura Ann mumbled, too intimidated to look directly at Carol.

"Well, we're not taking on any new clients now. But you really do need to put together a portfolio," Carol said gently. "Have you thought about going to Europe or Japan to get your book together?"

"It took all my savings just to get to Los Angeles," Laura Ann blurted out.

"Look," Carol said kindly. "I'll give you a list of photographers. You call them up and test with them. Get your basic book together and then try one of the smaller agencies. Then, after you get some experience, come back and see us . . . say in maybe a year or so."

Laura Ann took the photographers' list and walked slowly back to her car. She was going home. She had

had enough rejection for one day, she decided.

But the next few days were no different. Even the smallest agencies refused her without a portfolio or experience.

"I get five or more of you in here a day. You're all alike," the owner of a tiny agency in the valley told her, and after this final rejection, Laura Ann drove back to Marcus's apartment in tears.

"Marcus, what am I going to do?" she cried. "I can't get an agency to sign me because I don't have pictures. I can't get pictures because I don't have any money. And I don't have any money because I can't get a job. I'm caught in a circle."

"Precious, I've got an idea. I've got a friend who's a photographer," Marcus said slowly, pausing after each word for emphasis. "Maybe I can get you a job and pictures too."

"You're kidding! Oh, Marcus! Really," Laura Ann exclaimed, drying her tears.

"Now, I'm not promising anything. He's a very busy man and if he agrees you will have to do exactly what he says," Marcus said, looking sternly at her. "Exactly."

"Oh, I will, I will! I promise, Marcus," she cried, jumping up and down.

"Okay, I'll give him a call." He walked into the bedroom to use the phone as Laura Ann almost jumped up and down with excitement.

He returned a few minutes later. "Done," he said, tossing out the words as if they were nothing. "We'll go by the studio tonight. If my friend likes your look, you'll start shooting tonight."

"Oh, my God! Marcus, I love you!" She threw her arms around his neck and hugged him close.

As they headed for the studio, Laura Ann thought how downtown L.A. looked very different at night, taking on an almost movie-set quality. Everywhere she looked, fluorescent neon signs flashed and popped, in Spanish, in Korean, and in Japanese, and the pavements almost seemed to sweat with the muggy heat of the hot summer night. People churned and milled everywhere, crowding the theaters and bars. And in garbage-strewn doorways, the homeless sought sleep. On almost every street corner, girls lounged under the streetlights, and with the passing of every car, their eyes became alert as they searched for a trick.

A flashing neon sign advertising video games caught Laura Ann's eye as they rounded a corner. In the doorway beneath the entrance a group of boys stood in a circle kicking at a limp figure, and Laura Ann sucked in a breath and sat back in her seat, dreaming of the brighter daylight. Their car pulled up in front of a dark office building.

"Here we are, sugar."

"Are you sure?" Laura Ann asked doubtfully. "It doesn't look like it's open."

"Sure, it's open. Come on," he said, taking her hand and pulling her firmly from the car.

Marcus rang a buzzer on the wall next to the dark entrance, barred by an iron gate. After a few minutes, they heard a hushed voice through the grating.

"Marcus? That you?"

"Yeah."

The grating swung back, and they walked through the black opening into a dimly lit lobby.

"Come on," the voice said.

They followed the dark shadow up two flights of stairs and down a hallway lit only by an overhead light bulb, which revealed walls covered with stains and graffiti. They stepped through an unmarked door into a well-lit studio. The bare walls, floors and ceiling were whitewashed, and even the windows were painted over.

Marcus introduced her to his friend, Gene "Flash" Coulter, a short, skinny man in his late forties with a gray-streaked wiry beard and wearing round wire-rimmed glasses.

"So you want to be a model," Flash said. It was a statement rather than a question.

"Oh, yes," Laura Ann answered excitedly, "more than anything."

"You're pretty enough," he said flatly as he openly appraised her. "Turn around," he said brusquely.

Laura Ann pivoted, then quickly turned back to face him, her eyes wide and round, fearful that he would dismiss her.

"What do you know about photographic modeling?" he asked as he turned around and walked back to the living room area, leaving Laura Ann to trail shyly after him.

"Nothing really. I'm just starting out," she said honestly.

"I can see that. With the right guidance and advice you could work a lot." Flash still had his back to her, and she thought she might not have heard him right.

"Do you think so?" she asked excitedly. This was the first encouragement she had received in Los Angeles from a professional.

"Yes," he answered casually. "It all depends on the camera, though. You have to make it love you."

"How do you do that?" she asked, confused.

"Let's all sit down and get comfortable," Flash said, indicating a small couch in the corner. "Here, have a glass of wine, relax, and we'll talk some more."

Marcus and Laura Ann sat down on the couch while Flash poured three glasses of wine from a bottle he had taken from a small refrigerator. He gave a glass to each of them and pulled up a chair. "Like I said, Laura Ann, you have to have a love affair with the camera."

"Listen to everything Flash tells you, sugar. He's the master, the guru of photographers," Marcus said, draping his arm around Laura Ann's shoulders.

"Part of what makes the camera love you you're born with," Flash continued. "Your bone structure, the size

31

and spacing of your eyes, the shape of your nose in relationship to your face. But the rest is your attitude."

He took a sip of wine. "The camera has to turn you on. You have to seduce it and make love to it as you would a man. Here, have a little more wine." He refilled her glass.

"Do you think I have the right kind of look to succeed as a model?" Laura Ann asked anxiously.

"Yes, from what I see," Flash answered. "What I'm more concerned about is your attitude. You've got to relax and become uninhibited with the camera."

"How do I do that? Doesn't that just come from experience?"

"Partially," Flash explained. "But more than that, it's a state of mind. Let me tell you what all the top models do."

"What?" Laura Ann asked, taking a long drink of the wine, which was beginning to make her mellow. She wasn't feeling as nervous as she had earlier, and Flash was so confident, seemed to have all the answers.

"They pop a 'lude, smoke a little grass, or do a line of coke, and then they play."

"I beg your pardon?"

"You know, quaalude, marijuana, cocaine! Jeezes, Marcus, what closet have you had this girl stashed in?"

"I'm sorry." Laura Ann was embarrassed. "I just moved here from Iowa and—"

Marcus broke in. "Don't worry, Flash, Laura Ann's a smart girl and she'll do anything to become a model. Right, Laura Ann?"

She nodded.

Flash pulled a small bottle out of his pocket and shook out a white tablet that looked like a Tylenol. He handed it to Laura Ann. "Okay, okay," he said. "Anyway, a 'lude is no big deal. It just helps you relax for the camera. Here, take this. You'll see, there's nothing to it."

She looked at Marcus to see if it was all right.

32

"Go ahead, precious, take it," Marcus said, encouraging her.

She took the tablet and washed it down with the last of the wine in her glass.

"Like I said," Flash continued, "these girls get a little high and uninhibited. Then they have an affair with the cameras, and the sexual electricity comes through in the pictures."

Laura Ann was feeling very relaxed and very loose. Flash's voice seemed to float in the distance. She rubbed against Marcus's shoulder. The wine was making her feel warm and sensual. She giggled softly.

"Flash, I think maybe it would be a good idea if you took some test shots now," she heard Marcus say.

"Yeah," came Flash's voice.

"Come on, sugar. Flash is going to take some test shots." Marcus half lifted her from the couch, and Laura Ann threw her arms around his neck and nibbled his ear. As she ground her pelvis into him, she felt his hardness and she thought of the long nights of lying in his arms making love.

"Take her over to the bedroom setup," Laura Ann heard Flash say in a fuzzy, far-off voice.

Marcus walked her into the next room, and they sat down on a bed covered with satin sheets and pillows.

"Now, Laura Ann," Flash explained, "I want you to have an affair with the camera. Look at it like you would Marcus. Make love to it. Yeah, that's right. Good. You're doing fine."

Flash kept talking to her and snapping the shutter. The quaalude and wine made her feel wonderful, and everything seemed so natural.

"Unbutton your blouse, that's right; now take off your skirt. That's nice. Yeah, baby. Slowly unzip your skirt. Pull it down over your hips. Slower. That's right. Now, take it off. Good. Move around on the bed. Rub your pussy against the satin sheet. Feel its softness. Now, turn over, stay on your back and pull down your

33

hose, real nice and slow. That's good. Real good, Laura Ann. Now, I want you to play with yourself under your panties before taking them off. Make yourself feel real good. Wow, you're wonderful. You really are going to be a star. Lovely, yes. You're going to be famous!"

Flash kept talking and shooting, and Laura Ann kept making love to the camera, hardly aware of Flash. All she could think of was how good she felt. She slipped her hand between her legs and stroked herself, softly at first, then with increasing intensity as she felt her climax building. Suddenly, Marcus was there, naked, on top of her, pulling off her wet panties and making love to her. They came together in an explosion of lights. Exhausted, Laura Ann drifted off to sleep, and in her dream, she thought she heard Marcus and Flash talking.

"What did I tell you," Marcus said, pulling on his pants. "Is she a wild pussy or what?"

"Yeah, easy to turn as one, two, three," Flash agreed. "Got some hot shots here. Next time it'll be even easier."

"This cunt is great! I knew it the first time I saw her. These small-town chicks are all alike. You can put them right under, just like ether," Marcus bragged.

"Yeah, well, next time stick her on the top, so I can shoot more of her. I got a half roll of nothing but your skinny ass!" Flash snorted.

"Okay, sure," Marcus retorted. "Just fork over the cash or there won't be a next time."

Laura Ann whimpered a little in her sleep and then drifted off again. She smiled, knowing that she was dreaming. Marcus would never talk about her that way.

Chapter Two

A light fog hung below the treetops as the morning sun broke over the horizon, its warmth melting soft holes in the fog's gray cottony center. Within a few hours the fog had completely dissipated, leaving Santa Monica sparkling in the clear morning sun.

Helena poured herself a cup of coffee and leaned back on the couch, her hazel eyes gazing out of her apartment window at the pool in the courtyard. There was a quiet tranquillity this time of the morning. Doves cooed softly in the ficus trees, and somewhere across the courtyard a faint alarm clock awakened a sleeper. In his bedroom, Helena's nine-year-old son, Nicky, sprawled diagonally on his bed, clutching his spotted velvet puppy under an arm.

There was a crispness to the day that tugged at the memories sleeping within her, memories of her past in Seattle. Though it seemed like a lifetime ago, it had only been six months.

Sometimes she felt pangs of guilt and anxiety about breaking up her family and marriage. But the reality of what her life had been always reinforced her decision. For eight years she had totally supported the family through her husband's college and dental schooling and had given up her career dreams to fulfill her husband's and son's needs. She had struggled through years of grueling hard work and long hours, sometimes holding down two jobs just to make ends meet. She had done it willingly because she knew that when the time came and Kyle graduated, it would be her turn to follow her career.

But that time had never come, and there had been plenty of clues along the way that it never would. Like the late-night parties that her husband insisted he had to attend, and his inability to hold down a part-time job, even in the summer when school wasn't in session. "I need to hang loose for the next year" was the way he explained it. Of course there had been clues, but she had been so wrapped up in her family that she hadn't noticed them—not at first, anyway.

His graduation from dental school had come, and with it his halfhearted attempt at setting up a practice. But in the end, it was Helena who had added another job to her already bulging days. She had put his practice together while he was golfing, playing tennis, working out at the gym, anything with the guys, anything except building a life with her. She had finally realized she was trapped in a loveless marriage that closely resembled a never-ending baby-sitting job.

Nicky emerged from his bedroom, interrupting her thoughts. He was the epitome of the all-American boy, with his light-brown hair tumbling into his eyes, freckles sprinkling his turned-up nose, and his sky blue eyes. He rubbed his eyes sleepily and pulled his stuffed dog behind him by one ear.

"Hi, pumpkin," she greeted him when he stumbled and plopped down on the couch beside her. She gave him a big hug. "You ready for a little breakfast?"

He nodded, yawning.

She sent him off to dress with a kiss and went into the kitchen to prepare his breakfast.

"Dear Lord," she thought as she squeezed fresh orange juice for him, "I love that child so much." And she blinked back fierce tears as her mind wandered

36

back to the black, rainy predawn morning they left Seattle. She had packed her car with her belongings and a still sleepy Nicky. Kyle had been partying the night before and hadn't bothered to see them off. Armed with $962 and belief in herself, she had set out for Los Angeles, crying silently for the life she was ending. But there was no future for her there, only a selfish husband who never grew up; her dreams lay ahead.

She called Nicky to the breakfast table and sat down to keep him company. He was such a sweet, obedient little boy, and she knew how hard it had been for him to leave his father and his little friends. She had tried to explain to him that the divorce was the best for all of them, and he had said he understood. But Helena wondered, deep down, if he really did.

It had been a somewhat lonely existence for her, too, especially the first several months in L.A. During her last year in Seattle, Helena had worked hard to become Seattle's top model, and her work had kept her from being lonely. But before she had established herself fully here the empty hours between bookings had only emphasized her loneliness.

It had been scary, too, relocating to a new environment, even though she knew she could support herself and her son. After all, she had supported the whole family all those years. But she knew she was too old to pursue a serious modeling career in L.A., and all she could count on was that she looked years younger than her age and her maturity would help her land modeling assignments. She knew how to go about establishing herself and was certain it would only be a matter of time before she was working to capacity. She had a good portfolio and the expertise to back herself up. She had been proven right when Catherine Beck, one of Los Angeles's top fashion agents, immediately signed her and her list of clients grew.

Establishing friendships had not been easy either.

Though she had Nicky, she found it hard to get close to anyone else. Making friends with other models was difficult because they viewed each newcomer as a competitor. Also, being one of the few runway models who was a single parent didn't help. When the other models wanted to go out and play, she wanted to be with Nicky. But slowly she gained their acceptance and started to make friends. Best of all, she was working toward her goals, and for the first time in years, she felt alive, stimulated and proud of herself.

Nicky finished his breakfast, grabbed his lunch and was ready for school. Reluctantly Helena pushed her memories of the past six months away and drove him there.

Nicky seemed unusually quiet in the car.

"How is school going, honey?" Helena asked him as she drove down the tree-lined streets.

"Okay, Mommy."

"Are you making some new friends?"

"I guess so," he answered quietly.

Helena studied him for a moment out of the corner of her eye.

"Sometimes, sweetie, it takes a while for the kids to get used to a new kid, doesn't it?" she said.

"It sure does," Nicky replied. "Most of the kids have been friends since kindergarten."

"Just be friendly to everyone and they'll come around," Helena said. "I promise. By the way," she smiled, "I saw a sign-up sheet on the school bulletin board, for Little League Baseball. I thought maybe we'd go shopping for a ball and mitt this weekend. Then next week you could sign up for the team."

"Oh, boy!" Nicky cried, bouncing up and down on the seat. "Could I?" His little face brightened and his mood lifted.

"Of course you could!" Helena laughed, giving him a hug with one arm and steering with the other.

"Here you go," she said, pulling up in front of the

schoolyard. "You walk home after school and I should be back from my interview by then. Love you," she said, kissing him. "Have a good day!"

"Okay, Mommy!" he replied, jumping out of the car. "Love you, too!"

As she drove to her appointment she thought about the interview. Catherine Beck had called the day before with a cattle-call interview for models for a television miniseries. It wasn't a large part, just a few scenes. But Catherine said the studio had called every modeling agency in town looking for the right models and decided that Helena had the look they wanted. Helena had agreed to go but hated these kinds of interviews. Yet as a single parent with a small son to support, she had no choice. Money was important.

The call was for high-fashion models, but Catherine had told her that what the studio really wanted were girls who were sexy and glamorous. So instead of her usual sleek look Helena decided to leave her long brunette hair loose and flowing and she chose a dramatic sea green dress and cape that emphasized her pale complexion.

The interview, Catherine had told her, was not to be held at a casting office or studio, but by the executive producer at the writer's home office at the end of a private street in Beverly Hills. As she now made her way up the narrow, one-lane driveway, Helena had to pull to the side several times, to allow cars driven by beautiful women to pass. Finally, she reached the end. There were perhaps ten or twelve cars parked around the bright white two-story contemporary home. She parked her car and with portfolio in hand, walked up a flight of stairs that led to the second-level entrance.

The art deco reception area, done in triangles of gray and cream, had bookshelves lining the left wall and several vacant desks pushed up against the right wall. Straight ahead, at the far end of the room, was a receptionist, and behind her, a private office door.

Scattered in the rectangular room were folding chairs filled with eager models of all types and descriptions.

The receptionist looked up briefly as Helena approached, but then went back to her work without speaking. Helena signed in on the callsheet, noting her agent's name and her scheduled call time. Then she sat down with the others to wait her turn.

The models sat silently or talked quietly among themselves. Each time the receptionist called a name, the other models would surreptitiously study the woman, comparing themselves to her. They also noted how long she was in the interview.

After about twenty-five minutes, the door behind the receptionist's desk opened and a man entered the room. Tall and lean, with a head of full and wavy dark hair, he seemed to Helena to be in his late forties. He was wearing a beige silk shirt, open at the neck, with beige gabardine slacks to match. He was weighed down by a heavy gold chain, the epitome of the classic "Hollywood producer."

His eyes flicked casually over the room as he bent over and started to say something to the receptionist. He glanced briefly in Helena's direction and then away. Then his eyes flashed back and riveted on her. He straightened up and stared intently at her for what seemed like minutes. Helena caught his look and nervously smiled back.

"Are you next?" he demanded from across the room.

"No, Mr. Cramer," the receptionist intervened. "This one is." She indicated the blonde sitting next to Helena.

"Oh, excuse me," he said politely to the model. "Would you come with me, please." He held the door open for her and started to follow her, then turned back to the waiting room.

"You," he said, looking at Helena, "stay right there."

"I will." Helena nodded, almost feeling as if she should have saluted at his order.

Helena fidgeted in her chair and thought about Mr. Cramer and what he had said to her. He seemed to have taken special interest in her. The other models in the room certainly noticed. Maybe, she debated back and forth with herself, I have the look he wants. Or maybe I just imagined his interest in me.

A very short time later, the blonde returned. "You're supposed to go in now," she said to Helena.

"Thank you," Helena said, picking up her portfolio and walking into the office.

There was a small den with a spiral staircase leading down to the lower floor, which opened into a large living room completely furnished in white—white Berber carpeting, and white wool couches that matched bleached wood end tables. At the far end of the room was a fireplace flanked on either side by floor-to-ceiling sliding glass doors that opened onto a patio and pool. To the right of the room was an L-shaped formal dining room. Between the two couches was a large glass coffee table with an overhead light that spotlighted an Oscar, two Emmies, and numerous plaques. The walls were covered with photographs of famous celebrities.

The man looked up as she walked into the room.

"I'm Jaimie Cramer," he said, extending his hand.

"It's nice to meet you." She took his hand. "I'm Helena Sinclair."

"Won't you please have a seat," he said, indicating the couch across from him, his eyes watching her every move.

Up close, one on one, he was even more attracted to her than when he'd seen her sitting in the reception area. She had that cool, luminous, sexual magnetism that the young Grace Kelly had exuded. The kind that he had always found so challenging. She moved with a natural aura of grace and elegance on the outside, and he was sure she possessed a smoldering passion on the inside. He imagined burying his face between her creamy white breasts and slowly stripping the clothes

41

from her lithe body.

Helena, who was usually never at a loss for words, felt tongue-tied. There was something in his eyes that left her breathless. She felt trapped, as if the room were closing in on her, and she wished she could turn and leave; but she remembered Nicky and her monthly bills waiting to be paid, so instead she sat down.

"May I see your portfolio?"

"Yes, of course," she said as she hastily unzipped the portfolio and handed it to him.

Slowly he thumbed through it without comment, and she watched him, trying to think of something intelligent to say.

"Very nice," he said, closing the case. "Let me tell you a little bit about what we're looking for."

Helena leaned forward in her seat and listened attentively.

"There's a fashion show sequence in the miniseries, and we need four models to wear the designs of the lead character, who is a world-famous fashion designer."

"What sort of look do you want?" Helena asked.

"A glamorous Hollywood look," he replied. "We want models who know what they are doing and can handle themselves on a runway."

"Well, I can certainly do that," Helena said. "Runway modeling is primarily what I do."

"Would you mind walking for me?"

"Not at all." Helena stood up and walked to the end of the room, the sea green cape fluttering behind her. She executed a showy double turn, called a Double Dior, and walked back to the couch, and sat down.

"Very good," he said. "You have the type of look we want; but I do have quite a few others to see before I make a final decision."

"I understand." Though she knew he had others to see, her confidence was a little shaken and she hoped he would choose her.

He paused, lit a cigarette and finally said after what

seemed like an eternity, "I'll tell you what, Helena. If you're really serious about this part, why don't you come back later, say around three or so. I'll have a little more time and we can discuss the show in more detail."

"I'd be happy to," Helena said enthusiastically. "Thank you. Thank you very much. I really appreciate your taking the time to talk with me."

"You're welcome," he said, as he held out his hand for her to shake and dismissed her without looking up. "I'll see you at three, then."

Helena's feet barely touched the ground as she left the interview. She was used to the straightforward attitudes of Seattle, and it didn't occur to her that Jaimie was interested in anything other than possibly giving her a job. She was so excited about the prospect of a callback that she decided to drive straight to the agency and tell Catherine about her interview.

Reaching Catherine's, she parked her car and almost bounced up the sidewalk to the agency. As Helena pulled open the door she almost ran into a young, pretty blond woman just leaving the agency. Dressed in a stiff red suit and teetering on her high heels, she looked as if she were on the verge of tears, so Helena gave her a friendly smile as they passed.

"Hi, Catherine!" Helena called as she entered the agency.

"Hello, Helena," Catherine greeted her, watching the departing young blonde and shaking her head. "These young things show up in town with the hayseed still in their hair and think Los Angeles is just waiting for them to arrive. That one," she continued, "is so green that she'll be easy prey for the first wolf she runs into. I told her to go home where she belongs but she wouldn't listen. They never do."

Helena was too excited to give much thought to what her agent was saying. "Guess what, Catherine!" she blurted out. "I have a callback on my interview! I have to go back there at three today."

"Well, don't count your chickens before they're hatched," Catherine said with her usual dour pessimism. She took a drag on her cigarette and turned around without another word to hobble slowly back to her desk in a cloud of smoke.

As she said goodbye and left the agency, Helena refused to let Catherine's negative attitude pull her down. She decided to walk over to the little café across the street and have a light lunch. After that, it would be time to go to her callback.

At 2:45 P.M., Helena was filled with nervous energy, and with great anticipation she wound her way back up the narrow, private driveway. This time no cars passed her, and only one lone white Rolls Royce was parked near the house.

The waiting room was deserted, and Helena wondered whether she should wait there or go down to the living room. She decided to take the aggressive route and go downstairs, her heels echoing as she timidly descended the metal stairs.

Mr. Cramer was sorting through a stack of composites and looked up as Helena reached the bottom of the stairs.

"You're back," he said, glancing up briefly as he continued to thumb through the pile. "Have a seat." It was more of a command than an invitation.

Helena sat down on the couch opposite him.

"Would you like some coffee?" he said, finally looking up.

"Yes, thank you."

Almost immediately, an Oriental houseboy appeared with a tray bearing two cups and a pot of coffee.

Mr. Cramer waited until the houseboy had served the coffee and disappeared. "You know, Helena, I asked you back here because I see something special in you that I don't often see."

Helena sat at attention, hardly believing what she was hearing.

44

"You have a sense of poise and aloofness. But at the same time I see a childlike vulnerability just beneath the surface."

He took a sip of his coffee. "Vulnerability is the quality in an actor or actress that makes the audience want to root for them. Have you ever thought about making a transition into acting?"

"Well, I have done quite a few television commercials—" Helena started to say.

"Unfortunately," he continued on, almost as though he hadn't heard or even wanted an answer, "time goes by, and with every hurt and pain suffered, this beautiful vulnerability gets covered up by self-protection until it's completely hidden behind a brittle shell. Then the actor or actress is no longer able to open himself to the audience or even to another human being."

He got up and sat down next to her. "Hollywood is a tough town," he said, gazing intently at her. "It's full of vultures ready to prey on the weak and vulnerable. There are people who have been used and who turn around and try to do the same thing to someone else."

Helena hung on his every word, almost afraid to breathe for fear the spell would be broken. It was like a dream come true. This important producer saw her as someone special.

"As I said before, you have a certain charismatic quality, and I think you would be absolutely perfect for what we need." He leaned back and casually draped his arm on the back of the couch. "You know, you have a lot of raw potential. In fact, I'd like to see to it that you have all the classes necessary to make the transition into acting. Singing, dancing, whatever it takes."

In her excitement, Helena took a gulp of hot coffee and it went down her windpipe. She started coughing and Mr. Cramer patted her on the back.

"Are you okay?" he asked, genuinely concerned.

"Yes, Mr. Cramer," she answered, embarrassed. "I'm sorry, I swallowed my coffee the wrong way."

45

"Call me Jaimie," he said, his hand still resting on her shoulder. "I want to teach you about the business. I want you to learn to recognize the users and the con artists, and I want you to learn to protect yourself against them, so that you won't wind up bitter and used like the thousands of other girls in this town."

"Mr. Cramer—"

"Jaimie, please," he said. He moved a little closer and started to caress her shoulder lightly with his fingertips.

"Jaimie," Helena responded, beginning to feel very nervous and uncomfortable. Suddenly, her elation about the callback vanished, and she wished the interview were over. As naive as she was about the workings of Los Angeles, there was no mistaking his overt come-on, and she wondered how she could gracefully retreat.

"I think it's wonderful that you believe in me and want to help me. But," she said, taking a deep breath, "you know, I'm from a small town and you'll have to spell things out for me. What exactly do you want from me in return?" She didn't bother to mask her growing suspicions. She was a very direct person, and in her brief six months she had acquired some knowledge of the convoluted workings of the Los Angeles scene.

Instead of answering, in one motion he casually pulled her to him and covered her mouth with his. He forced his tongue between her teeth, kissing her passionately. The effect was electric, but Helena pushed him away in shock.

"Helena," he said, his hands still caressing her shoulders. "I want your head, your heart, and your body."

Dumbfounded and shaken, she had a sinking feeling in the pit of her stomach as reality hit her. He had no interest in her career. Save her from the vultures? He was one of those vultures, and she was gullible enough to have believed him.

46

Humiliated, she mustered all the panache she could. "Well, Mr. Cramer," she said lightly, trying to sound sophisticated instead of like the naive hick she felt she was. "You can have my head, and my heart, but as for my body, I'll keep that for myself. I'm sorry," she added, "I have to go now. I've had about all the instruction I can handle for one day. And," she said, trying to control her anger, "I don't believe in mixing business with my personal life. I think a person should get a job based on her own merit, not because of her talent in bed!"

"Great," Jaimie mumbled under his breath. "Two-hundred and fifty beautiful models to choose from and I pick the one that thinks she's a Sunday school teacher."

"What did you say?" Helena demanded.

"I said, no, I don't think every model has to sleep with the producer to get a job. . . . But," and he smiled slyly, "I never knew one who didn't."

"I want to thank you for taking the time to talk with me," Helena said stiffly, ignoring what he had just said and holding out her hand.

"Well, you can't blame me for trying." He smiled.

Helena just stood there silently with her hand out.

"I do think you have promise and I wish you the best of luck," he said, taking her hand.

"Goodbye," Helena said, through gritted teeth.

Holding her head high, she turned and walked out. Hot tears stung her eyes, and it was all she could do to keep from crying until she reached her car. As the tears ran down her cheeks, she wasn't sure which was a more bitter pill to swallow: that she wasn't going to get the booking or that she'd allowed Cramer to trample on her self-respect.

Jaimie watched Helena through the window as she marched stiffly to her car, her back straight, her head up. She made him smile. He had used his most successful approach on her. The lure of a movie role had always guaranteed him an afternoon of fucking and sucking—until now. He watched Helena slowly drive off. He would have bet any amount of money on that sparkle of excitement in her eyes when he had asked her to come back. Instead she had turned him down, but he liked that. In a city where willing, beautiful girls were there at the nod of a head, here was one with scruples. She intrigued him. And as far as he was concerned, the game had just begun.

Still furious when she arrived home, Helena called Catherine and complained to her about Jaimie Cramer's advances, expecting sympathy.

Instead, Catherine said, "It's all part of the business, dear. Just let it go. There will be other bookings."

And Helena tried to do just that. Within two days, she had almost forgotten all about Jaimie Cramer and on the third day, Catherine called.

"You got the miniseries booking. Be at the studio tomorrow morning at ten for a wardrobe fitting."

Helena was speechless.

Chapter Three

The pale apricot moon hung suspended in the cool, Spanish night and cast a path of light onto the smooth, Mediterranean beach. A thousand stars danced overhead, and a light breeze ruffled the bougainvillea and spread the scent of hibiscus into the air.

The sound of music from Regine's was so faint, it was almost like an unconscious throb, and a beacon of light radiated through the small diamond-shaped glass that was cut into the massive gold and silver mirrored entrance. This door was the threshold between reality and fantasy, dividing the "haves" from the "have-nots." For the rich, it was a place where they could go and mingle with their own. For those neither chic nor famous, it was just a fantasy.

For Kabrina Hunter, internationally known model, it was a stopping-off place, neither fantasy nor reality but something in between. As she led the way into Regine's, Jean-Claude, her photographer, and his assistant, Francois, followed close behind. Kabrina was a tall sliver of a woman with endless legs, and skin the color of rich molasses. Her delicate, sculpted features and her startling copper brown eyes, however, were what haunted onlookers. Tonight Kabrina seemed to flow like quicksilver, dressed in a simple cream silk shirt, harem pants that billowed behind her as she moved, and her waist cinched by a wide gold sash. Heavy gold loops adorned her ears, and she clasped a gold mesh bag to her side.

The front door to this exclusive club swung wide open without hesitation the moment she approached.

"Welcome, Señorita Kabrina," Julio, Regine's doorman, said, bowing low.

"Good evening, Mademoiselle Kabrina," Natalie, the hostess, added. "It's so nice to see you again."

"Thank you, Natalie." Kabrina paused and looked at Jean-Claude.

Without speaking he took out a thick roll of money, counted out a stack and handed it to Natalie.

"George has our best table ready for you, Madame Kabrina," she said, handing Jean-Claude a receipt, but Kabrina was already past the bar area and onto the steps where George was waiting.

"Such a beautiful woman," Julio murmured to Natalie.

"*Oui,* women like that are born, not made," Natalie observed. "I'll guarantee she's never known a hard day in her life and never will."

"People say that her family is one of the wealthiest on the African continent," Julio added, watching Kabrina's slim figure glide into the lounge area.

"Of course! Look how she carries herself. Without a doubt, she comes from money," Natalie exclaimed, closing the discussion.

George seated Kabrina, Jean-Claude, and Francois at the number one table facing the dance floor. A bottle of Dom Pérignon rosé sat waiting next to the table in a silver ice bucket, and a waiter hurried over with chilled crystal champagne flutes. He quietly popped the cork and poured the icy bubbles into each glass.

"Here's to many more successful and profitable shootings in exotic locations," Jean-Claude toasted.

"Here, here," Kabrina smiled, raising her glass.

The walls of Regine's were wrapped in ruby red

velvet and mirrors, and soft banquettes upholstered in the same deep red velour bordered the postage-stamp dance floor in the center of the room, packed with chic partners dancing to the throbbing beat as spotlights beamed blue and gold overhead.

Kabrina sipped her champagne and watched the dancers. The music acted as a tonic, and she felt the tensions of the long day slip away as she lost herself in the mood of the evening—until the disc jockey put on an oldie by Gloria Gaynor. Its lyrics haunted Kabrina, echoed in her mind. They told of a young girl's fear of being alone, her fear of dealing with life and everyday living, until she grew strong and learned how to survive on her own.

The words brought back a rush of memories to Kabrina, and Regine's temporarily faded. Seven years rolled away and she was back in her father's tiny clapboard house in a canyon above Los Angeles.

"You say what?" her father had said in astonishment.

"I said I want to be a model," she had repeated. "I'm going to take the money I saved for college and go to New York."

"You're not taking your money and you're not going to New York. You're staying right here and enrolling in college!" He stood with his face inches from hers.

"Look, Dad, I talked with a booker from the Madeline Parks Agency in New York." Kabrina had tried to speak calmly and slowly, but her heart had been pounding. "She was at school for career day and she said if I came to New York, they would definitely sign me and I'd get work right away."

"You'd work all right," he spat out. "I thought I raised you smarter. Those so-called modeling agencies are all alike. They'll be peddling your black ass all over town."

"No, Dad! It's not like that," she tried to explain patiently. "This is a legitimate agency. It's one of the biggest!"

51

He grabbed her by the shoulders and shook her hard. "Can't you get it through your head, girl? They're all cons! I see this shit every day of the week. In two days they'll have you tricking up and down Manhattan every time they snap their fingers. No way. No daughter of mine is gonna be a whore! I've worked too hard. You've worked too hard. Now make something of yourself!"

She pulled away from his grasp. "You don't understand," she cried.

"I said no," he shouted at her. "That's the end of the discussion!"

"I'm going—" she started to say. Instead she decided to leave the room.

Taking her arm, he jerked her so hard her teeth snapped together, biting her tongue. "You go and you don't need to come back when they finish with you."

She had never seen him so angry, never. His dark face seemed almost brick-colored under the sheen of perspiration. Without a word, she turned and stalked to her room, slamming the door behind her.

The next morning Kabrina withdrew all her savings from the bank, packed her bags, and, armed with a business card from the Madeline Parks Agency, hopped a plane for New York City. There, the agency found her a place to share with two other models, and then recommended a modeling school. Two days later she called her father from New York to let him know she was safe. She still remembered every detail about that call, even down to the tone of the operator's voice.

"Collect call from your daughter," the operator said, her voice bored and disinterested. "Will you accept the charge?"

Silence.

"You won't accept the call?" the operator persisted.

"I have no daughter," her father said and hung up.

"I'm sorry, miss, your party will not accept the call," the operator said, this time her voice gentle.

Kabrina quietly replaced the telephone as the radio in the background played Gloria Gaynor singing of life and survival.

And survive Kabrina did. At first she was afraid. She had never been away from home or her father. She knew she couldn't go back to see her father until she was a huge success, and that thought gave her determination. She'd show him how famous and rich she had become—and all without a college degree.

She enrolled in the modeling school to learn to walk properly and turn: to apply makeup for shows, for photography, and for everyday; to put clothes together; to present them to the best advantage; and how to play to the camera and to an audience. She spent hours thumbing through fashion magazines, selecting poses and practicing them in front of the mirror. In between, the agency sent her to "go-sees."

"What are go-sees?" she had asked the booker at the agency.

"A go-see means you have an appointment with a photographer to see if he is interested in testing with you or using you for a job," the booker replied.

"What do you mean, 'testing'?" Kabrina had asked, embarrassed.

"It's when a model shoots with a photographer for free. Each donates their time. That way, they both get free shots for their portfolios," the booker replied. "Eventually, if you do enough testing, you get your portfolio built up without spending thousands of dollars."

And her father had been right. She did peddle herself all over Manhattan, but not for sex. Each afternoon she would call the agency and get her list of go-sees for the next day. Starting early the next morning, she'd run from one appointment to the next, rain or shine. She'd meet with photographers, hoping she would spark enough excitement that they'd want to test her.

By the end of each day she was exhausted. Her feet

ached and her head pounded. Kabrina was shocked to discover the stamina a model had to have, both physically and mentally. In Los Angeles the attitude was laid back, but in Manhattan there was none of that sunny "have a good day" California attitude. Here business was business, and it was pursued with somber determination by models and industry people alike. It was a quick "you're right" or "you're not right."

Some mornings, she just wanted to pull the covers up over her head. She was sick of selling herself, sick of the rejection eight, ten, sometimes twelve times a day. She learned to put a wall up around her emotions, telling herself not to take it personally, that they wanted a particular look for a particular product. She knew that her turn would come and that she'd have to hang in there, and she did.

And she thought of her father's last words, "I have no daughter," and they spurred her on. Her bitterness made her strong, and she was determined to survive. While other women left New York, defeated, Kabrina persevered. She was driven. Nothing or no one would stand in her way, and day after day, she pressed on.

Finally one afternoon the agency called with her first booking. It was a fitting with the famous Italian designer, Roberto Franco. That booking was her turning point. From that day on she became Roberto's favorite model. He not only used her for fittings and showings but made her the star of his press show, and the press exposure broke the ice for her. Other bookings, for photography and runway, followed. Her face soon appeared on a hundred magazine pages and videotapes. At last she was really a model. It had taken her years but she had made it, and she had never spoken to her father again even with all of her success.

"Hey, *ma chère!* You okay?" Jean-Claude said, his sharp voice jarring her back to the present.

The song had ended and all that remained was a single tear that had escaped from the corner of her eye.

"Sure," Kabrina said, quickly brushing away the tear before anyone noticed. "I'm just tired." She stood up. "You guys stay. I'm going to call it a night. I'll see you in the morning."

The next day it was modeling as usual, although the setting was anything but usual. The luxurious Puente Romano Hotel, set on the Costa Del Sol, along the southern edge of Spain on the Mediterranean Sea, was a resort made up of Moorish white stucco villas. Nestled among lush, tropical vegetation hiding tranquil ponds and sparkling turquoise pools, it was the perfect hideaway for the rich and famous. European wealth and nobility oozed from every corner of the resort.

"Hold it!" Jean-Claude called as Kabrina stood beside one of the elegant swimming pools. "Francois, check that fold on her pareu, yeah. Straighten that piece of hair, okay. Great, chin up . . . terrific, wonderful," he said, clicking away on his Hasselblad and talking nonstop.

The hotel had hired them to shoot a new publicity brochure, and Kabrina, wearing an orchid, gold-and-orange pareu over a string bikini, reclined on one of the orange chaise longues at the edge of the pool. A small crowd of guests from the hotel gathered around. That was nothing new to Kabrina. She was used to people watching her work, and she knew how to tune them out completely. The only voice she heard was Jean-Claude's.

Smoothly, catlike, she moved from one pose to another as he focused and clicked the shutter. It was as if she and Jean-Claude were partners in a photographic ballet, sharing a comfortable rhythm between them. In between takes, Francois would dart in and out smoothing and straightening, pulling and tucking.

Gradually the crowd thinned out, and finally only one man remained. He was of average build, about 5'11", with thick dark brown hair that cowlicked at the crown. His face was interesting rather than handsome, with Slavic features. Kabrina saw him out of the corner of her eye and glanced over in his direction. They smiled at each other and he walked on.

"Okay Kabrina, I think we've got it," Jean-Claude exclaimed excitedly.

Kabrina stood up and stretched. "Can we break for a soda?" she called to Jean-Claude.

"Sure, *chère,*" he answered, snapping the lens cover on his camera.

They walked over to the covered poolside bar and sat down. Jean-Claude ordered *"agua con gas"* for all of them, and a white-clad waiter brought them iced glasses of soda.

"Oh, ask him for a straw, please," Kabrina said to Jean-Claude.

"Will this do?" Kabrina heard a boyish voice behind her say.

She turned around to face the man who had been watching the photography session earlier. Even as she turned to face him, he produced a straw from behind her ear with a quick twist of his wrist.

Smiling, she accepted it. "How'd you do that?"

"Magic, my dear," he said, winking. With another twist of his wrist, he produced a whole lime. "Would you like a squeeze of lime in your soda?"

"Yes, thank you," Kabrina laughed.

He cut the lime and squeezed it into her glass.

"You're a magician," she asked, sipping her soda.

"Sometimes," he said. "I'm Noel Wellsley from Los Angeles." He made a mock bow.

"I'm Kabrina Hunter from New York."

"You're very beautiful, Kabrina." He stared at her intently. "I couldn't help wondering who did your face."

"Who did my face? You mean my makeup? Francois did," she said, confused.

"No, I mean your bone structure. Who did your plastic surgery, your cheekbones and your nose?"

56

"I haven't had any plastic surgery," Kabrina snapped, irritated. "I was born with this bone structure. Now, if you'll excuse me, I have to get back to my shooting."

Nuts, Kabrina thought to herself, standing up. They're everywhere. And she started back to the poolside.

"Wait, wait, let me explain," Noel called. He jumped up and hurried after her, touching her arm lightly. "I didn't mean to be so rude," he said softly, "but when I'm not playing with magic, I'm a plastic surgeon. I guess I was just thinking out loud. I really didn't mean to offend you."

"That's fine," Kabrina said with a stiff smile, and she looked pointedly at his hand on her arm. He immediately dropped it to his side.

"I have to go." She turned and walked away.

"Look," he said, following her, but careful not to touch her again. "Let me make it up to you. Let me take you to dinner tonight."

Kabrina glanced at him doubtfully. "No, thanks."

"I really am harmless and you'll have a good time, I promise." He put his hand behind his back and with a twist of his wrist, produced a flower. "Look, a peace offering. Come on, what do you say?"

Kabrina studied him for a few moments. She was getting a little tired of spending every evening with Jean-Claude and Francois. "Well," she said hesitantly, taking the flower, "maybe just for a drink."

"I'll call for you at nine-thirty," Noel said, enthusiasm creeping into his voice, "in the lobby?"

"All right," she responded, wondering what she had gotten herself into.

By nine-thirty that evening, the flaming Latin sun had dipped down almost to the placid horizon of the Mediterranean, bathing the whitewashed boutiques and villas of Puerto Banus in warm pink and gold shadows. At the water's edge, long wooden docks, like keyboards on a piano, moored sumptuous yachts, the likes of which Kabrina had never before seen. The crème de la crème of Europe together with throngs of tourists milled back and forth in the narrow streets of the port. Open-air restaurants and quaint bars lined the streets facing the sea. Everywhere there was a bustling carnival atmosphere.

As they strolled the length of the port, Noel acted like a puppy, eager to please his master. He kept Kabrina laughing with interesting stories and funny anecdotes as they stopped to inspect menus at café entrances or to admire a moored yacht. At the far end of the port, Noel told her, was a bronze statue erected to José Banus, the founder and original owner and developer of the port. Beyond the statue was a walkway to a spit that led to a magnificent silver yacht, rumored, Noel said, to be owned by one of the wealthiest men in the world.

They sauntered back to the shop area and decided to have dinner outside at the Leon de Oro, the only Chinese restaurant in the port. They sat outside under the gay red-and-gold Chinese lanterns as a trio of strolling musicians serenaded the diners.

Kabrina was surprised to find herself having a wonderful time with Noel, whom she had first thought ordinary. Now he was anything but that. Funny, animated, and full of energy, he held her undivided attention with his charm and intelligence and also entertained the diners around them with his magic and sleight of hand. She hated for the evening to end, but as she glanced at her watch she realized how late it was.

"Back to your villa before midnight, huh, Cinderella?" Noel joked, catching her checking her watch.

"Yes," she laughed. "There are pots and pans still waiting to be scrubbed."

As they walked back to the entrance to Puerto Banus and the taxi stand, they passed the Sinatra Bar. A small rock band had set up equipment, and the night echoed with the sound of American music set to Spanish lyrics.

58

A festive crowd congregated around the bar, swaying to the beat of the music.

"Are you sure you don't have time for a nightcap?" Noel asked.

"Next time," Kabrina suggested.

"Next time? Then I take it that I've made enough of an impression that you'll see me again."

"Maybe," Kabrina laughed as they hailed a taxi back to the hotel.

"I've had a lot of fun, Noel," Kabrina said at the door, holding out her hand when they arrived at her villa.

"So have I, Kabrina, dear." He took her hand, and before she realized what was happening, he pulled her to him and kissed her for what seemed like an hour. Instinctively, she responded, and in that instant he was no longer the amusing dinner companion, charming everyone with his tricks. Instead, he was a confident, passionate man, in complete control of the situation. She was surprised and a little confused by his sudden role switch.

"I've wanted to do that since the first time I saw you," he whispered in her ear.

"I—I—" she stuttered, for once at a loss for words.

"Tomorrow night I'll show you the flamenco dancers."

"Thank you—I mean, all right," she stammered. "I mean, good night." Kabrina shut the door behind her and leaned against it. The evening had taken an unexpected turn. She had accepted the date with Noel out of boredom and now in a matter of seconds the situation had changed.

She'd have to think this out, but she smiled in spite of herself as she glanced down at the white marble floor. An envelope addressed to her had been slipped under the door. She picked it up and tore it open. It was a telephone message from Leon, Roberto Franco's assistant and lover.

59

"Kabrina," it read, "Roberto is gravely ill. Please come immediately. Leon." Kabrina felt a jolt, as if someone had thrown cold water on her. All thoughts of sleep and the evening left her mind. Roberto was her mentor, the man who gave her her start. More than that, he was one of the rare people in her life whom she trusted. She tried to keep her fingers from shaking as she dialed Roberto's number.

"Leon, I just got your message. What's happened to Roberto?"

On the other end of the wire, Leon burst into tears. "Kabrina, Roberto has AIDS!"

"But I just spoke to Roberto a couple of weeks ago," Kabrina said. "He said he had picked up a virus, but that was all."

"That's true, but he couldn't seem to shake it. He became so sick he couldn't even work. I finally convinced him to see his doctor. The test results came back positive, advanced. Kabrina, he's so weak he can't even lift his head from the pillow," he said. "Please come! I know Roberto wants to see you, and I need you here."

"I'm on my way!"

She hung up and immediately called Jean-Claude to apprise him of the situation.

"Of course you must go. I have enough shots to cover the brochure," he reassured her.

She booked a reservation on the next available flight that night from Malaga to Madrid to New York and hurriedly packed her bags. A limousine picked her up at the hotel and deposited her at the Malaga airport.

After boarding the plane, she took as usual a seat in the first-class section. She leaned back in the sleeperette and tried to relax, but she couldn't rest as her mind wandered back to her first meeting with Roberto.

"It's only for a fitting, honey," her agent, Madeline Parks, had said. "But if he likes you, it will be a start. His press shows are legendary."

Kabrina had never done a fitting, but she hadn't told the agency that. She had been so excited that she was ready hours before her appointed time. She had walked to Seventh Avenue, the heart of the New York "schmata" industry where laborers, wheeling racks of clothes, and patterns scurried from one building to another and trucks blocked side streets, their lights flashing, while bolts of fabric were unloaded and whisked inside buildings. Kabrina entered the building where the fitting was to take place and was propelled to the elevators by a surge of "rag" people. She got off on the eleventh floor and followed the arrows and sign proclaiming, House of Roberto Franco.

"I'm here for a fitting," she had told the receptionist.

"Go straight back," the receptionist said, pointing to a door behind her. "Mr. Franco is in the first office on the right."

The room beyond the door was like a big, open warehouse, with rows of sewing machines and scores of Oriental and Puerto Rican women sitting at the machines busily sewing. On one side of the room long tables were covered with bolts of fabric on which cutters were laying out patterns and cutting fabric. There was no air conditioning, and the windows were flung wide open. The hum of the machines working in unison meshed with the sounds from the street below. Sweat colored the workers' clothes, and waves of heat slowly rose to the ceiling and hovered there. Kabrina hurriedly walked through the partially open door on the right into an air-conditioned room. A worktable stacked with papers and fabric, and several racks of dresses filled the space. The walls were lined with sketches signed with the famous signature of Roberto Franco.

Six people, two women and four men, hovered over the worktable discussing a sketch.

"Excuse me," Kabrina said timidly from the doorway. Six pairs of eyes turned and looked up.

"It's the model, Roberto," one of the women said.

"Hello. Come in, come in," a small, slight man said, hurrying toward her with his hand extended. "I'm Roberto Franco," he introduced himself in a thickly accented voice. He stood very straight. His thick, black hair was glossed straight back from his forehead, and the pencil-thin mustache under his hook nose bristled as he spoke.

"I'm Kabrina Hunter." She shook his hand. "I'm pleased to meet you."

"Well, now that you're here, we can get started. I want to drape some fabric to see how it moves. Go ahead, get undressed.

"Rodeaka," he said to one of the women, "come with me to get the charmousse."

"I beg your pardon?" Kabrina said, thinking she had misunderstood.

"I said, take off your clothes. You can hang them on the rack. I'll be right back." With that, he and Rodeaka left the room.

Kabrina went behind a rack of dresses and slowly stepped out of her dress. She hadn't worn a bra, so all she had on was a G-string and pantyhose. She was embarrassed and didn't know what to do, so she stayed behind the rack of dresses. The others in the room had turned back to their work.

Roberto and Rodeaka walked back through the door, carrying long bolts of colorful silk charmousse in their arms.

"Kabrina, ready?" Roberto asked.

"Y-yes," she answered, stepping from behind the rack, her arms crossed to cover her bare breasts.

Everyone turned to face her.

"What are your measurements?" Roberto asked.

"I'm not sure," she said, feeling very insecure.

"That's all right. Leon can take them. Leon—"

The sight of six pairs of eyes looking at her as she stood there naked was almost too intimidating for

Kabrina. No one had told her this was part of modeling. Her face burned and perspiration, chilled by the air conditioner, rolled down her sides under her arms and beaded on her temples.

A fine-boned sparrow of a man stepped from the group, pulled a tape measure from around his neck, and started to measure her.

"Base of neck to waist, seventeen and a half inches," he stated in a monotone. "Arm down to your side, bend, please. Shoulder to wrist, twenty-four inches."

Kabrina had attempted to cover her bare breasts with one arm and held the other arm straight out.

"Bust—" Leon droned on, then paused. "Honey," he said to Kabrina, "you'll have to put your other arm down so I can measure your bust."

By this time, Kabrina was quivering with humiliation and embarrassment. She felt like a nonentity, a piece of meat being inspected. Tears welled up, and she made a choking sound in her throat, trying to hold back the tears.

Roberto looked up from the bolt of cloth he had been toying with. "Is this the first time you've done fittings?" he inquired, dropping the cloth and walking over to her.

Kabrina nodded, still trying to hide her breasts with her arm.

"Oh, I see. Come with me." He led her back behind the rack of dresses. "Here." He handed her a clean, white handkerchief. Then he took her hand and patted it. "Kabrina, there is nothing to be embarrassed about. There is no sex here. This is just work. Nothing here is personal. You're just a part of the team with a job to do, like Leon or Rodeaka or myself. *Capisce?*"

Kabrina nodded.

"Okay, little one." He smiled. "Let's get back to work. Leon—"

After her measurements were taken, Roberto draped fabrics on her and had her walk around the room to see how they moved. By the end of the day, most of Kabrina's inhibitions had left her. Roberto was right. No one was looking at her with anything other than a professional eye.

In time, he had become more than a mentor to her. He had been her only friend. In the dark beginning days of her modeling career he had believed in her and had given her a chance. She had never had the opportunity to repay him, and now he was dying. Her heart saddened as she thought about how much she loved her dear friend. How she wished the plane would fly faster, and with that thought she finally drifted off into a troubled sleep.

Ten hours later, a limousine dropped Kabrina off at Roberto's penthouse facing Central Park. She hadn't taken time to drop off her luggage at her apartment, so she left it with the doorman and hurried up.

"Thank God you're here, Kabrina!" Leon cried, tears welling up in his little bird eyes. "He's been asking for you." He led her to Roberto's spacious and beautifully decorated bedroom.

The frail figure in the bed did not remotely resemble the Roberto Kabrina knew. In the space of a few weeks his appearance had altered unbelievably. His perennial tan had turned sallow, and his skin hung loosely over his bones and looked so transparent that Kabrina could almost see the color of his veins. Raw, red blotches covered his face and neck.

"Is he awake?" Kabrina whispered to Leon.

"He floats in and out of consciousness," Leon replied. "Oh, Kabrina, why? He has so much to live for. He's worked so hard."

"I know, Leon, I know."

She walked over and sat down at Roberto's side, taking his cold, damp hand in hers.

His eyes fluttered open. "Kabrina," he whispered. "You came. We have to prepare the collection. I shall need you for your usual fittings." Then his eyes closed again.

"Of course, Roberto," she reassured him, patting his hand. It had been years since she had done any fittings, and she looked at Leon.

"He's hallucinating. He doesn't realize," Leon said, tears streaming down his cheeks. "I just don't know what else to do."

Kabrina gathered Leon in her arms and rocked him. "How long have you been here?"

"I haven't left his side since the doctor told him he had AIDS. I've sent out for groceries and medicines. I just couldn't bear to leave him alone."

"I'm here now, Leon. You've got to get some rest or you'll be sick, too. I'll stay with him."

"I couldn't—"

"It's my turn. I owe him so much. Let me do this, please," Kabrina said. "If you'll get a little rest, you'll feel much beter. Then you can come back refreshed."

"Maybe if I lay down for just a little while . . ." he said, obviously tired.

"I'll be right here. I promise I'll call you if there is the least little change."

Kabrina sat down to keep her vigil.

It took Roberto another week and a half to die, and Kabrina stayed by his side every day. She sat next to Roberto's bed, sometimes reading to him, sometimes just stroking his hand. He had lucid moments, and then they would talk quietly about the past. Other times he was incoherent. Mostly, he had no idea where he was or what was happening to him. Day by day he became weaker and weaker. Then Roberto took a turn for the worse. Kabrina, Leon, and the doctor were at his side. One moment he was awake talking to them in a soft voice, and the next, it was as if he had fallen asleep.

"I'm sorry," the doctor said, quietly, "he's gone."

Kabrina held Leon in her arms and they wept

together. The wall she had built around her feelings when she left Los Angeles crumbled with Roberto's death. He had been her first friend, the first one to believe in her, and she cared deeply for him.

Work was her comfort, and she drew solace from her bookings as the days passed and her sadness faded. Finally, only the sweet memories of her friendship with Roberto remained.

Chapter Four

Laura Ann awoke that day to the sounds outside and to the hot California sun burning brightly in the cloudless blue sky. The drone of commuter traffic had long since dissipated with the morning mist, and in its place the midday shift of motorists rushed from destination to destination, caffeine pumping in their veins and tempers rising with the heat of the day. For a few moments, she thought she was still at home in Iowa; then she heard voices beneath her window speaking in Spanish. No one in Iowa spoke Spanish, and with that she realized she *was* home—her new home, Marcus's apartment, in Los Angeles.

She lay in bed for a few moments, slowly waking up, trying to remember the night before, and her mind drifted back to the three weeks since she'd arrived. It was all a sort of blur. She remembered being at Flash's photography studio a couple of times with Marcus. Flash had explained about modeling the first time, and they all had drunk wine. Then Flash had given her a pill and Marcus had said to take it. She searched her mind now for the name of the pills. "Quaalude," she thought they had called it. After taking the pill, everything went hazy. She knew that Flash took some pictures of her both times, and she remembered making love with Marcus. There were vague memories of driving home which came after making love with Marcus. That couldn't have been right, they couldn't have made love at Flash's studio. And the pictures; she remembered that Flash was taking pictures of her for a portfolio. She wondered if he really had and why she couldn't remember for sure, even after all this time. And why she couldn't remember what had happened last night.

The apartment was silent and she called for Marcus, but there was no answer. She slipped out of bed, threw on one of his T-shirts, and walked through the living room into the kitchen. The apartment was empty, and a stale pot of simmering coffee, black as tar and almost as thick, sat on the coffee warmer. She poured herself a cup and sat down on the couch to think. Perhaps she couldn't remember what had happened over the past few weeks and last night because she was drunk. Maybe she had been making a fool out of herself and embarrassing Marcus. A feeling of nausea started in her stomach and increased with her fears. Yes, she decided, that had to be it. And now, maybe because of what had happened last night—damn, if only she could remember—

Marcus had left the apartment angry and not wanting to be around her. What was she going to do now? Where could she go? She curled up in a corner of the couch and struggled to hold back the tears. She tried to think of a solution. She would make it up to Marcus for whatever she had done. She would promise never to let it happen again. She berated herself over and over again. Oh, why was she so stupid?

She had no concept of how long she sat on the couch, comatose, tears quietly dropping into her coffee, silently cursing herself for her supposed stupidity. But eventually she heard footsteps in the hallway outside the door and a key turning in the lock.

"Laura Ann," Marcus exclaimed, smiling, as he opened the door. "You're finally awake."

68

He took a good look at Laura Ann and immediately surmised that she was on a low swing from the drugs. She obviously didn't know that the drugs caused depression. That depression coupled with her already low self-esteem made her a prime target for his manipulations.

Laura Ann looked up from her coffee, tears streaming down her cheeks. "I'm sorry," she cried, bursting into loud sobs. "I don't know what I did last night. But if I embarrassed you, I didn't mean it! Please forgive me!"

"Embarrassed me," said Marcus, sitting down beside her and putting an arm around her. "What are you talking about, precious? You haven't embarrassed me."

"L-last night," Laura Ann stuttered. "I can't remember what I did, but I think I was real drunk."

Marcus started laughing. "Is that what the problem is? Yes, you were drunk, and high, and wonderful. Absolutely wonderful. Flash got some great shots. I've got them right here. That's where I went. I got the contact sheets from Flash to surprise you!"

"Really," Laura Ann sniffed, wiping her eyes with the back of her hand. "Really?"

"Yes, they're great. Those shooting sessions really paid off." Marcus pulled some sheets of photographs from a big manila envelope. "Here, take a look at these." He sorted through the contact sheets and handed them to Laura Ann in sequence.

As Laura Ann started looking at them, her eyes widened with horror. "I don't have any clothes on!" she gasped. "Oh, my God!"

"They're terrific," Marcus exclaimed. "Look at the expression, the attitude!"

"Oh, no, Marcus," she cried. "And look at these. Flash took pictures of us, doing it!"

"Of course, they're the best," Marcus said calmly. "Laura Ann, *all* the top models get their start this way."

69

"I don't think—" Laura Ann started.

"Hey," Marcus said sharply, cutting her off. "I thought you were serious about wanting to be a model."

"I am," Laura Ann said quickly. "I just thought—"

"Flash told you what it took," he said, agitated. He dropped his arm from around her shoulder. "Now, I put my neck out on the line for you. If I would have known you weren't serious about modeling, I would never have wasted my time and Flash's time!" He stood up and began to pace back and forth for emphasis. "I didn't know you were a flake; just like ninety-five percent of all the other girls around!"

"Oh, no, no," she cried, jumping up and grabbing his arm. "I am serious about modeling, I'm not a flake. I promise. I was just a little shocked for a moment. Is that really how all the top models get started?" she asked timidly, trying to win back his favor.

"Of course it is," Marcus replied, pretending to be mollified by her words. He knew a little anger would bring her right around. The bitch was too insecure to question him. It was all so easy, not even a challenge, really.

"Besides," he continued, "it's supposed to be fun. You had a good time, didn't you?"

"I-I guess so," she replied, not completely convinced. "I really don't remember much of what's been going on."

"This is all fun and games. It's nothing serious," he said, knowing he held all the cards. "Now tonight, we'll really get some good shots."

"Okay," she said dubiously.

"Now get dressed." Marcus gave her a light slap on the backside. "We're going shopping. Gotta keep my jewel shiny."

Laura Ann dressed in record time. She was so relieved and happy that Marcus liked the pictures that she pushed any doubts she had to the back of her mind. Marcus had been so good to her that she was determined to keep him happy. He was her Prince Charming, she decided to herself; whatever Marcus wanted, she would do.

Marcus took her to lunch at a tiny coffee shop on Hollywood Boulevard. Outside, every type of person imaginable walked the boulevard.

"What do you do for a living, Marcus?" Laura Ann asked in between bites of her hamburger. "You don't seem to have a regular job."

"Oh, a little of this and a little of that," he replied evasively. "I believe in the free enterprise system. I guess I'm what you would call an entrepreneur."

"Oh, I understand," Laura Ann said, but she didn't. She hadn't the faintest idea what "entrepreneur" meant, but she didn't want Marcus to think she was dumb.

Just then, Marcus waved to a young girl outside on the street. She was dressed in shocking pink tights and high heels and a T-shirt that was cinched around her waist. Her bright strawberry blond hair was long and flowing and her face was heavily made up.

"'Scuse me, precious," he said, standing. "I've gotta talk to this girl for a minute. Business."

Laura Ann watched him step outside and engage the blonde in a conversation. They talked for a few minutes, and Laura saw the girl give Marcus a thick wad of bills. Then she kissed Marcus on the cheek and strutted off down the street.

Marcus came back into the coffee shop and stood above Laura Ann. "Ready? Let's go," he said, without explaining the girl or the money.

Laura Ann was afraid to question him, so she just nodded and quickly grabbed her purse.

Marcus took her to the famous Frederick's of Hollywood, the bright purple-and-pink edifice standing as a monument to the craziness of Hollywood. There Marcus picked out a set of sexy black un-

71

derwear: a lacy push-up bra, a G-string, a garter belt, and long silky hose. Laura Ann had never owned a garter belt or a G-string, and Marcus wanted her to model them for him, but she was too embarrassed and wouldn't come out of the dressing room.

"Come on," he coaxed her. "I told you, it's just fun, nothing serious. This is L.A. Get with the program."

Laura Ann finally came out of the dressing room. Maybe Marcus was right. This was L.A., her new life. It was time to put her old life in Iowa behind her.

That night, Marcus and Laura Ann, wearing her new black lingerie under her clothes, went back to Flash's studio. This time there was another "model" there.

"This is Ginger," Flash said, indicating a woman lounging on the couch. She looked about twenty-four or twenty-five. Her hair was shoulder length, auburn in color and permed to fall in crimped waves. She was covered with freckles and had a turned-up nose. She looked like the girl next door.

"Hi, guys," she called with a friendly wave of her hand. "What's doin'?"

"Laura Ann, honey," Marcus said casually, "why don't you go over and get acquainted with Ginger? I've got to talk to Flash for a few minutes."

Laura Ann obediently sat down next to Ginger. At first she felt a little insecure, Ginger being so pretty and vivacious; but Ginger soon put her at ease. She poured her a big glass of wine, all the while talking nonstop. Ginger was the first woman Laura Ann had met, and she was eager to make friends. Above Ginger's constant chattering, Laura Ann tried to catch snippets of Marcus and Flash's conversation. She heard the word "converter" and Flash say "she could turn a nun," but Laura Ann couldn't figure out who they were talking about. After a short time, they joined the two women, and by then Laura Ann and Ginger were starting on their second glass of wine and were giggling like old friends.

"Ladies, tonight is the night that we are going to get some outrageous shots of Laura Ann," Flash exclaimed in his best circus barker imitation.

Laura Ann grew excited at his words; he was going to shoot more pictures for her portfolio.

"And to help us along," he continued, his voice rising to a peak, "the whitest, the purest, the best toot money can buy!"

Ginger applauded excitedly. "Bravo, bravo, maestro," she giggled.

"What's toot?" Laura Ann asked.

"Blow, snow," Flash said, and when he saw the blank look on Laura Ann's face, he began, "Oh, God, Marcus—"

"Laura Ann, precious," Marcus said in a patronizing tone of voice, patting her on the shoulder as he would a child. "Just keep quiet. We're here to have some fun and take a few pictures. You want some more pictures for your modeling portfolio, don't you?"

Laura Ann nodded.

"Pictures," Ginger said. "Flash, you didn't mention pictures. That will be extra."

"Yeah, yeah, my ass," Flash said good-naturedly. "You can blow it up your nose, deal?"

"Deal," Ginger agreed.

Laura Ann couldn't figure out what they were talking about, but she was afraid of making Marcus angry, so she kept quiet.

Flash pulled a little square of tissue paper from his shirt pocket and carefully unfolded it. In the middle of the paper was a small pile of white powder. From the wall, he removed a mirror and took a safety razor from a drawer. Then he carefully dumped the powder on the mirror and chopped up all the lumps with the razor.

"Just a minute." Marcus dipped his index finger in the powder. "Laura Ann, open your mouth."

"Not so much," Flash whined. "This coke is precious."

73

"So's my Laura Ann," Marcus said, and Laura Ann's heart soared.

Marcus ran his finger over her lower gum line, and almost immediately, Laura Ann's gums felt numb and her teeth prickly.

"Feel good, precious?" he asked her.

"Feels funny," she answered, wide-eyed.

Marcus winked at her. "Okay, maestro," he said to Flash. "Continue."

Flash pushed the powder into long narrow lines and then produced a straw, which he handed to Marcus. "Guests first," he said.

Marcus pinched off one side of his nose, stuck the straw up the other side, and deeply inhaled half of a line. Then he did the same with the other side of his nose. "Fuck, that's good," he said, sniffing and carefully wiping any remaining particles from under his nose with his finger, then running the finger over his gums. He handed the straw to Flash.

"Hey, what happened to 'ladies first'?" Ginger protested, elbowing Laura Ann.

"There ain't no ladies here," Flash said, running the straw down the line of white powder.

Ginger laughed good-naturedly but watched him intently, waiting for her turn.

When it was Laura Ann's turn, Ginger helped her. "Come on, baby. That's right," she said encouragingly. She put her hand over Laura Ann's and helped her grip the straw.

Laura Ann nervously sniffed half the line of cocaine into each nostril and leaned her head back. Marcus wiped the few particles that clung to Laura Ann's upper lip and stuck them in his mouth.

Almost instantaneously, Laura Ann felt a rush through her body. She leaned back, feeling hot, and sexual, and throbbing. She became aware of soft hands unfastening her clothes, then stroking and rubbing her. She looked down and realized that the hands belonged to Ginger, but she didn't care. They felt good and they excited her.

Without a word, Ginger slipped out of her own clothes and led a naked Laura Ann to the bed. Behind her Laura Ann heard Marcus's voice say, "Get the camera, Flash. This is gonna be hot."

"What did I tell you, Marcus," she heard Flash reply. "Ginger is the best converter around."

Their words bounced off Laura Ann's numb mind without sinking in. All she could think about was sex. She craved it, wanted to taste it, feel it. The two women writhed on the bed, and Ginger's hot breath was everywhere, taunting Laura Ann. She ran her wet tongue around Laura Ann's nipples and down her stomach, stopping short of her pussy. The anticipation made Laura Ann crazy. She started at the silky inside of Laura Ann's thigh and moved upward until she finally reached Laura Ann's soft, moist mound. She kneaded it softly with her mouth. She raised Laura Ann to heights of sexual frenzy that she had never reached before, over and over again, and in her fuzzy mind's eye, Laura Ann saw Marcus instead of Ginger. Then suddenly Marcus was there. Together, they were a tangle of arms and legs and pussies and cock. Flash kept snapping pictures from all angles, roll after roll.

Finally the two women lay exhausted on the bed. Marcus got up and joined Flash at the mirror.

"I got some unbelievable shots," Flash said, inhaling a line.

"I knew you would. That Ginger's okay." Marcus took the straw from Flash and did a line.

"I tell you, that dike could convert Nancy Reagan," Flash replied, laughing at his own joke.

"Who'd want to," Marcus said dryly. He picked up his half-empty glass of wine. "Here's to dreams and drugs and dumb broads."

"And most of all money," Flash added, clinking his glass against Marcus's.

"Yeah," Marcus agreed, and after the last swallow of wine, he looked at his watch. "Well, time to take the dummy back home."

He walked over to the sleeping girls on the bed. "Laura Ann, Laura Ann, precious," he whispered, shaking her gently. "Time to go home."

He prodded her until she awoke. He helped her groggily slip back into her clothes and then half carried her down to the car. Once in the car, Laura Ann immediately fell back asleep.

The next morning when Laura Ann awoke, she remembered little of what had happened and felt mentally and physically fatigued and very, very depressed.

"Here, take a hit of this," Marcus said, pulling out a tiny vial of coke and measuring out a small amount with a tiny spoon.

Laura Ann remembered how it had made her feel the night before, and she eagerly waited to try it again. She had no idea that her severe depression and fatigue were caused by cocaine and the strain it placed on her body. All she knew was that it made her feel better and it gave her endless energy. This time when Marcus showed her the contact sheets, she looked at them with enthusiasm.

"Flash thinks he has a buyer for some of these pictures. Your modeling career has begun! Thanks to me."

"You're kidding," Laura Ann exclaimed excitedly. "Somebody wants to buy a picture of me?" A *nude* picture, a little voice in the back of her mind said. She inhaled another tiny spoonful of coke and the little voice stopped.

"I'm a model, a real model," she said, and she pulled Marcus to her and kissed him passionately on the lips.

"I'm so proud of you, precious," he whispered, and his words made her heart sing.

*   *   *

Shoots at Flash's studio became a daily routine. Sometimes Marcus would come, and other times he would have business to attend to. Sometimes there would be other "models" there, male and female. It didn't really matter, because after a hit of coke or a quaalude, Laura Ann felt like she *was* a top model, and Flash always paid her after the session. Of course she gave all the money to Marcus, thinking it was for their future together. The more she worked the more Marcus pushed her to work, and he always helped her along with drugs. When she started to come down from a high, she would feel depressed, insecure, and paranoid, but Marcus would always take care of things with another hit, and so she was almost always high.

Sometimes men would come to the studio and watch, and one day, one of them joined in her "photo session" and they had sex. Only this time, the man paid Laura Ann and it was much, much more than Flash had ever paid her for the photo sessions.

"Great, precious," Marcus exclaimed, reassuring her when she gave him the money. "This is a lot more than for just modeling and it's easier than the photo sessions. I love you, baby. But I love the way you take care of me even more!"

An alarm went off in Laura Ann's conscience, but she ignored it because his words gave her a high greater than any line of coke. He needed her and she promised herself she'd work even harder to keep him happy. After all, he was all she had in L.A. Without him, she was nothing.

Without Laura Ann realizing it, her photo sessions slowly dwindled while the sessions of straight sex grew. And it became so easy to have sex. She just did a little toot and started to fantasize. Sometimes she would imagine she was doing a magazine layout for a famous photographer, and other times she would fantasize that she was walking down a runway in a magnificent

77

designer gown while all around her, the audience applauded. She hardly noticed the men fucking her. Her fantasies were almost realities, and keeping Marcus happy and with cash in his pockets became her sole goal.

One morning while they were lying in bed, Marcus held her in his arms and Laura Ann thought about how they hardly made love anymore. It was strange, but lately she just didn't have the desire to make love. She only felt like it after she'd had a hit, and more and more frequently, the hit had to be stronger and stronger to arouse any passion. When she wasn't high, she was exhausted, but Marcus didn't seem to care. And she thought as she cuddled closer to him, if it didn't bother him, it was all right with her.

"Precious, I've been thinking," he said, interrupting her thoughts. "Why should we share our money with Flash? We don't need him. What does he really do for us? Nothing," he continued, answering his own question. "I think we need to branch out, so I've made a deal with the night clerk at the Las Palmas Arms Hotel on Hudson Street."

"Hmm?" she said sleepily.

"The Las Palmas Arms Hotel on Hudson. You can work out of there."

A silent voice cried out in her head, What about your modeling? That's why you came to Los Angeles in the first place! What about that? But she brushed it aside and nestled closer to Marcus.

"Anything you say, honey," she whispered.

After that, she didn't see Flash anymore.

Marcus introduced her to Izzy, the night clerk at the Las Palmas Arms Hotel. A loose-jointed, stringy-looking man with a pockmarked face, he leered at her with half-closed eyes. "I don't want no trouble here," he said in a flat voice. "Your room is number thirty-one, upstairs. The maid changes the beds once a night. A john pisses or pukes in your bed, that's your problem, I don't want to hear about it—and above all, no noise. I don't want no cops turnin' up here because someone complained about noise. Any cops and you're out. Any trouble and you're out. Got it?" He coughed and spit on the floor.

"Laura Ann won't be a problem, she's a good girl, aren't you Laura Ann," Marcus said.

She nodded. She was straight that day, and a sober look at the seedy hotel made her cringe inside.

Izzy showed them her room. The furniture consisted of a bed with a nightstand next to it and a dresser. The walls at one time had been papered, but it was impossible for Laura Ann to tell the color or pattern, and the floor was covered with a filthy avocado green shag carpet that was worn to the mat in places. Dusty, colorless curtains hung limply at the window.

"Well, it's not the Ritz," Marcus said, shrugging his shoulders. "But the important thing is that we love each other and we're building a future together, you and me. I always take care of my precious jewel, right?"

"Right," she answered quietly, staring at the room. She never questioned anything, because between the drugs and her own low feelings of self-worth, she felt she was getting as much as she deserved out of life. What would she do without Marcus to make her happy?

During the next month, a pattern developed for Laura Ann. By day, she would sleep late, watch TV or go out for lunch with Marcus or just lie around the apartment. By night, after a good, strong hit of coke, she worked the streets. Some of the men were repeats from her days at Flash's studio. Others she met at the neighborhood bars she dropped by, and still others she picked up off the street corners as they drove by. She got into the habit of standing on the corner of Hudson and Olympic. She felt comfortable there, as if it were her own corner, and her steady customers knew where to find her, too.

Standing on the corner gave her time to think of how much she loved Marcus, of how they met and how he had rescued her and taken care of her. She felt grateful to have the chance to show him how much she loved him, and it was a good feeling to know he depended upon her as much as she depended on him. Turning tricks wasn't so hard, she told herself on more than one occasion. And it gave her the chance to plan her modeling career and her future with Marcus.

For two nights it had rained, so business had been slow. But tonight there was a freshness to the balmy air. The rain had washed away the smell of rotting garbage and musky bodies. Street people strutted the streets and flashed their wares to prospective buyers as they cruised slowly by. Any kind of drugs, any kind of sex, any kind of trouble could be found on the streets.

Laura Ann leaned against a light pole. She had just done some blow and was fantasizing about her life with Marcus. She would become a world-famous fashion model, and he would be so proud of her. He'd never want to leave her.

Then a voice brought her back to reality.

"Hey, mouse, I said, 'You want to party?'"

Laura Ann walked over to the green Toyota and leaned into the partially open window, pressing her breasts against it and using the line Marcus had taught her: "Honey, for the right price, I'm the one who coined the phrase." They settled on a price, and Laura Ann slid in. They drove in silence to the Las Palmas Arms Hotel, and Laura Ann stole a quick look at her john. There was nothing unusual about him. In fact, the only unusual thing about him was the fact that he was so usual: colorless hair, colorless eyes, age anywhere from twenty-five to forty-five, no distinguishing marks.

When they arrived at the hotel and passed through

the lobby, Izzy was sitting behind the counter, but he didn't bother even to look up when they walked by him. They took the elevator to the third floor, and Laura Ann unlocked the paint-stripped door numbered thirty-one. Once inside, the man just stood in the middle of the room, staring at her.

Laura Ann ignored him and began to get undressed. Her mind was eons away in a fantasy about modeling for a famous designer. By rote, she unfastened her skirt and stepped out of it. She laid it carefully on the dresser and started to unbutton her blouse. Marcus had taught her that by taking her time undressing, she got the full attention of the john and at the same time, psychological control of the situation. In her fantasy, she was changing into a beautiful gown. She folded the blouse in half and laid it carefully on the skirt before she turned back to the man.

His hand snaked out of nowhere so fast, Laura Ann didn't even realize what had happened. Her head snapped sideways, and at the same time she felt herself propelled backward against the wall. Her head hit first, and she hung suspended a moment like a puppet on strings, then crumpled in a heap on the floor. There was a high-pitched tinkling in her ears, and a thousand flashbulbs went off behind her eyes. Then a blackness rushed up and over her.

Through the cottony black silence, she became aware of someone giggling. It was faint and high, as if a long way off. Gradually, it became closer. Her mind swam upward through the thick blackness, struggling to awaken. At first, she thought she was paralyzed when she tried to move her arms and legs. She started to cry out but her mouth was filled with something thick and dry. So she fought her way back to consciousness with her mind. All trace of the drugs she'd taken earlier in the evening disappeared, and her mind completely cleared. The giggling continued, and Laura Ann finally pinpointed the sound as coming

81

from her left. She strained to look in that direction, but found her left eye was almost swollen shut. She was lying facedown, her arms and legs spread out and tied to the four corners of the bed with strips of what looked like her bra and garter belt.

"Here mousie, mousie," he called in a soft, falsetto, breathless voice. "Nice mousie, mousie."

The man moved into her line of vision. He was completely naked, and a fine sheen of perspiration covered his hairless body, making it almost glow a mottled pinkish red in the dim light. She tried to catch his eye, but even though he was looking directly at her, it wasn't her he was seeing. There was a glazed look in his eyes, and he seemed tuned inward into his own thoughts. He ran his hand down the length of her back, starting at her neck, as if he were stroking an animal. He continued to giggle to himself.

"Poor little mousie," he gurgled in a woman's voice. "Little mousie got caught in my trap. Now Mama has to punish the little mousie."

"No, no," a child's voice cried. "Please don't punish me!" For a moment, Laura Ann thought there really was a child in the room, but as she strained to look up, she saw there was only the man.

"But I have to punish you," the woman's voice said calmly. "You were bad."

"Please don't, Mommy," the child pleaded. "I'll never do it again, never."

"It's too late," the mommy voice said.

Laura Ann struggled with her bonds, but that only seemed to excite him more. He scratched her behind the ear as one would an animal, and she twisted her head, trying to escape his touch. He continued to mutter under his breath in his mommy voice, but stopped stroking her and moved out of her range of vision. She heard the strike of a match, and she strained to see what he was doing.

"Don't, Mommy, don't!" the child's voice begged,

and Laura Ann smelled cigarette smoke.

"I have to teach you right from wrong," the mommy voice giggled.

Suddenly she felt a searing pain on her left leg, and she screamed silently, choking on the cloth in her mouth. She writhed and twisted, but the searing continued. Somehow, she managed to loosen one leg and twisted and kicked out at him. But he caught it in a steel grip and held it down, so that she was turned half frontward and half backward.

"When you struggle, mommy has to punish you more," he said in his woman voice. "You have to learn, every time you're bad, mommy has to punish you."

In this new position, Laura Ann could see what he was doing to her. In a glance, she saw the whole picture in slow motion. His eyes were glassy, and his face had a rapt look to it. In his hand he held a cigarette, and he was calmly pressing the lighted end to her bare leg. In the wake of the smoldering tip, the skin was blistering and popping and peeling back. The odor of burning flesh filled her nostrils. He was still giggling to himself, but now his breath was coming in heavy gasps. He was completely naked, and his erect penis was swaying back and forth as he moved. A closer glance and Laura Ann realized that what she first mistook for a mottled flush on his body was really scars; hundreds upon hundreds of small circular scars covered his arms, his legs, everywhere, even his penis. They were scars made by cigarettes, she concluded in horror.

The man ground the burning tip of the cigarette once more into her leg, and Laura Ann, crazy with pain and terror, went wild. She writhed and bucked, trying to escape the cigarette as the bonds holding her cut into her flesh.

Suddenly, all at once, the strips of cloth that had been loosely holding her wrists gave way, propelling her backward to collide with the man. The force of her momentum broke the final bond on her leg and she fell against him. The cigarette flew out of his grasp and caught unnoticed in the dusty, dry curtains at the window. In an instant they erupted into a sheet of flame.

The force of Laura Ann's lunge threw the man off balance. He fell backward to the floor, and Laura Ann wildly clawed at his face and chest. Furrows of his skin pulled away under the onslaught of her nails. The back of his head hit the floor first, stunning him, and he lifted a feeble arm to ward off her blows. Then his eyes slipped back in his head and he lay still.

Laura Ann, who had landed on top of him in the struggle, rolled off him and scrambled away. She had been screaming hysterically the whole time, but not a sound could be heard through the gag that was still stuffed in her mouth. Frantically she ripped it off and looked in horror at the inferno raging around them. The crumbled and yellowed wallpaper was on fire, and they were surrounded by a wall of flames on three sides which licked hungrily at the shag carpeting and started to consume it around the edges.

Propelled by the instinct to survive, Laura Ann rolled across the floor and grabbed her clothes off the dresser. Then, on her hands and knees, below the rising smoke, she crawled to the door, opened it and fell into the hallway. Black smoke rolled out behind her as the flames, stoked by the air in the hallway, roared into an angry blaze. Laura Ann wrapped her blouse and skirt around her and staggered unseen down the back stairway and into the night.

She didn't remember the walk back to Marcus's apartment or the fire engines screaming by. She only remembered him opening the door and stumbling into his arms. She was barefoot, crying hysterically, and so cold she was shivering. He wrapped her in a blanket and rocked her in his arms until she calmed down. In between sobs, she told him what had happened.

"Are you sure he was dead, precious?" he asked, still rocking her. "Maybe he came to and got out after you left."

"Marcus, there was no way! There was blood all over him, and when I looked back into the room, it was all in flames!" She began to sob uncontrollably again.

"My God," she said, holding up her hands for him to see. "Look at my hands! They're covered with his blood!"

Her nails were ripped and splintered. Dried blood covered the cuticles, and remnants of flesh hung from under the torn nail edges. Her finger pads and palms were stained red. She began to shake involuntarily, and her teeth chattered.

Marcus carried her into the bedroom and laid her on the bed. "I'll be right back."

He returned a few seconds later. "Here, I want you to take these, Laura Ann. They'll calm you down." He handed her two red capsules and a shot of brandy mixed with water.

"Now lie down. Everything will be all right. Marcus'll take care of everything. You'll be all right," he crooned.

Her sobbing slowed to whimpering as he stroked her hair. Within seconds, she was asleep.

Marcus looked at the sleeping young woman. Her cheeks and eyes were red and swollen from crying, and she was rolled up on her side in a fetal position. Her hands were open and held upward, as if she were afraid they would contaminate the rest of her body if they touched it. The bloodstains on them were turning a deep rust as they dried. On her left leg, from the calf to almost the top of her thigh, were a series of perfect circles the diameter of a cigarette. Some were raised with large, watery blisters, and on others the blisters had broken and the skin had literally peeled back, revealing bloody flesh beneath. He pulled a blanket over her and she shuddered quietly in her sleep.

"Shit, of all the rotten luck," he muttered to himself. "The stupid bitch will never want to go back on the streets, after all my work."

Then a plan came to him and he smiled slyly. He bent down and turned off the bedside lamp.

Laura Ann wasn't sure when she awoke. One moment her mind was below the level of consciousness, and the next, it had slipped above. She lay there, too exhausted and numb to move. She played and replayed the events of the night before in her mind as tears rolled down her cheeks. She saw the man trying to ward off her hands. She saw his eyes roll back in his head as it hit the floor, the image making her sick to her stomach. Then Marcus walked into the room.

"Hi, you awake?" he asked solicitously.

She nodded.

"Good, then let's get you put back together."

He gently cleaned around the cigarette burns and put a dab of ointment on each. He gently bathed her hands with a wet washcloth and carefully removed all the blood. Then he kissed each finger gently, murmuring tender endearments.

"Now that we've got your leg and hands taken care of, let's have a little talk," he said soothingly.

He stroked her hair back from her forehead. "You know, precious, you've had a bad scare. This was a one-in-a-million situation. If you would have read him right, none of this would have happened. You gotta look in their eyes at the beginning and make a judgment right then, before you get to the room. Now the next time—"

"Next time! What are you talking about?" she cried.

"Now, calm down, Laura Ann. Honey, I love you. I need you," he said, calmly, following the plan he had mapped out earlier in his mind. "I need your help."

"I can't, Marcus, I just can't," she said and began to cry.

"Precious, we need that money for our future together," he said, pressing on. "Think of our future."

"Marcus, no! No! NO!" she screamed, sobbing.

Marcus grabbed her shoulders and shook her hard, until her teeth rattled. "Listen to me! I'm going to point out a few facts of life to you."

"But—" she interrupted.

"No," he said cruelly. "You listen! Last night, you murdered a man in cold blood. I'm the *only* one standing between you and the electric chair. *I'm* your alibi. Without me, you'll fry!" And he threw her back against the bed.

"But he attacked me," she cried.

"Do you think the police would believe that?" He spat out the words. "You're a transient, a whore. They'll say you lured him up there to roll him; you botched the job, panicked, killed him, and then started the fire to cover up.

"Now, you're going to do exactly what I say. You're not even going to piss unless I tell you it's okay." He grabbed her by the front of her blouse and lifted her off the bed into the air. "I need you, but you need me even more." He threw her back down on the bed. "Got it?"

This was a Marcus she had never seen before. His voice was flat and emotionless, but his face was flushed red. There was a strange light in his eyes that scared her. At that moment, she suddenly knew nothing would stand in the way of anything Marcus wanted, least of all herself.

He stroked her face with shaking hands, and she knew he was struggling to control himself. Then he held her chin so tightly that it pinched, and whispered in her ear, "You just keep working, precious, and Marcus will take care of you. Marcus won't let anything happen to his little jewel. You understand?"

Laura Ann nodded in pain, but knew better than to

87

cry out.

"That's better, precious," he whispered. "You know I love you. You love me?"

"Yes, Marcus," she whispered hollowly.

Marcus gave her almost a week to recover from her harrowing night with the pervert before he insisted she go back on the streets. During that time, he found another hotel for her to work out of, the Wilcox Park Motor Court. It was even sleazier than the first hotel.

After that horrible night, their relationship took on another aspect. He was sometimes still sweet and considerate, but only as a thin veil masking more and more demands. He pushed her relentlessly to turn more tricks, and he kept a tight account of the money she brought in. If it was less than usual, he would question her and watch her reactions closely to see if she was telling the truth.

Laura Ann was sure there were other women, too. Several times, she found evidence of them in the apartment—wineglasses with lipstick stains on them, a pair of lavender bikini panties under the bed—and once when she called Marcus on the telephone, she could hear music and a woman laughing in the background.

When she questioned him about it or their relationship, he would fly into an angry rage and remind her of the night of the fire. Several times, he lost his temper and slapped her.

She did everything in her power to appease him, anything to keep from provoking him. During the day, she literally tiptoed around the apartment, making herself as inconspicuous as possible, waiting for night to come so she could escape to the streets.

But even the streets held no reprieve. They were filled with faceless men waiting to use her for a price. Laura Ann also found out that she could not trust the other hookers. Everyone seemed to know Marcus, and everyone seemed eager to give him a report of her actions.

She was trapped. She had no one to turn to, no one to talk to. Even the drugs she took to make life bearable didn't always help. When she came down off them, reality was always there waiting. She searched her mind for a way out, but every route led to a dead end. She imagined that a knight in shining armor would materialize and take her away, but as the days passed, she only descended further and further into the nightmare of the streets.

Finally the only place she found any peace was in her fantasies.

Chapter Five

While Laura Ann was lying in Marcus's bed, trying to remember what had happened to her at Flash's studio, Helena was making her way through the morning traffic to the Burbank Studio. The Pass Boulevard entrance to the studio was plain and unassuming. It could have been the entrance to a factory anywhere in the U.S. It was just a lone wooden guardhouse, beyond which loomed big warehouse-like buildings, except these "warehouses" held the magic of the movies. Looking at them made Helena shiver with excitement. Any moment, she expected to see Spencer Tracy or Dorothy Lamour step out onto the narrow street that ran between them.

The old guard at the gate was straight out of Central Casting, circa 1940, too. Perhaps, Helena mused, he was once an aspiring actor who had never risen beyond the position of studio guard.

"I have a wardrobe appointment at ten A.M., in Building One," she said to him as she pulled alongside the guardhouse in her car.

"Your name, please," he asked politely.

"Helena Sinclair," she answered, trying to assume a casual attitude, as if she went to movie studios every day.

He scanned his clipboard.

"Here it is, yup, Building One," he confirmed to her. "You can park in the visitor's lot on your right. Then walk straight back. It's on the right."

"Thank you," Helena said, shifting into first gear and slowly pulling away.

"Good luck," he called pleasantly after her.

Helena parked her car in the lot and walked down the street in the direction the old guard had indicated. She passed a series of identical nondescript beige buildings that reminded her of old project housing from World War II. Each one was labeled as to its function: Editing, Screening Rooms, Film Labs, and finally Wardrobe.

The main wardrobe office was at the end of a narrow corridor, and her footsteps echoed loudly on the linoleum floor. The door was open so she walked in. The room was light and airy, its walls covered with fashion sketches and pictures of actors and actresses in costumes. Three desks were in the room but only the back desk was occupied. A thin, middle-aged man sporting a flat-top haircut looked up as she entered.

"Hello," Helena said, a little nervously. "I have a ten A.M. fitting."

"Yes," he said, rising and coming toward her with his hand out. "You must be Helena. I'm Jersey O'Day."

"It's nice to meet you," Helena said, taking his hand.

"Let's go into the fitting room," he said, walking toward a closed door. "I've pulled several gowns from wardrobe, but now that I've seen you, there's one in particular that I think would be perfect for you."

"Great," she answered, following him into the fitting room.

From a closet at one end of the room, Jersey pulled one of the most beautiful dresses Helena had ever seen. It was a strapless black chiffon. Its bodice was shirred and encrusted with black pearls and beads and the skirt wasn't really a skirt at all, but palazzo pants made of yards and yards of rippling silk chiffon.

91

"This gown takes someone with a certain elegance and lots of height to carry it off," Jersey said, holding it up for Helena to see. "And this black chiffon against that milk white skin . . . it'll be exquisite."

"It's gorgeous," she breathed.

"A gorgeous dress for a gorgeous lady," he replied. "Here, try it on."

Helena quickly took off her clothes and slipped into the dress. The fit was perfect everywhere, except for the bust. Jersey rummaged through a drawer in the closet and came up with a pair of bust pads.

"Here, dear." He handed them to Helena. "Put these in. What God didn't give you, Hollywood will."

Helena laughed and stuck them in the top of the gown.

"Incredible," he raved. "Simply incredible!"

He added black jet and pearl earrings and a pair of black peau de soie sling-back pumps to the ensemble.

"There," he said with a wave of his hand. "Walk for me."

Helena walked a few steps and did a turn for him.

"Oh, my God," he exclaimed, clasping his hands toward the ceiling. "I've done it again! I've created another masterpiece. Jersey, you're a genius!"

Helena started laughing. Jersey made her feel glamorous and completely at ease.

"Okay, Helena. You're all set. You can put your own clothes back on now," he said, helping her out of her dress.

"You be here at seven-thirty A.M. tomorrow morning for hair and makeup. Though with a face like yours, you don't need any." He gave her cheek a pat.

"Thank you," she said, and left the fitting room with a smile on her face.

Helena's fitting left her in an effervescent mood. Jersey had really made her feel like a star. As she passed the old guard sitting in the guardhouse, his feet propped up, reading a magazine, she waved gaily to him. He grinned and waved back. "See you in the movies!" he called after her car.

Helena fairly sailed through the day, running errands and straightening the apartment. Before she realized it Nicky was home from school.

"Nicky," she exclaimed, hugging him as he walked through the door. "I've had such a great day that I think we should celebrate! I think we should have one of our famous ice cream dinners tonight."

"Oh, boy!" he cried. "Can I have fudge brownie *and* peppermint?"

"You certainly can," she replied. "You go do your homework, and as soon as you are finished, we'll go."

"Okay, Mom," he cried excitedly and ran off to his room.

Helena's enthusiasm carried through dinner at Baskin Robbins and bedtime. As she tried to fall asleep, anticipation of the following day kept her awake. It wasn't just the fact that she would be getting a substantial day rate; it was also the fascination and lure of the film industry. She couldn't help imagining that this booking might be the beginning of something important. One thought led to another, however, and the memory of Jaimie Cramer drifted into her mind. He was a dark blot on her enthusiasm. Helena couldn't understand why, after she had bluntly rebuffed him, he would still recommend her for the job. She wondered if she would see him again, and then finally she drifted off into a restless sleep.

The next morning she woke Nicky up early and got him ready for school. She left him watching television and made him promise not to forget to leave for school on time.

When she pulled up to the studio gate, she was greeted by the same old guard.

"See, I was right," he grinned as she drove up. "I am going to see you in the movies."

"You'll only see me if you don't blink," she laughed,

93

but she was pleased that he remembered her. "It's not exactly a starring role."

"Who knows," he answered. "It only takes one role for someone to discover you."

Helena smiled politely.

"What was your name again?" he asked.

"Helena Sinclair."

He consulted his clipboard. "Here it is." He checked it off. "Studio Three. You can park in the same lot. Then go down to the stop sign, turn right, then left at the second building. You'll see the sign."

"Thank you."

"Good luck," he called after her again.

She parked her car and then followed the guard's directions down to Studio Three. The outside reminded her of a huge beige barn. Over the door was a red light reminding people not to enter if the light was flashing; at the moment, it wasn't. The inside was like a barn, too, except instead of a hayloft, the ceiling was crisscrossed with wires and lights and scaffoldings. All the lights were dimmed except at the far end of the building, where there was a hub of activity. A scene had been set up duplicating a ballroom, complete with a lighted runway surrounded by row upon row of chairs. Huge overhead lights lit up every corner of the set. Several of what looked like small prefab trailers on blocks were set at the sides of the set, and people were scattered everywhere. Some were carpenters working on the set itself, others adjusted cameras and lights, and still others stood around talking.

Catherine had told Helena to report to the assistant director, and she looked around trying to spot anyone who seemed to be in charge. But everyone seemed to be working at their own tasks independently. Finally she stopped an electrician and asked who the assistant director was.

"That's him over there." The electrician jerked a thumb toward a bearded man in jeans and sweatshirt who was deep in a conversation with another man.

She walked over to the two men and stood behind the other man until she caught the A.D.'s eye.

"Yes, may I help you?" the A.D. finally asked. The other man turned to face Helena, and to her dismay, it was Jaimie Cramer.

"Good morning, Helena," Jaimie said. "How are you today?" His voice and manner were polite, but his eyes twinkled mischievously.

"Good morning, Mr. Cramer," she replied formally, while to herself she thought, Why does that sleaze have to be here? She turned to the A.D. and in her warmest voice said, "I was told to report to you. I'm—"

"This is Helena Sinclair," Jaimie interrupted, smiling broadly. "She's one of the professional models I've hired for the runway scene. Helena, Ken Richards, the assistant director."

She realized he was laughing at her, but at the same time, she couldn't help noticing Jaimie had dimples when he smiled.

"Yes," she said stiffly, "and I want to thank you for hiring me, Mr. Cramer."

"I always try to give beginners a break," he replied earnestly. He wasn't even embarrassed; in fact, he seemed to be enjoying her discomfiture. Helena couldn't help glaring at him.

"It's a pleasure to meet you, Helena," said the A.D., unaware of the undercurrent to the conversation. "Mr. Cramer certainly has an eye for hiring beautiful women."

"Thank you," she said and moved ever so slightly, so her back was toward Jaimie, but she could still feel him staring at her.

"No one can ever accuse me of having bad taste," Jaimie said, undaunted by her deliberate snub.

She could hear the laughter in his voice and it infuriated her, but she also realized that as the producer, he called the shots, so she forced herself

95

to smile.

"Helena, why don't you go over to trailer four and wait," Ken said. "Someone will come and get you when they're ready for you in makeup."

"Thank you, Ken. It's nice to meet you." She turned and started walking toward the prefab trailer.

"It was a pleasure to see you again, Helena," Jaimie called politely after her.

"Yes, and you, too, Mr. Cramer," she responded by rote over her shoulder, refusing to look at him.

She climbed inside the prefab trailer to wait. It was small, with a couch at one end and a dressing table and a lighted makeup mirror at the other. Someone had left a magazine, and Helena thumbed through it while she waited, but she couldn't concentrate. Her mind kept wandering back to Jaimie Cramer. She wondered if he was going to be on the set the whole time. She hoped not, because he made her extremely nervous. She worried that he would make more passes at her, and the more she thought about it, the angrier she became. She was nervous as it was, without Jaimie Cramer's presence adding to it.

After half an hour, a young woman came to take her to the makeup artist. As they picked their way through the props and the set to the makeup area, she happened to glance across the set and caught sight of Jaimie. She steeled herself for another meeting, but he didn't see her. Instead he seemed deeply involved in a conversation with a tall, tanned girl with long blond hair. They stood very close and the blonde gazed at him with rapt attention. Helena was greatly relieved that he didn't see her.

The makeup area was a series of mirrors with a tall director's chair in front of each of them. Two other models were already there. One was Gayanne Leigh, a model Helena worked with often. The other, Helena had never met before.

"Hi, Helena," Gayanne called out when she saw

Helena approach.

"Hi, Gayanne," she said, sitting down in the vacant chair next to her. A makeup artist introduced herself to Helena and started to work on her face. She complimented Helena on her skin and her eyes and her beauty, and hearing Gayanne's makeup artist doing the same to Gayanne, it occurred to Helena that everyone on the set seemed prone to giving large doses of ego-stroking.

Helena, Gayanne, and the other model, Andrea, were gossiping together about modeling and shared bookings, and discussing makeup techniques with the makeup artists, when the blonde Helena had seen talking with Jaimie earlier came over. She introduced herself as Lisa, the fourth model hired for the runway sequence.

"Mr. Cramer, he's the producer, said he thinks I have star potential," Lisa said, tossing her mane of blond hair. "This job is just my first step to bigger parts. I'm really an actress, you know."

"Oh," Helena and Gayanne said together, giving each other a knowing look. In Los Angeles, everyone was a model or an actress.

"Yes, Mr. Cramer said he sees a very special quality in me," Lisa continued, gazing at herself in the mirror.

"A sort of vulnerability," Helena finished for her in a tight voice, recognizing the words.

"Oh, yes," Lisa said, checking the angles of her face. "There, you see it too! It's an omen!"

"Oh, man," Gayanne muttered under her breath.

"Oh, brother," Helena moaned.

"No, *not* my brother, silly," Lisa said, "Mr. Cramer."

"Say," she said to her makeup artist. "Would you be sure to line my eyes in gray? It brings out the blue in them for the camera."

"Of course, honey," her makeup artist said. "You know, you have the most incredible eyes I've ever seen."

"Thank you," Lisa replied, fluttering her eyelashes at him.

Lisa's remarks left Helena speechless. It was bad enough for Jaimie Cramer to feed her that whole line and bad enough that she had almost fallen for it, but to find out that it was his standard line left her steaming. She was relieved when the subject was dropped, although she was curious as to whether he had given Gayanne the same come-on. Helena didn't ask until she and Gayanne were walking back to the prefab to wait for Jersey and their wardrobe.

"What did you think of the interview for this booking?" she asked nonchalantly.

"I understand over two hundred and fifty girls showed up," Gayanne said. "We were very lucky to be booked."

"Yes, I guess so," Helena replied.

"I was so nervous," Gayanne continued. "But Mr. Cramer was so easy to talk to. He's really a nice man, isn't he."

"I guess so," Helena agreed, slightly confused. She wondered if they were talking about the same man. "Did you notice anything strange about him?" she asked.

"No," Gayanne answered. "In fact, he went out of his way to put me at ease. Why?"

"Oh, no reason," Helena said, remembering his kiss.

The four models sat in the trailer until after lunch. Jersey had stopped by for a moment and explained that they wouldn't be shooting the runway scene until that afternoon.

"That's the nature of this business," he laughed. "It's hurry up and wait. We rushed to get you here early this morning; now you have to sit and wait until it's time to use you." And he rushed off.

About 2:30, Jersey and his assistant came in with the

98

wardrobe, and the women dressed for their shot. Helena observed that while her gown was by far the most elegant, Lisa's was certainly the sexiest. It was backless and the front was slit to the waist, showing her ample cleavage.

A makeup artist came by and touched up their faces, and they sat around until 3:30, when Ken came to get them. He took them to the set and introduced them to Chuck, the director.

"Okay, ladies," Chuck explained briskly to them. "We're going to line you up backstage and start the music. On cue, you'll walk down the runway one by one, do your thing, turn at the end and then walk back to the head of the stage and take a pose. After all of you have walked and are posing on the stage, our star, Melissa Sloan, will be introduced. At that time, the extras in the audience will applaud; you will applaud. Melissa will smile and take a bow and then everyone will hold their places, applauding, until the camera goes to black."

"Any questions?" he asked.

They shook their heads.

The runway was an exact replica of a real runway in every respect, except it was shorter. It was covered in white fabric and outlined in miniature white lights. Extras, dressed in evening attire, sat in the rows of chairs in the audience.

Ken lined the models up backstage in order of appearance: first Gayanne, then Andrea, then Lisa, and finally Helena. He explained that he wanted lots of snobbish attitude. Then the women ran through the sequence with the music twice so they would get a feel for the runway and the music before the actual filming.

Helena watched the other models before her work. Gayanne looked wonderful as usual, and Andrea was good, too; but when Lisa walked down the runway Helena could immediately tell she hadn't done many fashion shows, if any. Her walk was uneven and bumpy

99

and when she turned, she held her arms out stiffly away from her body. When it was Helena's turn, she felt the beat of the music and moved smoothly down the runway in time with it. As she reached the end, she gazed out past the "audience" of extras. There in the back, leaning against a set wall, was Jaimie Cramer. He smiled pleasantly at her, but Helena quickly averted her gaze to another direction. On cue, the audience applauded wildly. Helena walked back and took her place on the stage. Melissa Sloan was introduced, the audience clapped and the director yelled, "Cut! Let's try a take!"

Ken held up a slate with the name of the film, the scene number and the take in front of a camera and "slated" the information on the slate.

"Action," Chuck shouted.

Again Gayanne and Andrea walked, then Lisa. This time, however, Lisa looked directly into the camera and gave it a big smile.

"Cut!" Chuck yelled. "Lisa, honey," he said, walking up to her. "We need attitude here. The mood is snobbish not friendly, and avoid looking directly into the camera. You understand?"

"Yes, Chucky," she responded, giving him a pouting smile. "I was just trying to give it my all."

"I know, honey," he said, squeezing her arm. "And I appreciate that."

"And you, Helena," he said, looking over at her. "I want you to turn an extra time at the end before coming back because the fabric has a nice movement to it."

"Oh, Chucky," Lisa said, "my dress is the same fabric, too, do you want me to turn an extra time, too?"

"No, Lisa," he answered. "Once is enough. Okay, guys, let's take it again."

Ken slated the second take and they started again. This time things went smoothly. When Helena walked down the runway she held the full pants out on either side. The chiffon rippled and billowed with her momentum. After two graceful turns, Helena walked back up the runway and took her place on the stage, closest to the podium. The star was then introduced and everyone broke into applause. At that moment, Lisa, who was assigned the spot farthest away from the podium and Melissa, crossed in front of everyone and edged her way in between Helena and Melissa. She gave Melissa a hug, all the while mugging for the camera. Helena was elbowed to the back of the stage and completely blocked from the camera's view by Lisa. There was nothing she could do without making a scene.

"Cut," the director shouted and walked over to the stage again.

"You know," he said thoughtfully, "that last bit with Lisa walking over to congratulate Melissa wasn't in the script, but I don't mind it. It looked spontaneous. I think we'll keep it. It's a print! Next scene." And he walked away.

With that the crew members immediately started breaking down their equipment. The extras walked off the set and Melissa Sloan vanished to her dressing room.

"Ladies," Ken said to the models, "thank you very much. You were all wonderful. Lisa, you were beautiful, sweetie, beautiful."

As he walked away, he added over his shoulder, "Oh, Lisa, Chuck said to tell you he'd see you at home, later tonight."

Helena, Gayanne, and Andrea all looked at Lisa.

"Chucky's my boyfriend," she said, and she tossed her mane and wiggled back to the dressing room.

"Can you beat that?" Andrea said, staring after the retreating figure. "That bimbo almost trampled you getting in front of the camera."

"You should have tripped her," Gayanne added.

"Oh, well, it doesn't matter," Helena said. "This booking wasn't exactly a career move for me." She glanced over the other women's shoulders and caught sight of Jaimie at the back of the set. His eyes met hers and he smiled pleasantly, but she pretended she didn't see him.

"I'd better get going; my son will be wondering when I'm coming home." She turned back toward the dressing room. She didn't want to stand around the set under Jaimie's scrutinizing eyes. She felt relief, too, although she didn't understand why, that Lisa was Chuck's girlfriend, and not Jaimie's.

It was almost five o'clock so she hurriedly changed back into her own clothes. She hated to leave Nicky alone too long. She gathered up her things and paused at the door to say her goodbyes.

"By the way," Gayanne said, "are you doing the show at the Del Coronado Hotel on Thursday?"

"Yes," Helena said. "I hate the thought of having to be there at seven A.M."

"Me too," Gayanne agreed. "What time is the show supposed to go on?"

"Around noon. That's what Catherine told me. But who knows if it will be on time. See you there." And she turned to leave.

Jaimie had come up behind her while she was talking, and when she turned to go, she bumped directly into him.

"Oh, excuse me," she exclaimed politely; then she realized who it was.

"I just stopped by to tell you what a nice job you did." He smiled. "You were by far the most professional."

"Thank you very much," she replied with a cool smile. "Now you'll have to excuse me, I have to go." She squeezed past him and walked away.

Jaimie watched Helena. She certainly was the best, and her pride made her all the more intriguing to him— a real challenge, unlike most of the actresses and models in Hollywood. Thursday, he had overheard her

102

say; twelve noon at the Del Coronado Hotel. Maybe he would take a ride down and see a fashion show. So far, it was Helena two, Jaimie zero, but the game had just begun.

Helena pulled at one of the ornate brass handles centered in the massive mahogany double doors to the California Ballroom of the Del Coronado Hotel. It swung open on silent well-oiled hinges and she looked inside. The beautiful old hotel was heralded as one of the most elegant and genteel hotels in southern California, and the interior of the ballroom reflected its Victorian heritage. Even in the early morning darkness, she could make out the dark wood paneling and deep red velvet tapestries. Thick plush carpeting stretched from wall to wall, muffling sounds. It was hard to imagine that in just a few hours this immense, dark, cavernlike ballroom would sparkle with bright lights and vibrate with the conversation of hundreds of charity patrons. Now, not even the waiters had arrived to start assembling the tables.

She picked her way through the forests of stacked chairs and empty tables toward the dim lights illuminating the stage at the far end of the room. A small group of about a dozen models sat sipping coffee and waiting for rehearsal to begin.

She always marveled at these early morning rehearsals. Most of the models rolled out of bed and came sans makeup, and without it, most of them looked almost scary. They didn't even remotely resemble the colorful peacocks they were onstage. Helena had always likened putting on makeup to painting on a blank canvas; only some of these girls were starting out one step below an empty canvas.

She dropped her bag and sat down on a chair between Linda and Pam. At least she thought they were Linda and Pam, she laughed to herself. Linda, whose trademark was luminescent skin and thick wavy tresses, had her hair tied up in sponge rollers and a hair net. Her normally milky-looking skin was pasty and was sprinkled liberally with red splotches. Pam, who was famous for her incredibly big eyes and long lashes, was almost unrecognizable with no eye makeup and her eyes hidden behind thick glasses.

"Morning," Helena said, reaching for an empty cup and pouring herself some coffee from the setup the hotel had left on the table for them.

"Hi!' answered a couple of the other models from around the table.

"I don't see why we have to be here at seven A.M.," Susan was grumbling as she stared mesmerized into her cup of coffee. "The call time isn't until eleven-thirty."

"I heard we have to be out of here by ten so they can set up the room," Gayanne mumbled, resting her chin on her arm and gazing trancelike at the far wall.

"I don't see why we had to have a rehearsal at all," Linda added from across the table. "These charity shows are all alike anyway."

"I had to leave my house at five A.M. That means I was up at four, washing my hair," Helena grumbled, sipping her coffee. "I couldn't find anyone to stay with Nicky until it was time for him to go to school, so I just set the alarm. I hope he hears it." She checked her watch. She decided to wait a few more minutes, then sneak away and call Nicky to see that he was up and everything was okay.

"You can bet Michael wasn't on the road at five A.M.," Linda complained.

"No," Gayanne said, rousing herself from her trance. "Michael told me he and his new assistant, Seth, were coming down yesterday morning to relax and get some sun."

"Yeah, I'll bet he was getting something and it wasn't sun." Linda laughed slyly.

"Shhh," Pam cautioned, motioning over her shoul-

104

der. "Here he comes."

A tall, slender man with flowing white waves of hair entered the room, dressed completely in black: black baggy European-cut slacks, tight at the ankles, a black linen shirt, and black Italian tasseled loafers. The only accent was an ornate Kesselstein-Cord silver-and-alligator black belt. He was followed by a very handsome, square-jawed young man in jeans.

"Oh, my God!" he exclaimed, stopping abruptly at the edge of the circle of light in mock horror and throwing his hand up in front of his face. "Who let you witches in? Where are my beautiful models?"

"Very funny," Susan said. "What do you want at seven A.M.?"

"How about masks?" Michael retorted dryly. "All right, ladies, and I use the term loosely," he said, taking the handsome young man by the arm and pulling him forward. "This is Seth, my new assistant."

"What a waste," Linda muttered to Helena.

"What was that?" Michael demanded.

"I said, 'What good taste,'" Linda said.

"You'd better believe it." Michael winked as he possessively draped his arm around Seth's shoulder. Seth gazed adoringly into Michael's eyes.

"Oh, God," Linda whispered under her breath to Helena, rolling her eyes.

"Seth, dear, will you please hand out the lineups to the girls?" Michael said sweetly. Then he turned back to the models. "I want the first six girls on the stage, pronto: Misha, Pam, Susan, Helena, Suzanne, and Linda," he said sharply.

"Lights!" he shouted to a light man in the black room behind him. Magically the stage was bathed in light.

The back of the stage had been set up with geometric pedestals of varying heights. Some stood on the floor of the stage while others were as high as four feet off the floor with steps leading down to the floor.

"When the curtain rises, you'll all be posed on or by a

105

pedestal. Then one by one you will leave your pedestal and work the runway.

"Misha, Helena, you go to the platform on the left. Helena, you sit on the taller one, and Misha, you stand next to her."

Helena and Misha took their places on their assigned pedestals.

"Susan, Pam, you two take the two pedestals on stage right. Suzanne and Linda, take the middle. Linda, I want you to lie on the pedestal, and Suzanne, you lean against it."

The models all took their assigned places and struck dramatic poses. Helena, on a block pedestal four feet off the ground, sat profile to the audience with her head thrown back. Misha, standing next to her, faced the audience straight on. Susan and Pam across the stage, stood back-to-back, sideways to the audience. Linda, center front, lay prone with her head resting on one elbow with Suzanne leaning, half sitting, at the foot of the pedestal.

"Here, Suzanne," Michael said, handing her a cigarette holder. "I want you to use this as a prop.

"When the curtain rises, the smoke machine will start. Hold the pose for about five seconds; then Linda, you lead off," Michael said, and he began to pace back and forth on the runway, gesturing wildly with his arms as he explained the routine.

"When she is about halfway back, Helena, you start; then Pam, then Misha, then Susan, and finally Suzanne. Every time you pass a girl on the runway, I want you to turn simultaneously. Suzanne, you will be the pièce de résistance! After working the runway, go back to your platform in the center, lean back and hold a pose. By then, the smoke will swirl up around you and we'll go to a blackout."

"Is there going to be smoke all down the runway or just on the stage?" Susan asked.

"All down the runway, of course, darling," Michael

replied. "For what that machine costs me I'm going to get my money's worth."

"Shit, Michael," Misha said, "between the spotlights and the smoke, we're not going to be able to see anything."

"Everyone will be in red and it will look absolutely spectacular with the white smoke and white pedestals," Michael said, ignoring her.

The six girls looked at each other, exasperated.

"We're not going to be able to see the end of the runway. What if one of us ends up in the audience?" Susan persisted.

"Don't be ridiculous! Now pay attention," he continued. "I want to show you the kind of walk and attitude I want. Allen! Allen!" he shouted into the black ballroom. "Play the opening music!"

"Right," a voice at the back of the room replied. The music started slowly, and then, about ten measures in, hit a strong throbbing beat.

"Now watch me!" He sashayed down the runway, his hips swaying to the beat of the music.

Linda looked over at Helena. "If he could be wearing one of the dresses, he would!" she whispered loudly.

"Get out of here," she laughed.

"It's the truth," Misha said behind her. "When I was working for him in New York, I know he used to put on the dresses at night. He and his little buddies would have Drag Balls."

"Great," Helena said sarcastically. "He probably looks better in the clothes, too."

"I heard he fits them on his assistant," Susan offered. "Isn't that so, Michael?" she called to Michael as he walked back up the runway.

"What's so?"

"That you put the clothes on Seth," Susan said.

"No, I take clothes *off* Seth," Michael said wickedly. All the models groaned in unison at his words.

"Don't be jealous, girls, some of us just have more

107

sex appeal than others," he said loftily. "Now, did you all watch me? That's what I want. Let's take it from the top. Allen, start over! Lights!" he shouted as he hopped off the stage. "Poses, girls!"

As the music built into a crescendo, the runway spotlights grew brighter and brighter. As the music and lights peaked together, an undulating, pulsating beat moved in under the intro music.

"There's your cue, Linda, go!" Michael shouted above the music.

Linda gracefully rose from the platform and moved down the runway in sync with the music. As she turned to come back, Helena dropped her pose and started down. As the two passed each other, they turned simultaneously and one by one each model followed.

"One turn," Michael called from the audience. "I only want one turn when you pass each other."

Finally only Suzanne was left. After working the runway, she made her way back to the center platform and took a languid pose, pretending to smoke a cigarette.

"Go to black, now!" Michael shouted, frantically waving his arms to the light man in the back of the ballroom. "Good, Suzanne, off the stage. Next segment."

Segment by segment they went through the show, rehearsing their routines, working with timing and music and lights. There wasn't a spare moment for Helena to make a quick call to Nicky, and she hoped he had gotten off to school on time.

For the finale of the show, Michael wanted all the models out on the runway, one immediately after the other. The effect would be to bombard the audience with breathtaking evening gowns. Each model would take a prearranged spot on the runway and twirl. The ending would climax with a crescendo of music as Pam, in a spectacular wedding gown, walked to the end of the runway, turned, and walked back. The other

108

models would peel off alternately and follow her offstage.

"Quick," Michael shouted, checking his watch. "We only have ten more minutes and our hour is up. I don't want to have to pay you prima donnas for a second hour."

"Line up, starting with Susan," Seth said. He read off the order in which the models were to appear onstage.

Susan led the way, followed by all the other models, took a spot at the end of the runway, and began to turn. One by one, the others joined her on alternating sides of the runway and began turning.

"Where's Pam?" Susan asked. "I'm getting so dizzy that in a minute I'll be falling off the runway!"

After a long pause, Pam finally appeared through the curtains and slowly walked the length of the runway. At the end of the runway, she posed, then turned around to lead the procession back up the runway and off the stage. Susan fell in behind her, then a girl from the opposite side, then one from Susan's side and back and forth.

"Jesus Christ!" Helena heard Susan say to Pam as they proceeded back up the runway. "I thought you were never going to appear. I was getting motion sickness from all that twirling! Next time don't take so long."

She didn't hear Pam's reply, for at that moment Michael called for everyone to start over with the finale segment.

"One more time; and this time let's have a little enthusiasm, you girls are dragging along like this is a funeral march!"

Seth repeated their order, and everyone lined up and waited for the music to start.

"Remember," Helena heard Susan say to Pam loudly, "don't make a career out of one walk down the runway."

109

Helena glanced at Pam, curious as to what her reaction would be to Susan's words. Pam said nothing. Instead, she looked the other way, as if she hadn't heard Susan.

The music started, and Susan led the way through the curtains and down the runway. Each model followed, took her assigned spot on either side of the runway, and began turning. Again there was a long pause before Pam appeared to lead the procession offstage.

"Michael," Susan called, stopping in her tracks. "Don't you think it would be better if Pam got out here sooner, so we aren't out here twirling forever? The audience is going to get bored."

"Bored!" Michael said huffily. "Bored with *my* creations? Of course not! Pam's timing is just perfect!"

"But—" Susan persisted.

"But nothing!" Michael interrupted sarcastically. "Things would go much faster if you'd stop trying to walk and talk at the same time! It's a little too much for you to handle. Now move, move, move!"

Pam, who had said nothing, shot Susan a triumphant glance and with a grand flourish, turned and strutted back up the runway. Susan, red-faced and steaming, followed her offstage.

Once all the models were backstage and the music ended, Michael joined them. "Call time is eleven A.M. I want everybody's hair slicked back, except Linda's and Julie's. I want your hair down and full. Everyone's eyes should be smoky, lips bright red. Any questions?"

"Michael, don't you think—" Susan began.

"Listen, big mouth, I told you what I think," Michael said pointedly, "and if you don't like it, you don't have to be in this show, or any of my other shows!"

Susan blanched white, but didn't say a word. She finally realized silence was the best course of action.

"And who said models weren't dumb?" Pam said under her breath behind Susan, but loud enough for everyone to hear her.

Susan whirled around and glared at Pam, but Pam stared straight ahead, refusing to look at her.

"Any more questions?" Michael said, looking directly at Susan.

She avoided his eyes. No one else said anything.

"In that case, put your bags in the dressing room; the waiters need to set up the tables." With that, Michael disappeared behind the curtain.

The models picked up their belongings and trudged backstage to their dressing room, which in reality was a small linen and utensil pantry off the kitchen. The walls were lined with floor-to-ceiling metal racks that held extra pots and pans and linens.

Walking through the kitchen, Helena noticed the floors were covered with wood slats. They made the kitchen safer for the employees because any liquid or food fell through the slats to the floor beneath. But for the models, it meant treachery because they would have to pick their way over the slats in high heels. One false move and they could end up with a twisted ankle or worse.

The pantry opened directly off the kitchen.

"Terrific," Misha said to Helena and Linda, as they walked through. "This makes it easier for the waiters to get a better look at us dressing."

"That's a wonderful thought," Helena muttered.

"We could probably make more money charging the waiters admission than doing the show," Linda said sarcastically.

Helena dropped her bags and surveyed the tiny room.

"We're going to be bumping into each other throughout the whole show," she said. "Just once, I'd like a decent place to dress."

"Forget about the space," Misha replied, already blotting her forehead. "Wait until this place starts to heat up. It'll be like a sauna."

111

"So what else is new," Linda countered.

Helena, Misha, Susan, and Linda had decided earlier to go to the hotel coffee shop for a light breakfast before the show. They left their model's bags backstage by their racks of clothes, grabbed their purses and headed down to the coffee shop in the basement arcade in the hotel. The hostess led them to a table. Across the room, Allyson, Suzanne, Pam and Gayanne were already seated, and they waved to them.

"Look at that bitch gloating," Susan fumed, dropping into her chair. "What does she care if we're out there spinning like idiots until we fall off the stage?"

"She doesn't really have a choice," Misha said. "It's Michael's idea."

"Bullshit, that cunt is the biggest kiss-ass I've ever seen," Susan continued, shooting venomous looks in Pam's direction. "She probably gives Michael and Seth blow jobs at the same time. She blows everyone else."

"Susan!" Helena and Linda choked out in unison.

"It's the truth! She certainly doesn't get bookings on her modeling ability!" Susan said, craning her neck to see what was happening at the other table. "That girl walks like a cow!"

Helena shot Linda a "here we go again" look. Susan caught the look, and it added fuel to her ire. "I'm not kidding! That runway was shaking when she came lumbering down the middle."

"You certainly have a way with words," Linda said dryly.

"Look, it's just a show," Helena said soothingly. "In a couple of hours, it will all be forgotten."

"In a couple of hours," Linda said, taking her cue from Helena and changing the subject, "I'll be on my way to the airport to pick up my sweetie."

"*I'm* not forgetting anything," Susan said darkly, refusing to be swayed.

"Is he flying in for that party at Club Privé?" Misha

112

asked Linda, trying to move the conversation in a new direction.

"He wouldn't miss it. Everyone in the agency will be there," Linda said, buttering her croissant. "The agency invited every account we work with. Catherine said this party will really help our bookings."

"What about you, Helena? You going?" Misha asked.

"No, I promised Nicky we'd go to a movie," she answered. "I haven't been spending as much time with him as I'd like. What about you?" She directed her question to Susan.

"I don't know," Susan said, tearing her eyes away from Pam at the other table. "Trace has been working late a lot and I don't know what his schedule for tonight is."

As she spoke, Helena noticed she nervously folded and refolded her napkin. "It's so strange, I'm beginning to think that . . ." Her sentence trailed off without being completed.

For a few moments, no one said anything, waiting for her to continue, but she didn't.

Finally Misha looked at her watch. "Eleven twenty-five, girls," she said. "Showtime."

They paid the bill, collected their purses, and started to walk back to the ballroom. Misha and Linda were in the lead, deep in a discussion of the upcoming agency party. Helena had moved to catch up with them when Susan pulled her back.

"I didn't want to say anything in front of Linda and Misha, but I think Trace is seeing someone," she said, her voice quavering.

"What makes you think so?" Helena asked.

"Well," Susan said, taking a deep breath, "for about the last two weeks, he's been real short-tempered and edgy. And our sex life has been nonexistent for almost three weeks. Usually, we can't keep our hands off

113

each other."

"Maybe he's just under a lot of business pressure," Helena said as they walked through the lobby to the ballroom. "I know when I'm very involved with work, the last thing on my mind is sex. And pressure from work puts me in a terrible mood."

"I thought about that, but then I found this on the floor of his car." She pulled her hand out of her pocket and held a wide silver loop earring studded with turquoise stones and engraved along the rim.

"I think that when I find the mate to this earring, I'll find the reason why Trace has been working late and why he has no interest in fucking me at least." Susan dropped the earring back in her pocket.

"Anyone could have dropped that earring in his car," Helena said hopefully. "There could be a completely innocent explanation. Did you ask Trace about it?"

"Of course I did. He got very defensive. He said he'd never seen it before and to quit badgering him. Besides the earring," she continued, "I've noticed a particular fragrance on his clothes when he comes home late. I've smelled it before, but I just can't place it. I do know that it's not his cologne. I've been going crazy worrying about this! What do you think I should do? Should I follow him?"

"You could," Helena said carefully. "But if you do, you'd better be prepared. You may find what you're looking for. There's an old saying, Don't ask questions if you don't want to hear the answers."

"You're right," Susan said, shaking her head. "How come you're always so together? You always have the right answers."

"It's always easy to be objective with other people's lives," Helena laughed. But not always with your own, she added silently.

"Whatever," Susan said. "But thanks for listening to me."

"Anytime. We'd better hurry."

114

The dressing room was its usual organized pande-monium. Most of the models were already back. Some were sitting at the makeup mirror slicking their hair back into low chignons, while others were applying heavy stage makeup that would show up under the bright spotlights. Michael was assigning dressers as Helena and Susan walked in.

"Consuela," Michael said to a short, round Mexican woman. *"Vestirá a Helena.* Helena, here's your dresser, Consuela."

"Hello, Consuela," Helena called. "Come here and let me explain how I want you to dress me." She motioned for Consuela to come over.

"¡Hola!" said Consuela, smiling. *"¡Hola!"*

"Michael," Helena said, "I don't speak Spanish. How can I tell her what I want?"

"You don't have to, she knows what to do," Michael replied, dismissing her. "Gayanne, I have your dresser."

"That cheap queen imports the dressers from his factory. That way he doesn't have to pay them," Linda said from the floor, where she was taking her shoes out of her model's bag. "They're probably illegals anyway," she added cynically.

"Hola, Consuela," Helena said to her. *"Me llamo Helena.* Well, that's the extent of my Spanish," she said to Linda.

"Good luck." Linda shook her head.

"Do you speak any English?" Helena asked.

"Sí," Consuela said, bobbing her head up and down.

"Thank God," Helena said. "Okay, here are my changes. They are lined up left to right." She pointed to her first change. "This is my first change." Then she pointed to her last change. "And this is my last change."

She looked at Consuela to see if she understood. Consuela was listening intently, so she continued on. "I'll put the shoes that I'm wearing for each change under each outfit. I'll take care of my shoes, you don't

115

have to worry about them. I'm putting the jewelry for each outfit in the corresponding shoes, so they won't get lost. You just hand it to me after I'm dressed," Helena said. "And don't worry about hanging up the clothes until I'm back out on the runway. Do you have any questions?"

Consuela just smiled and bobbed her head.

Linda, who was undressing next to Helena, snickered.

"What are you laughing about?" Helena turned to her in mock anger. "Your dresser doesn't speak English either."

"Yes," Linda said, smirking. "But I speak just enough rag Spanish to get by. Ha-ha!" she added.

Helena made a face at her and turned back to Consuela. "Please make sure everything is unbuttoned. ¡Mira!" She unfastened the first dress and motioned for Consuela to unfasten the others.

Consuela nodded and followed suit.

Helena picked up her makeup bag and brush and walked over to the mirrors that were propped up against one wall and squeezed in between Anita and Pam.

"Do your dressers speak English?" she asked as she pulled her hair back into a tight ponytail.

"No," Anita replied, "but I grew up with a Mexican nanny, so I speak fluent Spanish."

"Mine speaks a little English," Pam said.

"Just my luck." Helena rolled her eyes.

After securing her hair with a covered rubber band, Helena back-combed the ponytail and lightly smoothed it with her brush. Then she twisted it around the base of the ponytail and secured it in place with hairpins.

"Is that how your chignon always looks so full?" Anita said, watching the process.

"Yes. Ratting it makes it stay in place easier, too," Helena replied, as she sprayed the chignon with hair spray.

116

"It would serve Susan right if her dresser doesn't speak English or Spanish," said Pam, who had been deep in her own thoughts. "What's with her, anyway? It's not my fault Michael wants all of you to keep turning until you're ready to drop."

"I don't think it's personal," Helena said carefully, remembering her conversation with Susan. "I just think she has a lot of things on her mind right now."

"Maybe she's not getting laid," Anita joked.

Helena silently continued to line her eyes with black pencil.

"Who knows," Pam said, matting down the shine on her face with translucent loose powder. "All I know is that she'd better leave me alone."

"Pam," Gayanne called from her clothes rack across the room, "may I borrow those rhinestone bow earrings from you?"

"Sure," Pam answered. She unzipped her jewelry case and rummaged through it, looking for the earrings. Heléna happened to glance down at the case and with a jolt, saw a silver-and-turquoise earring exactly like the one Susan had showed her earlier.

"That's an interesting earring," she said, pointing to it.

"Yes," Pam answered. "It's one of my favorites. I had them specially made for me in Mexico, but I've lost one somewhere."

"Oh," Helena said, wishing she'd never seen the earring. "That's too bad."

She continued applying her makeup, and her thoughts drifted to the earring and Susan and Trace. Even though Susan didn't seem to consciously know that the earring belonged to Pam, Helena wondered if the knowledge was being triggered on a subliminal level. It wasn't like Susan to be as bitchy as she was today. It would only be a matter of time before she put it together. Helena debated with herself as to her own course of action. She liked both Susan and Pam,

117

although she was not a close friend of either. Should she tell Susan who the owner of the earring was, or should she tell Pam who had her other earring and how she had obtained it? She finally concluded that her best course of action would be to say nothing. Experience had taught her that the bearer of bad tidings was always resented regardless of the final outcome of a situation.

Then her thoughts drifted on to Jaimie Cramer. There had been something very intriguing about him, the way he had kissed her at their first meeting; and then, during the studio shoot, he had treated her like a lady. In retrospect, she had liked the way he kissed. But he was so confident, it made her angry all over again. She didn't know why she even bothered to think about him. She would never see him again. They traveled in different circles, and with that thought she dismissed him from her mind.

She quickly penciled in her lip line and filled it in with a clear red lipstick. Then she finished off her makeup with translucent powder. She dipped her powder brush in the loose powder one more time and tapped it down and left it sitting out in case she needed it in between changes. She also left out a comb and hair spray. Then she gathered her things together and went back to her rack.

Consuela was there talking in animated Spanish to another dresser. Helena pulled out the extra pantyhose she would need for her changes, and her makeup hood.

"Consuela," she said, tapping the woman on the shoulder.

"Sí," Consuela said, turning.

"Don't worry about my pantyhose." She pointed to them. "I'll take care of them." She rolled the legs up so they would be ready to step into in a flash and laid them on top of the shoes she would wear them with.

"And I'll step into everything that I'm able to, so I won't mess up my hair. Okay?"

118

"Sí," Consuela said, still smiling.

Helena wondered how much she really understood.

"I want everyone in their first change," Seth called. "Michael says we're going to start in about seven minutes."

Helena quickly stepped into her first change, a red satin dinner suit with bugle bead trim. She added a pair of flashy red rhinestone earrings that would show up well on the runway, then checked herself in the mirror.

"Line up, everyone. Linda, Helena, Pam, Misha, Susan, and Suzanne. I want all of you out here, now!" Seth yelled from the doorway.

The women hurried through the kitchen and stood in line behind the curtains. Michael was already there, waiting to be introduced. Out front, people in the audience were finishing their lunch as the chairman of the affair began his introductions. He droned on and on, five minutes, ten minutes. Backstage, the models, who were mentally set to start the show, began to grow impatient.

"Oh, God," Helena heard someone behind her whisper. "Is he going to introduce the entire audience?"

"If we don't start soon, this show is going to go into overtime," Michael moaned.

"If I would have known we were going to be here this long, I would have brought my jammies," Susan quipped, leaning against the wall.

Helena started thinking about Nicky, and how she missed seeing him in the morning. She hated it when she had these early morning bookings and he had to wake up to an empty house. But she had no choice. She had to work as much as possible during the fashion season so she would make enough money to tide her over during off season.

Pam's voice broke into her thoughts. "Shit, if we don't start soon, we'll hit the rush hour traffic going back into Los Angeles."

Michael began to pace back and forth. "I told that

old goat we had to start right on time," he whispered as he paced.

Finally, after what seemed like hours, the chairman began to wind down his acknowledgments, and Michael dashed back to his position behind the curtains. The chairman introduced Michael. As he said a few words, the models hurriedly took their places on stage and waited for the curtain to rise.

Helena seated herself on her assigned geometric block, and Misha posed next to her.

"Now there's a happy couple," Misha whispered, nodding her head toward the opposite side of the stage. Helena glanced across the stage to where Pam and Susan posed back-to-back. Both women ignored each other, and there were forced smiles on their lips.

Helena started to reply but then they heard the applause as Michael finished his speech and the curtain began to rise. Behind them, Seth started the fog machine. White smoke billowed out and filled the stage and silently rolled down the runway. Helena took a deep breath and held her pose.

The music swelled and expanded as the throbbing underbeat caught on and grew until it became the predominant beat in the introductory measures. On cue, Linda languidly slipped to her feet and swayed down the runway, her hips undulating with the beat of the music.

As she turned back, Helena rose and started down the runway. When the two passed, they turned; then Helena continued down the runway, and Linda left the stage. As Helena started back up the runway, she glanced ahead at the others on the stage. Pam broke her pose with Susan, and as she began her walk down the runway, she "inadvertently" elbowed Susan in the small of the back. Helena saw Susan wince, but she held her pose. Pam continued on down the runway, turning in sync with Helena when they passed.

Helena had no time to think about Susan and Pam.

In fact, it barely registered with her, so intent was she on dashing back to her rack of changes. Consuela was standing there, but she hadn't even taken Helena's second change off the rack.

"Consuela, my next change," she exclaimed as she stripped off her first change and pantyhose and grabbed her next pair. She wriggled into the pantyhose and reached for her next change from Consuela, but it was still hanging on the rack. Consuela stood looking at her with her arms hanging at her sides.

"Consuela," she cried, "help me!" But Consuela just looked her, not comprehending. Helena tore her second change from the hanger and threw it on, buttoning it as she ran to the door of the dressing room. She pushed her way through the waiters loitering there.

"Get out of here," she said to them angrily. "Don't you have anything better to do than gawk?" They just looked at her and slowly shuffled back a few steps.

"Those fools act like they've never seen a woman before," Gayanne said, passing Helena on her way back to the dressing room. "Go away, or I'm complaining to the manager," she said to them without breaking her stride. "And I know all of your names!" she added, looking pointedly at one of the waiters' name tags. With this, the waiters slothfully shuffled back to their appointed tasks.

Helena arrived at the curtain as Seth was calling her name. She turned to Susan behind her. "Is my hair all right? My dresser is absolutely no help whatsoever."

"That bitch elbowed me in the back!" Susan whispered, ignoring Helena's question. "I swear she not only walks like a cow, she is about as graceful as one, too!"

"Maybe it was an accident," Helena said, trying to smooth her hair without the help of a mirror.

"Helena, go!" Seth whispered.

Helena worked the runway and dashed back to her next change. Consuela was nowhere in sight.

121

"Consuela," Helena called, madly pulling off her clothes and dropping them to the floor so she could grab her next change. She slipped it on as she heard Seth calling her name. She ran back to the entrance of the stage just in time to go on.

Helena's fourth and fifth changes were the same, with Consuela nowhere in sight. When she returned from the stage to put on her finale gown, Consuela was back. As she stepped out of her change, Consuela slowly removed the finale dress from the rack and started to shove it over Helena's head.

"No! No!" Helena cried, struggling to get out from under the dress. "I told you I want to step into everything I can so I don't muss up my hair and makeup." She grabbed the dress and stepped into it in a flash. "Zip me up! Quick!" she exclaimed.

Consuela just stood there, but Helena had no time to waste with explanations and strained to zip herself up. She grabbed her earrings, slipped into her heels and hurried over to the mirror for a final check.

Her hair from the dress was pulled out of the chignon in places and standing straight up, and her lipstick was smeared across her cheek. Behind her, Seth started calling her name.

"Coming! Two seconds," she shouted over her shoulder. In record time, she repaired her makeup and smoothed her hair and gave it a final mist of hair spray.

"Helena, now! You're on," Seth shouted.

"Coming!" she called, and she sprinted through the kitchen at a dead run, clipping on her earrings as she ran.

"Zip me!" she cried to Seth.

Seth zipped her and gave her a shove onstage. "Go!" he whispered.

He pushed her so hard, she almost stumbled, but she caught herself and regained her composure as she stepped through the curtains. She floated gracefully down the runway, executing a smooth double turn at the end before starting back up. Someone in the audience started to applaud, and in seconds, the entire audience was clapping enthusiastically. When she reached the base of the runway, she turned and addressed the audience one last time before exiting. Then she retired through the curtains to the backstage area.

"Line up for the finale," Seth said.

Helena took her position behind Misha.

"You have the most graceful walk I've ever seen," Misha said enviously. "You just seem to float down the runway."

"Just like a fairy," Helena said, embarrassed, trying to turn the compliment into a joke.

"You really do," Misha persisted.

"Thank you," Helena answered dryly.

"Everybody, move," Seth hissed as the music changed.

Susan led the way and all the other models followed. At the end of the runway, Susan took her assigned position at the end of the runway and started to twirl. The other models peeled off alternately and took their spots on each side of the runway. They continued to turn for what seemed like hours until finally Pam appeared at the curtain, a vision in wedding white lace and a long tulle veil that trailed behind her. She made her way slowly down the runway between the models as the lights came up. The audience applauded over and over. Pam paused at the end of the runway, then turned and began walking back.

Susan was the first model to fall in behind her and Helena the second. Helena was never able to say whether it was planned or an accident, but as Susan turned in behind Pam she stepped firmly on the middle of the gossamer train that trailed behind Pam. Pam took a step and the veil was ripped from her head, dropping toward the floor. Pam turned and caught it in midair, at the same time shooting Susan a murderous

123

look. Then, holding the fallen veil, she continued down the runway and off.

Back in the dressing room, she turned on Susan. "You cunt!" she screamed. "You did that on purpose!"

"I don't know what you're talking about!" Susan retorted and turned to walk away.

Pam grabbed her arm and whirled her around. "You've been on my case all day!"

"Get your fucking hands off me!" Susan yelled, jerking away.

"Come on, girls." Helena stepped between them. "Pam, it was an accident. Susan wouldn't purposely step on your veil."

"Yes," Susan said, standing nose-to-nose with Pam. "You don't need my help to screw up. You do well enough on your own, you clumsy cow."

"That's it!" Pam cried, giving Susan a sharp shove.

Susan reeled backward and fell against the makeup counter, and makeup and jewelry flew in all directions. Susan caught her balance. "Wait'll I get you!" she said murderously between clenched teeth.

Fortunately, Michael appeared. "Fabulous, fabulous show, ladies," he exclaimed. Then he stopped short at the sight of all the models standing around and the look on Susan's and Pam's faces.

"What's going on here?" he demanded.

Both Susan and Pam began talking at once, each trying to sway Michael to her own point of view.

"Forget it!" Michael cried, holding up his hands in exasperation. "Forget I ever asked. You bitches work this out yourselves. Just get out of my dresses, *now!* You ruin those dresses and you'll be paying for them!"

"But—" Susan cried.

"I don't want to hear it, big mouth!" Michael cut her off and walked away.

"Let it go, Susan. It's over and done with." Helena steered her toward her rack of clothes.

Linda pulled Pam away. "Come on, Pam. It's just

124

been a bad day all around."

"I don't know why she's on *my* back," she grumbled as she allowed Linda to lead her away.

The other models went back to their racks. Usually after a show adrenaline was pumping and spirits were high. Today, however, there was no joking, no laughter. Everyone dressed quietly and packed their model's bags.

Helena quickly gathered her things together and left the dressing room. She walked back to the coffee shop, intent on getting a cup of coffee before starting home.

Behind her, several feet back, Jaimie trailed her. He had driven all the way down to the Del Coronado Hotel with the idea of staging a casual, unplanned meeting. He had watched her in the show. Her elegance and grace made her stand out from the other models, and it only intensified his determination to win her over. And win her over he would. He had supreme confidence in his ability to talk anyone into anything, and Helena would be no exception. He would get her into bed yet. He watched her sit down at a small booth in the coffee shop, and then he moved in for the approach.

Jaimie started to walk past her booth, pretended to look down casually, and then exclaimed with surprise, "Helena, what are you doing here?"

Helena glanced up, and a look of dismay crossed her face. "Oh, ah—hello, Mr. Cramer."

Jaimie immediately sat down and glibly continued the conversation. "You know, I thought that was you in the fashion show, but then I thought, no, they wouldn't bring the models all the way down from Los Angeles. They must think very highly of you. Did you have to leave at the crack of dawn?"

"I had to leave at five-thirty this morning," she answered grudgingly. She didn't want to continue their conversation, but his friendly, open manner made it hard for her to be rude to him.

125

"You know, I have to tell you," he continued, appealing to her ego, "you looked absolutely radiant on that runway. You really stood out."

"Thank you." Finally she couldn't contain her irritation at seeing Jaimie. "What are you doing here, anyway?"

"The organization sent me an invitation. I'm one of their biggest supporters," he boasted. "And I want to tell you again," he continued, "that if there is anything I can do to help you, please let me know, no strings attached."

"That's as opposed to the strings you had attached the last time," Helena said dryly.

"It was all a misunderstanding last time," he said, verbally tap dancing.

"Oh, really," she answered, sipping her coffee.

"Of course. I don't know what came over me. Believe me, I've never acted that way before," he said, trying to mollify her.

"Look, Los Angeles is really a small town and our paths are bound to cross again. Let's start over, okay?" He held out his hand and waited for her response. This was his moment of truth.

She looked at his outstretched hand and weighed his words. Maybe she did overreact. He did apologize, and he was making an effort to be a gentleman. And he was right. Los Angeles was a small town as far as work was concerned. Maybe it was better to give him the benefit of the doubt. She accepted his hand. "Okay."

Gotcha, Jaimie thought to himself as he took her hand.

"Good," he said, pushing his luck. "Look, what are you doing tomorrow at lunch? Do you have plans?"

"Well," she said, trying to think up a quick excuse. "Well—"

"That's great, I'll pick you up at twelve noon sharp. There's some things I want to talk to you about, if you're going to make it in L.A.," he said, not giving her

126

a chance to make any excuses. "What's your address?" he pressed, pulling out an appointment book.

Helena hesitated.

"Please," Jaimie said meekly, with a boyish smile on his face.

The smile worked and Helena relented, giving him the information.

"Wouldn't you rather talk right now?" she said lamely.

"No, I haven't the time right now, I'm late." He stood up to leave. "Gotta get on the freeway and try to miss the traffic. You'd better leave soon, too, or it will take you hours to get home. It was a pleasure to see you again. I'm looking forward to tomorrow."

"See you then," she said.

As he walked away, Jaimie thought to himself, Helena two, Jaimie one. I'm gaining.

She watched Jaimie walk away. Now why did I agree to have lunch with him?

Helena asked herself that question over and over, throughout the drive home and while she prepared dinner for Nicky and herself. Even while she and Nicky cuddled together on the couch and she read to him, Jaimie Cramer's face kept creeping into her mind. Again and again, she replayed their various meetings and conversations. She wondered if she really could have misinterpreted their first meeting, but his kiss kept coming back to haunt her. She told herself that she would have a casual lunch with him and then firmly discourage any further meetings.

The next day, she was no closer to forming an opinion on Jaimie Cramer than she had been after their chance meeting in the Del Coronado coffee shop. But she dressed with extra care and had to admit to herself that she was excited about the prospect of their luncheon date. At the worst, she told herself, he was a fascinating man and she would have an interesting lunch. At best, perhaps he really would take a professional interest in her. He certainly seemed well established in the entertainment industry, and he might be a good contact for her. She dressed very conservatively in white silk pants and a matching high-necked silk blouse. She pulled her hair back in a simple ponytail. She wanted to make sure that he in no way construed their lunch as anything other than a casual, nonsexual appointment.

Jaimie arrived at her apartment promptly at noon. He, too, had taken special pains to create the right impression. He had made reservations at the elegant but intimate La Scala restaurant in Malibu, only a half hour from Helena's apartment, and that extra time was perfect for Jaimie to use in his campaign to win her over. He picked her up in his white Rolls Royce Corniche convertible, knowing it would have to make quite an impression on a small-town girl.

Throughout the ride to Malibu, Jaimie kept up a steady stream of questions about Helena and her life. He had a disarming way about him, and Helena found him extremely easy to talk to. In no time, they were at the restaurant.

La Scala Restaurant of Malibu echoed the original La Scala Boutique in the heart of Beverly Hills, or so Jaimie told her. The walls were covered with caricatures of famous people who had dined there, and the red leather booths were cozy and private. The hostess greeted Jaimie by name and led them to one of the booths in a corner. Jaimie ordered a Chardonnay for Helena, but he, Helena discovered, was a teetotaler.

"I've just never liked the taste of liquor," he told her. "And during business lunches, it's an extra asset to be the only one whose wits aren't dulled by alcohol. More deals are done socially in Los Angeles than in any other city. The more the other person drinks, the better for me."

He's right, Helena thought, and she filed his words away for future reference.

128

They dined on the house specialty, Leon's Chopped Salad, garnished with hot crusty bread, and throughout lunch, Jaimie held her spellbound with stories about the famous people he knew, the important deals he had made, the suggestions he had for her career. His grasp of human nature was astounding, and Helena, like a sponge, soaked up every one of his insights. Jaimie's magnetism and charm thoroughly won her over, and before she knew it, the hours had flown and it was time for her to get home before Nicky arrived from school.

"I want to thank you for lunch and for all your suggestions," she said, smiling, when Jaimie dropped her off at her apartment.

"The pleasure was mine." He offered his cheek for her to kiss, Beverly Hills-style. "And remember, you're a very, very bright young woman and you have great career potential. Anything I can do to help you, don't hesitate to let me know." He patted her hand.

"Thank you, again." She kissed his cheek chastely. "Goodbye." She closed the car door.

Jaimie slowly pulled away.

"Jaimie Cramer and Helena Sinclair, two up," he muttered to himself, grinning.

Helena stood at the curb and watched the white Rolls pull slowly away. She felt someone take her hand, and looked down. Nicky stood at her side.

"Who was that, Mom?" he asked.

"My mentor, I hope," she answered, still staring at the car.

The following three weeks flew by for Helena. By day, she traveled all over the general Los Angeles/Beverly Hills area, modeling, and her evenings were taken up with Nicky and motherhood. He still hadn't made many friends, and Helena tried to spend as much time as possible entertaining him. Each day, she tried to organize one special activity for him to look forward to.

129

After a month, Jaimie called and asked her to lunch again, and she readily accepted. Again, Jaimie was the perfect gentleman, treating her like a lady, and at the same time mesmerizing her with stories of the rich and famous and of lessons to be learned and applied in her everyday business dealings. Other lunches followed, and it got to be a biweekly then weekly habit that she eagerly anticipated.

One day, Jaimie casually made in passing a comment about his wife.

"Your wife," she said in surprise. "I didn't know you were married."

"Oh, I thought you knew," he said offhandedly. "I've been married for thirty years. I have a married son in his late twenties. My life is an open book; anything you want to know," he said with an innocent look on his face, "just ask."

Helena was shocked, but she quickly recovered. "What does your wife do?" she asked politely.

"Oh, she spends money," he laughed. "Now, then, I want to talk to you about people and the value of money," he said, changing the subject. "You've heard the old adage, 'money talks and bullshit walks'?"

Helena nodded, but her mind wasn't on his words. Married? She had no idea. But then, she reasoned with herself naively, all the better; now he will be sure to think of our friendship on a father/daughter basis.

One day, after lunch, Jaimie told her he had to stop by a friend's apartment to pick up a script. The apartment was located on a tree-lined little side street in Beverly Hills. He parked the Rolls and they walked up to the door. Jaimie rang the security buzzer, but no one seemed to be home.

"I guess my friend already left for Las Vegas," he said, pulling a key out of his pocket. "It's all right, though, I've got an extra key."

They walked through the lobby to the elevators and Jaimie pushed P for penthouse. Once on the roof, Jaimie led the way to a door marked P-1, unlocked it and they stepped inside.

It was a dramatic apartment, very masculine yet contemporary and stylish, done in earth tones of beige, gray and ivory.

"Have a seat," he said casually, indicating the pearl gray leather couch. "I'll be right back."

He disappeared into another room and returned with a bottle of wine and a glass. "Have a glass of wine. I just want to read the script before we go."

Jaimie sat down beside her and poured her a glass of wine, but instead of reading the script, he continued to chat. She sipped the wine as they talked, and he kept refilling her glass. Her big lunch and the wine made Helena very mellow, and she rested her head on the back of the couch as they spoke.

Abruptly, Jaimie stood up and took her hand. "Come with me."

"Where are we going?" she asked, but she obediently stood up.

Without answering her, but still holding her hand, he led her into another room, the master suite. They stood in the doorway before he answered her question. "We're going to bed," he said, and he kissed her before she could react.

It was a strong, masculine kiss, yet vulnerable and sweet, and instinctively, she responded. The wine or the kiss, Helena wasn't sure which, made her weak in the knees, and she clung to him for a moment for support as a heady warmth flowed through her. Jaimie started to move toward the bed.

"No, no," she said, "I thought we were going to be just friends."

"But we are friends," Jaimie said persuasively. "We're just going to be closer ones."

"I can't," Helena said, afraid at the change of events,

131

afraid because he was married, uncertain that she wanted to get involved. "I have to go home. Nicky is waiting."

"School isn't out until three-thirty," he answered smoothly, playing with a lock of her hair. "It's only one-thirty now; we have plenty of time."

"I have to go see Catherine, my agent," she stuttered.

Jaimie kissed her again and held her close, gently stroking her face. "No, you don't," he whispered in her ear.

"But--but--" Helena stammered, but she had no more willpower and she held her face up for him to kiss.

He kissed her lips, her cheeks, her forehead and her neck, all the while slowly unbuttoning her blouse and then her skirt.

"You dress like a Sunday School teacher," he whispered in her ear. "But we're going to change all that."

He pushed her gently down on the bed and lay down beside her. Without missing a beat, he undressed himself while he continued to stroke her naked body.

She was completely under his spell as Jaimie took her hand and put it on his hard cock. His skin was warm and soft like velvet to her touch, and his cock pulsed with a will of its own. She gently stroked the long shaft while Jaimie covered her body with kisses and nibbled and massaged her nipples with the touch only an experienced lover has. The exquisite pleasure of it took her breath away. His fingers slipped between her legs and he gently probed. She moaned in pleasure and guided his big cock inside her, wanting the passion of this moment to go on forever. Above her, Jaimie thrust his cock in and out, his breath coming faster and faster. She felt herself building and building, her climax coming closer, until she could no longer hold it back. He, too, could no longer control himself, and they came together, holding tight to each other and rocking back and forth, trembling.

They lay together for a time, silently floating on clouds of sexual release, dozing.

He broke the silence first. "I think we may have something here," he quipped softly, and a little voice in the back of his mind whispered, Touchdown, Jaimie three, Helena, two.

Helena, completely unaware of the game, smiled sweetly.

Chapter Six

"How do you get to Park Avenue?"

Kabrina turned to face the voice of a young man in his mid-twenties. His tousled dark hair fell in ringlets on his forehead, and his eyes crinkled as he spoke.

"Where's Park Avenue?" he repeated, smiling.

"It's up that way two blocks." She smiled back and pointed to the left. As she lifted her arm to point, the cuff on her jacket slid back to expose her watch, the diamonds on its pavé face sparkling and dancing in the late afternoon sun.

"Thanks." He winked and sauntered off to her right.

Kabrina smiled to herself, flattered, and wished she had thought of something clever to say. But in a few minutes, she'd dismissed the incident from her mind.

New York City in the late afternoon was hectic, with thousands of people jostled to and fro, each one on a private mission of utmost importance. As Kabrina walked on, she had the premonition several times that someone was watching her. It was just the seed of a feeling, a tiny sliver of thought, all but submerged in her unconscious, surfacing only as a shiver in the warm sunlight.

She walked up Lexington Avenue toward Bloomingdale's and wandered in and out of the small boutiques and shops that lined the avenue. Once, when she came out of one of the stores, she thought she caught a furtive movement in her peripheral vision, but she never really saw anything definite. So instead, she ignored the nebulous sense of impending trouble. Her slender figure cast a long shadow on the sidewalk as she briskly strolled on, refusing to allow herself the childish luxury of looking over her shoulder. She cut across Lexington and pushed through the huge brass revolving doors of Bloomingdale's. Inside, the bright lights and security of a hundred shoppers reached out to seduce her into calmness.

"What an imagination!" She laughed to herself. "Who knows what I'll be thinking up next!"

Lulled by the conviviality of the store, she spent the next hour meandering through its various departments. Without her realizing it, the minutes sped by, and soon the store was closing. Then, with her purchases in hand, she left through the same revolving entrance.

Outside, dusk dipped down to meet the brown exhaust of a thousand engines, and the crowds swarmed about in their hurry to leave the city. Unable to find a cab during the rush hour, Kabrina began a leisurely walk back to her apartment, enjoying the rich fall twilight. She crossed Lexington Avenue and headed up toward Madison Avenue, and by now, the sidewalks were almost deserted, in the lull before the start of the dinner hour.

She was so caught up in her own thoughts that she failed to notice the dark shadow sliding silently in and out of the shadows across the street and behind her. First the figure kept a half-block distance behind her and merely watched. Then, as the crowds thinned out, he narrowed the gap between them. He darted across the street behind her, scrambling between two parked trucks and melting into the gray shadows of a small darkened shop. He paused for a moment in the doorway and wiped away a trickle of nervous sweat

135

that rolled down the corner of his right cheek, his fingers leaving brown streaks on his face. He breathed through his open mouth, taking short silent gulps of air, as if normal breaths would be too loud. He crept forward, closing the distance between the two of them.

Kabrina felt his presence at the same instant she heard the low voice in her ear.

"Do you know the time?"

She whirled around at the same time, taking a step backward. "Yes," she involuntarily replied, gazing into his partially averted face.

It was the young man who had asked directions earlier in the day. For a fleeting moment, she was flattered. He had been attracted to her and had come looking for her. But in an instant, her mind raced with questions. How had he found her in the sea of people? He'd said he was looking for Park Avenue and she wasn't on Park Avenue. Had he been following her? An alarm in the back of her mind sounded. The feeling of being followed earlier; the shadow that seemed to fade in and out of her sight; the dark, deserted street that they were standing on. Nevertheless, she shifted her packages to her other arm and lifted her wrist to see the time. The small diamonds in the face of the watch twinkled and shone in the twilight.

"Six forty-five," she said brusquely. Now she was very uncomfortable and was eager to be rid of him.

"What didcha say?" He stalled and crabbed a step toward her, his lips twisting into a tight smile. His eyes never met hers and were riveted on her wrist and the watch.

"I said six forty-five." Suddenly, she realized that this man was not interested in the time, nor in her, but in her watch.

"Huh?" he said and edged forward.

It was like the slow speed on a video recorder. Kabrina knew the man was after her watch, but at the same time she hesitated, torn by her ingrained sense of politeness. She stepped back and he lunged, grabbing her wrist with his right hand. She instinctively threw up her right arm to block him, her packages scattering to the ground. He pulled back his hand, his fist clenched so tight that forever afterward, Kabrina could re member the paper-thin skin stretched across finger bones blanched white in the fall twilight. The fist hurtled toward her. She held up her right arm in front of her, and the involuntary defense saved her from a direct blow. His fist bounced off her arm and caught the right side of her nose. She heard a sharp crack inside her head and the force of the blow threw her off balance, but the man's hold on her left arm kept her from falling to the ground. The blow mobilized her adrenaline.

"Stop it!" she screamed.

She grabbed at the fingers of his right hand, which held her wrist in a viselike grasp. Her long nails dug into the tendons of his hand and left deep, bloody furrows. Three nails splintered with the force of her fingers as they scraped upward and caught on something. Whatever it was gave Kabrina a handhold on his arm. In one movement, she twisted her wrist inward against his thumb, breaking his hold, and shoved him backward, throwing him off balance. He landed half on the sidewalk, half in the street and was caught suspended in the headlights of a passing taxi.

Whether it was the unexpected fight Kabrina put up, or the headlights of the taxi, Kabrina didn't know. But the man clawed his way to his feet and without a word, fled down the street and disappeared into the night.

Kabrina pressed against the cool, smooth stone of a building, taking deep gulps of night air. Her heart pumped furiously, and she silently willed herself to calm down. Gradually, she gained control of herself. Her pounding heart slowed and only her shaking, weak knees remained.

After a few minutes, she bent to retrieve her broken

packages, forgotten in the midst of the struggle, and she realized she still held something in her hand. A man's gold wristwatch with a broken leather band ticked on in her open palm, its shattered crystal face reflecting the blinking streetlights overhead.

For a moment, Kabrina smiled at the ironic twist of events. Then she felt droplets of blood trickle over her upper lip and drop onto the watch. She reached up and touched her nose. It was numb, and her fingers came away smeared with blood. She frantically searched her purse for a mirror, but she could only find a tiny compact, and in the dark it was impossible to see how injured she really was. She rushed over to a streetlight and peered into the cloudy compact, but all she could make out was a swollen mass in the middle of her face. Finally she held a tissue to her nose and hurried home on rubbery legs.

Once inside the safety of her apartment, she looked in the mirror. A battered face which she hardly recognized gazed back at her. The bleeding had stopped, but both eyes were turning black and blue, as the rising pain throbbed with increasing intensity and the shock began to wear off. Her nose was swollen almost twice its size and it seemed to tilt strangely to one side. She stared into the mirror, horrified.

The shrill ringing of the telephone in the background wrenched her away from the mirror. She instinctively picked up the phone and held it to her ear, but she couldn't speak.

"Hello? Hello," she heard a man's voice say. "This is Noel Wellsley. Is Kabrina Hunter there?"

The sound of his voice jolted her out of her trance and she burst into tears.

"Kabrina? Kabrina, dear," he said, "is that you?"

The sound of concern in his voice brought on more tears, and she sobbed out her story.

"Kabrina," he said, very slowly his tone professional yet gentle. "Calm down. You're all right. It sounds like

138

your nose might be broken, but you're okay!"

"Oh, God, no!" she wailed.

"Kabrina, listen to me," he said soothingly. "I want you to put ice packs on it for the next twenty-four hours. It will make the swelling go down. I'm going to contact a New York associate of mine to take a look at it immediately and prescribe some medication. Then I want you to fly here to Los Angeles."

"I can't," she cried, beginning to sob all over again. "My face is my career."

"You forget, I'm a plastic surgeon, and a damn good one, too," Noel retorted firmly. "I'm going to take care of you. You'll stay in my guest room. Everything will be fine. I'm going to make you just as beautiful as ever. Trust me."

"B-but my bookings . . ."

"You'll be back working in no time. The cast will be off in a week," he said confidently. "By the end of the second week, your bruises will be gone and you'll be working again."

"Are you sure?" she asked dubiously.

"I guarantee it," he answered. "You know, Kabrina, dear," he continued with a smile in his voice, "since our date in Spain, I've called the Puente Romano Hotel, harassed your agency and called every 'Hunter' in the Manhattan telephone directory, trying to locate you for the past three months. I finally badgered Jean-Claude into giving me your telephone number. Now we're finally going to get together, but I have to tell you, this is a heck of a way to do it.

"Come on now, give me a little smile over the phone. You'll be fine. Trust me. And look at it this way," he added jokingly. "Now you have two watches, one for New York time and one for Los Angeles time."

"Okay," Kabrina said.

"I'll call you in a couple of hours to see how you're doing," he said, and hung up.

Kabrina had never felt so alone. She realized that in

139

her determination to prove herself, to become successful, she had cultivated no one she could turn to and call a friend. Only this funny man, 4,000 miles away in a city she had forsaken, held out his hand in friendship to her. Life was ironic, she thought. She put ice packs on her face as Noel had told her to and tried to relax.

Noel was true to his word. Within a few minutes, Dr. Cohen, a New York associate of Noel's, called.

"You're just a few blocks away," he said when she gave him the address. "I'll be there in ten minutes."

Those few minutes later, her buzzer rang. It was Dr. Cohen, a jovial, rotund man in his fifties.

"Yep, your nose is broken all right, and you're going to have two real shiners," he announced after he finished examining her. "I'd like to see the other guy," he joked, trying to lighten the situation. His words brought a little smile to Kabrina's face in spite of herself.

She told him the whole story. "And all I got from the deal was an old watch," she said ruefully, holding up the watch for him to see.

"Let me see that for a moment," Dr. Cohen said, taking the watch and inspecting it closely. "I'd say you did all right for yourself. This is a Bushe Gerold. It's a very expensive watch. I think your mugger came out on the short end of the deal."

"Maybe that will teach him a lesson," she said, her sense of humor returning.

Dr. Cohen nodded. "I want you to take one of these every four hours for pain and keep an ice pack on your nose," he said, lapsing back into his professional manner. "Noel told me he's making arrangements for you to fly to Los Angeles tomorrow, where he'll take over."

Kabrina nodded, stifling a yawn as the events of the evening caught up with her.

"I can see that it won't be necessary for me to give you anything to help you sleep. I'll let myself out," he said, patting her hand and getting up to leave. He looked at her closely once more.

"I can see why Noel is so concerned about you. You're a very special lady. Good night, Kabrina." Then he was gone.

His words kept echoing in Kabrina's head: "Noel is very concerned about you." It had been so long since she had been concerned about anyone, or had imagined that anyone was concerned about her. During all her years of modeling, she had shut herself off from personal relationships. She had had such a drive to prove herself and to protect herself from further pain that she had closed off the part of herself that could give, could feel. Then, with Roberto's death, and now, with Noel's sympathetic concern, she wondered if she had really done the right thing. It had seemed right at the time. Sometimes, that wall was the only thing that kept her going. With those thoughts running through her head, she fell into an exhausted sleep.

The next morning, Kabrina awoke to the sound of Noel's cheery voice on the telephone, announcing that she was booked on the noon flight to Los Angeles.

"I'll never be ready in time," she said groggily.

"Yes, you will," he answered. "Just toss a few things into a suitcase. You're going to be recuperating most of the time anyway. We can buy anything else you'll need."

She dragged herself out of bed, her muscles stiff and sore from the struggle the night before. She went into the bathroom, turned on the bath water, then steeled herself for a look in the mirror. "Oh, God," she wailed. Even her voice sounded funny and nasal.

She swallowed hard to keep from crying again. For all she knew, her struggle with the mugger could have cost her her whole career. She had given up everything for it—her life in Los Angeles, her relationship with her father, even any closeness she might have had with friends. Everything had gone into succeeding in

141

modeling, and now, in the space of a few minutes, it might all be destroyed. Why had she struggled? Why hadn't she just given him her watch?

Kabrina turned off the faucets and leaned back in the tub, the steeping water covering her up to her neck, the warmth penetrating her aching muscles and relaxing her troubled mind.

One of her father's favorite sayings had been not to worry about things one cannot change. He had drilled it into her all through her childhood, and now his words came to her rescue.

"Enough," she said out loud, her voice reverberating against the pale blue tiles of her bath. "The mugging is over. The damage is done. There is nothing I can do to change last night. Berating myself is not going to help. Noel setting my nose *is* going to help. There is nothing I can do about my career until I see the results of the operation. So I stop worrying until after my nose is healed."

Somehow saying the words out loud made Kabrina feel better as she got out of the tub, then quickly dressed. Repeating that remembered phrase gave her the strength she needed to carry on.

Kabrina quickly packed her bags and called for a limousine. When it arrived, the chauffeur glanced curiously at her swollen face, but said nothing.

Kabrina slept throughout most of the long plane ride, and when she arrived in Los Angeles, Noel was waiting at the gate. He protectively guided her to his Mercedes and whisked her off to his home at the end of a winding tree-shaded lane in Bel Air.

Even in her distracted state of mind, she couldn't help but admire Noel's beautiful home. It was brick and wood—Tudor-style, Kabrina thought it was called. The grounds around it were neatly landscaped with trim hedges and shade trees, a far cry from the

142

homey little crackerbox cottage that she grew up in only a few miles away in Nichols Canyon.

Maria, the housekeeper, met them at the door and led Kabrina to the guest room. Like the rest of the house, it was solid and traditional, stylishly decorated in earth tones, although lacking a woman's touch. Still, it was very comfortable.

She lay down to rest on the four-poster bed and the next thing she knew, Maria was calling her to dinner. She quickly changed into fresh clothes and joined Noel in the dining room.

Throughout the meal, Noel entertained her with anecdotes and clever conversation, and Kabrina found herself forgetting her plight and laughing.

After dinner, Noel took a closer look at her nose. "Just as I thought," he said, gently touching and inspecting it from all angles. "It's not serious. In fact, I'll take care of it tomorrow, if the swelling is down enough. Two weeks, and you'll be back modeling, I promise."

"Are you sure?" she asked anxiously.

"Positive, Kabrina, dear," he answered.

The following morning, Noel was right. The swelling in her nose had almost disappeared, and he could operate in his office operating room in Beverly Hills.

Barbara, Noel's O.R. nurse, deposited Kabrina, dressed in a paper gown, in a darkened cubicle. She gave Kabrina a sleeping pill to relax her and to prepare her for surgery. A little later, Noel had stopped by to check on her.

"In about fifteen minutes, Jerry, my anesthesiologist, will be in to take you into the operating room, Kabrina, dear," he said, gently stroking her forehead. "He'll give you Sodium Pentothal intravenously. You'll be in a twilight sleep. You'll be able to hear what's going on around you and answer any questions, but you won't feel any pain. In half an hour, you'll be better than before. I promise."

143

Jerry came in later with a gurney and wheeled her slowly into the O.R. With Barbara's help, he transferred her to a table and draped a white sheet over her body. Kabrina had expected the room to look like those she had seen in the movies, dark and closed-in except for bright lights over the operating table. Instead, the room was light and airy and warm sunlight streamed through the windows, sprinkling the sterile linoleum with prisms of light. Vivaldi softly played in the background.

Jerry strapped her arms down, and she felt the dull prick of the IV needle.

"Now, Kabrina," Jerry said. "I want you to count backwards, starting with one hundred, ninety-nine, ninety-eight . . ."

She looked up into the face above her, which was almost totally covered with a blue mask. Only his soft brown eyes looked down at her. She felt vulnerable and afraid and wished she were safe back in her apartment in New York; but she obediently began to count.

Vaguely, she heard Noel come in and tried to open her eyes, but the overhead light was so bright, she closed them again. She heard Noel's voice, light and vaporous above her.

"Kabrina, you may feel some pressure, but that should be all. If you feel any pain, you tell me immediately and I'll put you under a little more. Okay?"

She floated in and out, feeling some pressure, but no pain. Noel's hands were steady and tender. At one point, she opened her eyes just to prove to herself that she was in control enough that she could do it, but she quickly closed them again, afraid of what she might see. The last thing she remembered was Noel and Jerry talking in quiet voices above her, and the first thing she remembered was lying in the four-poster bed at Noel's house.

Her nose had a splint on it and it was covered with

144

tight bandages. The insides of her nostrils and sinuses were packed with cotton, which made breathing very difficult.

"I know how uncomfortable the packing is," Noel said sympathetically, "but I want to keep your nose packed for at least five days and the cast on for a week or longer. It will be better for the swelling in the long run."

Noel, with Maria's help, tended to her every need. He was the strong, professional doctor, the gentle and sensitive nurse, and the comical magician, healing her with laughter. Every day, Kabrina saw a new facet of his personality, and her trust and appreciation of him grew. To her, he seemed to possess everything—strength, gentleness, intelligence, humor, self-confidence, and humility.

After a full week, Noel removed the cast from Kabrina's nose in the privacy of his home. First he loosened the adhesive with minute strokes of a cotton swab dipped in adhesive remover. Then he carefully lifted off the cast.

"See, just like I told you," he said triumphantly, handing her a mirror. "In fact, better than before. In a few days, the swelling will be down and the bruises gone. No one will ever know."

Kabrina inspected her face closely in the mirror. Noel was right. Except for some swelling and minor bruises under her eyes, she was back to normal.

"Oh, thank you," she exclaimed and impulsively hugged him. An electric shock jolted her as their bodies touched. Up until this moment, she had thought of Noel only in terms of a dear friend. Now her feelings had changed. Suddenly she felt rather than saw another facet to him, the sexual. It was so unexpected that it caught her off guard, and she abruptly dropped her arms to her sides.

Noel didn't seem to notice. "Come on, let's celebrate with a little champagne!"

145

He grabbed her hand, led her to the kitchen, and plopped her down at the round granite table. He poured tall flutes of Moet-Chandon, and they toasted to her continued success in modeling, to his talents as a plastic surgeon, and then to Spain and their meeting.

Then, in a breath between a toast to New York and one to Los Angeles, Noel leaned over and kissed her. Without a moment's thought, her head buzzing from the champagne, she responded. They sat there breathlessly around the kitchen table, illuminated only by the dimmed overhead lamp, kissing. The champagne slowed everything down, and each kiss lasted an eternity for her. She felt each delicious, soft line of his lips, the warmth of his wine-scented breath, and the gentle, insistent probing of his smooth tongue. She found herself wanting more. His voice, soft and gentle, responded to her need, and he took her to his bedroom.

The love they made seemed almost mystical to Kabrina. Slow and languid, they discovered each other's bodies, touching with their hands and lips. It had been a long time since she had been with a man, and Noel caressed her body as a violinist would stroke a rare Stradivarius. He aroused her in ways she could never remember having been aroused before, and she was on the verge of begging him to enter her when he slowly did. The night left her breathless and contented.

"You'll stay here with me, won't you?" Noel whispered as they drifted off to sleep in each other's arms.

"Uh-huh," she murmured drowsily, happy and fulfilled.

The days that followed were some of the happiest and busiest Kabrina had ever had. Noel convinced her to stay in Los Angeles at least for a few weeks, so as soon as her bruises disappeared, she made an appointment to see Carol McMahon at the William Halsey Hallowell Agency. Her New York agency, Madeline Parks and Associates, had already notified Carol that

Kabrina was in Los Angeles and would be calling her about representation. "Sure," Carol had said when Kabrina called, "come in whenever it's convenient. We'd love to talk with you about representation."

Kabrina chose a short black cashmere skirt and a soft black leather jacket, edged in red and lined with a white silk that was patterned with black Japanese lettering, for her appointment with Carol at the Hallowell Agency. To complete the outfit, she added a black silk knit turtleneck, black opaque hose, high black pumps, and red-and-black earrings. She dressed carefully, although she knew she wouldn't have a problem getting them to represent her. She had worked extensively on the East Coast, and she knew that her portfolio was impressive.

She parked in front of the agency, grabbed her portfolio, and went inside. There was a California freshness to the agency—lots of green plants, sunlight, and white walls. It was very different from her smoky, closed-in New York agency. The receptionist, noting her confidence, her dress, and her professional manner, pointed out the Fashion Department without hesitation.

Carol was different, too, from her New York agent, bubbly, enthusiastic, and positive in her attitude.

"Clients always like new faces, especially from New York," she said. "So you might as well take advantage and work as much as possible now. In a few months, they'll forget you were ever in New York."

Carol was right. Fashion coordinators and designers, impressed with her background, clamored to book her, and Kabrina found she was working almost constantly. From morning to late afternoon, she raced from one end of Los Angeles and Beverly Hills to the other.

Most of the fashion and commercial photography studios were located in mid- to downtown Los Angeles, and being in the area brought back memories of her childhood and her father. Once she was at a booking, her memories were forgotten, but during the drives to and from bookings, the memories would tumble out.

There was Tiny Naylor's Drive-In, long abandoned, but its pink pillars still stood, a tribute to the grilled cheese sandwiches and strawberry shakes her father used to buy her. Sometimes, he'd take her for a ride in his black-and-white squad car and they would stop there for a snack. The waitresses would always joke with him, but there was a tone of respect in their voices.

"This here's my new partner," he'd tell them, pointing a thumb at Kabrina and slapping his hat on her head. "I handle the tall ones and she handles the small ones!"

"Looks pretty tough to me," the waitresses would invariably reply and laugh uproariously.

Kabrina used to half believe him, and she'd sit as tall as she could in the seat and try to look serious, as she thought a real policewoman would.

She passed the May Company on Fairfax and Wilshire, where she and her father had shopped for her school clothes. She even went so far as to stop at Cantor's Deli on Fairfax. The air was still heavy with the fragrance of kishke, and corned beef, and chicken soup. She swore the same little Jewish ladies she'd known from her childhood stood in the bakery line and clucked their tongues in Yiddish at the price of bagels. Her mother had died long before she ever knew her, and so it was her father who was at the vortex of these swirling memories.

Her curiosity pushed her to drive past her father's house, but her stubbornness held her back. She wouldn't give him that satisfaction. Once, when she was on her way to a fashion show in downtown Los Angeles, she thought she glimpsed him in his old beat-up Buick, but there was a young blonde sitting in the passenger seat, so she decided that it had to be someone else.

148

By day she played the fashion model and by night, she just played. She rushed through each day to spend her nights with Noel. Some evenings they would spend quietly at home; but more often, they would go out on the town, sometimes with his friends, other times alone. Noel was always up, always such fun to be with. At dinner, he would entertain the waiter and diners around them with clever magic tricks. After being the center of attention all day, Kabrina was more than happy to let someone else bask in the limelight, and Noel loved it; he fed off the attention.

When they returned home, he would pour himself a nightcap and Kabrina a soda; they would sit around his kitchen table and talk, and he would entertain her with her own private magic show that culminated in passionate lovemaking.

"I love doing magic tricks for you, Kabrina, dear, because you have such a child's sense of joy," he told her one night, as he pulled a rainbow of silk scarves out of nowhere.

She would gaze at his escapades with wonderment and encourage him. He brought a lightness and sense of fantasy to her life that had been missing. She would beg him to show her the secrets of his tricks, and he would laugh and refuse. Her days and weeks were full of joy and abandonment.

One day after she'd been in Los Angeles for two months, he broached the subject of her career in New York. "It seems to me," he said carefully, "that it's a waste of money for you to keep an apartment in New York. Do you really have any ties keeping you there?"

She hesitated for a moment, but for just a moment, before answering. "No, not really." She smiled, anticipating his next words.

"Great," he rushed on, "then why don't you go back to New York, pack up your things, sublet your apartment, and come back to sunny California for good!"

149

"I could do that," she said with forced casualness. "Do you have any suggestions on where I should live?"

"Here, of course," he exclaimed. "Is tomorrow too soon for you to go?"

"No," she replied, and they started giggling like two children.

Within a couple of days, Kabrina found herself back in New York City. After her fairy-tale weeks in Los Angeles, Manhattan seemed lonely and colorless. The days were warm and the sun was shining, but the mammoth buildings seemed to absorb the sunlight before it reached the streets below. Waves of humidity rose from the city's concrete pavement, and there were no gentle breezes from the Hudson River to cool its inhabitants. Everyone who could left Manhattan for the summer, and the weather helped to ease any regrets she may have had about leaving as she packed her belongings.

She contacted her agency and had them place her on their inactive list unless they received a booking for her that was too extraordinary to pass up. She also told them that she wanted to sublet her apartment, and with the tight housing situation in Manhattan, the agency almost immediately found a model in from Europe to take over her apartment.

She was a little sad to leave her apartment and the city that had been her home for so long, but her excitement in returning to Los Angeles and Noel kept her from dwelling on it. Although she had many social acquaintances, outside of Roberto she really had no close friends; so in less than a week, she had all her loose ends tied up and was ready to leave.

A limousine took her to the airport again, like so many times before, but this time, for all Kabrina knew, it would be the last. She felt a little twinge of melancholy as she watched the scenery go by; the rows of identical brick houses; the tiny mom-and-pop businesses eking out a living along the humming thoroughfares; even the abandoned cars, stripped of everything removable and left like tortoise shells along the roadside. All these things were as familiar to her as her own living room, and she couldn't help wondering what her future would bring.

The plane ride to Los Angeles was interminable, and with every mile Kabrina's sentimental feelings for New York diminished and her hopes for Los Angeles increased. Even first class didn't help the time to pass more quickly. She tried to watch the movie and couldn't. She tried to read a book and couldn't concentrate. Even the food bored her.

Daydreams of Noel kept creeping into her head. He was so intelligent and yet off-the-wall, the total antithesis of the stable, conservative New York male. Yet, she mused, he was stable too. After all, how could one be a respected surgeon and not be stable? She had always been taught that professional people, doctors, lawyers, and such, were the pillars of the community. Fine examples to be revered. More than his stability and intelligence, however, was his fun-loving nature. He was always in a great mood, always the center of attention, always the clown at any party. He thrived on attention. In fact, Kabrina thought, he almost seemed to crave it. Well, she dismissed the thought, everyone had little quirks.

After what seemed like an eternity, the flight attendant announced their arrival at the Los Angeles International Airport. Kabrina hurried up the ramp, eager to be back in Los Angeles, back to Noel. As she reached the gate, she heard her name over a loud-speaker.

"Kabrina Hunter! Stop right there!"

The lounge area was crowded with people swarming over arriving passengers so she couldn't pinpoint where the voice had come from. She stopped short to hear if the announcement would be made again. Again, the loudspeaker announced her name. She craned her neck

151

and stood on tiptoes, looking for a courtesy telephone. Someone had to be paging her.

A crowd had gathered to one side of the waiting area and it caught her eye. She heard her name once more, and this time it seemed to be coming from the center of the crowd. She walked hesitantly toward it, and the people parted. There, in the center of the crowd, dressed in black tuxedo tails, a silk top hat, and white high tops, was Noel, holding a microphone in one hand and a kazoo in the other. On his chest was a huge, hand-painted sign that read: LOS ANGELES WELCOMES HOME KABRINA! When he saw her, he started to play the kazoo and tap-dance. The crowd laughed hysterically when they realized she was the woman he was waiting for, and then broke into a round of applause.

She was embarrassed, then started to laugh goodnaturedly, assuming that her arrival would end the floor show. But she was wrong. It heralded only the beginning. As she reached him, he pulled a huge bouquet of daisies from the silk top hat and presented it to her. She started to give him a hug, but he was already into his act. He began to juggle the microphone and the top hat while playing the kazoo. The crowd cheered, encouraging him on. Kabrina didn't quite know what to do, so she stood to the side with the crowd and applauded. Finally, people started to grow tired of the act and began to disperse, and Kabrina, finding a lull, broke into his act.

"This is the most wonderful welcome home I've ever had," she exclaimed in laughter, and at the same time she took his arm and maneuvered him toward the exit.

"I just wanted you to know that you've got my attention and I'm very happy that you're back," he said, still giggling at himself.

Kabrina smiled, but she couldn't help wondering whose attention he was trying to attract, hers or the crowd's.

152

Chapter Seven

LAURA ANN STEPPED OUT ONTO THE
RUNWAY. THE AUDIENCE GASPED. SHE WAS
WEARING AN AQUA GOWN OF CHIFFON.
YARDS AND YARDS OF FABRIC BILLOWED
BEHIND HER AS SHE WALKED. GLITTERING
DIAMONDS AROUND HER NECK CAUGHT
THE SPOTLIGHTS AND SHOT THE PRISMS OF
LIGHTS BACK TO THE MIRRORED WALLS OF
THE BALLROOM AND BACK AGAIN. AS SHE
GLIDED DOWN THE RUNWAY, THE AUDI-
ENCE BURST INTO APPLAUSE. ONE BY ONE,
THEY JUMPED TO THEIR FEET IN A STAND-
ING OVATION AS SHE PASSED. THEN THEY
BEGAN TO CHEER . . .

"Augh, augh! I'm coming, I'm coming! Jeezes
Christ!"

The ballroom scene burst like a soap bubble, and
Laura Ann opened her eyes just in time to see a dribble
of sweat slide to the end of the oily fat nose directly
above her, dangle there for a moment, then drop off
onto her cheek. With a grunt, the man rolled off her
and lay like a pig, catching his breath. As his
mountainous breasts heaved up and down, little
rivulets of sweat carved paths beneath the wiry black
chest hairs and down the white mounds of flesh.

"Jeezes, what a load! I've been walkin' around with that one for the last two weeks," he puffed.

Laura Ann didn't bother to reply to the slob. He wasn't looking for a conversation. She wiped her cheek with her hand, stood up and walked across the filthy, cracked linoleum to the sink in the corner, then wet a paper towel and wiped herself off. Behind her, she heard the rustle of cloth as the man dressed.

"Not bad, bitch. Maybe I'll give you another tumble in a coupla weeks," he said as he adjusted his shorts. He gave her a slap on the ass and slammed the door as he walked out.

She stepped into her red skirt and hiked it up to mid-thigh level, then slipped her jacket on. She left it unbuttoned almost to her waist, so that anyone interested would get a good look at her breasts pushing out of the black lace bra. As she started to leave, she caught a glimpse of herself in the faded, scratched mirror above the dresser.

My interview suit, she thought. I remember walking into Dupois' Family Department Store and instantly knowing it was the perfect interview suit for modeling.

Modeling, she thought sarcastically. She gazed into the cloudy mirror and hardly recognized the woman who stared back at her. The skin still had the firmness of a young woman's, but the pink blush was gone from her cheeks, and in its place the skin was pale and pasty as if it hadn't seen the light of day in months. Her eyes no longer sparkled; instead they had a flat, haunted look to them that was emphasized by dark circles of hard living.

What a fool I was to believe I could ever really model, she thought in a burst of honesty. Who would want someone like me?

She sighed and dropped her gaze from the mirror. She didn't like looking at herself in the mirror too long. Instead she preferred to imagine how she used to look.

If I hurry, I might be able to get in one more trick

154

tonight, she mused to herself. That should make Marcus happy.

She pulled out a tiny brown vial and carefully shook out a tiny bit of white powder on the dresser. She chopped up all the clumps in it and pushed it into two long, thin lines with a razor. Then she tightly rolled up one of the ten-dollar bills left by the john. She held one end of the bill against one of the lines of white powder and the other end in one side of her nose and inhaled one of the lines. She repeated the procedure with the other line in her other nostril. Then she wet her finger and ran it along the dresser to pick up any stray particles she might have missed and licked the powder end of the bill. Finally she slipped the vial back in her purse and walked out the door.

She exited and took her usual place against a back wall of the motel on the corner. Barbie and Che Che, two other hookers whom Laura Ann knew slightly, were just leaving.

"Hi, Laura Ann," Barbie called. Black and petite, she had a button nose and a wide smile.

Che Che, the older of the two women, just nodded her blond head in acknowledgment and coolly adjusted a garter on her purple mesh hose.

"Hi," Laura Ann answered.

"We're gonna call it quits. Tonight's been as slow as a john's second come," Barbie quipped. "What about you?"

"I'm going to hang around for a while longer. I think I'd better try for one more trick before I go home."

"If you wouldn't spend so much time daydreaming, precious, you'd have made your quota by now," Che Che said nastily. "You can't keep that man of yours happy with pipe dreams." With that, she tossed her mane of strawberry blond hair and sauntered off, leaving Barbie to trail after her.

Laura Ann watched the two women disappear down the block. Most of the working girls were fairly nice,

155

and there was a camaraderie between them; but Che Che had disliked Laura Ann from the beginning, and she never missed a chance at a dig. She knew Marcus, too, and took it upon herself to keep him informed of Laura Ann's actions. Laura Ann suspected that at one time Che Che and Marcus had had something between them that Che Che wasn't ready to end.

A battered old brown Buick pulled up, and the driver rolled down the window.

"Hey," he called to Laura Ann. "You want to talk?"

Laura Ann walked over to the car and sized up the driver instantly. He was a big black man, and by the crags and furrows on his face and the gray in his kinky curls, she put him in about his mid-sixties. He was dressed in a neatly pressed plaid cotton shirt and beige windbreaker. She looked into his eyes, searching for any clues to the man behind them—crazy or sane, cop or john—and decided he looked all right.

"Look, it's late and I'm tired," she said to him flatly. "You want a car date and a frenchie, I'll give you a deal. But let's get going."

The old man shrugged his shoulders noncommittally, and Laura Ann took that for agreement. She scrambled into the old Buick.

"Drive around the block and pull into that parking lot," she said, pointing down the street. "In the far corner."

The man barely got the engine switched off before Laura Ann had his fly unzipped and a fantasy started in her mind. SHE STOOD THERE FOR A MOMENT, BATHED IN THE PINK SPOTLIGHT . . .

"Hold it," the old man said, covering her hand with his and removing it from his fly. "I want to talk to you for a few minutes."

"Are you kidding?" she said, trying to act tough, but a little nervous at his unexpected actions. "This is a car date, not a blind date. Do your talking at home."

"I just want to talk for a couple of minutes," he said,

156

unimpressed by her toughness. "My name's Norris Hunter—"

"Talk all you want," she said nervously, opening the car door. "I'm taking a hike." She got out of the car and started to walk away.

Norris watched the young blonde slide out of his old sedan and slam the door. She had put on quite a show of bravado, but he could see behind that, to the tired vulnerability quivering beyond, like deep water beneath a sheet of thin ice. Her tough facade would crack with any pressure he applied, but he didn't want to break her, just help her. He watched her square her shoulders, but with each trudging step away from him, they slumped a bit more. Those weary, young shoulders loosened a hundred memories that pulled at his heartstrings.

From the moment he had first seen her, several days ago, she had reminded him of his own daughter. Physically they had no similarities, except maybe the height and delicate bone structure. Other than that they looked nothing alike. His daughter was black, this girl was blond. Instead, it was a mannerism, a vulnerability covered by a facade of toughness that had attracted him. Seeing her had opened a wound he had long thought healed. It was an emptiness he had tried to fill with long hours of work; he had almost succeeded until he saw this young girl three days ago.

He had been looking for a whore. He might be old, but he had his needs, too. And like everyone else, he was a creature of habit. For years, by day he had patrolled that area, so it was only natural that he should seek it out by night. But what he wasn't looking for was the memories; and now they haunted him as if they had just happened yesterday.

His daughter's face floated before his eyes and he heard a man's voice shout, "No daughter of mine is gonna be a whore," and he realized the words came from him.

"You don't understand," she had tried to explain.

157

But his authority was threatened and his anger whetted. The words flew out of his mouth by themselves, and it was too late to take them back.

"I said no! That's the end of the discussion," he had exclaimed angrily.

Her eyes flashed that particular amber color that was hers alone. "I'm going," she had said defiantly and shook off his grasp.

Her manner goaded his anger. "You do and you don't need to come home!"

He pulled her back and shook her by the shoulders, so angry he could hardly speak. She had a way that pushed him to his limits. He looked in her face and saw the uncertainty behind her show of determination and felt certain she wouldn't go.

But the next day, she was gone. Two days later, her call came, but he had hung up, determined to teach her a lesson. He had been sure she would come home with her tail between her legs. But that had been years ago.

And now here he was. He felt the same pain, but it was another time, another place, another girl. He felt this girl was reaching out to him for help without realizing it. She was giving him an opportunity to partially soothe his conscience. This time he wouldn't fail. He glanced down. She had left her purse, and he took it as an omen.

"Hey," Norris called to her. "You left your bag."

Laura Ann turned around and walked back to the car, feigning arrogance to cover her embarrassment and her surprise at his honesty. "Thanks," she mumbled gruffly.

"Come on," he coaxed her, "get in the car. It's late. Let me drive you back to your corner. No talking."

Laura Ann studied him suspiciously for a minute.

"I promise, no funny business," Norris exclaimed, throwing his hands up in surrender.

"Okay," she said, surprising even herself. "Take me back to where you picked me up."

She hopped into the car, and Norris pulled out of the lot. He knew enough not to start any conversation, and they drove in silence to her corner. Laura Ann jumped out at the red signal light, gave Norris a quick smile and mumbled a thank-you.

Norris watched her walk down the street. There would be other times, and he knew where to find her.

A week or so later, Laura Ann was slowly walking back to the apartment in the early hours of the morning. It had been a slow night and she had spent more time on her feet than on her back. She didn't like that, because it gave her too much time to think. Besides, Marcus got nasty when she came back with only a little money and accused her of holding out on him. She heard a rattling old car pull up next to her, and she looked over. It was the old black man again, Norris whatever-his-name-was.

"Hey, kid, you want me to drop you somewhere?" he called through the open window.

It was late, her feet ached, and he had been safe enough the last time, she told herself. "Why not," she said, and she got in.

"Where do you want to go?" he asked.

"Burwell and Rose," she answered, leaning back and closing her eyes to indicate she didn't want any conversation.

"Long night?" Norris asked.

Laura Ann nodded without speaking, too busy thinking about how to keep Marcus calm when she handed him the few dollars she had made. She jumped out at the red light at Burwell and Rose.

"Night, kid," Norris said.

"Thanks," Laura Ann smiled.

She waited until he drove off before she headed for the apartment. All she needed was for some john to know where she lived—or, she added to herself, for Marcus to see her getting out of a car.

She quietly opened the front door, anticipating a

159

confrontation, but to her relief, the apartment was empty. She mentally gave a prayer of thanks and fell into bed.

Almost a week later Laura Ann was again on her way home. She was in a good mood. The night had been busy, but easy; a couple of straight johns, three blow jobs, and one nut who just wanted to jerk off on her stomach. As she turned the corner, the familiar sound of an old car caught her attention.

"Hey, kid, you want me to drop you somewhere?" Norris called to her.

"You're beginning to be my private taxi," she smiled and slid in. "Look," she said. "I've had an easy night; you want a frenchie, on the house?"

"No," he answered, then hesitated a moment and took a chance. "What I would like is a cup of coffee and a little company. Do you want to join me?"

She looked at him a moment and then shrugged. "Why not."

They pulled up to the Copper Penny Coffee Shop on Highland and Sunset. Norris parked the car and they went inside the almost totally deserted restaurant.

"Take your choice," the waitress called, indicating the whole restaurant.

They sat down in one of the red vinyl booths, and Norris ordered coffee and apple pie à la mode for both of them.

"I really shouldn't have pie," Laura Ann said.

"Live a little." He smiled.

"I haven't had pie à la mode since I was a kid back home," she said.

A memory of herself at six or seven flooded her mind. She and her father were sitting at the counter of Olberg's drug store, the air so heavy and warm with the smell of frying hamburgers that you could almost cut it and serve it up on a plate. She was feeling all grown-up,

160

because she got to sit on one of the shiny black stools at the counter. If you pushed against the counter, the stool would swivel around in a circle. And if you closed your eyes, it was kind of like the Teacup Ride at the carnival.

Around and around, Laura Ann spun. Then the waitress came over, wearing a green-and-white uniform, her hair ratted into a tall beehive and a tiara of starched cotton crowning it. "Honey, I bet you'd like a slice of that homemade hot apple pie with a big scoop of vanilla ice cream on it," she had said to Laura Ann.

Laura Ann was too shy to say anything to her, but it sounded awfully good, so she just nodded and kept twirling on her stool.

The waitress set the pie and ice cream down in front of her, and the warm smell of cinnamon and apples mixed with the cool, sweet vanilla fragrance filled her nose. The steam from the pie had melted the edges of the ice cream, and it flowed down the sides of the crust and puddled in the hot juice of the apples like oil on water. She felt her father tuck a paper napkin under her chin.

"Don't spill, Laura Ann," he had said in his deep, gruff voice. "Make Daddy proud of you." He gently brushed back a stray wisp of hair from her cheek with a warm, rough hand.

"I won't, Daddy," she had promised, looking to him for approval. She had felt so safe.

"I said, where's home?"

Laura Ann blinked back to the present. "What, ah . . . Iowa," she answered without thinking.

"How long you been here?" Norris asked.

"Oh, I guess about eight or nine months," she said. Nine months and four days, to be exact, she thought to herself. A lifetime. Out loud however, she said, "The days seem to go by so fast here. I remember back in Iowa, everything seemed to go by so slowly. You could sit out on the front porch and almost see the flowers

161

and trees grow. It was so peaceful," she said wistfully. "It was a world away from here."

"Why did you come to Los Angeles?" Norris questioned her, trying to find out as much as he could while she was being so talkative.

Laura Ann smiled wryly. "I came with the naive dream that I could become a model. I thought that a top agency would immediately sign me and in a couple of months, I would be rich and famous. I couldn't get any agency to sign me, let alone a top one. And the only runway I'm walking is Olympic Boulevard at midnight."

"That's hard to believe, from a girl as beautiful as you are," Norris said, leading her on. "By the way, what's your name?"

Laura Ann gave him a dry look. "Laura Ann, and for your information, in Los Angeles, everyone is beautiful. Every pretty girl and handsome guy with a dream comes to Los Angeles to find it. In Iowa, I was the prettiest girl in my town. Here, the streets are paved with the broken dreams of beautiful people."

"Then why don't you go home?" Norris asked.

Laura Ann laughed bitterly. "I can't go back. It's too late; everyone back home thinks I'm a model. I can only go forward. Or down," she added quietly.

"Then why don't you get a legitimate job and work toward becoming one?" Norris said encouragingly. "One step at a time. I could help you find a job."

"I wouldn't know how to start," she said, beginning to get nervous. "Besides, my boyfriend, Marcus, would never let me go."

"Yes, he would," Norris warmed to his subject. "If you—"

"No," she cried, remembering the fire at the Las Palmas Arms Hotel, the still form of the pervert on the floor with his eyes rolled back in his head, and the flames licking hungrily at them.

"I can't," she cried in panic. "I have to go. Marcus

162

will be waiting for me!"

She got up, knocking over her coffee in her hurry to leave, and fled from the restaurant. She fought to hold back the tears as she hiked back to the apartment. She prayed that Marcus would be asleep.

Norris sat back and thoughtfully watched her rush out of the coffee shop.

The waitress arrived with their apple pie. "What happened to your friend?" she asked. "Wasn't she hungry?"

"I guess not," Norris replied. "But I am. Put the pie down."

She shrugged her shoulders and set the plates down with a clatter and left. Norris started to eat the hot pie and contemplated his next move with the young hooker.

His cop's instinct had been right from the beginning. She wasn't an ordinary whore. Something or someone had a hold on her. He saw the homesick look on her face when she talked about Iowa, and he saw the fear and heard the terror in her voice when he suggested she get a legitimate job. It made him more determined than ever to ferret out the truth. Let her run away tonight. He knew where to find her. He knew her haunts, her favorite corner, even the fleabag motel she worked out of. She was a creature of habit; she'd return to them.

He hadn't been able to help his own daughter. He had been too emotional, and he hadn't taken time to listen to what she had said to him. Now she was lost to him forever. With this girl, he had a chance. This time he would listen and he would act accordingly.

Laura Ann carefully closed the front door of the apartment. She had learned that if she lifted the doorknob and turned it to the left as she slid the door closed, it wouldn't creak. She quietly stole through the living room into the bedroom, holding her breath. The only light was a slit coming from beneath the bathroom door. Her goal was to get undressed and in bed before

163

Marcus came out of the bathroom, and she almost succeeded.

"Hi, precious. You're a little late, aren't you?"

She jumped at his voice, soft as velvet in her ear.

Marcus stroked her bare arms gently. "Did my little sugarpop have a busy night tonight?" he asked, gently.

"Yes, Marcus, business was good," she answered, her stomach tight, afraid of what was going to happen.

"It had better be all business. I'd hate to think about what would happen if I found out some dude was lickin' on *my* sugarpop for free," he said menacingly. He massaged an inch of the flesh of her upper arm with his thumb and index finger, then twisted it cruelly.

She bit her lip to keep from crying out. She'd learned that any sound from her would only goad him. "I'd never do that, Marcus," she managed to gasp.

"Good, because I love you and I don't like hurting you," he said, letting go of her arm. "All I really want to do is protect you, you understand?"

"Yes, Marcus," she whispered, rubbing her bruised flesh.

"Now," he said in a businesslike voice. "How much do you have for your daddy?"

She handed him the roll of bills and watched him as he counted them.

"That's a good girl," he said solicitously. "Now you get some sleep. You must be real tired." He ran a fingertip softly down the curve of her shoulder and over her breast, and she shuddered inwardly.

Two nights later, Laura Ann was standing on her usual corner with Barbie and Che Che. Barbie was telling them about a kinky john she had just had, and Che Che was teasing her. Laura Ann hung back, only half listening to the other two.

She was trying to cut back on the amount of coke she had been doing, so she was straight and depressed. After her conversation with Norris in the Copper Penny Coffee Shop, grim reminders of the past months

164

in Los Angeles kept crossing her mind. Life in Los Angeles was so different from what she had imagined it to be. She had seen and done so much in the past few months that she hardly remembered the fresh-faced young woman who had hopped off that bus from Iowa. She thought back to how sweet and considerate Marcus had been, and she knew now that it had all been an act. The real Marcus was short-tempered and moody. If he was having a bad day or if she didn't bring home enough money, she could expect him to knock her around the apartment a few times. And he never missed the chance to let her know he was the only one standing between her and prison.

There were other women, too, and he didn't bother to hide the evidence anymore. Cigarette butts with lipstick on them, strange lingerie—they were all there in plain sight. She knew better than to question him about anything, least of all other women. She didn't care anyway. It just meant she didn't have to service him as often.

He had his spies, too. Che Che for one. She never missed a chance to fill Marcus in on Laura Ann's actions, so she always had to be on her guard. She was trapped.

"Hey, Laura Ann," Barbie said, nudging her out of her reverie. "That john's talking to you."

"What?" Laura Ann said, startled out of her thoughts. She turned to the car at the curb.

"I said, you want a ride someplace?" Norris repeated.

"No," she exclaimed firmly.

"Strictly business," he said, pushing open the door on the passenger side. "Get in."

"No," she repeated.

"Get a load of Miss Precious, turning down business," Che Che taunted behind her. "Wait 'til Marcus hears this one."

Laura Ann could still feel Marcus twisting the flesh on her arm and his words ringing in her ears.

165

"Okay," she said and got into the car. "Strictly business, though. What do you want, a frenchie?"

He put the car in gear and they slowly drove off. For a few minutes, he said nothing. Laura Ann was beginning to think he had forgotten her question, and she started to repeat it. "I said—"

"I heard what you said," Norris said. "I want to talk to you."

"Stop the car! I want out right now," she said angrily, grabbing at the door handle.

"Calm down." He grabbed her arm and held on to it. "I just want to talk for a few minutes. Talk can't hurt you. I'll pay you for your time, God damn it. Just calm down." He thrust some bills into her lap.

"What is it you want from me, anyway?" she said more calmly. "Why can't you just leave me alone?"

"Because you don't want to be left alone. Whether you know it or not, you're crying out for help. It's written all over you," he said gruffly. "You're not a professional girl. You don't have the mentality."

"Hooking is the only thing I do have," Laura Ann retorted. "Can't you see that?"

"No, I can't. You're caught by something or someone, but you're not a hooker by choice."

His words were touching too close to the truth. He was putting her thoughts into words, thoughts she'd denied. She thought of Marcus and felt cornered.

"Stop the car and let me out," she demanded. "We've talked enough."

"What is it, Laura Ann?" he said. "Who or what's got a hold on you? And why?"

His voice was soft and calm, but he continued relentlessly probing. "We're going to get to the bottom of this. You're going to tell me the truth or we'll circle Hollywood all night. Then try explaining that to Marcus, or whatever your boyfriend's name is." He grabbed her wrist and held on to it.

"There's nothing to tell," she cried, her voice

quavering. She didn't know who scared her more, Norris or Marcus. She tried to jerk her arm away but his fingers held her tightly.

"Tell me! Tell me why a pretty, corn-fed farm girl comes to Los Angeles to model and nine months later is hooking on the Boulevard," he pressed on. "It's an old story, I know, but I want your version."

"Because I murdered a man," she blurted out. "And I'm trapped!" The whole story tumbled out in a flood of tears. "So you see," she stuttered through sobs, "I can't go anywhere, because Marcus is the only one between me and jail. He's my only alibi."

"So you don't really know if the man died in the fire," Norris said.

"He had to be dead. I told you, he hit his head and he didn't move," she repeated. "The fire was everywhere."

"But Laura Ann, even if he did die, it was self-defense," Norris told her.

"Who's going to believe that," she said hopelessly. "No one would believe me!"

"I believe you," he said.

"You don't count," she insisted. "You're not a cop."

"But I am," he blurted out. "That is, I was," he amended quickly, pulling his identification from his jacket pocket. "I'm a retired cop."

"Oh, my God," Laura Ann cried in horror, jerking at the door handle. "Let me out!"

The door flew open, and at the same time Norris made a grab for her, but she slipped out of his grasp and jumped from the car. She tripped and hit the pavement with her shoulder and rolled. The force of her fall knocked the wind from her and she lay on the sidewalk for a few seconds, gasping for air. Behind her, she heard the screech of brakes as Norris's car slid to a stop. The sound drove her to her feet and she fled into the night. Behind her, she heard Norris shouting, and she ran faster. She ran and ran until she could run no more—down an alley, around a corner, up streets.

167

How could she be so dumb, she berated herself. How could she confess to a murder to begin with—and then to confess to a cop! But there had been something about him that seemed so safe and comforting, she argued with herself. He had been so understanding and sympathetic; it seemed like the natural thing to do at the time. Now look at her; she had lost her purse, and her clothes were filthy and torn.

She limped into an all-night gas station, where the attendant stared at her curiously but didn't say anything. Once in the ladies' room, she washed off the dirt and grime and repaired her makeup as much as possible. She straightened her clothes and tried to smooth her hair. Her shoulder throbbed painfully, but she ignored the pain. All she could think about was how to explain to Marcus why she had no money. She couldn't just tell him that a cop picked her up and she confessed to murder. She thought about telling him that things were just slow, but that would set him off. In desperation, she finally devised a thin story that she thought might work.

Finally she reached the apartment door and took a deep breath to steady herself before entering. "Marcus, Marcus," she cried out, on the verge of tears. It wasn't hard to cry. All she had to do was think about how stupid she had been tonight and the fury of Marcus's temper. That fear alone brought her to tears.

"What the hell are you bellowing about," he said sourly as he ambled in from the next room. Behind him, the television blared.

"Oh, M-Marcus," she stammered between sobs. "I was walking down an alley and someone mugged me and snatched my purse with all my money in it!"

"What! And you didn't stop them?" he screamed. "You fucking cunt! What the fuck were you doing in an alley anyway?"

He grabbed her by the hair and jerked her head back. She winced in pain and cried harder. Her crying

168

seemed to add fuel to his rage, and he slapped her, making her teeth snap together and forcing her backward. She stumbled halfway across the room to the floor, and he descended upon her.

"I'll teach you to be so stupid, bitch," he shouted, kicking her viciously in the stomach, and then stomped away from her.

"Marcus, please," she implored him, doubling up in pain. "Oh, please don't hit me anymore. I'll never let it happen again. I'll work twice as hard and make it up to you."

She crawled across the floor to him and grabbed his legs. "Please, Marcus, please. I promise."

"Well, okay, cunt," he relented grudgingly. The sound of the television in the other room seemed to have caught his attention. "I'll let it go this time. You're just lucky I love you so much."

He kicked her away, walked into the other room, and threw himself down in front of the television set.

Laura Ann crawled to a corner of the room, where she rolled up into a ball and shoved the edge of her hand into her mouth to keep from sobbing. The pain in her stomach was so excruciating that she felt nauseous. The coppery taste of blood filled her mouth and she swallowed hard, willing herself to stop crying. In the next room, Marcus snickered at Johnny Carson, and to take her mind off the pain, she forced herself to fantasize. . . .

SHE WALKED OUT ON THE RUNWAY AND THERE WAS THE FLASH OF A HUNDRED CAMERAS; THE APPLAUSE WAS DEAFENING. THEY WERE APPLAUDING FOR HER. . . .

Chapter Eight

Jaimie leaned back in his black leather chair and absentmindedly stared out the window of his penthouse condominium at the spectacular skyline. Located above Sunset Plaza Drive, his condominium gave him a panoramic view of West Hollywood and Beverly Hills; but today, he didn't notice it. He shuffled through the papers on his green malachite desk, but nothing held his interest. He stood up and restlessly paced back and forth in front of the desk, then wandered out of his office into the rest of the condo. His secretary, Lila, looked up questioningly as he walked past her desk, but then went back to her typing. He wandered aimlessly through the dramatic black-and-white art deco living room into the black lacquer dining room and into the kitchen that, like the rest of the condo, was done in jet black—granite floors and countertops, black cabinets, black appliances. It was a New York chic apartment accented with California glitz. He took a red ceramic mug from the cupboard and poured himself a cup of coffee. Across the hall, in the den, he could hear his wife, Donna, planning an upcoming dinner party with the cook. He idly tuned in to fragments of the conversation.

"Russian beluga caviar is the kind I want," Donna was saying. "The Stillers served ossetra last night and it was the worst. It was so salty, no one could eat it. Why they cut corners on such important things, I'll never know."

Jaimie could hear the Filipino cook murmur in agreement.

"Now, Mr. C. wants you to buy the caviar from French's," she droned on. "He'll give you the best prices on caviar. God knows, at his prices, we're probably putting his kids through college."

Donna has such a whiny, bored way of talking, Jaimie thought to himself. Not her fault, really; it came from a lifetime of socializing with other spoiled, bored Beverly Hills matrons. They competed to see who could complain the most, and Donna was definitely a top contender.

He tuned in again. "And don't forget," she was saying. "Make sure you tell him we want the freshest he's got and Mr. C. doesn't want any that's been on the shelves for more than five days."

I don't even like caviar, Jaimie thought to himself.

He picked up his coffee mug and went back to his office. Sitting down behind the desk again he thumbed through a script that a writer had messengered over for him to read.

I wonder what Helena's doing, he thought to himself. Two days ago, after his conquest, he had decided not to call her again. It was his usual modus operandi; conquer and leave them. He believed in keeping things simple. Now he was having second thoughts. She was convenient, he rationalized to himself, and he didn't feel like making the effort to find another conquest, going through the whole routine. She was great in the sack, so maybe he'd see her a couple more times. She was kind of fun to be around, too. A little small-town, naïve, but she had a bright, quick mind and she hung on to his every word. It made him feel like Professor Higgins with Eliza Doolittle.

"Yes," he decided out loud. "I think I'll give her a

call." After all, he was doing her a favor. Any girl would consider herself lucky to have an affair with someone of his caliber.

He buzzed his secretary on the intercom.

"Yes, Mr. Cramer," Lila immediately replied.

"Pick up your phone," he said, so he could speak to her without being overheard. "Where's Donna?"

"She's in the den talking with the cook," Lila answered after checking.

"Okay." He hung up and dialed Helena's number.

But he had to be careful. He never knew when his wife might walk in on him. He swore that she had radar. Whenever he tried to make a call he didn't want Donna to know about, she was right there hovering over him, listening. And he was positive that sometimes she listened in on an extension, which was easy for her to do. They had nineteen telephones scattered about the condo and each time someone picked up a telephone, a red light on all the other phones went on. But he was so good at covering his tracks that he couldn't imagine she suspected any of his escapades. She was just nosey.

In the past two days, Helena had given Jaimie a lot of thought, too. Making love with him had been incredible, and he was fascinating to be around. His charismatic personality drew people to him and there was never a dull moment. She knew, however, that she was playing with fire. Morally, she believed in the sanctity of marriage. She had had the strength to leave an unhappy marriage, and she believed that was a better path to take than to stay and lead a life of deception. She had heard the numerous mistress stories and she didn't want to be part of the statistics, but she was also very attracted to him.

"Helena," Jaimie said, assuming she would surely recognize his voice. "How are you?"

172

"Fine." She hadn't been expecting him to call at that moment, but there was no mistaking his voice, and she felt butterflies in her stomach.

"I have an appointment in Santa Monica today. Why don't we have lunch." He made it a statement. It didn't occur to him that she might not be available.

"Well . . ." She hesitated, quickly debating with herself. One more lunch couldn't do any harm—and besides, each lunch with him was like going to school; she always learned something interesting. "Great," she finally answered. "What time shall I be ready?"

Jaimie checked his watch. "I'll pick you up at eleven-thirty."

"Okay. Goodbye."

Jaimie hung up the telephone. I wonder why she hesitated? he thought. She's gotta know how lucky she is.

Jaimie picked her up at precisely 11:30 and drove to an open-air seafood restaurant near the beach.

"I have to watch my weight," he explained to her, patting his stomach. "I've put on ten pounds in the last year, since I stopped smoking."

"I think you look fine," she said politely, "but I like eating light, too."

"You know, Helena," Jaimie said after the waitress served their jumbo shrimp cocktails, chopped green salads and Diet Cokes. "You need to think about your future, what you're going to do with your life. You've got a young son to support and you can't model forever."

"Well," she countered carefully, "actually, I have plenty of time to make that decision. I can model for the next fifteen or so years, if I want."

"Oh," he said, eating his shrimp and thinking, That wasn't what I was working toward.

"Yes, age isn't as much a problem with runway

173

models as it is with photographic models. In fact, couture models are normally a little older, because they have the sophistication and presence to wear the clothes that younger women don't. The women that go to fashion shows find it difficult to identify with young models."

"That's very interesting," he said. "But I was thinking in terms of becoming a success in any walk of life. You've heard all the homilies like money can't buy you happiness and the meek should inherit the earth and always go by the rules?"

Helena nodded.

"Bullshit." He tapped his finger on the table for emphasis. "It's all bullshit. Those are quaint phrases that the rich have made up from time immemorial to keep the poor in their places."

Helena leaned forward, listening intently.

"Don't kid yourself. The rich are happy. The only thing money can't buy you is poverty," he continued. "Rules are made to be broken. The rich and the successful are rich and successful because they make up their own rules as they go along. They don't always stay within the guidelines of morality. The more people they can convince to stay in their places, the less competition they have."

"I never thought of it that way," she said, completely mesmerized by his words.

"Yes," he said, hitting his stride. "And if you want to be successful, you have to learn to step away from everyone else, to be strong enough to live life the way you want, rather than the way everyone else wants you to. Because the majority of the people want you to be poor or unsuccessful. They find comfort in those little pat homilies and security in numbers. When their friends pull ahead and become successful they take it as a reflection on themselves. It makes them insecure."

"It's a little hard to believe that my friends wouldn't want to see me successful," she said questioningly. "I

174

always wish for their success."

"Are you going to listen to what I say, or are you going to interrupt?" he retorted impatiently. "I told you before, I see something special in you. I want to see you successful, but you have to pay attention to me and do just what I say."

"I am listening," she said, thinking how bright and worldly he was. He had such a knowledge of human nature. She'd never met anyone like him anywhere, and he took such an interest in her. That in itself was very flattering and seductive. She was like a coveted princess on a pedestal. Any problem, big or small, he'd handled and she had watched his maneuverings. It was such an opportunity to learn.

Jaimie, on the other hand, had a dual purpose in mind. What he had said was true. He did indeed see a special potential in Helena, and he did sincerely want to see her succeed. But he had also made the decision to continue his relationship with her, and he was laying the groundwork for that. He knew that Helena would have to take a lot of criticism about their relationship, and he wanted her strong and influenced by him enough to ignore the comments. He also knew that a woman as beautiful as Helena would have scores of single men pursuing her. If he was to keep her, he would have to make sure she was completely involved —not just physically and emotionally, but with a woman as bright as Helena, mentally, too.

Just looking at her eager, beautiful face made him want her. "Come on, let's go," he said, signaling for the check.

Helena wondered where they were going, what they were going to do, and if they were going to make love. And she pushed the thoughts of Jaimie's marriage from her mind.

Jaimie parked his Rolls and they entered her apartment.

"What time is your son coming home from school?"

175

he asked, taking off his jacket.

"About three-thirty."

"Good," he said, checking his watch. "Enough talking for today. I've got a little body language I want to show you."

He took her by the hand and pulled her into the bedroom. There he confidently took off her clothes and pushed her gently down on the bed. He made love to her gently, passionately, for once forgetting about manipulation, and she responded in kind, forgetting all her logical promises not to get involved with him as passion took over.

All too soon, it was three o'clock and time for them to dress. Jaimie grumbled a bit at her insistence that they hurry.

"Couldn't you send Nicky somewhere?" he said, pulling on his socks.

"Of course not. I'm gone enough as it is when he gets home from school. I want to be here for him, every chance I get. Look, let me make us some coffee."

"All right," he gave in grudgingly. He was used to getting his own way.

They were sipping coffee in the living room when Nicky arrived.

"Hi, Mom," he exclaimed, slamming the front door.

"Hi, pumpkin. How was your day?"

"It was okay," he replied, unenthusiastically.

"I want you to meet someone," she said. "Nicky, this is Jaimie. Jaimie, this is Nicky."

"It's nice to meet you, Nicky," Jaimie said, smiling and holding out his hand. "You're really a big boy."

Nicky put down his books and solemnly took Jaimie's hand. "Yes, sir," he said, sizing Jaimie up. "Do you work with my mom?"

"Jaimie is the man who hired me for the television show I did a few weeks ago," she interrupted.

"Oh." Nicky seemed satisfied with this new bit of information. "Is that your Rolls Royce in front?"

"Yes, it is," Jaimie replied. "Would you like a ride in

176

it sometime?"

"Wow, could I?" Nicky exclaimed excitedly.

"Next time, you've got a deal. Right now, I've got to go. Helena, I'll call you later. Nicky, it was nice meeting you."

"It was nice to meet you, too," he replied, adding, "When are you coming back?"

"Maybe tomorrow."

"And I could have a ride then?"

Jaimie nodded.

"Oh, boy!" Nicky jumped up and down.

Helena walked Jaimie to his car. "That was very nice of you to offer to take him for a ride."

"Anytime. He's a cute kid." He gave her a quick kiss.

But as cute as the kid was, he said to himself as he drove off, he was going to have to figure out how to keep that kid away from home more, or he was going to cramp his style.

The next morning, he called Helena. "Hi," he said when she answered. "I'll pick you up for lunch about noon."

"I'm sorry, Jaimie. I can't have lunch with you to-day. I have a show to do at the Beverly Wilshire Hotel."

"You're kidding," he said, disappointed. Helena had been on his mind all the night before and through the morning. He had hardly been able to wait until Donna was busy, so he could call her.

"No. If you want to," she suggested shyly, "you could come with me and watch the show. Then we could have coffee afterward."

"No way. I'm no stage-door Johnny, waiting around for some girl to get off work. I've seen those guys. Everybody laughs at them. It's not my style."

"Oh." She'd never heard anyone say that.

"Besides," he finished, "there's too many people that know me around Beverly Hills to be seen."

"Oh," she said again. That sounded more like the real reason.

"What time will you be home?"

"I should be home by three," she said, calculating her times. It was a 1:00 call, 1:30 show. The show had to be over by two-thirty or it would go into overtime, and it would take her a minimum of one half hour to get home from Beverly Hills.

"Can't you get home any sooner?" he demanded in an irritated voice. "Your kid will be home at three-thirty. We won't have any time at all."

"I'm sorry, Jaimie," she answered, feeling guilty. "That's the best I can do."

"All right," he grumbled. "I'll see you at three, then. Don't be late."

Helena hung up the telephone. Jaimie's dictator-like tone upset her. She enjoyed being with him immensely because he was so fascinating and knowledgeable about all facets of life. Every day with him had been a new learning experience, and she looked forward to the time they spent together. But she was also a mother and she loved Nicky very much and wanted to spend as much time as possible with him, too. She never put demands on Jaimie about the time he spent with his wife, yet he selfishly pressured her to spend every available moment and then some with him.

She mulled it over and over in her mind. Without her really being cognizant of the transition, her relationship with Jaimie had evolved into a steady affair, and she had become the mistress of a self-centered married man. She wasn't sure how she felt about this transition, and so she decided to let things ride for the time being.

The days slipped by, and seeing Jaimie became a daily routine. If she didn't have a show, Jaimie would come by and take her to lunch. Then they would come back and talk or make love. Nicky would come home at three-thirty, and then Jaimie would leave around five or five-thirty. Although Jaimie and Nicky didn't develop the close friendship Helena had hoped for, they did seem to get along.

178

Helena and Jaimie became increasingly close as the months passed. Jaimie began to buy her expensive gifts and to take her shopping for clothes. She never asked for anything, and her pride made it very difficult for her to accept his gifts. Initially, they had argued over her difficulty in accepting them.

"But I like buying you things," Jaimie had told her over and over, exasperated. "Just take it. What's the matter? Don't you like to see me happy?" he had joked.

Helena felt uncomfortable accepting the expensive gifts that she couldn't afford to purchase on her own. And she didn't want Jaimie ever to think she was seeing him in exchange for gifts when the truth was that she was falling more and more in love with him. His charismatic personality and vibrant sophistication when coupled with his singular interest in her were seductive and intriguing. He was a one-of-a-kind person, and he kept her attention as no one else ever had. Finally she gave in rather than argue anymore.

It made Jaimie happy to see the excitement and joy on her face when he bought her something lavish. He loved to see her dressed to the nines in expensive clothes. He would escort her about on his arm (where he wouldn't run into anyone he knew socially) and watch with obvious relish as the heads turned when she walked by.

He was generous with Nicky, too, although Helena suspected he was more interested in currying favor with Nicky than in the boy himself. The important thing to Helena was that he treated Nicky well.

Nicky, too, was friendly to Jaimie, though not overly enthusiastic. Helena realized, however, it would take Nicky a while to adjust to anyone she dated, that it was normal for him to compare every man with his father. And she tried hard to balance her time between Nicky and Jaimie and at the same time promote her career.

A couple of months after their first meeting, Jaimie suggested to her that she and Nicky move to an apart-

179

ment in Beverly Hills.

"I can't do that," she said.

"Why not?"

"Because living in Beverly Hills is not within my budget, that's why."

"I'll help you out," he said generously. "I want you to have the best."

"Sorry," she said firmly. "I want to pay my own way."

"Look, it would be more convenient, too," he continued, trying honesty. "It takes me half an hour to forty-five minutes each way to get to your apartment; that's too far away."

"I'm sorry, I really can't," she maintained stubbornly.

"Why are you so stubborn?" he said, exasperated.

"Because I want to pay for things on my own."

"You know," he said, trying another tack, "the schools in Beverly Hills are the best public schools in California. No other school comes close."

"Really?" she asked, becoming interested.

"Positively," he answered knowledgeably. "Education is so important, I'm surprised that you wouldn't want the best for Nicky."

"Of course I do."

"The education Nicky gets now will be the foundation for the rest of his life," he continued. To himself, he thought, Bullshit on driving forty-five minutes each day, each way.

"Well," she said slowly, "I didn't realize that Beverly Hills had such a good school district."

Gotcha, he thought. "Sure it does. The rich are the only ones around willing to spend money on the schools," he said, closing his sales pitch. "When are you going to learn to listen to what I say?

"Now," he said, not waiting for an answer. "You go out and find a place you like and let me know."

"All right," she agreed, though still suspicious of his motives. "What you say seems to make a lot of sense,

180

and I do want Nicky to have the best education possible."

So she found a modest little fourplex on Oakhurst Drive, a quiet street lined with beautiful old jacaranda trees that bloomed periwinkle blue in the spring. The apartment, a large old two-bedroom with a well-kept front yard, cost her double what she had been paying, but was low enough that she could cover it without Jaimie's help. Best of all, the manager had no objections to children.

"Perfect," Jaimie pronounced when he saw the apartment. "It's only ten minutes away from my condo."

"And I can afford it myself," she added.

"Strike!"

"Are you kidding?" Helena exclaimed with mock anger. "That ball wasn't within three feet of the plate!"

"Mom, if that ball was any closer, it would have hit the bat without you swinging," Nicky called. "And besides," he added. "You're choking the bat."

"Oh," she said, readjusting her grip. "Okay, Babe Ruth, pitch another. This time I'm ready for you!" She pounded on the old towel they were using for home plate and swung the bat through the air several times for emphasis.

Nicky pulled his Seattle Mariners baseball cap down low on his forehead and let go with his best pitch. The ball wobbled slowly through the air toward her.

Helena stood positioned to the right of the plate, her bat cocked, ready to connect with the ball. Down at the end of the block, Jaimie's white Rolls Royce turned the corner and sped toward the two of them, honking. Helena turned to face the car, and Nicky's ball whizzed past her and fell heavily to the ground behind her.

"Hey, guys," Jaimie called from the car.

"Hi, yourself," she said gaily, dropping the bat and

walking over to the car. "What brings you over to this neighborhood? I thought I wouldn't see you until tomorrow."

"I was able to break away and I thought I'd stop by for an hour or so." Jaimie grinned as he stepped out of the car. He was dressed in white jeans, a white Swiss linen shirt, and white handmade Italian loafers. The only other color he wore was the heavy gold chain around his neck and the gold, diamond-studded Rolex on his wrist.

"You look sort of like the Good Humor man," Helena joked.

"I am the Good Humor man," he shot back suggestively and winked. "I've come to put you in a good mood."

"Oh, boy," Nicky cried. "You could play ball with us. Do you want to be the catcher? Mom's the batter and she's got two strikes against her!"

"I, uh, came by to talk to your mom for a while, Nicky."

"Well, you could be the pitcher, if you want," Nicky said, compromising. "I really had enough of pitching. I could catch."

"We've just started playing, Jaimie," Helena said. "And I promised Nicky we'd play ball for a while. Come on, you'll like it!"

"Helena," Jaimie said, smiling stiffly, "I'm sure I would, but I only have an hour or so and I want to sit down and talk to you."

"Well," she said hesitantly.

"Oh, please, can't we play just a little longer, Mom, please?" Nicky begged.

"Maybe—" She looked from Nicky to Jaimie.

"Helena," Jaimie said sharply, "I want to talk to you, now."

"I know. Why don't we all go in and have a dish of peppermint ice cream."

"I want to discuss some things about your career,

182

alone," Jaimie insisted.

He turned to Nicky. "You understand, don't you? Sometimes adults need to talk about adult things. Why don't you call up one of your buddies to play ball with?"

Nicky shook his head, looking forlornly down at the ground and kicking at home plate.

"Nicky is still making friends at his new school," Helena explained. Then she turned to Nicky. "It just takes time, pumpkin. I changed schools when I was your age and it took me almost the whole year to make new friends. But some of them are still my friends. You'll have plenty of friends. You just wait and see."

"I know, Mom,' he said with a small smile. "Maybe I'll go watch TV."

"Well, actually, Nicky, I want to talk to your mom in the living room. I'll tell you what. Why don't you go down to the store and buy yourself a candy bar or a comic book." He extracted a thick wad of bills from his pocket, peeled off one, and handed it to Nicky. "Go on now," he said. "That's a good kid."

Nicky took the money. "Thank you," he mumbled and turned, walking slowly up the street.

It tore at Helena's heart to see the little figure, head down, feet dragging, walking up the street.

"Oh, Jaimie, look at him," she said and started to go after him.

Jaimie grabbed her arm. "Leave him alone, Helena. Kids are resilient. It just takes them a little time. He'll bounce back. In a few months, he'll forget all about Seattle. Let's go inside. I gotta be home by six for a dinner party at the house," he said. "We're wasting our time standing out here."

"But—"

"The kid's fine, I tell you. Come on," he said, dismissing the subject of Nicky and pulling her into the apartment. He slammed the door behind them and pinned her against the wall, kissing her passionately.

183

"I couldn't wait to do that," he whispered gruffly in her ear.

She kissed him back absently, but her mind was on the dejected little figure. She knew how hard it was to be the new kid at school. Nicky didn't complain, but she knew he missed his friends. He missed his daddy and grandparents, too. She tried to believe Jaimie's words about kids being resilient, but guilt gnawed at her.

"What was it that you wanted to talk with me about?" she said finally, maneuvering Jaimie around so he was at arm's length.

"I have been talking to you," he whispered, pulling her to him again and nibbling on her ear. "It's called body language. He pushed his body against hers and pulled one of her hands down to his crotch. "Feel it," he asked seductively. With his other hand, he undid the buttons on her blouse and slipped a hand under her breast, fondling it.

"Yes, but, Jaimie, it's so hard for Nicky to be in a new school and not know anybody," she said, slowly extracting his hand and maneuvering him again to arm's length so that she could explain about Nicky.

"Are we still talking about kids? You know, that's the problem with women today," he exclaimed, exasperated. "A man tries to be sensitive and romantic and you women's libbers walk all over his feelings." He warmed to the subject of himself. "It's not easy for me to break away, but I took the chance just to see you."

"I'm sorry, Jaimie. I know it's not easy for you," she said, turning her attention to him. "I guess I wasn't thinking."

"That's okay, honey, I forgive you," he said, grabbing her hand and shoving it down the front of his jeans. "Let's go fuck."

He took her by the hand and pulled her toward the bedroom. Once in the bedroom, Jaimie quickly started to peel off his clothes. Then they heard Nicky's little voice.

184

"Mom," he called through the front door. "It's me."

"Oh, shit," Jaimie muttered under his breath, his jeans around his ankles. "Is he back already?"

"Just a second, Nicky." She looked at Jaimie with his pants around his ankles and his socks up to his knees and started giggling. She hurriedly buttoned her blouse and ran to open the front door. Jaimie trailed behind, zipping up his fly.

"Look at the rad comic book I bought." Nicky held up an already wrinkled comic book for them to see. "Thanks a lot, Jaimie!"

"Any time, Nicky. You know," Jaimie said, devising another plan to get rid of the kid, "I wonder if you would do me a favor."

"Sure, anything you want," Nicky replied, thumbing through his comic book.

"Would you mind going back to the store? I just remembered some things I need."

"Could I read my new comic first?"

"Why don't you let him sit down and read it for a few minutes," Helena said. "Then he can go back to the store."

"No, I need the things now," Jaimie said, pulling out a pen and madly scribbling out a list of articles for Nicky to buy.

"Here's the list and some money," he said when he finished. He pulled the wad of bills out again and extracted a couple of them.

"You can keep the change, but you have to go now."

"Okay, I guess," Nicky said reluctantly.

Jaimie walked him to the door. "Take your time, pal." He scooted him out the door, shutting it and locking it behind him.

He turned to Helena, a determined look on his face. "Now about that body language that I was going to show you," he said quietly, pulling her against him.

*   *   *

185

Time passed quickly for Helena and with each passing day, she became more and more attached to Jaimie. She knew he was sometimes selfish and self-centered, but he was also generous, protective, and such fun to be with. He spent more time with her than her husband ever had. Though they couldn't always go to the trendy spots in Beverly Hills, he would take her anywhere else she wanted to go, and when they were together, the time seemed to fly. They never seemed to tire of each other's company.

She would accompany him to business meetings, and after the meetings, they would discuss what had transpired. Jaimie would ask her opinion and consider what she had to say seriously. She was the brightest woman he had ever met, he told her over and over. She considered that a compliment, considering Jaimie grew up a generation ahead of her, in a chauvinistic time, when business was a man's world.

She vacillated back and forth with their relationship. She had never met anyone as intriguing as Jaimie. It was like a full-time job just to keep up with his active mind. Often, she wished they could be together forever. He made life full and joyful. Other times, she wished she had never met him. She realized the seriousness of falling in love with a married man. It was a dead-end street; Jaimie had never made her any promises about the future of their relationship, and she had never asked. She loved and resented him at the same time, and consequently tried to be strong enough to keep a part of her detached.

Jaimie was very generous, too, and that made things difficult for Helena. On the one hand his wealth was seductive, offering a way of life she could have only dreamed of back in Washington, but it was also a trap. She was careful never to become dependent on him or what he gave her or Nicky, because she sensed that Jaimie was a compulsive opportunist and if he had complete control over her, he couldn't help but take

186

advantage. He was a giver, but he also took more than he gave, and even in love he needed to hedge his bets.

Nicky was the third part of the triangle of Helena's life. She loved him dearly and felt guilty for having uprooted him from his friends and family. She realized the difficulty he had making new friends, but she also believed what she did was for the best. She firmly believed that she had to be happy before she could make Nicky or anyone else happy.

She also understood that as a parent, she couldn't build her life around her child. Eventually a child grows up and leaves the nest to begin his own life. A parent who hasn't planned for that could end up bitter and alone.

It was hard balancing those logical ideals with her traditional upbringing, and at times she found herself guilt-ridden for trying to pursue her own career and identity in Los Angeles. And she wondered how Nicky really felt about Jaimie. It had to be upsetting to see his mother with another man other than his father. She tried to draw Nicky out and to explain her relationship with Jaimie in terms he would understand. Nicky would nod and seem to comprehend, but in the back of her mind, she wondered if he was just giving her lip service.

Another week passed, and as May rolled into June, Helena found herself looking toward spending the summer alone. As soon as school ended, Nicky would be flying to Seattle to spend the summer with his father, and Jaimie would be leaving soon afterward to make his annual pilgrimage to the south of France with his wife. Although she would miss both of them terribly, Los Angeles would be a calmer place without both of them vying for her attention.

When it came time for Nicky to leave, she did her best to be strong and hold back the tears as she put him on the plane. She watched his innocent little figure, clad in shorts and knee socks, march down the ramp, clutching his faithful velvet spotted puppy under his arm. Just as he entered the plane, he turned and gave her one last wave before disappearing inside. As soon as he was out of sight she immediately burst into tears on Jaimie's shoulder.

"He'll be fine," Jaimie told her, patting her tenderly. "At the end of the summer, he'll be back and excited about starting school."

"I know," she sniffed, trying to stop crying. "I just miss him already."

"Me, too. He's a good kid," Jaimie agreed solemnly. "Hey, look," he continued, brightening. Out of sight, out of mind was his motto as far as Nicky was concerned. "If we hurry and get back to your apartment, we can make love before I have to leave."

She looked at him, astonished at his abrupt mood change. "Right," she said sarcastically.

Jaimie ignored her inflection. "Let's go," he said, heading off down the corridor at a fast pace.

A week later, she was saying her goodbyes to Jaimie at her apartment. The next morning, he and Donna were leaving for Cannes, and Helena hugged his tall, lean frame. As frustrating as he sometimes was, she cared deeply for him and was sorely going to miss him.

"Cheer up," he said, relishing her tears. "When I leave, you can date all these single, swinging Beverly Hills bachelors. They'll be glad I'm out of town." He watched her reaction closely to see if she looked happy. To his relief, she still looked miserable.

"But be careful, because all they're interested in is fucking you. And of course they all have diseases," he added, just in case she was considering dating.

"I'm not interested in dating anyone," she said, her lower lip quivering. "I'm just missing you—and you

188

aren't even gone yet."

Jaimie left the next morning, and the following week dragged by for Helena. The summer was off season for runway modeling, and she only had one booking that week, so she had plenty of time on her hands. At first, she enjoyed her freedom from her lover and her son. She met Linda and Gayanne for lunch one day and another day she relaxed in the sun.

Very early one morning, about a week after Jaimie left, she awoke to the sound of the telephone ringing. It was the overseas operator with a person-to-person call from Jaimie.

"Hello, hello," she heard Jaimie say over the crackling of static.

"Hi, Jaimie," she exclaimed, overjoyed to hear his voice.

"Hi, baby," he said. "How are you?"

"Fine, but I really miss you," she confessed.

"That's what I'm calling about. I knew you were probably miserable without me, so I've arranged for you to fly over here." He couldn't bring himself to be open enough to tell her he was lonely without her, so he turned things around.

"Really?" she cried excitedly. "Are you kidding?"

"Of course not. I never kid. Now listen carefully. I haven't got much time before Donna gets back. I want you to leave this Tuesday. I've already made reservations on Pan Am's eight A.M. flight, direct to Nice. There'll be a prepaid first-class ticket waiting for you at the reservations desk."

"Tuesday," Helena broke in. "You want me to leave Tuesday? I don't know if I can be ready by then!"

"You will and you'll be on that plane or else," Jaimie growled. "Now listen to me and quit interrupting. I won't be able to meet you at the Nice Airport, so hire a taxi and tell him to take you to the Martinez Concord Hotel in Cannes. I've made reservations for you there. You got that?"

Helena grabbed a pen and scribbled down the information, repeating it after him. "Martinez Concord, Cannes. Tuesday, eight A.M. flight, Pan Am to Nice. I've taken down the information, but I can't guarantee that I'll make it."

"I don't want any arguments, Helena," he countered, bristling.

"I'm just telling you," she began, her anger rising. How could he just assume she could drop everything and come at his beck and call?

"Gotta go, baby," he interrupted, whispering. "Donna's back!"

Helena heard a click as he hung up.

She thought it over for the rest of the day and slept on it before making her decision. She didn't like his manipulations and chauvinistic attitude, but she was lonely in Los Angeles with him and Nicky gone. She also felt that what she would gain would outweigh his attitude and in the end she decided to go.

The international gate at Pan Am was a crowded cacophony of people from all walks of life and all corners of the world. The air was stale with the muskiness of many bodies pushed together into a small area, and there was an aura of anticipation. Every available seat was taken, and people leaned against the walls and pillars. There were people being greeted with hugs and tears and being bid farewell with hugs and tears, and other people were scurrying everywhere.

She felt as if she were in the middle of the United Nations instead of the airport waiting room. In one corner, an Indian family waited patiently for the arrival of a plane. A gaggle of Japanese tourists with their perennial cameras waddled by with their interpreter. In another corner, a group of students sat against the wall amidst their carry-on luggage, arguing loudly in Spanish. By standing still and concentrating, Helena could tune in to a half dozen different dialects, none of them English.

At 7:50 A.M., the gate attendant announced the boarding of her flight, and it suddenly hit her. She felt like hugging herself. A lifelong dream was coming true. She was actually on her way to Europe. So she boarded the plane immediately, half afraid that her reservations were a fluke and at any moment a flight attendant would ask her to vacate her seat and return to the boarding area. But after twenty minutes that stretched into hours for Helena, the plane took off.

The nine-hour flight gave her time for her mind to catch up with her body. Jaimie had called so suddenly and insisted that she leave so quickly that she hadn't had any time to contemplate or anticipate the trip. With something so wonderful happening to her, it would have been fun to relish the thought of Europe for several weeks before actually leaving, she mused to herself.

The steady roar of the airplane engines lulled her into a light sleep, where fragments of unspoken thoughts made their way into her dreams like air bubbles popping on the surface of a still pond. Everything always revolved around Jaimie, what Jaimie wanted to do, where Jaimie wanted to go. She was always giving and Jaimie was always taking, but somehow, he always craftily turned things around, that he made himself out to be the giver and her the taker.

Nicky's little face appeared in her dreams, and she dreamed that he was calling to her, but she couldn't come because Jaimie held her in a cage made of satin cords. She awoke with a jolt as the stewardess tapped her on the shoulder to ask her if she wanted breakfast. Her nap left her more exhausted than before, with an inexplicable uneasy feeling in the back of her mind.

When the plane arrived on the airstrip, hot summer air enveloped her as she descended the steps and

191

walked across the field to the terminal of the Nice Airport. She passed through customs and then looked around for Jaimie. He had told her that he didn't think he could get away from his wife to meet her, but she had crossed her fingers hoping he would just the same. It was frightening being in a foreign country alone and unable to speak the language, but Helena told herself to grow up.

The Nice Airport was much smaller and more modern than she had expected. She had had visions of massive pillars and carved cornices, dripping with European tradition, but instead, the interior could have passed for any small, modern American airport, except for the French policemen, armed with rifles, stationed around the airport.

Armed with her own form of ammunition—her Berlitz *French for Travelers* handbook—Helena followed her porter to the taxi station. She explained in halting French, reading from her handbook, that she wanted to be driven to Cannes on the Riviera. True to the French reputation, the taxi driver indicated that he understood her and flirted with her outrageously, without uttering a word of English.

The drive from the Nice Airport to Cannes took about half an hour, and the view, when Helena's eyes weren't glued to the road ahead, was beautiful. The driver kept up a running monologue over his shoulder while driving 60 miles per hour on the curves. Helena nodded politely with a forced smile, while she clutched the door handle with one white-knuckled hand and her French handbook with the other.

The highway twisted in and out of the countryside, and the driver continued to call out scenic points of interest in French, which Helena couldn't understand. Eventually, the road wound into the city of Cannes. The boulevards were lined with giant old shade trees, and each block was crammed with small shops, boutiques and apartments. Townspeople and tourists

192

sat side by side leisurely sipping cool drinks in shady sidewalk cafés.

The taxi rounded the top of the last hill, and suddenly, as far as she could see, the Mediterranean Sea lay glittering before her, like a dark blue sapphire in the late afternoon sun. The taxi jostled through the narrow streets, then turned left onto the palm-lined croisette. There were people everywhere, dressed in chic playclothes and swimwear. To the right, the Mediterranean stretched out to meet the horizon, its beaches sprouting colorful beach umbrellas. To the left, fairy-tale names leapt out at her: the Palais de Festival, home of the Cannes Film Festival; the Festival Bar; the Carlton Hotel, with the legendary Carlton Terrace; Felix's Restaurant; and finally the white walls of the Martinez Concord Hotel. The driver pulled around the horseshoe-shaped driveway to the entrance of the hotel, and Helena stepped out of the taxi.

A porter immediately took her bags and led her through the entrance into a bygone era. The lobby had an old-world grace about it, its architecture reminding her of the early 1920s. But the furniture was left over from the fifties and was quite an eclectic combination. At the far end of the lobby, a white marble staircase with ornate wrought-iron railings stood side by side with its modern counterparts, two elevators.

Helena made her way to the old-fashioned wood reservation desk.

"*Bonjour,* mademoiselle, may I help you?" the desk clerk inquired, looking her up and down with typical French snobbishness.

"*Bonjour,*" she said, a little intimidated. "I believe you're holding a reservation for me—Helena Sinclair."

"Ah, yes, Mademoiselle Sinclair," he replied, making a big production of thumbing through the reservation files. "Here it is; room eight-oh-three. Mr. Cramer was by this afternoon to check the room."

She was touched by Jaimie's attention and it dissipated her anger a bit at his blatant manipulations of her. "Was he really," she asked. "That was so sweet."

The clerk shrugged noncommittally. "Please sign in, and the bellman will take you to your room," he said, with the air of a monarch dismissing one of his subjects.

Helena followed the bellman to her room, where the entrance opened into a narrow hallway that ended in a large high-ceilinged living room. Tall French doors at the end of the room opened onto a tiny terrace, and the sleeping alcove was separated from the living room by an archway; beyond that was a large pink-tiled bathroom. The suite was huge by American standards, and the furniture was antique. There were no closets, only a huge rosewood armoire.

On the coffee table in the center of the living room was a gigantic bouquet of summer flowers. Helena pulled the card from the flowers, already knowing they were from Jaimie, and tore open the envelope. The note said: "Take off your clothes and hop into bed, I'll be there soon after this is read." She laughed out loud. It was so typical of Jaimie—one minute precise and businesslike, making sure her room was right, and the next minute corny and romantic.

She unpacked her suitcases, opened the French doors, and leaned out over the terrace. The sun was beginning to sink low over the water, and the view was breathtaking. The headlights from the traffic on the croisette lit up the dusk. Directly below her, the shopkeepers were closing up for the night, and across the way, a festive red-and-green sign flashed the name of a local nightclub called La Chunga. Next door on the corner was a crowded open-air restaurant called Vesuvius Pizza. The fragrance of baking pizza wafted up and reminded her that she hadn't eaten for hours.

Rather than venture out and chance missing Jaimie, she ordered a light dinner from room service, but by the time she finished eating, Jaimie still hadn't arrived. So

194

she took a leisurely bath and puttered around the room. Finally eleven hours of traveling caught up with her, and though she fought to stay awake, she gave up at last and went to bed.

It seemed as if her head had barely touched the pillow when she heard someone pounding on her door. Glancing at her travel alarm she read 1:30. She stumbled out of bed, threw on her robe, and hurried to the door. "Who is it?" she asked, trying to clear her head of sleep.

"It's me," she heard Jaimie whisper on the other side of the door. "Open up!"

She unlocked the door and barely got it closed behind her before Jaimie had her backed up against the door, his mouth hungrily searching out hers.

"I thought you were never going to get here," he said huskily, cupping her face in his hands. "I've missed you so much."

His hands slipped down her neck and beneath the satin of her robe to the soft skin of her breasts. Her body was still warm and drowsy from sleep, and his hands felt cool against her skin. His fingertips caressed the tips of her breasts, and he pressed himself against her. She felt him growing hard through his light trousers.

"Come with me" she whispered, drawing him down the narrow hall to the living room. She started toward the bedroom, but instead, he led her to the sofa and laid her back against it. He knelt down on his knees in front of her, gazing at her in the pale moonlight.

"I love you, Helena," he murmured, stroking her face tenderly. "I've missed you so much."

It was the first time he had ever told her that he loved her, and was as much a surprise to him as it was to her. Somewhere in the past few months, the game of wits Jaimie had been playing had fallen by the wayside without him realizing it, and it had taken a separation from Helena for him to finally acknowledge it.

195

"I love you," he whispered over and over, understanding the meaning of the words.

He stood up and quickly stepped out of his clothes, then knelt before her again, parting her gown and kissing her breasts and sucking on her nipples, feeling them grow hard in his mouth.

She moaned with pleasure and caressed his chest and kissed his nipples. Her hands fluttered down to his stiff cock, and she longed to feel it inside her. She nibbled on it, stroking it with her tongue. She felt the sharp intake of Jaimie's breath as he felt her lips on his hard cock.

He pulled her mouth to his, crushing her lips in a passionate embrace. She moved her body against his and felt his cock slide into her warm wetness; the exquisite feeling left her breathless. She moaned and pulled him closer. He plunged his cock deeper and deeper into her, making her realize how much she had missed their passionate lovemaking. At that moment, she never wanted to let him go. Behind them, the gentle night breezes off the Mediterranean softly billowed the sheer curtains.

Helena awoke alone at ten A.M., to warm rays of sunlight streaming through the open French doors and the sounds of laughter from the streets below. The incredible lovemaking of the night before seemed almost like a dream, except for the fragrance of Jaimie on the pillow next to her. She luxuriated in the pink satin bed linens and planned her day. Jaimie had said he would meet her on the beach about eleven o'clock, or as soon as he could get away. That gave her an hour to shower, have breakfast, and get a spot on the beach.

She picked up the ornate telephone next to the bed and called room service, ordering a continental breakfast of croissants, fresh orange juice, and coffee. Then she hopped out of bed, slipped on her robe and walked out on the terrace.

Far below her, people looking like tiny toys strolled

196

down the side street. La Chunga, which the night before had echoed with Latin music, dozed quietly in the morning sun. Across the way, a French family breakfasted on their terrace. The view to her left was so breathtaking and exquisite that it almost brought a lump to her throat. The Mediterranean sparkled before her as far as her eyes could see. In the hazy distance, a graceful yacht bounced and dipped on its moorings. The beach in front of the hotel was already dotted with gaily striped yellow-and-white umbrellas. The entire view looked like a picture postcard, and she wished Nicky were there with her to share it.

She gazed at the view and reminisced for a moment about the change her life had taken. Less than a year had passed since she left Seattle, and yet it seemed like a century. The French Riviera was so far from Bremerton, the little Navy town outside Seattle where she had grown up. Who would have thought, she mused, that in the span of one short year, I would leave my marriage, move to Los Angeles, begin a love affair with a married man, and spend the summer on the French Riviera. Life was truly full of strange twists and turns, and it left her with mixed feelings. She loved Jaimie and was grateful to him for the attention he lavished on her, both materially and emotionally, but his selfishness and overdeveloped ego made her angry. She was beginning to resent his demands for her time more and more.

A sound behind Helena brought her back to the present. She whirled around as a waiter set up a breakfast table.

"Excusez-moi, s'il vous plait, mademoiselle," he said bowing and indicating the table. "Your breakfast is ready."

"Merci, garçon," she replied. "I didn't even hear you knock."

The waiter shook his head as if he didn't understand. Helena later came to realize that the waiters never knocked; they just walked right in.

Everything was different in France, even the croissants. They were exceptionally light and buttery, and Helena could undestand why the French were famous for their food. The coffee was very, very strong and black and was served with a pitcher of hot milk. She quickly realized she'd have to order the coffee American-style, with an extra pot of hot water to dilute it.

After breakfast, she quickly showered and pulled on a string bikini and a cover-up. Then, armed with suntan lotion, a novel, and a few francs, she headed for the beach.

The beaches on the French Riviera were nothing like American beaches. Each hotel not only had its own, but each area was designated by a different color umbrella and mattress. The Martinez Concord had yellow-and-white umbrellas and mats; she saw the green of the Miramar, the red and white of the gay beach next door, and farther on, the blue and white stripes of the Carlton, where Jaimie was staying. There were two public areas, one several beaches down to the left, and another about a mile to the right, near the Palais de Festival. Both, Helena discovered later, were small and dirty and crowded to the point of overflowing. At night, students slept on the public beaches next to their campfires.

For a small fee, a muscular towel boy, clad only in shorts, deposited Helena, with a mattress, towel, and umbrella, among the rows of sunbathers. She slathered on suntan lotion and joined the ranks of brown bodies baking in the sun like rows of hot dogs on a grill. The fragrance of coconut oil mingled with the salt of the Mediterranean and floated in on the lazy winds. Tanned young waiters scurried about, delivering cold drinks to the sunbathers. Children of the wealthy played in the gentle lapping waves at the edge of the water, their laughter tinkling on the breezes. Now and then, African hucksters dressed in caftans and flat native hats picked their way through the bathers, hawking their wares in a hodgepodge of French, pigeon English, and what she assumed was an African language. On every side of her, Helena could hear fragments of conversations in French, German, Italian, Swiss, and Arabic. Everywhere there was a lazy, hedonistic sophistication. It was a far cry from the frenetic beaches of Southern California with its surfers and Frisbee players.

She picked up her novel and began to read, pausing from time to time to glance up the beach for Jaimie. Then she saw a familiar, chubby figure jogging toward her at the water's edge. Jaimie dropped down beside her, and she leaned over to welcome him with a kiss.

"Sorry," he said, backing away from her. "Someone might see us."

"Oh, that's right," she said, a little disappointed. "I forgot."

"That's okay. So, what have you been doing?"

"Nothing much." She smiled. "Though I did have the most wonderful dream last night."

"Is that so? What did you dream?"

"I dreamed that a sexy man came to my room and made passionate love to me," she giggled.

"Really," he said with a straight face. "I had an interesting dream, too. I dreamed I was walking down the croissette and an ugly old broad grabbed me, pulled me into her hotel room, and forced me do all kinds of kinky things to her. I couldn't get away."

"Ugly old broad, huh," she said with mock severity. "I'll remember those words the next time I hear someone whining at my door in the middle of the night!"

"Don't look at me." He raised his hands in surrender. "From now on, I'm using the balcony."

"You and Romeo," she finished, and they both started laughing.

"Look," he said, changing the subject. "I've made arrangements with Felix for you to have dinner at his restaurant. Everybody goes there. Afterward, you can go for a walk on the croissette. Everyone strolls the croissette at night; you'll like it. By then, jet lag will have caught up with you and you'll be ready for bed. But try to stay awake as long as you can, so you can get your hours turned around."

"What are your plans for tonight?" Helena asked, hoping maybe Jaimie would be able to get away and see her.

"Oh," he said casually, "we're meeting some friends on the Carlton Terrace for drinks, then going to the Palm Beach Casino for dinner and a little gambling."

"That's great," she said not feeling great at all.

"I've gotta go." He abruptly stood. "Gotta get back before Donna comes looking for me. I'll be back again in a couple of hours."

He turned around and jogged back down the beach toward the white dome of the Carlton.

Throughout the day Helena would watch Jaimie jog down the beach to see her then back up the beach to see his wife. Then he'd jog back down the beach and then back up the beach. If she wasn't so bothered by the situation she would have laughed. She wondered what his wife was like and was tempted to casually stroll down the beach and have a look, but she didn't. She didn't know how she would handle seeing them together. In Los Angeles, at least, she didn't have to face the reality that his wife was so nearby, waiting for his return. But being here brought home the cold fact that she was a married man's mistress.

"A few more weeks of this," she told Jaimie when he had jogged back to see her for the third time, "and you'll be ready for the Boston Marathon." She said it with a smile, but she didn't feel like smiling.

In between Jaimie's visits, she took a swim and explored the nearby beaches, but she couldn't quite

200

bring herself to walk up the beach past the Carlton and chance seeing Jaimie with his wife. It was a long day without anyone to talk to, but Helena did her best to occupy her time. Most of the other bathers had already left the beach when she finally packed up her things to return to her room and dress for dinner.

Felix's was a small but internationally known restaurant on the croissette. The walls were lined with red leather booths, and wall sconces added an intimate glow to the interior. The outside patio was a popular late night rendezvous for dessert and an aperitif after a stroll on the croissette.

Helena stepped up to the maître d's desk. Felix, the maître d' and owner, a pleasant, middle-aged man, looked up. *Bon Soir,* may I help you?" he asked with a heavy French accent.

"Yes," she replied. "I think I have a reservation. Helena Sinclair."

"Oui, mademoiselle," he said with a slight bow. "I've been expecting you. I have our best table waiting for you."

He led her to a cozy booth in the corner where she could watch the comings and goings of the glamorous people around her.

The food was exquisite: buttery escargot, fresh caught pompano, asparagus from local truck farms, and rich Strawberries Romanov, a specialty of the house, all complemented by an icy white Burgundy. The meal was memorable and the restaurant the most romantic. Helena couldn't help wishing she had someone to share it with. She tried to tell herself that it really didn't matter that she was alone. The important thing was that Jaimie cared enough about her to want her to see France. She had almost convinced herself that she liked dining alone; then the check came.

She opened her purse to pay the check, and to her

horror, she had forgotten her wallet. She sat there stunned for a moment and contemplated her next move. Then she got angry, angry at herself for forgetting her wallet and angry at Jaimie because she was alone. Then embarrassment and humiliation replaced her anger because she would have to explain to Felix, owner of one of the most elite restaurants in Cannes, that like a true hick she had forgotten a minor thing like money.

The waiter, noticing the stricken look on her face, hurried over to her. "Mademoiselle," he said. "You look pale. Is everything all right?"

"Everything is fine," she replied, smiling wanly. "Would you ask Felix to step over here, please?"

The waiter hurried off to get Felix, and Helena took a deep breath and gathered together all the poise she could muster. She wondered whether she should try to bluff her way through and be haughty and indignant or if she should throw herself on his mercy and grovel. In the end, she was too embarrassed to try anything except sincerity.

"Yes, Mademoiselle Sinclair," Felix said when he reached her booth. "What can I do for you?"

"I'm sorry, I have no money," she said, trying to be calm and at the same time speak in a low voice so the diners around her couldn't hear. "That is," she amended, "I don't have any money with me. I have money. I just forgot to get it from the hotel safe. I'm staying at the Martinez Concord."

Felix said nothing and Helena nervously rattled on. "If you will just give me a few minutes, to run over to the hotel, I'll be right back with my money." She searched his face for a clue to what he would say. "You can call the hotel to verify that I'm a guest there."

She tried to think of something else that might convince him of her honesty, and she silently prayed that he wouldn't make a scene.

"That won't be necessary, Mademoiselle Sinclair," he said.

Helena breathed an inward sigh of relief. "It will only take me five or ten minutes and I'll come right back," she promised him.

"It's no problem. Don't hurry; take twenty minutes, half an hour," he said magnanimously. "I trust you."

"Oh, thank you," she said in relief. "I'll be right back."

She stood up and started to walk out the door.

"Oh, Mademoiselle Sinclair," Felix called after her. "I'll just keep this until you return."

He casually snatched her purse from her shoulder and put it on a shelf under the maître d's desk. Several people at nearby tables glanced curiously in their direction, but no one said anything.

"Of course," she stammered, embarrassed, and left the restaurant.

Trusts me, huh, she thought to herself dryly as she hurried back to the hotel.

After removing her traveler's checks from the hotel safe, she went directly back to the restaurant. Felix was not in sight, but a hostess came up to her as she entered. She started to explain the situation, but the hostess seemed to know the whole story. Helena quickly paid the check and added a large tip, just to prove she wasn't destitute. Then she collected her purse and left the restaurant.

By then, her sense of humor had returned, and she smiled at the situation. These things are only supposed to happen in books, she thought to herself as she walked down the croissette.

The night was warm and sultry, and it seemed like half of the south of France was out for a stroll. Sidewalk vendors displayed their wares, and the strollers jockeyed for positions and bargained for prices. Across the street, a fire-eater gathered a large crowd as he blew flames high into the starry sky. Everywhere, there was a carnival atmosphere. Lovers sauntered arm in arm, blocking traffic long enough to reassure each other with a kiss. The crowd was like a slow-moving tide, ebbing and flowing, curling around obstacles in its path, then slowly moving on. Helena joined the flow, allowing it to move her along without a purpose. She passed the white walls of the Carlton. The terrace was almost empty; the fashionable cocktail hour had ended. A flood of light poured from the tall windows and arched entry of the hotel, spilling out over the line of waiting limousines, but not quite reaching a woman with her baby, who was begging in a dark corner of the hotel wall.

Farther on, Helena passed the Blue Dolphin and the Festival Bar. Both were jammed with carefree people enjoying the balmy French night. The laughter and good times seemed to infect everyone except Helena. Instead, it made her feel lonely. She wished she had someone to talk with, someone to share the evening with. She knew she would talk with Jaimie the next day, but it wasn't the same.

"Being by myself," she told herself philosophically, "is a good opportunity to build character." But she didn't believe it.

She wandered on, immersed in her own thoughts, not noticing that the crowds had thinned out at this end of the croissette. Suddenly, a man blocked her path and pushed his face close to her, saying something in French. Startled, Helena looked at him and shook her head to indicate that she didn't understand.

"How much do you want?" he repeated in heavily accented English, his breath laden with garlic and wine.

Helena took an involuntary step back. "What?" she asked, confused.

"One thousand francs," he said.

Helena looked at him blankly.

"One thousand five hundred," he said peevishly.

Helena looked around her. She had been so deep in thought that she had passed through the brightly lit tourist district. The street that she was now on was quiet and lit only by an occasional streetlamp. The shops were all closed for the night, and dark shadows stood in their doorways. At the end of the block, under a dim streetlamp, two women in miniskirts and spike heels stood haggling quietly with a man. In the distance, Helena heard a woman's throaty laughter. It took her only a moment to realize she was in a red-light district. At the same time, the man in front of her took hold of her arm, as if to lead her somewhere.

"What's with you," he said in an irritated tone. "I said how much?"

"Let go of me," she exclaimed with more bravado then she felt, jerking her arm away and starting to walk off.

"Wait a minute!" he cried, following her.

With that, her show of bravery melted and she took off at a dead run. Behind her, she heard him laughing in the darkness.

Rounding a corner onto the croissette, she collided with a vendor selling sugar-coated peanuts. Peanuts flew everywhere.

"Watch out," he screamed at her in French.

"I'm sorry, she said and tried to scoop up the peanuts as they rolled across the sidewalk and into the gutter.

"Idiot," the vendor roared. "Get out of here!"

Helena at that point decided it was best to go back to her hotel.

"Ah, Mademoiselle Sinclair," the concierge called out as she entered the hotel. "How was your evening stroll?"

"Very interesting," she told him dryly as she made her way to the elevators.

That night, Jaimie came by again in the wee hours of the morning, and Helena tried to tell him about her evening, but he was more interested in making love than in conversation.

*   *   *

205

After a month had slipped by and the summer sun had turned her skin to a golden brown, Helena looked more and more European and had become lonelier, sometimes wishing she had never come to France.

Jaimie still jogged down the beach to meet her, and they would steal a few hours together occasionally in the afternoon or in the middle of the night. But other than that, Helena was alone. It seemed that most of the other guests were with friends or loved ones, and they had no time for a beautiful, unattached young woman. She tried to explain her feelings of loneliness to Jaimie, but he couldn't or wouldn't understand.

"You should be happy just being here," he told her impatiently. "Any other girl would give her right arm to spend the summer in the south of France in the style I've shown you. Who else would do this for you?"

"I really do appreciate everything you've done," she tried to tell him. "It's just . . . that I don't have anyone to talk to. Most people don't speak English, and if they do, they aren't interested in talking to a stranger."

"You can talk to me," he told her arrogantly. "I should be enough for you."

He made her feel guilty and ungrateful but at the same time she was angry that he refused to acknowledge her point of view. Everything was always his way. He refused to see her loneliness or empathize with the stigma she felt at being his mistress. Finding that she was getting nowhere with him, she dropped the subject and vowed not to be such a baby.

One day as she was lying on the beach reading, she heard a deep voice above her say, "Hi! Do you speak English?"

Helena looked up into the smiling face of a man standing above her. "Yes, I do." She smiled politely.

"May I sit down?" he asked and not waiting for her answer, plopped down in the sand beside her.

206

"Well, sure," she muttered, looking around to see if Jaimie was coming. He wouldn't be thrilled to see her talking to another man. Yet it had been days since she had talked to anyone, except for a few brief conversations with Jaimie.

"I'm Richard Rosenfeld, from Los Angeles," he said, holding out his hand. He was fairly tall and well built, with curly brown hair and a dark tan that brought out his light gray-green eyes and curly lashes. She stared at his profile and noted that he had model-perfect bone structure and a warm, friendly smile.

"I'm Helena Sinclair," she said, taking his hand and noticing that his fingernails, like Jaimie's, were well manicured.

"How long have you been here?" he asked.

"Oh, about a month."

"I've seen you before, and I thought you were French but today I noticed your book was in English, so I took a chance." He smiled, showing his white, even teeth. "Are you here alone or with friends?"

Helena hesitated a moment, deciding how to answer him. She was here because of Jaimie, but technically, she was alone. Before she could answer him, a shadow fell over them and they looked up.

"Jaimie Cramer! How are you?" Richard exclaimed, standing up and shaking Jaimie's hand. "I didn't know you were here in Cannes!"

"Hello, Richard," Jaimie replied.

"Jaimie Cramer, I'd like to you to meet Helena Sinclair," Richard said, assuming Jaimie had stopped by to speak to him. "Helena, Jaimie Cramer."

"How nice to meet you," Jaimie said, formally extending his hand with a straight face.

"It's nice to meet you, too," she said, smiling and carrying on with Jaimie's charade.

The three of them chatted for a short time. Helena found out that Richard was a successful entertainment attorney and that he didn't live too far from her in Los

Angeles. Jaimie continued to treat Helena like a stranger.

After a few minutes, Richard checked his Rolex. "I'm sorry, I've got to go; I have an appointment. But Helena, would you like to join me for dinner at the casino tonight?" he said, turning to her. "I can't have a beautiful woman dining all alone on the French Riviera."

Helena looked at him in surprise. "I don't—" she said, starting to refuse him.

"That's a great idea," Jaimie interrupted. "You'll like the Palm Beach Casino, Helena."

She looked at him in amazement. "All right," she said to Richard. "Thank you very much."

"Great, I'll pick you up at the hotel about seven. Jaimie, nice to see you again." And he left.

"I can't believe you," she said to Jaimie, shaking her head. "What did you do that for?"

"This is perfect," he said. "Richard can be our beard."

"Our what?"

"Our beard. Our cover. Richard can cover for us. He doesn't need to know about us, but at the same time he'll take you out, show you a good time, and I won't have to listen to you complain about sitting home all the time in your hotel room. This is great. If we should ever meet, Richard will say he introduced us."

"Well, I guess it's a good idea," she said dubiously.

The more Helena thought about it, the better the idea seemed. She was lonely and bored, and it would be nice to have company at dinner for a change.

She dressed carefully that evening in a white linen backless halter dress, pulling her hair back in a long, simple ponytail, with white linen and rhinestone earrings as her only accent. At exactly seven, the telephone rang; Richard was waiting for her in the lobby.

"I thought you were very pretty when I saw you on the beach," Richard said admiringly as she stepped from the elevator. "But you're a knockout!"

"Thank you," she replied, embarrassed.

208

"I thought we'd stop by the Carlton Terrace for a drink before dinner," he said as he escorted her to a glossy black Mercedes limousine waiting outside the hotel. "Have you been there?"

"No." An uneasy feeling came over her. She didn't know Jaimie and his wife would be there, but she knew they generally did have a cocktail there before dinner. It was almost a ritual with them. She didn't think she wanted to face seeing them together.

They drove the few short blocks to the Carlton, and as they pulled up, red-liveried doormen hurried to open the limousine doors. They stepped out, and the driver took his place in the ranks of waiting limousines, which stood like so many black beetles in a row.

They crossed the driveway, climbed the short flight of steps to the terrace, and paused at the side entrance. The Carlton Terrace was the place to be seen, and all eyes were on them. The domain of the American and European jet set, this was not a place that catered to tourists. That was left to the Festival Bar and the Blue Dolphin or a dozen other places. This was where the rich and famous went to see and be seen.

There was even a caste system to the seating arrangements. The tables nearest the hotel entrance were the cherished ones; and were often reserved for regular clients. The farther away and the closer to the croissette, the less important the table. The patrons were varied, young and old, men and women, but they all had one thing in common: the poise and self-assurance of wealth.

Richard waved to a group of people who had been trying to get his attention at one of the head tables, and Helena glancing in their direction received a sharp jolt. Sitting at the next table was Jaimie. He hadn't noticed them, and Helena hoped that Richard wouldn't see him and suggest they say hello. Thankfully, he didn't. Instead, Richard signaled Roland, the terrace's maître d', who was almost as famous as the terrace itself.

Roland led them to a reserved table that was directly facing Jaimie's table. As she sat down, she tried to catch Jaimie's eye but he was oblivious to her. He sat with his arm casually draped across the back of the chair of the woman sitting next to him.

Helena studied the woman and observed with a start that the woman looked like an older version of herself. She had the same dark brown hair, fine bones and big eyes, although there was a bitter twist to her mouth. She was chicly dressed, expensive jewels glittering at her ears and throat. Helena knew that the older woman was Donna, Jaimie's wife, and although she wasn't able to catch Jaimie's eye, she did catch Donna's, and she returned Helena's stare with a cool nod of her head. Helena dropped her eyes in embarrassment. She felt almost nauseated by the sight of her lover with his wife.

"Helena," Richard asked, looking up from the wine list, "what kind of champagne would you like? Chrystale? Laurent Perrier?"

He noticed the strained look on Helena's face. "What's the matter?" he asked quickly. "Are you okay?"

"I—I'm fine. Will you excuse me for a moment?" she said, standing up. Without waiting for him to reply, she got up and made her way through the tables and into the hotel lobby to the ladies' room.

She locked herself in one of the cubicles and leaned against the door, taking deep breaths. She had always known that someday she would see Jaimie with his wife, and she had tried to prepare herself. But it still hurt. She heard the door to the restroom open and someone walk in. She stayed in the cubicle for a few more moments until she felt composed enough to leave. Then she unlatched the door and walked out. There was a woman in front of the mirror, freshening up. Helena glanced at her in the mirror as she walked over to the sink, and the reflection stopped her dead in her tracks. It was Jaimie's wife.

"Men," Donna said breezily, touching up her

210

makeup. "As fast as I put on makeup, my husband messes it up. That man can't keep his hands off me!"

Helena nodded faintly, reading between the lines. She knew that Donna had caught her staring and was letting her know that Jaimie was taken.

She must be very insecure, Helena thought sympathetically. And she has every right to be, judging by Jaimie's behavior.

She suddenly realized she was identifying with her rival, so she quickly washed her hands and walked out without replying. As she passed Jaimie's table, he looked up with a start, and she felt his eyes following her to her table. She willed herself to look straight ahead and maintain her composure. She arched her back and walked a little straighter.

"Helena." Richard stood as she sat down. "I was beginning to think you got lost."

"Not on your life," she said, devoting her full attention to him. She could feel Jaimie staring at her, so she moved her chair slightly so she couldn't see him even if she tried.

Jaimie saw Helena return from the ladies' room and it gave him a jolt. At first he panicked at seeing her; then he remembered that Donna knew nothing about their affair, and he calmed down. He watched Helena glide through the room and saw the reactions of the people around him. All eyes turned in her direction. He felt a possessive pride and wished that she were on his arm so that everyone would know she belonged to him.

Donna returned and sat down next to him. She noticed the people around them staring at Helena. "Look how skinny that girl is," she sniffed cattily. "She's probably anemic or bulimic or both. I don't know what any man would see in her." She watched Jaimie closely to see what his reaction would be, but he pretended not to hear her.

*   *   *

211

From the Carlton Terrace, Richard took Helena to the Palm Beach Casino, where they had supper in the elegant, gilded dining room overlooking the roulette wheels and chemin de fer tables. This was where the crème de la crème of Europe toyed with gambling. Unlike the bawdy atmosphere of Las Vegas, the Palm Beach Casino was sleek and sophisticated. Here, too, fortunes were made and lost with the spin of the roulette wheel, but it was done with total nonchalance.

After supper, they walked down the steps to the tables. Helena had a glorious time. Richard taught her how to play chemin de fer and insisted she blow on their roulette chips for good luck. Later, they went into another part of the casino to a disco, and they danced until Helena thought she would drop from exhaustion.

The stars had disappeared and the night was fading when Richard's limousine pulled up in front of the Martinez Concord. Across the side street, the La Chunga Bar had just closed, while farther down the street, lights in the back of a *pâtisserie* flicked on as a baker began his day. On the opposite side of the street, a produce truck was parked next to the hotel, and truckers conversed in country French as they unloaded fresh produce. The air was clear and fresh with the smell of salt water.

A sleepy doorman opened the limousine door, and Richard walked her to the elevator. "Dinner tomorrow night?" Richard asked as she stepped into the elevator.

Helena hesitated only a moment before answering. "I'd love to."

"Good. Unfortunately, I'm leaving the day after tomorrow, but I'd like to see you one more time before I leave. See you on the beach," he called to Helena as the elevator doors closed.

"Thank you," she called. "I had a great time tonight."

She leaned back against the back wall of the elevator, smiling, and thought about what a wonderful time

212

she had had. Richard was young, attractive, and such fun. So easygoing and undemanding, not like Jaimie, who always wanted everything his way. But thinking that way made her feel disloyal. After all, she reminded herself, Jaimie was the one who had brought her over here, and Richard was only a beard. Jaimie was the one who truly cared for her. But he also had a wife. It had hurt Helena to see them together. Even though she had imagined it over and over in her mind, the reality of it made her heart ache. She wondered how Jaimie's wife would feel if she knew Jaimie had a girlfriend. Helena had been a wife, and she knew she would never condone a cheating husband.

With these conflicting emotions warring inside her, she opened the door to her room and spied two folded slips of paper that had been slid under the door. She opened the first one. The time on it was 11:30 P.M. "I stopped by to see you but apparently you aren't home yet. Love, J."

The second note was also from Jaimie. "It's one-thirty A.M., time for good little girls to be in their *own* bed. Wherever you are, you'd better be behaving yourself! I'll talk to you in the morning. J."

The tone of the second note definitely was not happy. On the one hand, Helena felt guilty for not being there when Jaimie came by. She felt a responsibility and a loyalty toward him, not to mention her emotional involvement. On the other hand, she had done nothing wrong. It was Jaimie's idea that she go out to dinner with Richard. And she was glad she had. It was difficult having no one to talk to. Jaimie had his wife to talk to. What right did he have to supervise her actions as if she were a child? And why was it always Jaimie's wishes that had to be catered to?

She had slept late and the sun was almost directly overhead by the time she got down to the beach. She hadn't been there ten minutes when Jaimie showed up.

"Where were you so late last night?" he demanded, sitting down on the foot of her mattress. "I said you could go out for dinner with the man, not spend the whole night."

"I didn't," she said. "We just went dancing after dinner and I lost track of time."

"You know," he said, laying on the guilt, "it's not easy for me to get away. I went to a lot of trouble to come by twice, last night, so we could spend some time together."

"I know," she replied. "And I'm really sorry. I know it's not easy for you."

"I brought you to the south of France so we wouldn't have to be apart," Jaimie continued, surreptitiously stroking her leg while looking around to make sure no one saw him. "I know how hard it would be for you to go the whole summer without making love with me."

She saw him casing the beach, making sure no one saw them together, and it hurt and infuriated her at the same time.

"Jaimie, it *would* be very hard for me to spend the summer without you," she agreed, "but can't you understand how hard it is for me being in a foreign country and not having anyone I can talk to? And on top of everything else, I have to see the man I love with his wife and watch him pretend not to notice me," she added.

Instead of answering her, he chose to ignore what she'd said. "In fact," he continued in a seductive voice, "I think maybe we'd better go up to your room right now."

Making love was the last thing on her mind. "I just came down to the beach!"

"Are you saying you don't want to?" he said raising his voice. "After all the trouble I've gone to just to spend a little time with you?"

"No," she said, feeling guilty and giving in. "Of

214

course I want to."

"Okay then," he stood. "Let's go. I haven't got much time."

Helena picked up her things and followed him.

Half an hour later, they were back on the beach.

"By the way," he said as she deposited her things on the mattress and started to sit down. "What are you going to do tonight? Grab a bite to eat and get a good night's sleep." He made it a statement rather than a question.

"Well, no." She knew he wasn't going to be happy when he found out she had accepted another dinner date with Richard. "Actually, Richard asked me out to dinner tonight."

"He what!" he shouted. "When were you going to tell me that? I suppose you kissed him good night, too."

"Of course I didn't." She glared at him. "Besides, you're the one who told me to go out with him."

"Well, I didn't ask you to make a career out of dating the guy," he said angrily. "The only reason he's asking you out is because he figures he can score with you."

"I'm not making a career out of it," she retorted. "And he's leaving tomorrow. Anyway, what makes you think he's only asking me out to try to get me into bed? Maybe he likes my company."

"I know how men think," he said nastily. "He can go to a bar if he wants company."

She didn't reply. She just stared straight ahead, a determined look on her face.

Jaimie could see he wasn't going to get anywhere with her, so he backed off a bit. "Well, I guess you can have my permission to go out for dinner, but that's all," he said grudgingly. "I didn't bring you all the way over here just so you could go out with a bunch of young studs."

Helena threw her arms around his neck, knowing that he was feeling insecure. She felt sorry for him and wanted to reassure him. "Thank you." She hugged him.

215

"I really am excited about being here! And you know I'm only interested in you," she said, meaning every word.

"Don't do that," he said in an angry tone, shaking off her arms; but Helena could tell he was pleased. "Someone may see you!"

"I'm sorry," she said contritely.

"I've got to go, baby," he said, sufficiently mollified, and stood prepared to leave. "You have a nice evening. Behave yourself, and I'll try to talk to you before you go out. If not, I'll see you on the beach around eleven tomorrow morning."

"Bye." She watched him jog up the beach. He was so infuriating sometimes, but she understood him so well. Beneath the self-centered, brash front, he was vulnerable and insecure. She had seen the gradual change in their relationship and sensed his deepening feelings for her, from casual companionship to love. She knew it was difficult for him to show his feelings so he covered them up with his abrasiveness. Understanding him helped her to tolerate his behavior—but for how long, she wondered.

She lay back on her mattress and started to read a book. After a short while, Richard came by.

"Hi," he said, sitting down next to her. "I was wondering when you were coming down. I came by earlier but I couldn't find you."

"Oh," she stuttered, thinking fast. "I had lunch at the hotel before coming to the beach."

"I hope you didn't eat too much," he smiled. "I made reservations for dinner at the Moulin de Mougins, a five-star restaurant near the little village of Mougins, not far from here. You can't go to the south of France without at least having one dinner there."

"It sounds wonderful," she answered enthusiastically.

"Great. I'll pick you up about seven. We'll stop for cocktails in the old port of Cannes and then go on to

216

the Moulin de Mougins after that."

"Okay," she said happily, thinking how easy Richard was to be with and how really refreshing that was.

Richard picked her up promptly at seven, and they drove directly to the old port of Cannes. The chauffeur dropped them off down by the water's edge, and they walked for a while. It was early yet, and the streets were empty in the lull before the dinner hour. Helena wished she had brought her camera; it was all so picturesque.

Narrow stone streets climbed upward from the main drive that ran along the water. Quaint shops, tiny restaurants, and small apartments were all squeezed together on the winding streets. As dusk settled on old Cannes, the lit candles on the restaurants' tables made them intimate and inviting.

They stopped at a cozy little restaurant called the Machou and cracked a chilled bottle of champagne before continuing on to Le Moulin de Mougins. When they finished their champagne, the limousine was waiting for them at the end of the street to whisk them off to the restaurant on the hillside.

The Moulin de Mougins had an old-world elegance with its antique furniture and wonderful old hunting tapestries. Bouquets of country flowers were scattered throughout the restaurant, the tables in the main dining room were covered in pink linen tablecloths and the flowered tapestry chairs echoed the pink in the tablecloths. The maître d' seated them at an intimate candlelit corner table, accented with a crystal vase filled with homegrown roses.

The dinner was indeed the most delicious Helena had ever eaten. Starting with a chablis-glazed rabbit cake, she then had a minted frog-leg soup, followed by a salad of torn greens. By the time their waiter brought the entrée, Helena didn't think she could eat another bite, but she forced herself to eat the grilled sweetbreads with truffles.

"Enjoy it," Richard laughed when she told him she

couldn't eat any more. "This is a once-in-a-lifetime meal. You'll never find one like it in California."

"Thank goodness," she replied, joining his laughter. "If I ate like this in California, I certainly wouldn't be modeling long."

"And you have to save room for the tarte tartin; it's the specialty of the restaurant," he reminded her.

"Oh, no," she groaned. "I can't eat another bite."

"Yes, you can. You have to try a little of it," he insisted with a wicked grin.

The evening flew by, and before she realized it Richard was saying good night to her at the elevator.

"May I call you in Los Angeles?"

She had had a wonderful evening and did want to see Richard when she returned to the States; but she also knew she was asking for trouble. Richard had no idea she was Jaimie's mistress, and Jaimie certainly wouldn't stand for her dating Richard or anyone else. But then again, Jaimie had a wife.

She mulled things back and forth in her mind for a brief moment and finally took a deep breath. She couldn't bring herself to turn Richard down. "Okay."

He leaned down and kissed her gently on the lips, and she responded briefly before quickly pulling away.

"Good night," she said. "I had a wonderful time."

"So did I." He smiled. "I'll call you before I leave tomorrow."

Helena smiled to herself as she watched him walk away, then pushed the button to her floor and watched the elevator doors close.

From behind a pillar, Jaimie watched the exchange between Helena and Richard. He had come by for a little midnight romance with Helena and was just leaving when they had pulled up in Richard's limousine. He had just had time to duck behind a pillar when they walked through the lobby. He couldn't hear what was being said, but he could tell by the looks on their faces that they were more than a little interested in each

218

other. He had to hold himself back from confronting them when he saw them kiss. He felt threatened and no longer in control of Helena, and he wasn't about to take a chance on losing her.

"I think I'll have a little talk with Mr. Richard Rosenfeld," he muttered to himself.

He waited until the elevator door closed before slipping out of the hotel.

The next morning, while Helena was having breakfast in her room, Jaimie was ostensibly strolling through the pastel dining room of the Carlton. As he had hoped, he found Richard having breakfast.

"Hello, Richard," he said in his friendliest tone of voice.

"Hi, Jaimie." Richard looked up from his coffee and brioche. "Sit down; have some coffee with me." He poured Jaimie a cup from the pot on his table.

"Thanks." Jaimie took a seat opposite him. "How have things been going? I haven't seen you for a few days."

"Things have been great," Richard said enthusiastically. "Unfortunately, I'm scheduled to leave today."

"That so," Jaimie said, sipping his coffee.

"I've had a great time with Helena the last two days; she's quite a lady," Richard went on. "I only wish I had met her earlier."

"Yes, I've been meaning to talk to you about her." Jaimie feigned an offhanded attitude. "I want to thank you. It hasn't been easy for Helena with nothing to do in the evenings. It was nice of you to take care of my baby."

Jaimie noted the look of shock on Richard's face and smiled inwardly. That should take care of this stud, he thought to himself.

"Excuse me. I'm afraid I must have missed something. Your baby?"

"Yes," Jaimie said innocently. "You mean Helena didn't tell you? She's my girlfriend. I brought her over here so she wouldn't be lonely without me. You know how women are. It's just a little difficult with Donna and everything."

"No, Helena didn't tell me," Richard confirmed. Jaimie could see his temperature rising. "I'm glad I could help out. Anytime."

"Well, I've got to be going." Jaimie checked his watch and rose from his chair. "I have to run over to Helena's hotel and keep her happy." He gave Richard a knowing wink.

Richard gave him a tight smile and a wave.

Jaimie smiled to himself as he walked out of the dining room. That should take care of any ideas that schmuck had.

Helena had expected to hear from Richard, but he hadn't called. And when Jaimie stopped by, he casually mentioned that he had run into Richard in the dining room at breakfast.

"Yes, I thanked him for taking care of my baby," he said, stroking her cheek and watching her reaction closely.

"Oh," she said, slowly stiffening. "You told Richard that I was your girlfriend?"

"Yes." Jaimie slowly unbuttoned her blouse. "It wasn't a secret, was it?"

"No, of course not," she said with a sinking feeling. "What did he say?"

"Nothing." Jaimie, nibbled on her breast. "Let's fuck. I know what my baby wants."

No wonder he didn't call to say goodbye, Helena mused. Well, she told herself, now she wouldn't see Richard when she got back to Los Angeles. And she was furious that Jaimie had taken it upon himself to inform Richard of their relationship. After all, he had a

220

wife, she fumed to herself, and that led her to think about his motives for telling Richard. She knew he felt threatened and insecure, and that was why he went out of his way to squelch her friendship with Richard. But what right did he have to control her life?

With Richard gone, Helena returned to spending her days and evenings alone. Jaimie suggested she go out by herself, which she did, but it really wasn't much fun.

One afternoon, Helena and Jaimie were sitting on the beach chatting when a distinguished older man with silver-white hair and chiseled features walked by.

"Gerard, Gerard Sardonne," Jaimie called, waving to him.

On hearing his name, the old man turned around, saw Jaimie, and walked over to their mattress. "Jaimie Cramer, what are you going here?" he said in heavily accented French.

"I come to the south of France every summer," Jaimie replied. "What about you, what are you doing here?"

"I live here now," Gerard told them.

"No more Beverly Hills," Jaimie said.

"Nope, I've had enough of Beverly Hills and the motion picture industry."

"Gerard, this is my girlfriend, Helena Sinclair," Jaimie said. "Helena, this is a very famous actor, Gerard Sardonne."

"Well, perhaps not that famous," Gerard protested, flattered by Jaimie's words.

Helena smiled politely and held out her hand. "It's very nice to meet you, Gerard."

"And you, *chère.*" Gerard kissed her hand instead of shaking it. "Jaimie, your taste has finally improved."

Jaimie beamed with pride, and as the three of them chatted for a few minutes, a solution to his problem with Helena flashed in his mind. "Say, I just had an idea," Jaimie said. "Helena is here alone and I can't spend evenings with her, so Gerard, why don't you take Helena out to dinner tonight—my treat, of course!"

"Jaimie," Helena chided him, embarrassed. "Gerard probably has plans of his own without having to baby-sit me."

"Nothing would give me greater pleasure," Gerard quickly cut in. He was always up for a free dinner. "Of course, I wouldn't hear of you paying for our dinner," he added without much enthusiasm.

"No, no," Jaimie insisted. "After all, you would be doing both of us a favor."

"Well, if you insist," Gerard relented without an argument. "I know all the quaint little restaurants that the locals go to, the spots that the tourists don't know about."

"It's really very sweet of you," Helena told him. "Are you sure it wouldn't be an imposition?"

"Of course not," Gerard replied.

"Then it's all taken care of," Jaimie said. "Why don't you pick Helena up here about eight."

"Fine," Gerard said. *"À bientôt,* Helena."

"Thank you, Gerard, see you tonight." She held out her hand, but instead, Gerard kissed her on both cheeks, European-style.

As Gerard walked off down the beach, Jaimie said, "He's such a cheap prick; I knew he'd go for the free dinner routine."

"Jaimie," she hissed, shocked. "Shhh, he'll hear you." She was seething. He was palming her off on yet another man and manipulating her life again. How was she ever going to get him to stop? By leaving him, a voice deep inside her answered. But Helena wasn't ready to make that decision. She just couldn't break away from him yet. Would she ever be able to? She wondered.

*   *   *

222

Gerard called for Helena promptly at eight. He took her to a charming French café. Jaimie had given Helena money for their dinners, and true to what Jaimie had said, Gerard allowed her to pick up the check. Helena didn't mind, though; he was charming and he had hundreds of stories about old-time Hollywood. He brought along old publicity clippings to show to Helena, of when he was a big star.

After dinner, Gerard took her down a winding, narrow street to the Circus Circus Disco. "This is *the* place to go in Cannes," he explained.

Inside, giant screens flashed pictures in beat with the music and colored lights swirled around the room. The gyrating dancers were dressed with casual sophistication, and Helena felt like a child in a candy store with no money to buy candy. She was envious of the lifestyle she knew most of them led, and she longed to be a part of it.

The host knew Gerard and immediately led them to a table. Gerard ordered them nightcaps and sat back to watch the dancers. Helena was dying to dance, but Gerard declined.

"No, no," he said, laughing. "I'm much too old."

Helena was disappointed, but she let it go; it was exciting just being there and watching all the beautiful people. The time flew by and all too soon Gerard checked his watch and suggested it was time to go.

By the time he dropped Helena off, it was almost two A.M. She thanked Gerard, kissed him on both cheeks, and hurried into the hotel. Jaimie had been by again and had left a note under her door.

The next day, Helena was still in her room when Jaimie came by.

"What time did you get in?" he demanded when she opened the door. "I came by at midnight, so we could make love."

"Hello."

"Don't hello me," he snapped. "When I brought you

223

over here, it was so we could be together at my convenience, not so you could be out until all hours."

"I'm sorry, Jaimie." To herself, she couldn't help wondering how much Jaimie cared about whether she was having a good time. He seemed more concerned with whether he got laid on a regular basis.

"You know it isn't easy for me to get away," he continued as he paced around the room. "And when the opportunity arises I expect you to be here."

"I know, Jaimie," she said, trying to appease him and keep her anger in check. "I know it isn't easy for you to get away, and I know I should be around. I really am sorry. It's just that it's so hard being by myself day in and day out."

She watched him pace back and forth in the room. She decided that it would be best to say nothing more until he cooled down.

After a few minutes, he came up with another idea. "Listen," he said. "I'm going to introduce you to my wife, Donna, as someone I met on the beach. I'll tell her you're all alone here and invite you to come along with us."

"Oh, Jaimie," she said, with an awful feeling in the pit of her stomach. "I don't think that's a good idea at all."

"Sure it is." The more he thought about it, the better it sounded. He'd have his wife on one arm and his girlfriend on the other.

"Jaimie, I don't think I could handle being with you and your wife and pretending that I was a stranger."

"Of course you could. Think of the adventure. It would be great," he said, trying to sell her on the idea, and thinking he'd be the envy of every guy he knew.

"I don't think I could take it, and what if Donna found out? Think about what she would do. She'd scratch my eyes out and I wouldn't blame her."

"There's no way she would find out." As far as he was concerned, the decision was made.

224

"Jaimie, I don't—" she argued.

"You're going to do what I say. That way, I can keep an eye on you," he interrupted. "You said you didn't want to be alone; now you won't have to."

"But—" She tried again.

"I'm beginning to wonder how much you really care for me," he said, twisting the subject around. "I thought you wanted to be here with *me*. Now I'm beginning to wonder. It seems like you're always out on a date when I'm around. I feel like I'm being used."

"You know that's not true! You're the one who arranged the dates," she cried, throwing her arms around his neck.

"Then it's all settled." He thought he had her just where he wanted her.

"I'm not going to do it and I mean it." She removed her arms from his neck.

"Okay, okay." There's more than one way to skin a cat, as the saying goes, he thought to himself. So he dropped the subject and went on to other things.

"Well, gotta get back," he said after a few minutes. He started ambling back up the beach. "I'll be back in a while."

As Jaimie walked back up the beach, he concocted a plan whereby that afternoon he would walk down the beach, pick up Helena at her beach, and walk with her back toward the Carlton beach. When they were close to the Carlton beach and before Helena could retreat, he would catch Donna's ever watchful eye and casually wave to her to come over. Then he would introduce Helena to Donna and invite Helena to have dinner with them. What a coup, he thought, I'll have them both.

Later, he returned to Helena and persuaded her to take a walk with him. She agreed and they strolled, talking and watching the sun worshipers on their multicolored mattresses. Jaimie could see Donna watching them approach from far down the beach, and he waved her over before Helena realized what

225

was happening.

"Hi," he called to Donna as she approached. "Meet Helena Sinclair. She's from Beverly Hills, too. Helena, meet Donna."

"Hello, Helena," Donna said coolly.

"It's nice to meet you," Helena said, nervously extending her hand. She was in a rage that Jaimie had gone ahead with his plan, but there was nothing she could do.

"Helena is here in Cannes by herself and so I invited her to join us for dinner," Jaimie told Donna.

"Is that so," Donna said, raising her eyebrows at Helena.

"Yes," Helena said. She had no choice but to continue the charade. "I hope it won't be an imposition."

She hoped that Donna would protest, feeling physically ill from meeting her. This was the woman that Jaimie left her each day to go home to. She wished that she didn't care for Jaimie; then it wouldn't hurt so much.

"Didn't I see you a few nights ago on the Carlton Terrace?" Donna asked sharply. "I think we spoke in the ladies' room."

"Oh, yes," Jaimie said, speaking for Helena. "She was with a friend, but he left to go back to the States."

"Oh." Donna was apparently satisfied with Jaimie's response. "That's too bad; yes, why don't you join us?"

"Thank you," Helena said with a sinking feeling.

Jaimie looked from one to the other. This is going to be great, he told himself. What a coup: my wife and my girlfriend. What other guy could do that?

That night, Jaimie took them to the Colombe d'Or Inn for dinner. Situated high in the hills in a little medieval village with cobblestone streets, the stone inn served delicious French cuisine on a terrace overlooking a valley below. Over the years, famous artists had resided there at different times, repaying the innkeeper with works of art. Helena marveled at the splendid artwork.

After dinner, they walked around the ancient village, Jaimie holding both Helena's and Donna's hands. He kept squeezing Helena's hand, and she wondered if he was squeezing Donna's hand, too. The thought made her angry and frustrated and she struggled to hold back the tears. How dare he do this to the both of them! She swore that tomorrow she would tell him that she would never do this again. If he didn't like it, he could send her home. Anything was better than this.

When they dropped Helena off, Jaimie called as they drove away, "Goodnight, Helena. We'll see you tomorrow."

That's what you think, Helena thought to herself, barely making it to her room before she burst into tears. Her trip of a lifetime to France wasn't at all what she had anticipated. She couldn't understand how Jaimie could put her through this. Couldn't he see how it hurt her? She finally cried herself to sleep.

The next day, her eyes were so swollen from crying that she had to keep her sunglasses on. She lay down on the beach and tried to read, but her mind kept going back to the night before. What kind of an egotistical monster would put someone he professed to love through an ordeal like last night? Jaimie's selfishness and lack of conscience were becoming more and more apparent to her. And what about Donna? After she had warmed up, she had been relatively nice to Helena. Helena was sure that she would be devastated if she knew they were having an affair. Didn't Jaimie have any conscience? And what about me? Helena asked herself. What about my conscience?

"Boy," Helena said aloud. "I could write a book about this." Then she thought about her words seriously. Not a bad idea, she mused. Maybe I'll just do that when I get tired of modeling or modeling gets tired of me.

Later in the morning, Jaimie arrived where she was sitting. "That worked out well, didn't it?" he said, referring to the night before.

"Are you kidding?" she blurted out in frustration. "It was one of the worst evenings of my life. How could you even think it was all right? And I don't think Donna was particularly happy to have me around, either."

"Donna will do what I say. And you will, too."

"Jaimie, I'm not going out with you and Donna again," she said firmly.

"You are the most selfish person I've ever met," he exclaimed, turning the situation around. "Everything is always what you want. You never think about anyone else but yourself!"

"That's not true," she protested.

"Yes, it is. I bring you all the way to France, just so you won't be left alone in Beverly Hills. I show you the time of your life. You live a lifestyle like you've never in your whole life dreamed of, and this is the thanks I get," he said, pretending to be furious. He knew exactly how to control the situation. "You're just selfish! You have no appreciation for how hard it is for me!"

"I am not," she protested, forgetting all about her resolve in her haste to defend herself. "I really do appreciate everything you've done for me. But you've also put me in situations I've never even dreamed about. You've humiliated me and you've hurt me!"

"When are you going to quit giving me such a hard time and do what I say?" He was sure he knew what the answer would be. People were so easy to control, and the truth was, he did love Helena and he wanted her with him, regardless of the cost.

"I don't want to talk about this anymore," she retorted in clipped tones. "And if you keep it up, then I'm going back to Los Angeles now!"

228

Jaimie was surprised by the strong, determined tone of her voice, and he realized that he would get no further with her. He had no choice but to drop the subject. He knew he would rather spend a little time with her each day than to have her return to Los Angeles, where she would be completely out of his reach.

A few times after that, Helena accidentally bumped into Donna on the beach and they exchanged pleasantries. If Donna minded Helena's presence, she didn't let on. After a while, Helena came to like Donna, and that made her relationship with Jaimie even harder. It was true that Donna had the mentality of a spoiled Beverly Hills wife, but she was nice, too. She was also the only woman around whom Helena had to talk to. In her moments alone, Helena began to wonder if the price she had to pay for Jaimie's love was too high.

The last month slowly passed, and finally it was time to return to Beverly Hills. She was leaving a week before Jaimie and Donna.

"I'll give you a call when I get back into town," Donna told her casually.

Helena didn't really expect her to—not because she suspected anything, but because she felt Donna was cordial to her only to appease Jaimie.

As for Helena, she was relieved to be going home. She was tired of the strain she had been under the past few weeks, and she missed Nicky terribly. She was glad summer was almost over.

On the plane back to the States, she thought about Nicky's coming home and mulled over the thought of writing and vowed to give it a try.

Chapter Nine

Kabrina's new life in Los Angeles was idyllic. Noel was warm and sharing, and he catered to her every wish. Kabrina couldn't remember when she had ever been as happy as she had been in the past two months since returning from New York with her belongings. Her happiness was reflected in her attitude toward modeling, too. In the past, she had always guarded her privacy, always acting cordial, but staying aloof from the other models she worked with. Now along with her new love, she found herself opening up to her colleagues.

The Los Angeles models were friendlier than the New York and European models, more laid-back and more interested in each other's personal lives.

In New York, the models were interested only in business. They didn't take the time to chat before or after a show. They wanted to get in, get out, and get their money.

Modeling in Europe was incomparable with Los Angeles. The American models in Europe were decent enough, but to compete with the European models Kabrina had to be really tough. The Europeans resented the American models coming to Europe and taking away their bookings, and they weren't shy about making their feelings known. More than once, Kabrina had seen the American women "accidentally" knocked off the runway by European models. Heaven help the girl who was hesitant about holding her own during those shows. Even with all the resentment she had against her father, there were times when she silently thanked him for teaching her to be street smart and to stand up for herself.

Being black was both a blessing and a hindrance. It was a blessing because the white European models were less likely to take her on. Her aloof attitude made them give her a wide berth. It was a hindrance because black models still tended not to be booked because of their style and walk as much as for their skin tone. On more than one occasion, Kabrina was not booked for a show because the designer didn't want any blacks, or wanted only a few token blacks. In Los Angeles, at least, there were fewer black models and therefore less competition.

The models looked different, too. On the East Coast and in Europe, the models dressed low-key. One could almost pick them out from the crowd by their plain, unadorned appearance. But Los Angeles models were like glamorous peacocks. Kabrina supposed it was the result of the film industry's influence. These women were decked out in the latest fashions and were celebrities in their own right. They sparkled and played the role. Wherever they went everyone knew they were models. The majority of them were warm and outgoing, and Kabrina, with her newfound happiness, began for the first time in her career to reach out in friendship to the other models.

Kabrina, returning from running errands in Beverly Hills, drove up the long private driveway and parked her white Porsche in of the house, as Lily, the maid, waved to her from the front doorway.

"Miss Kabrina, telephone for you."

Kabrina grabbed her packages and hurried into the house. Dropping them on the antique breakfront in the

231

entryway, she took the telephone receiver from Lily.

"Thank you, Lily," she said, holding her hand over the receiver. "Would you mind putting my packages in the bedroom?"

When Lily was gone, Kabrina turned back to the phone. "Hello," she said into the receiver.

"Hi, Kabrina. This is Carol," her agent said on the other end of the line. "I've got a booking for you."

"Great. Just let me get my appointment book." She put the telephone down and hurried to get the book, pulling it out of her model's bag and then picking up the receiver again.

"Your booking is this Thursday," Carol told her. "It's a fur extravaganza at the Pagnini Fur Salon. The store specifically requested you. All you need to bring are black evening shoes, a black leotard and tights to wear under the furs, and your jewelry.

"Fendi furs are being featured, and when the Fendi sisters heard you were in Los Angeles they sent word to the salon that you were to be booked."

"Oh, that was so nice of them. I've done their press shows many times in Europe. It will be wonderful to see them again."

"Oh, they aren't going to be here this time," Carol corrected her. "They just want to make sure that you will be one of the models wearing their furs. They told Gregory Pagnini that he just *had* to book you to wear their furs in the show."

"My goodness," Kabrina joked, "I didn't realize I was so important."

"It's the truth," Carol went on. "I saw you work recently in Michael Noverese's show and you were wonderful!"

"Thank you," she replied modestly.

"Rehearsal is from five to six; call time is at eight, and the show will start at eight-thirty P.M.," Carol explained. "And be prepared. I've heard a rumor that an organization against using animal pelts for coats

232

may picket the salon. Gregory has asked all the models to enter through the alley entrance so they won't be hassled."

"Wonderful," Kabrina commented, dryly. "It's not like we're out there personally trapping the animals; most of the animals are raised expressly for their pelts."

"I know," Carol said. "All I do is take the bookings."

"And all I do is wear the clothes," she answered.

"Anyway," Carol finished. "Good luck. I wouldn't be surprised if the press shows up. You may see yourself on the eleven o'clock news."

"Thanks, but I hope not. Bye." She hung up the telephone.

Kabrina forgot about the fur show as she changed her clothes and got ready to meet Noel for dinner. They were meeting at the trendy Ivy Restaurant in Beverly Hills, so Kabrina decided to dress accordingly. She put on an oversize black ribbon silk shirt that had a slit up the middle of the back to the yoke and added a pair of Noel's baggy black linen trousers. She tucked the front shirttails into the front of the pants and belted them with a carved black leather belt. The back of the shirt hung free and billowed open behind her as she walked. She slipped on a pair of black-and-silver tasseled flats and a pair of heavy silver earrings. Then she completed her ensemble with a little black shoulder bag with ornate silver trim.

Noel was already waiting for her when she pulled up in front of the Ivy and left her car with the valet. The Ivy was romantic and intimate, with quaint wrought-iron tables and chairs scattered around a small brick courtyard. Heat lamps were placed about the court-yard, too, but the night was warm and balmy and there was no need for them. Noel, sitting back in a cozy corner, already sipping on a Dewar's and water, waved gaily to her.

"Kabrina," he called, flagging her down with a wave of his arm. "Over here."

People glanced up at the sound of his voice, and then they did a double take when they saw Kabrina gracefully move through the tables to Noel. In a town where beauty was the norm, Kabrina still got more than her share of admiring looks.

"Kabrina, dear." Noel stood and gave her a low, exaggerated bow as she approached.

"Hi, Noel," she exclaimed happily, brushing his lips with hers. She sat down in the chair that he had pulled out for her. "How was your day?"

"My day was phenomenal, absolutely incredible," Noel answered. "In fact, let's drink a toast to it."

"It must have been great," she laughed. She had never seen him so up. "I'll be glad to, just as soon as you order me a glass of wine!"

"No matter, I'll drink to my toast while we're waiting." He held his glass high.

It seemed to her that Noel had already had a couple of "toasts" before she arrived. He was really flying.

"What happened to put you in such a good mood?"

Noel spotted their waiter and flagged him down before answering her. "Acacia Chardonnay for the lady, garçon," he told the waiter. "And another Dewar's for me. It's just been one of those days where everything went right," he continued without pausing. "I did a face-lift that turned out terrific, took ten years off the man. Then I sucked some fat out of a woman, you know, liposuction, and the rest of the day I had consultations."

"It sounds like you had a busy day," Kabrina responded politely.

"Busy day, hell. People don't realize the stress I'm under," Noel said, his mood changing abruptly. "I spend all day listening to sick people; all I ever hear are complaints. Nobody ever thinks about the doctor and how he's feeling. All they care about is themselves.

234

"Sometimes I get so tired of it all! And the hours! Do you realize I work twelve and fourteen hours a day?" Noel explained to her vehemently. "I don't even go out for lunch. My nurse orders in a sandwich for me while I do paperwork!"

He gestured wildly with his hands for emphasis, and several people at adjacent tables looked over curiously. Kabrina had never heard him go off on a tirade like this. The waiter brought their drinks and hovered near their table to see if they were ready to order, but Noel waved him away without breaking his monologue.

"You really should try to get out at lunch, Noel—" she started to tell him.

"I can't," he interrupted. "I haven't enough hours in the day!"

"I'm sorry, Noel," she said soothingly. She glanced around to see if anyone was listening to his outburst. "It sounds like you did have a hard day."

"No, no," he said in a resigned tone. "It just goes with the territory. People just don't appreciate me."

"I appreciate you," she told him, trying to cheer him up. "In fact, I'm crazy about you!"

"Maybe we should order," he said, ignoring what she had said and signaling the waiter.

Kabrina was quiet through dinner. It was the first time she had ever seen such a mood swing in Noel. He had always been such an enthusiastic, positive person. She decided he must have had too much to drink. She knew his work was pressure-laden, and she promised herself that she would be more understanding and sympathetic. She also noticed that his mood had affected his appetite. He continued to drink, but he only picked at his dinner.

After dinner they went home and sat around the kitchen table. Noel showed her a new magic trick he had been practicing, and later, they made love. But the earlier conversation at dinner seemed to hang over their lovemaking. Noel was somewhat distracted. He

235

initiated their lovemaking, but he didn't seem really involved. Kabrina's mind was preoccupied with Noel's strange mood swing, and she didn't notice their abbreviated lovemaking. Later, after Noel had rolled over to his side of the bed and was snoring soundly, the thought did briefly cross her mind, but she attributed its brevity to overtiredness on both their parts.

Late Thursday afternoon, Kabrina arrived at Pagnini Fur Salon in Beverly Hills for her booking. She pulled around into the alley behind the salon and noted that the salon had hired valet parkers to handle the parking.

The show was being held in a huge white tent behind the salon. A catering service had set up a temporary kitchen next to the tent and was preparing hors d'oeuvres and cocktails. Inside the tent, a stage and runway had been erected about five feet off the ground, and workmen were in the process of setting up rows of white folding chairs. The models' dressing room was behind a partition at the back of the stage.

Some of the models were already sitting on the edge of the stage, waiting for the rehearsal to begin. Kabrina put her model's bag behind the stage in the dressing room and joined the others. She recognized some of the models from recent shows: Raymond, Sean David, Linda, Gayanne, Susan, and Misha. There were some models she hadn't met, too. They were in the middle of discussing their favorite topic, modeling.

"You're lucky," Gayanne was telling Raymond and Sean David. "All you guys have to do is show up."

"Yes," Misha agreed. "We have to lug around our makeup, jewelry, hose, and God only knows how many pairs of shoes. It's a wonder we all don't have back problems."

"Tisk, tisk, ladies." Raymond smiled. "Can we help it if we're naturally gorgeous without any help?"

"Please," Susan said, "give us a break."

"I've been thinking of hiring my son, Nicky, to carry

236

my bags to my booking," quipped a model Kabrina hadn't met, named Helena.

"What are you complaining about?" Susan said, turning to Helena. "You've got a rich boyfriend. Tell him you need a maid."

Kabrina thought she noted an edge to Susan's tone, and she wondered how Helena was going to answer.

"I don't think that's on his list, and I know food and rent are at the top of mine," Helena replied lightly, brushing off Susan's comments.

Smart girl, Kabrina immediately thought, liking Helena's smooth style.

"Clothes are at the top of my list," Gayanne offered. She, too, had caught Susan's jibe and decided not to give Susan a chance to counter with another remark.

"Sex is at the top of my list." Sean David grinned wickedly.

"It figures," Gayanne told him. "And we have to undress in front of this animal?"

"Sweetie, not only do you have to undress in front of me, I brought my camera to take pictures for future reference." Sean David laughed.

"Oh, God," Gayanne said in mock horror, rolling her eyes skyward. "Kabrina, did you have to put up with male models like these in New York?"

"No," she answered. "In New York, they were all gay; they only hit on each other."

"Well, Kabrina, we're not all gay here," Sean David said lasciviously eyeing her. "How about if we have a drink after the show and I'll show you my portfolio?"

"Welcome to L.A." Helena said, and they all started laughing.

By now, the other models had all arrived, and Gregory Pagnini came out to organize the rehearsal. It went smoothly, but it was going to be a fast show. All the women wore black leotards with tights and high black evening pumps; the men wore black turtlenecks and black slacks. They would work the runway in groups of twos and threes to the contemporary, upbeat music. It promised to be a high-energy show.

Kabrina was paired with Helena for several sequences, and they discovered that they had similar strides, so they worked well together. In one upscale sequence, Kabrina, Helena, and Sean David came out together and each woman played off Sean David, flirting with him outrageously, knowing the audience would love it. Promptly at six, the rehearsal broke.

"Everyone back at eight," Gregory called. "The show will start at eight-thirty."

The models broke off into small groups to go get a snack. Kabrina, being new and still a bit of an outsider, hadn't made plans with anyone. So she decided to go to the coffee shop in the Beverly Wilshire Hotel and get a cup of coffee; then she heard her name being called.

"Kabrina," Helena said. "Some of us are going to run over to Chez Andre's. Do you want to join us?"

"Thank you, yes." She was touched by Helena going out of her way to include her.

The two women hurried to catch up with Susan, Linda, Sean David, and Raymond, who had already left ahead of them.

"It's hard being the new kid on the block," Helena told Kabrina as they were catching up with the others. "It takes a while for everyone to get used to a new model. They sit back and check things out to see if you're in competition for their bookings or not."

"I'm hardly the same type as any of them. I'm the only chocolate one here," Kabrina laughed. "But I know what you mean; believe me, this isn't the first time I've gone through this."

They caught up with the others just as they were being seated, and Raymond ordered white wine all around. "It'll put us in the mood," he said, referring to the show.

"I'm always in the mood," Sean David said, winking at the women.

There was a round of groans from everyone.

"You're always in heat," Linda corrected him.

"No, I'm not, sometimes I sleep. And not alone, if possible," he added.

"Speaking of sleeping," Linda asked, "do you still have jet lag from your trip to France, Helena?"

"No, it's taken me a week, but I think I've just about caught up," Helena replied.

The mention of Europe caught Kabrina's attention. She was just about to ask Helena about it when Susan cut into the conversation.

"Yes, it must be nice to have a rich boyfriend who flies you all over the world at the drop of the hat," she said snidely.

"It must be nice to have good friends who don't look for reasons to cut you down," Kabrina broke in pointedly.

"Touché," Gayanne laughed. "You asked for that one, Susan."

"Everything has its price," Helena said calmly, refusing to be ruffled by Susan's remarks. "It just depends on what you're willing to pay."

Susan made a face but didn't say anything.

The waiter cut short the conversation by bringing their wine, and the rest of their wait time was spent laughing, joking, and talking about modeling. Before long, it was time to go back to Pagnini's for the show.

Having coffee with the models had been a good opportunity for Kabrina to study them, to get to know them a little better.

She felt that Sean David went out of his way to demonstrate he wasn't gay, which led her to believe that perhaps he was. Raymond was quiet, and she hadn't formed an opinion about him. Linda and Gayanne both seemed very friendly, and they had great senses of humor. Susan was definitely troubled. Kabrina felt she had some sort of personal problem but had no idea what it was. Of all the models at the table, however, Kabrina liked Helena the most. She was warm and levelheaded. She thought about things before she spoke, as she had demonstrated with Susan; yet at the same time, she hadn't allowed Susan to walk all over her.

As they returned to the show, Kabrina saw Susan draw Helena away from the others and begin to talk earnestly to her. She saw Helena pat her on the shoulder sympathetically. Kabrina deduced that it had something to do with Susan's bad mood, and though she was curious, she knew it was none of her business.

The dressing area behind the stage was small and crowded. As usual, both male models and female models dressed together. The modeling industry was no place for modesty, as Kabrina well knew.

Kabrina undressed and put on her black leotard and tights. Sean David was dressing next to her, and when she took off her clothes to put on her leotard he gave her a wolf whistle. It reminded her of the first time she had undressed in front of people as a model in Roberto's showroom, when she had cried. This time she just gave Sean David a withering look and said, "Take a tranquilizer, hot stuff," with a smile. Boy, have I come a long way, she thought to herself.

Gayanne was dressing on the other side of her and she started giggling. "I'm glad you have to dress next to him instead of me."

"Thanks a lot," Kabrina said dryly.

The salon had placed several full-length mirrors in the dressing area behind the stage, and the models crowded around them trying to finish their makeup and touch up their hair. Gregory Pagnini and two of his salesmen wheeled the racks of magnificent furs into the dressing area. Outside, Kabrina could hear the sounds of the guests as they milled about, impatient for the show to begin. It was going to be a wonderful show, and Kabrina wished she had asked Noel if he would like to attend. He seemed to have been under a lot of

240

pressure the past few days, and the diversion of the show might have been good for him. Next time, she thought.

Gregory called for everyone to line up so he could hand out first changes. He gave Kabrina a full-length Russian lynx-belly coat, with a matching muff. She would be tripling in her first change with Helena and Sean David. Gregory gave Helena a coordinating lynx-belly coat with a matching hat, and Sean David a Russian lynx jacket.

After first changes had been given out, all the models stood around sweltering in the fur, waiting for the show to begin.

"I can't imagine when it would ever get cold enough to wear a coat like this in Southern California," Kabrina said to Helena, trying to fan herself with her muff.

"Believe me," Helena told her, "the weather has nothing to do with it. If you have a fur, you wear it, regardless of the weather! This is Beverly Hills."

"Shhh," Gregory said, peeking through a crack in the backdrop. "They're going to start the music. Get ready, everyone. Remember, I want a fast show and I never want to see the runway empty. Move! Move! Move!"

"Don't forget," Sean David said, coming up to Kabrina and Helena. "Play to me, I'll do the rest."

The music started, and the first model slipped through the curtains and took a pose; then the next one went, and the next one, until it was Kabrina's, Helena's, and Sean David's turn.

The three of them stepped through the curtain, took a pose at the head of the stage, and paused to let the audience get the full effect of the scene. Kabrina and Helena posed on each side of Sean David, clinging to him possessively. Then Sean David and Helena started down the runway arm in arm while Kabrina waited at the top. When they reached the end and started back,

241

Kabrina started down. As she passed them, Sean David pretended to pause and do a double take while Kabrina flirted with him and ran her hand across his shoulders and down his arm. When she reached his hand, she took it and pretended to steal him away from Helena. Helena acted insulted and continued on her way to the top of the stage, while Kabrina and Sean David worked the end of the runway. Helena turned around, went back down the runway, and picked them both up. The three of them then posed at the top of the stage and exited. The audience loved their little tableau, and the three of them raced backstage to change into their next furs.

"Not bad, huh," Sean David said to Kabrina as they changed their furs.

Kabrina smiled and gave him the okay sign.

The rest of the furs were equally stunning. Most of them were the trendsetting Fendi furs, the Fendi sisters being noted for their unusual and sumptuous use of fur. The coats had huge collars and oversize sleeves, and nothing was skimped on, including the price. Fendi furs were number one, and the rest of the pack followed.

Later in the show, Kabrina and Helena worked together again, making a striking pair. They matched each other in height and build, one was dark as the other was fair, and they worked the runway in exact shoulder-to-shoulder timing. Gregory had given Kabrina a Fendi golden Russian sable and Helena a matching one in natural dark sable.

"This is the most beautiful coat I have ever seen," Helena said to Gregory, stroking the fur. "And it's so light."

Kabrina had to admit it was striking on Helena, the color of the sable matching Helena's hair exactly and accenting the pale creamy glow of her skin.

"That coat should belong to you. We'll have to see what we can do about that," he told her with a

242

mysterious look.

Kabrina and Helena looked at each other. Helena shrugged her shoulders at Kabrina to signify that she didn't know what Gregory meant by that remark.

The show was fast-paced and the music pulsating, and over almost before Kabrina realized it. She was taking off her leotard and tights and putting her street clothes back on when Susan came up behind her.

"Is that your earring?" she demanded in a loud voice, pointing to the floor.

Kabrina didn't know what she was talking about and looked down to where Susan was pointing. On the floor next to her bags was a silver-and-turquoise loop earring with intricate carvings on it.

"No," she said, picking up the earring and examining it before handing it to Susan. "I've never seen it before."

"Are you sure?" Susan persisted in a nasty tone of voice. "Are you sure you're not just covering up."

"Look, chicky," Kabrina said, beginning to get angry at Susan's innuendos. "I told you I've never seen it before, and I don't appreciate being called a liar; so fuck off!"

Helena and Gayanne had been changing nearby and were attracted by the angry tones of voice. They walked over to the two women.

"Let me see that earring," Gayanne said, taking the earring out of Susan's open palm. "That's my earring, Susan. What's your problem?"

"My problem," Susan said, her face flushed with anger, "is that I have the mate." She reached into her pocket and pulled out an identical earring. It was the one that she had shown Helena a few months earlier, the same one that she had told Helena she found in her boyfriend's car.

"No, you don't," Gayanne told her. She rummaged around in her jewelry bag and pulled out the mate to her earring. "Here it is."

243

Susan blanched white.

"And I think you *do* have a problem," Gayanne continued. "It's jumping to conclusions. Where'd you get that earring, anyway? It looks like Pam's."

"What do you mean?" Susan demanded.

"Pam brought me these earrings from Mexico when she was there last year. She had them specially made— a pair for me and a pair for her."

"Pam, huh," Susan said in a rage. "No wonder I can't get along with that cunt! Just wait until I get ahold of her!"

"Calm down, Susan," Helena said soothingly, speaking for the first time. "Pam may have a logical explanation for all of this."

Helena doubted it, though. She remembered that she had overheard Pam say that she had lost the mate to her silver earring. "Susan found that earring in her boyfriend Trace's car," she told Gayanne and Kabrina. "She thinks that he's been fooling around with whoever has the other earring."

"Oops," Gayanne said. She had noticed that Pam had been secretive lately, and Gayanne had suspected that Pam was seeing someone on the side. Now the pieces fit into place.

"No wonder that bitch was going out of her way to make me look bad," Susan muttered.

"Think things through," Helena said, "before you rush into anything, Susan. You'll only lose by reacting emotionally. Think about what your options are. Decide where you really want to go from here."

"I know, you're right." She took back the lone earring and tucked it back into her pocket. "I'm sorry," she said to Kabrina and Gayanne. "I guess I over-reacted."

"That's okay," Kabrina said.

"Yes, forget it," Gayanne agreed, turning back to her clothes.

Kabrina watched Helena thoughtfully for a minute,

admiring the way Helena had calmed the situation. She was a straight shooter and Kabrina liked that.

Helena looked at Kabrina. "Never a dull moment, huh."

"I guess not," Kabrina agreed. "You did a good job of calming Susan down," Kabrina said quietly. "I think if Pam had been here, Susan would have gone for her throat."

The two women smiled at each other, and a bond of friendship slowly began to form between them.

Gregory Pagnini hurried up to Helena. "Thank goodness you're still here," he exclaimed.

"Why?"

"I had a telephone call from Jaimie Cramer this afternoon. He told me I was to pick out the fur that was the most exquisite on you in the show and present it to you with his compliments." Gregory held out the dark brown sable coat that Helena had worn in the show. "And this is it."

"You must be kidding," Helena said, at loss for words.

"Not at all," Gregory replied. "Sable is your fur."

"I can't accept this," Helena objected.

"Yes, you can," Gregory insisted. "Mr. Cramer said I was not to take no for an answer. Helena, every woman should have at least one fur in her wardrobe."

"At least one," Kabrina agreed, tongue in cheek.

Helena looked at them, exasperated. "A lot of help you two are."

"We are being helpful," Gregory told her. "Mr. Cramer can well afford it, and as I understand it he thinks extremely highly of you; so here, take it."

He thrust the coat at Helena as a couple of the models noticed the exchange. Helena looked around, seeing the curious looks.

"Okay, okay," she said, quietly, "but not now. How about if I come back tomorrow when no one is around and pick it up."

245

"Promise," Gregory pressed.

"I promise."

"Okay," Gregory said, taking the coat back and leaving the dressing room. "Don't forget, now," he called over his shoulder.

"I have enough trouble with jealous models as it is," Helena sighed to Kabrina, "without having everyone see me leave with a sable coat."

"It's really no one's business but yours," Kabrina told her. "They should be happy for you."

"You're right," Helena agreed, "but unfortunately, it doesn't always work that way." She liked Kabrina and her directness.

Everyone finished dressing at about the same time, and a group of them left together. They had no sooner walked out of the back entrance to the fur salon than a group of picketers descended upon them. They were carrying hand-painted signs that proclaimed "Stop the senseless killing of animals" and "Ban Beverly Hills Animal Killers." The picketers started chanting "Animal killers! Animal killers!" and several blocked their paths. One stood nose-to-nose with Sean David.

Sean David started to make a sharp comment, but Kabrina stopped him. "Don't incite them," she told him quietly. "The television stations are here, too."

Sure enough, a Channel 12 mobile unit had pulled up and a camera crew was filming the entire episode.

"Move out of the way, please," she said in a clear voice to the picketers who were blocking her way, holding her head high and looking them directly in the eye. "We'd like to get through," she said in a firm but neutral tone of voice.

Their eyes wavered before her steady gaze. She held her ground, and the picketers grudgingly moved aside. Then she moved calmly through the crowd, the rest of the models following.

A newscaster stuck his microphone in her face as she passed. "What do you think of the picketers?" he asked.

She ignored him and kept walking. She gave the valet parker her ticket and waited for her car.

"Not bad," Sean David quipped. "Remind me to stick around you in a crisis."

"Right," Kabrina said dryly, holding out her hands to show him they were shaking.

The valet brought her car around.

"Say," Sean David said, "you want to go somewhere for a drink?"

"Thanks, but I think I've had enough excitement for the evening."

She could hardly wait to tell Noel about the show as she pulled up in front of the house. All the lights were on and the stereo was blasting. Noel was sitting in his study.

"Hi, honey," he called out when she walked in.

"Wait'll I tell you about the show tonight," she said as she sat down in a chair opposite him.

"Hold it, hold it," he said, shoving some papers into a drawer and standing up. "Let's go into the other room."

"All right," she said.

He quickly steered her out of the room.

"Why are you in such a hurry to get me out of that study?" she asked jokingly.

"I'm not," Noel said defensively. "I just think we'd be more comfortable at the kitchen table."

It didn't matter to Kabrina, so while Noel poured himself a nightcap, she told him about the evening.

"You were wise not to speak to the newsman," Noel agreed.

"There was really no point in it," she said. "It would have only incited the picketers more."

"Yes, and what if they had found out you were my girlfriend?" Noel continued, taking a big gulp of his scotch. "It wouldn't help my practice any to have my patients think I'm political."

She looked at him in amazement. "It didn't have anything to do with you, Noel."

"Well, I have to be very careful about my reputation, Kabrina. A lot of people know me. In fact, wherever I go, people recognize me."

She decided to let the subject drop. "How was work today?"

"Great." He finished off his scotch and poured himself another. Then he launched into a detailed description of his operations. In the middle of the conversation, he abruptly stood up. "I'll be right back," he said, and walked out of the room.

"Where are you going?"

"Stay right there," he called from the study door as he closed it. "Don't come in here, don't come in here."

"I won't," she said, mystified by his insistence.

She heard the key turn in the study lock and wondered what he was doing in the study and why he wanted her to stay out. After a moment, he came back out but in the short time he had been in the other room, the scotch must have hit him all at once, because he was very high.

"Lemme show you this new magic trick," he exclaimed rushing back into the room. "Wait'll you see this one! It's called coins through the table," he slurred as he lurched and sat down at the table. He drained the rest of his drink and turned it upside down; then he proceeded to show her the trick. It fascinated her and she forgot her curiosity about why he had locked himself in the study.

Time passed and Noel continued to show her tricks nonstop. Finally Kabrina looked at her watch. It was after three in the morning.

"Noel," she said, yawning. "I am exhausted. I have got to get some sleep; I can't keep my eyes open."

"Just one more," he insisted. "I've got one more I have to show you."

248

"Okay," she stifled a yawn, and laid her head down on the table, struggling to keep her eyes open.

Noel was on a roll and didn't seem the least bit tired. He performed one trick after another without a break. Finally Kabrina couldn't stay awake any longer. When she left the table, Noel was still performing magic tricks and didn't even notice her leave.

As the next few days passed, it became a habit for Noel and Kabrina to sit around the table talking, and Noel drinking. After a while, he would abruptly retire to his study for five or ten minutes and return drunk. He would always nervously insist Kabrina stay at the kitchen table when he went into his study, and she would hear the lock turn in the door. Finally one night, she'd had enough of him insisting she stay in the kitchen. When he came back into the kitchen she decided to confront him.

"Noel," she said, exasperated, "when have I ever followed you into your study when you didn't want me there? And what are you doing in there anyway?"

He ignored what she said and pulled out some magic props. "I have a new trick to show you."

Another week passed and the late night acts gradually took on a stranger tone. One night, Noel came out of his study dressed only in khaki shorts, a top hat, and his magic wand. He turned on the stereo and began to do a magic routine. Kabrina thought his costume was a little strange, but she assumed he thought he was being sensual and exotic, so she hesitated to embarrass him by asking why he was wearing it.

As she watched, he ended his magic routine by beginning a striptease. He danced around the room twirling the rainbow-colored silk scarves from his magic act; then he took off his shorts. Under them, he was wearing black silk jockey shorts. His eyes were glazed and he was oblivious of Kabrina. He continued to dance and wave his scarves. He pulled off his black jockey shorts to reveal red bikini shorts. He pranced around the room, gyrating his hips to the sound of Linda Ronstadt in the stereo. He was off in his own world, no longer aware of Kabrina sitting there.

The song changed and so did his costume. Off came the red bikini shorts and under those he was wearing a woman's black lace G-string. His actions changed, too; his movements became more affected and feminine. He pranced and pirouetted about the room, waving the silk scarves through the air above his head.

Kabrina was speechless. She was L.A. street smart, thanks to having a cop for a father, and she was sophisticated from her years of modeling; but neither had prepared her for Noel and his bizarre actions. Here was a man whom she had opened herself to and trusted enough to move in with. He had been there for her when she needed help, operated on her and nursed her back to health. Could this prancing, ridiculous buffoon be the same man? She tried to keep an open mind about him. He had been under a lot of pressure, lately, she told herself as she watched him gliding about the room. And maybe he really did think his strange behavior was erotic. She even tried to joke with herself about it. Perhaps he was practicing to audition for a part in *Salome's Last Dance*, but the bottom line was that she didn't find it erotic. She found it weird, and she'd had enough for one night. She stood up and said good night to Noel, but he didn't hear her. She went upstairs to their bedroom and undressed and got into bed.

She didn't know what time it was when Noel came to bed, but he was still high and in a great mood. When he got in the bed, he cuddled up to her and nibbled on her neck. She was tired, but he continued to play with her, arousing her from a deep sleep. When he began to make love to her, her memories of the past few hours dropped away and he brought her to sublime heights of passion. His dancing only seemed to have heightened his sensuality.

A pale dawn was breaking when they finally fell asleep. Only a few hours later, Noel's answering service called with his morning wake-up. Kabrina was too tired to move, but Noel bounded out of bed and dressed for work. Kabrina couldn't imagine where he found the energy, and she fell back asleep.

Fortunately, Kabrina didn't have a booking until the afternoon so she spent the morning sleeping in and recovering from the late night before. Contrary to what most people believed, models needed to take good care of themselves if they were to enjoy any longevity in their career, and Kabrina was no exception.

She was still a little blurry-eyed when she arrived at her booking at Neiman Marcus in Beverly Hills. She was the first one to arrive and as she waited, the events of the previous night kept flashing back. She couldn't understand what would possess Noel to act the way he did. She wished she had someone she could talk to about it.

One by one the other models began to arrive. First Helena, then Gayanne and Misha, and then the others. The show was for the Ungaro collection in the couture department, and the models were assigned dressing rooms to change in.

Kabrina and Helena shared one dressing room between them. As before, Kabrina found Helena very easy to be around, and there seemed to be an instant rapport between them. The show went smoothly, and even in the close quarters of the tiny dressing room, there was no tension between the women. Kabrina's intuition told her that Helena was someone she could trust, and she made up her mind to ask Helena if she had time for coffee after the show. She needed to share the events of the night before with someone.

"Sure," Helena said, checking her watch. "I have

251

time for a quick coffee. Do you want to go to the café right here in the store?"

"That's fine," Kabrina answered.

The two women packed up their model's bags, said goodbye to the coordinator and the other models who were still packing to leave, and headed for the café.

The hostess seated them, and they ordered cappuccinos.

"Did you get things straightened out regarding your sable coat?" Kabrina asked Helena as they sipped their cappuccinos.

"Yes, I tried to explain to my boyfriend, Jaimie, that I couldn't take such an expensive gift," Helena told her. "But he wouldn't listen. I finally decided it was easier to take the coat than to continue arguing."

"You know," Kabrina said carefully, "I don't want to sound like I'm prying, but I've heard that he's married."

"It's common knowledge," Helena said guardedly, and wondered what Kabrina was getting at.

"Well, that's neither here nor there," Kabrina told her. "The point I wanted to make is that it salves his conscience. It's the only way he can show you he cares. He can't give you one hundred percent of his time, so this is the only way he feels he can make it up to you."

"But it's not necessary for him to do that. I know he loves me," Helena protested.

"But it's necessary for his own head," Kabrina said. "Let him do it."

Helena thought about Kabrina's words for a few moments. "I guess you're right. Relationships are sometimes so hard to understand."

"You're telling me," Kabrina said, thinking of the night before.

"Yes," Helena said. "I'm great at analyzing other people's relationships, but when it comes to my own I can't see the forest for the trees."

"We're all like that," Kabrina agreed, signaling to the waiter for another cappuccino. "Speaking of which, I had something strange happen last night with my boyfriend."

"What was that?"

Kabrina related the events of the night before to Helena as she listened closely.

"I don't know, Kabrina," Helena said when she had finished her story. "It all sounds very strange. It doesn't sound like he's drinking just liquor. I think something is happening when he goes into the study."

"It's like his mood changes when he comes out of it," Kabrina said. "He's over the edge. And then when he came to bed . . . I just wanted to sleep and Noel jumped on it," she exclaimed, referring to their lovemaking.

Although Helena realized the seriousness of the situation to Kabrina, she couldn't help but laugh at Kabrina's slang.

"'Jump on it,'" she choked, giggling.

"Yes," Kabrina told her, lightening up. "You know, make love. Listen, I was so tired of watching him dance, I felt like telling him to get it from rosy palm and leave me alone."

"Who's Rosy Palm?" Helena asked, confused. "Now I'm lost. You didn't mention another woman."

"Rosy palm, you know," Kabrina said, making a fist with her hand and jerking it up and down.

Helena understood and collapsed in laughter. "I have never heard that before," she sputtered when she could talk again. "Where do you come up with these expressions?"

"Who knows?" Kabrina grinned. She had forgotten how much a good girl talk always helped. "I just wish I could figure out what to do. I thought I was in love with Noel. You know, I left New York so we could be together."

"I think you should wait until you and Noel are relaxed, and then have a talk with him," Helena suggested. "I would act very neutral and tell him how you feel without being accusing. Ask him what he's doing in his study with the door locked, and reassure him about how much you care for him."

"That makes the most sense," Kabrina agreed. "I don't know why I didn't think of it myself."

"It's hard to think clearly when you're emotionally involved with someone," Helena said, then looked at her watch. "Oops, I've gotta go, Jaimie will be waiting for me and he hates to be kept waiting. Here's my telephone number; if I don't see you soon, give me a call and let me know what happened."

"I will," Kabrina promised. "Thanks for your advice."

"Thank you for *your* advice. Bye."

She watched Helena go. Helena was nice and Kabrina liked her a lot; her advice was levelheaded and made sense. Kabrina vowed to try it that night.

Kabrina decided that it would be best to wait until after dinner before approaching Noel on the subject, but she didn't get the chance. After dinner, he poured himself his customary scotch and water and Kabrina a Frangelico. Then they went into the living room to relax. Kabrina contemplated how to open her discussion, but before she could speak, Noel excused himself and made his way to the study, locking the door behind him. He came out about ten minutes later with a movie projector.

"Kabrina, dear," he said seductively, "I've got a little surprise for us tonight."

"What's that, Noel?" She had a feeling she knew what he was leading up to.

"I've got some X-rated films that I thought might be fun to watch." He plugged in the projector. "Variety is the spice of life, they say. Have you ever seen an X-rated film?"

"Well, not recently," she said cautiously. This evening was not going according to plan.

"You'll like these; they're very sexy. They really turn me on." The scotch was affecting him, and he gave her

254

what he thought was a seductive look.

Kabrina poured herself a glass of wine. She had a premonition that she was going to need strong fortification to get through this night.

Noel started the projector and then turned on the stereo for background music. He leaned back on the sofa and put his arm around her. "You have to understand that these are not polished porno flicks," he said. "They have no sound, so I put on the stereo for background music."

He was right, she thought as she watched the films. Home movies was a closer description. She had seen X-rated movies before, but these were the worst. Noel, however, was enjoying them immensely and watched them with rapt attention. He guzzled down his drink and poured himself another without missing a beat. One reel ended, and he quickly set up another, and then another.

Kabrina tried to feel some sexual interest, but they were beginning to bore her. Maybe if they were professionally done, she told herself. Or if they had a little plot I might be able to get into them. But they were strictly fuck and suck movies.

After three reels, Noel jumped up. "I've got some others that are really different. They're not your run-of-the-mill films. You want to see them?" he asked hopefully.

Anything had to be an improvement, Kabrina thought to herself. "Sure."

He hurried to his study and as usual carefully locked the door behind him.

"What can he be doing in there?" Kabrina thought to herself.

Ten minutes later, he opened the door, bare-chested and dressed in his khaki shorts again. This time he had tied the rainbow-colored scarves around his neck. Kabrina could tell by the glazed look in his eyes that he was flying.

255

"Wait until you see these, Kabrina, dear," he exclaimed excitedly. He lurched over to the projector, the reels under his arm. He pulled off the old reel and put on a new one. "These are black-market films that a friend of mine got me. It's terrific!"

"Are you all right?"

"Of course I'm all right," Noel said peevishly. "Watch this!"

The new movie depicted men with women who not only had full breasts but also male genitalia. Transsexuals, Noel impatiently told her. They were fucking and sucking and doing things that Kabrina had never imagined in her wildest fantasies. Noel, however, loved the movies. He got up and started dancing to the music on the stereo in front of the projector, so that the images were projected on him. When he started to strip again, Kabrina had had enough. She quietly got up and went to bed. She was filled with confusion. What had happened to the gentle, funny man she had met in Spain? This wasn't the man she cared so deeply for.

She started to drift off to sleep and then awoke with a jolt. Noel was next to her, still dancing, but at the same time completely into himself, oblivious of her. He stripped off his bikini underwear and Kabrina looked down. He was wearing one of *her* G-strings and pretending he had no cock. Kabrina was in shock and then became angry.

"Give me those," she exclaimed, ripping her underwear off him.

Noel didn't seem to notice that she was upset and obliged without comment, dancing out of the bedroom. Kabrina was enraged as she stuffed the G-string under her pillow and tried to go back to sleep.

Sometime, hours later, Noel came to bed. Kabrina lay stiffly on her side of the bed without touching him, then finally drifted off into an uneasy sleep. The next morning, Noel acted as if nothing had happened.

Kabrina decided to wait a few days to let herself calm

256

down so she could approach Noel rationally. But the next few days brought more mood swings. One minute, he would be exuberant and funny, like the Noel Kabrina remembered. Then abruptly, his mood would change and his disposition would become nasty and mean-tempered. He began to ridicule her in front of people without cause.

One night, about a week after Noel's first striptease act, they were having dinner with his friends at the fashionable Morton's on Robertson Boulevard when Noel became so loud and boisterous that people around them began to stare.

"I think maybe you should talk a little quieter," she suggested to him politely in a low voice. "Everyone can hear you."

"And I think you should shut up," he said in a loud voice. The other people at their table looked at him in embarrassment.

Kabrina was humiliated and furious that he would talk to her that way, but she said nothing.

"Oh, look, my little black jungle bunny is giving me the silent treatment," he gloated and turned to the others at the table. "Typical woman. Look at her pout!"

It took all of Kabrina's self-control not to make a scene. Instead, she quietly excused herself and went to the ladies' room. She entered a stall and struggled to control her rage. She had never, ever heard Noel refer to her like that. He had never made reference to her skin color; it had never been a part of their relationship. Just let me get through this evening without a scene, she promised herself, and tomorrow he and I will have a talk. She went back to the table. While she was gone, the others must have had a talk with Noel about his obnoxious behavior, because his mood had switched again to a conciliatory and apologetic one.

"I'm sorry, Kabrina," he said. "I don't know what came over me. You know I didn't mean what I said. I don't know, I just opened my mouth and the words came out . . . from somewhere. Please believe me. I guess I just had a little too much to drink."

He looked so stricken and he was so contrite that Kabrina grudgingly accepted his apology, but she still made a mental note to talk with him at a later date.

The next morning, Noel's answering service woke him very early, and he was up and gone before she had a chance to speak with him.

When she did get up, she was extremely depressed and needed to talk with someone. She had an all-day booking, but she was too upset to keep it, so she called Carol and asked to be replaced.

"Are you all right, honey?" Carol asked.

"I'm sorry, Carol," she said, "but I have some personal things that I have to take care of. You know I wouldn't do this if it wasn't an emergency."

"Okay, I'll replace you. Let me know if you're okay."

"I will," Kabrina promised.

Then she called Helena to see if she had time for coffee. Over the past three weeks, the two girls had become close friends. For Kabrina, Helena was not just a friend, but her only friend, and Kabrina had to talk to her.

"Sure, I can meet for coffee," Helena told her when she called. "Just let me get Nicky off to school, and then I'll have a few hours before I meet Jaimie."

They met at the Old World Restaurant on Sunset Boulevard and ordered coffee.

"I don't know, Kabrina, it's all very weird," Helena said, shaking her head after Kabrina had told her the latest. "From what you've told me, everything hinges on Noel's study. There's where your answer is."

"At first I thought it was just pressure from work, but now I'm convinced that he's doing something when he goes into his study, and I have a strong feeling that something is drugs," Kabrina declared. "I don't know how much more of this I can take. I'm going to go

258

home, and while Noel is at the office, I'm going to go over that room with a fine-tooth comb."

"Normally, I'd say don't snoop or you'll be sorry," Helena said. "But in this case, you may be sorry if you don't."

"I think you're right," Kabrina agreed. "I can't take much more of this."

"I'll be home all afternoon," Helena said. "Call me if you need to and let me know what you find."

"I will."

As Kabrina drove home, her mind was a jumble of thoughts. Why was Noel having such personality swings? Pressure from work? Maybe, she thought. But then there were the mysterious trips to his study late at night, and after weeks together he was suddenly showing strange sexual tendencies and a penchant for porno movies. It was all so confusing.

She parked her car in its usual place at the side of the house and walked in. Lily had the day off and the house seemed so empty. She threw her bag down on a chair in the living room and went right to the study.

"I might as well get it over with," she told herself.

The study door was closed, and she hesitated before opening it. This is silly, she thought to herself. I've gone into Noel's study a hundred times before. This time, though, she was looking for something in particular— something she didn't want to find. The door swung open on silent, well-oiled hinges. Everything was as it should be—the bookcase with all the books lined up in neat rows, his desk, void of papers, the pen-and-pencil holder filled with neatly sharpened pencils, even the credenza in the corner of the room topped with a vase of fresh flowers that Lily changed every few days. Nothing seemed different.

"Let me see," Kabrina whispered. "If I were going to hide something, where would I hide it?"

She went over to the desk. She knew she was alone in the house, but instead of feeling comfortable she had an eerie feeling. She opened the top drawer. There was nothing of interest in it, only some stamps, odds and ends such as paper clips and rubber bands, a pair of scissors and a letter opener. The drawer on the left held two blank legal tablets, typing paper, some letterhead paper and envelopes. Nothing important there, she told herself. The right drawer was no better. It was almost empty except for a few alphabetized file folders holding monthly bills and receipts. She thumbed through them but could find nothing suspicious, glancing up every few seconds, expecting to see Noel standing in the doorway.

Now she devoted her attention to the bookcase. Most of the books were medical journals. A corner of the bookcase held some fiction and current best-sellers, and she looked over the titles. He had good taste in books; several of them Kabrina had been wanting to read. Next to the fiction was a small group of magazines. She pulled them out and went through the stack title by title. As she started to replace them, one of the covers caught and bent back. She pulled it out to straighten the cover, then started to put it back and realized that though the cover said it was a journal on plastic surgery, the pictures inside were anything but medical. It was a men's magazine. Not just an ordinary magazine like *Playboy* or *Penthouse* or even *Hustler*, which Kabrina had seen millions of times before, this had pictures those magazines would never print, pictures like Noel's stag films. Transsexuals and men in all sorts of pictures, in all sorts of positions. She was disgusted by them. Well, at least I'm getting warmer, she thought dryly, and put the magazine back exactly where she had found it.

She leaned back on the top of the desk, taking deep breaths and surveying the room, trying to decide where she should look next. There was a creak somewhere in the house and it made her jump. Her hand brushed the pencil holder and it fell to the thick carpet with a dull thud. She laughed shakily.

"Nothing like having a guilty conscience," she told herself. She went around the front of the desk and got down on her knees to pick up the pencils and holder. Lying among the pencils was an ornate key. She picked it up and looked around the room, wondering what it unlocked. It wasn't the desk; all the drawers were unlocked. She tried the file cabinet behind the desk. It was unlocked, too. She quickly searched through it, but there was nothing unusual in it.

Then she spied the antique credenza. She had never really looked at it closely before. She walked over to it and examined it. Sure enough, it had a keyhole. She pulled on the handle, but she knew it was locked. Slowly she stuck the key in the keyhole and turned it. She took a deep breath as she heard the lock click. For a minute, she wished the key hadn't fit. She sensed that whatever she found behind the door would forever change her relationship with Noel. She wished things could be the way they were in the beginning, but she knew things would never be the same again. She pulled the cupboard open.

It was almost empty except for Noel's projector, some reels of film, and several pairs of underwear. Kabrina knew what was on the film, and she recognized the red bikinis and the black silk jockey shorts. There were also several pairs of women's panties and a big, dingy white lace bra that looked to be size 40. She also found her G-string, which Noel had worn the night before. In addition to the lingerie, there was a small paper package tied with string.

Kabrina was beginning to feel sick. A vision of Noel dancing around in her G-string floated before her eyes. She forced herself to pick up the small package. She carefully untied it, unfolded the paper, and then opened the little box. It was filled with white powder. Kabrina was positive she knew what it was, but she wet her finger and dipped it into the powder just to make sure. She touched it to her tongue and the tip of her tongue immediately got numb. It was coke.

Finally she understood the erratic mood swings and the late nights. She knew the reasons behind the secretive trips to the study and why when Noel came out of the study he was so high. She had no time to contemplate what her next course of action should be, because suddenly she heard a noise above her coming from their bedroom. It sounded like someone had dropped something on the floor.

"Oh, my God," she muttered in terror under her breath. "Noel must be home!"

Her fingers shook as she hurriedly rewrapped the package and put it back in the credenza, just as she had found it. Now that she was concentrating on sound, she could make out other faint noises, which she hadn't noticed before, coming from the master bedroom above her. She relocked the credenza, ran over to the desk, and quietly replaced the key in the pencil holder. Then she looked wildly around the room to make sure everything was as he had left it.

Kabrina had started to leave the study when she heard footsteps coming down the stairs. She barely had time to jump back into the study. She closed the door and hid behind the couch in the corner of the room. Through the closed door, she heard soft padding as someone walked by the door in bare feet.

"I'll be right back with more scotch, sugar," she heard a woman's husky voice call.

Kabrina tiptoed to the door and opened it a crack, just enough for her to get a look at the woman when she came back past the study on her way to the bedroom upstairs. She didn't have to wait long. Kabrina heard her footsteps before she saw her.

She was a black woman the same shade as Kabrina, but she was shorter and stockier—and stark naked. In one glance, Kabrina made a mental note of everything about her: the bottle of scotch in her hand, her long hair, her heavy pendulous breasts, her curly pubic hair, and her cock. The woman had already walked by, oblivious of Kabrina, before Kabrina fully realized what she had seen.

Black like me, she thought, bigger breasts and a cock. Big breasts and a cock . . . a cock. A cock, she thought in horror. The woman's face flashed in her mind, and Kabrina realized she had seen her before. She was the transsexual in Noel's sick porno films.

Her first impulse was to run from the house, and she started to leave, but instead her legs carried her unwillingly up the stairs toward the bedroom. The rational part of her told her to get out of the house, while her curiosity drove her on. A part of her had to positively confirm what the rest of her mind refused to acknowledge.

She crept stealthily along the hallway, the plush carpeting muting the sounds of her footsteps. One of the double doors to the master suite was ajar, and she heard muffled voices and the rustling of fabric. She wanted to turn and run, but her feet propelled her onward. A cold sweat broke out on her forehead as she inched her way around the edge of the double doors and peeked in.

As she watched, mesmerized in morbid fascination, Noel danced around the room in pink lace panties. He was higher than she had ever seen him, his eyes glazed and unfocused. The woman/man lay on the bed, encouraging him on. Even as Kabrina watched, Noel dropped to his knees in front of the transsexual and parted her legs. As Noel started to go down on her, Kabrina could stand it no longer.

She turned and fled. She didn't care if they heard her or not, though she thought they were probably too engrossed in what they were doing to hear anything. She picked up her purse in the hallway and made it through the front door, slamming it behind her, before she was sick. She fell to her knees, retching. She heard a ringing in her ears and fought to keep from fainting. She put her head down between her knees and took deep gulps of clean air. She felt numb. She had not just cared deeply for Noel; she had loved him. He was the first man she had opened up to since her father, and she had left a life thousands of miles away to be with him. And now, in the space of an hour, she had uncovered a whole secret life. All the pieces fell into place: the trips to the study followed by mood swings, his hostility toward her, the inappropriate highs, his unusual behavior. It all made sense now. How could she have missed the signals?

Kabrina made her way to her car, got in and pulled away. She drove aimlessly around, unable to think clearly. She had no idea where she was going, what she should do. Why hadn't she seen the signs? Had she somehow unwittingly been the cause? She didn't know if she should go back to Noel's and confront him or if she should just leave and never return. She had no place to go. In her flight, she had taken nothing but her purse. She had to talk to someone, someone calm and rational. She spotted a pay phone, pulled over, and dialed Helena's number.

Helena was just saying her goodbyes to Jaimie when Kabrina's call came through. At first, Helena couldn't make out who was calling. All she could hear on the other end of the line were deep, gasping breaths as if someone was making an extreme effort to speak.

"Hello? Hello," Helena repeated over and over into the receiver.

"Who is it?" Jaimie whispered behind her with his usual curiosity. "Who's on the phone?"

"Shhh, Jaimie." She covered the receiver. "I can't hear with you talking in the background."

"Don't say my name over the telephone," he exclaimed in irritation. "It could be Donna!"

Helena didn't reply.

"Who is it?" he nudged. "What are they saying?"

"Jaimie, please," she again said with her hand over the receiver. Now he was irritating her. "Shush! I can't tell who it is! The only one I can hear talking is you!"

"Shit," Jaimie hissed, throwing his hands in the air. "Now the whole world knows I'm here."

"H-Helena," Kabrina finally gulped over the open telephone line. She took a deep breath and tried again. "This is Kabrina."

"Hi, Kabrina." She could sense from the tone of Kabrina's voice that something was terribly wrong. "What's the matter? Are you all right?"

"I-I-I," she stuttered, then finally burst into tears. "I have to talk to someone," she blurted out between sobs.

"Come over, right now," Helena said.

"I don't want to bother you; if I could just talk to you a few minutes on the telephone, I'll be okay," Kabrina cried.

"You're not bothering me. That's what friends are for. I insist." She gave Kabrina her address. "Where are you now?"

"On Sunset, by Westwood."

"You're only about fifteen or twenty minutes away," Helena told her firmly. "I'll be waiting."

Helena hung up the telephone.

"What's the matter?" Jaimie asked behind her.

"It's my friend, Kabrina."

"Couldn't you have talked to her on the phone?" Jaimie said peevishly. "She's going to spoil our afternoon."

"Jaimie," she said, exasperated, "she's my friend and she needs help." She went on to explain to Jaimie what she knew about Kabrina's situation.

"Now I understand," he said sympathetically. "I can tell you right now without hearing the rest of Kabrina's story. Her boyfriend is heavily into drugs. Those are not the actions of a straight person. He's a real sicko; this town is full of them!

"See," he continued, campaigning on his own behalf,

265

"these are the kinds of single weirdos that I'm trying to save you from. You should thank me!"

Helena looked at him in affectionate disbelief.

Kabrina pulled up in front of the address Helena had given her. She had calmed down a bit, and she took several deep, ragged breaths to steady herself before she walked to the second-floor landing and rang the doorbell. Helena answered immediately.

"Come on in," she said, holding the door open for Kabrina. "This is my boyfriend, Jaimie Cramer."

"I'm so sorry to bother you. I didn't know you had company."

"Don't be silly," Helena told her. "Jaimie's family. Sit down and tell us what happened!"

Kabrina related her entire story.

"I had no idea," she sobbed. "I thought it was pressure from work or maybe I was doing something without realizing it; but after the lingerie, the films, and then what I saw today . . . I just want out of there. What am I going to do?"

"The first thing you're going to do is realize that none of this has to do with you," Jaimie said. "This town is full of the walking wounded."

"Walking wounded," Kabrina repeated with a blank look on her face. "What are the walking wounded?"

"They're people who walk around with a facade of normalcy. They act like you and me, so you think they're okay," Jaimie explained. "But inside their heads, they're wounded. It could be from their childhood, or past relationships, or who knows."

"Jaimie's right," Helena agreed and then she added, firmly, "I think you should spend the night here. Then, tomorrow, go back to Noel's house, pack all your things, and move out. You can stay with me until you find a place to live."

Now what have I got myself into? Jaimie thought. I didn't mean for Helena to suggest that Kabrina move in! Between Nicky and Kabrina, I'm not going to have

266

any privacy with Helena.

"Maybe Kabrina has a relative or someone she'd rather stay with," Jaimie suggested, hopefully.

Kabrina thought of her father but she couldn't contact him now, not after today. "No," she said slowly. "I don't have anyone else. But I'd hate to be an imposition."

"You're not an imposition," Helena exclaimed. "Is she, Jaimie?"

"No," he said grudgingly. What could they do, put the poor girl out on the street?

"I'm sure it won't take me long to find an apartment," Kabrina said.

"Then it's all settled," Helena said, taking her friend's hand.

That night Helena and Kabrina stayed up half the night talking, as Kabrina tried to get over the shock of what she'd learned. She didn't bother to call Noel and let him know where she was. He probably wasn't even aware she was gone, she told herself cynically.

The next day, she drove to Noel's. It was strange, she mused to herself, how something can change so radically in the space of one short day. She used to love the look of Noel's house, with its stable, traditional Tudor styling. Now it looked heavy and forbidding, she thought as she unlocked the door.

"Miss Kabrina," Lily called, running to meet her at the door. "Where have you been? Dr. Wellsley has been so worried!"

"I'm sorry to hear that," she said, but made no effort to tell Lily where she had been. "Now, if you will excuse me, Lily, I have some things to do."

She left Lily standing in the foyer in astonishment as she went upstairs, pulled her suitcases from the closet, and began to pack.

She had almost finished when she heard a voice

behind her.

"Where have you been? I've been so worried," Noel said from the doorway.

Kabrina had been deep in her own thoughts, and the sound of his voice startled her. She whirled around.

"Lily called," he continued, "and I rushed right home. I couldn't imagine where you were." He walked toward her with his arms out to hug her.

"I couldn't imagine a lot of things, like coke and half men/half women," she said, her eyes blazing.

He dropped his arms to his sides, and the color drained from his face. "What are you talking about?"

"I know, Noel." Her voice rose in anger. "I know everything—the coke, your little pinup playmate! I came home early yesterday and saw the two of you."

"You were spying on me," he shouted, trying to put her on the defensive. "How dare you spy on me! What kind of woman are you, anyway? And coke, I don't know what you're talking about. I don't do coke."

"Cut the bullshit, Noel," she said flatly, realizing what he was trying to do and infuriated even more by it. She went back to her packing, fit the last few pieces of clothing into her bags, and fastened the lock.

Then she stood up and faced him. "I believed in you, Noel, and I trusted you, and you're full of shit! No, you're worse than that; you're really sick. How could you abuse your body with drugs like that and then turn around and perform delicate operations on unsuspecting patients? Patients who put their lives in your hands! What kind of a sicko are you, anyway?"

Suddenly Noel collapsed before her, sobbing. "Please don't go," he pleaded. "Don't leave me! I only tried coke that once; and as for the other, it was just a fantasy. I just wanted to see what it was like!"

"That wasn't the first time you tried coke. For weeks, I've been trying to figure out what was the matter. I was just a little slow, but I've got your number now."

"No, no, I swear, Kabrina, dear. That was the first

268

time. I can stop anytime I want," he said.

"Noel, it's not just the coke, it's everything: the lingerie, the sick porno movies, and that thing with you yesterday."

"Sherilyn doesn't mean anything to me," he cried desperately. "I swear!"

"Well, she sure meant something to me," Kabrina told him. "I *saw* you giving Sherilyn or whatever you call *him* a blow job!"

Kabrina picked up her suitcases and stepped over Noel, who was lying on the floor, sobbing pitifully. When she got to the door of the bedroom, she wavered for a moment and turned. Then the memory of Noel ridiculing her in front of their friends flashed before her eyes.

"Get some help, asshole," she said charitably. And she walked out, slamming the door behind her.

Chapter Ten

For the next week and a half, Laura Ann avoided the bars and corners where she usually hung out, positive that the police were looking for her. She constantly peered over her shoulder, watching for Norris in his old Buick or the police in their squad cars.

She had also tried to cut down on the amount of drugs she was taking, but it wasn't easy. The drugs dulled her mind enough so she could cope with the nightmare of turning a half dozen tricks a night; but they made it impossible for her to keep a sharp lookout for the police. She finally settled on taking one hit at the beginning of the evening; the rest of the evening she would go cold turkey, regardless of how disgusting the johns were. She chided herself for being so stupid as to confide in a policeman.

Unfortunately, the new places and her being straight didn't prove to be so lucrative, and she brought home less money than usual. It made Marcus grouchy and short-tempered.

"I don't understand why you aren't bringing in more bread," he grumbled at the end of a night when she handed him the few dollars she had earned.

"I don't know either, Marcus. There just aren't that many johns around. Maybe people are all on vacation," she tried to joke. She couldn't tell him she'd been

270

avoiding her regular haunts because she'd told a cop she murdered someone and now the police were probably looking for her.

"Vacation? You stupid bitch," he said, exasperated.

The next evening, as Laura Ann was getting dressed to leave, he said, "You'd better do better tonight. Pull that front down more, so your tits show."

He grabbed the front of her sweater and yanked it down so there was a good view of her cleavage. "There, that's better. It pays to advertise, you know," he said and laughed at his own joke.

Laura Ann made a point of laughing too. She was willing to do anything, laugh at anything, if it would keep Marcus in a good mood.

"Come here," he said, going to his dresser drawer and pulling out a little bottle. "Let's have one for the road, a little something to send you on your way."

He shook out a small amount of coke, chopped it fine and arranged it in four long lines. Then he pulled a wad of money from his pocket and peeled off a bill.

"I'll use a hundred, for luck," he said, rolling the hundred up into a narrow straw. Then he sucked a line up each nostril and handed the rolled hundred to Laura Ann. "Go for it, precious," he said. "Take a toot of this, it's the best."

A line of coke was the last thing Laura Ann wanted, but she didn't want to risk ruining Marcus's good mood, so she obediently inhaled one of the two remaining lines.

"What's the matter, baby?" he asked. "How come you only did one line? Don't you want the other?"

"Of course I do," she replied, thinking quickly. "But I was saving it for you. I've got to keep my man happy, right?"

"Now you're thinking," he said, his ego puffing up at her words. "You're finally getting the idea."

Laura Ann opened the apartment door. "I'm going now, Marcus," she said. "See you in a few hours."

"Right," he said, snorting the last line. "Just be sure you bring home more bread."

Laura Ann quietly shut the door and leaned against it, taking a deep breath. How was she supposed to bring home more money when she had to spend all of her time ducking the police and hanging out on out-of-the-way corners? She didn't know the answer, and she started down the steps to the streets.

Behind her, around a corner of the hallway, Che Che quietly watched Laura Ann disappear down the steps. Then she strutted over to Marcus's door and knocked.

"Laura Ann," Marcus called through the door, "that you?"

"No, honey," Che Che said through the door. "It's me, Che Che."

"Che Che," Marcus exclaimed, throwing open the door. "What's hanging, baby?"

"I just came by to see how you were hanging. I haven't seen Laura Ann around lately, and I wondered what you were up to," she said, her eyes taking in the whole room. She saw the bottle on the table and walked over and picked it up. "How about a little toot, for old times' sake?"

"What do you mean, you haven't seen Laura Ann around?" he asked, ignoring her request.

"Just what I said," Che Che replied. "I never see her at the hot spots. Oh, yeah, I did see her once up on San Mateo Avenue, but you know no one drives through that neighborhood. I figured you must have retired. Come on, how about a little hit?"

"San Mateo Avenue, fuck. No wonder she hasn't been bringing any bread home."

"Marcus, baby," she whined, "you've got a shitload of blow here. How about parting with a line or two for your Che Che?"

"Yeah, yeah," he answered distractedly. "Help yourself."

"Thanks, baby." She quickly measured out some

coke on the table before Marcus could change his mind.

"You deserve a big hit for the information you brought me," he said generously.

Che Che took two huge hits of coke and squirreled a little away for the road when Marcus wasn't looking.

"Look, doll face," she said. "You'd better get that bitch back in line. Knock her around a bit. Sometimes those young ones need to be shown who's the boss, so they know you care. Now, anytime you want to see the action that blue ribbon experience brings, give me a call," she said, giving him an inviting wink. "I could do things you've only dreamed about."

"Save it for your tricks," he said, giving her a playful swat on the backside as she went out the door.

Laura Ann still stayed away from her usual haunts, so it was another slow evening. When she returned home, Marcus was waiting for her.

"How was business tonight, Laura Ann?" he asked, watching her closely.

"Not good, Marcus. I don't know where the johns are."

"Why don't you try hanging out on your usual corner? Maybe that's where they're waiting."

"What do you mean?" she asked fearfully.

"I mean Che Che tells me she hasn't seen you around in days," he sneered, his anger growing. "I mean I'm going to beat the shit out of you if you don't come up with some good answers, and now."

"Well—well—" she stammered, frantically searching her mind for a plausible excuse and backing away from him. "I heard that business was better on San Mateo and—and I thought I'd give it a try."

"You'd better stop thinking and start working, or there won't be enough of you left to do anything." He grabbed her arm and twisted it up and behind her back.

273

"You got that?" he said, emphasizing each word with a cruel upward jerk of her arm.

"Yes, Marcus, yes," she cried in pain. "I got it, I promise, I promise."

"Okay." He shoved her across the room. "Now get to bed."

After that night, Laura Ann went back to her regular haunts. She kept a close lookout for Norris and the cops, but she saw neither. Business was better, and that kept Marcus happier, which in turn made life easier for Laura Ann.

Several days passed uneventfully, and she was lulled into a sense of security. Perhaps Norris had given up, or maybe he thought she was just babbling. Whatever, she didn't really care. The important thing was that she was being left alone. Marcus was acting indifferent toward her, which was much better than having him slap her around.

One night, about a week after returning to her regular hangouts, Laura Ann was leaving the tired old motel where Marcus had secured a room for her. It had been a hard evening so far. It seemed that the tricks were getting stranger and stranger. The john she had just finished with didn't want to screw; he just wanted her to tie him up and jerk him off. He had been a thin, smelly man, and Laura Ann had found it hard to breathe in the tiny closed room.

It had started to drizzle, and the normally smog-laden air was refreshing after the stuffy motel room. She took several deep breaths to clear away the man's stench from her lungs. As she passed the hotel driveway, a hand reached out of the dark and grabbed her arm, pulling her around a corner and pushing her against the back wall of the motel. She closed her eyes and opened her mouth to scream, but a hand clamped itself over her mouth.

"Shhh, don't scream. It's me," Norris said quietly to her. "Norris."

She opened her eyes, first one and then the other. Then she slumped against the wall. "What do you want?" she asked defiantly

"I've been looking all over town for you," he said.

"I'll bet you have," she said angrily. "You and half the cops in Los Angeles."

"I want to talk to you. Come on," he said, taking her arm.

"I'm not going anywhere with you," she said and planted herself firmly against the wall.

"Sure you are, kid," Norris said, half dragging and half walking her over to his parked car, then shoving her in.

They drove down Olympic Boulevard in silence. A few minutes later, they pulled into the same coffee shop where they had stopped before. Norris parked the car, grabbed Laura Ann by the arm and pulled her out of the car after him. By now, she was much calmer. If he were going to arrest her, she reasoned, he would have taken her directly to the police station. If he were going to shake her down for money or sex, he certainly wouldn't have brought her to an all-night coffee shop. But she couldn't figure out what he wanted.

"Two coffees, black," Norris told the waitress.

Laura Ann sat stoically in the booth, saying nothing.

"What was the name of that fleabag hotel where you supposedly killed the pervert?" he asked her after the waitress set down two hot mugs of coffee.

Laura Ann refused to answer him. Instead, she kept her eyes on her hands clutched tightly in her lap.

Norris grabbed her shoulder and shook her hard. "Hey, I'm talkin' to you, kid!"

She jerked her shoulder out of his grasp and continued to stare at her lap. "There was no hotel. There was no man," she mumbled sullenly. "It was all a joke."

"The hell it was," he exploded. "Now you listen to me and you hear every word I'm saying. Read my lips if

275

you have to!" He grabbed her face and forced her to look directly at him. "Either you tell me here and now, or I'm going to have you run in on a solicitation charge. You'll have to have your almighty Marcus come down and post bail. How do you think he'd like that?"

She tried to glare at him defiantly, but her eyes wavered under his gaze.

"I said look at me," he commanded. "You think he bats you around now, sister? You'll be dog meat when he finishes."

God, she thought to herself. He was right. Marcus would beat her to death for sure. But if she admitted anything to Norris, he would have her arrested. Her mind flipped back and forth, trying to decide which was the less dangerous choice of the two. In the end, she cowered against the corner of the booth in fear.

"For Christ sakes," Norris exclaimed. "I'm not going to hurt you! I'm trying to help you. Tell me the name of that hotel."

"The Las Palmas Arms Hotel," she finally mumbled from the corner of the booth.

"Son of a bitch, I was right," he crowed triumphantly. "There's been no report of a murder or death at the Las Palmas Arms Hotel in the last six months. There was a fire there all right, but no one was killed in it."

"But I saw him," she said emphatically. "I saw his eyes roll back. The room was on fire!"

"Yes, but you told me you didn't wait around."

"No, but—"

"He must have escaped, just like you," he continued. "I checked the police log for the night of the fire, and several people did report seeing a naked man in the neighborhood. But shit, the way that street is, the police just figured it was one of the regulars."

"You mean he didn't die?" she exclaimed in disbelief. "I didn't murder anyone?"

"Of course not. In fact, my inquiry wasn't the first

276

about someone dying in that fire. The telephone log showed that a man, who wouldn't give his name, called right afterward and questioned the duty officer closely about the fire. I listened to the tape of the conversation myself. He was extremely persistent about the details. I think it was Marcus," he concluded firmly.

"Marcus?" She couldn't believe her ears. "Marcus knew and he didn't tell me? He just let me go on suffering, believing I killed someone?"

"Sure, why not? It's as good a hold on someone as anything else."

Something snapped inside her and she started to cry with relief. Thank God, she prayed silently. I didn't kill anyone. I'm not a murderer; the man lived. She cried for all the months of being wound tighter and tighter, of not being able to let loose, of always having to look over her shoulder, and of cowering beneath Marcus's constant barrage of physical and mental torture.

And she cried for her lost dreams. She'd come to Los Angeles with dreams and goals, but Marcus had fed upon her insecurities and she'd pushed those dreams back until they were only pale fantasies behind a drug-induced haze. It all came out in a wash of salty tears.

Initially, Norris awkwardly patted her on the shoulder, but she clung to him sobbing, and compassion overcame him. He held Laura Ann close, stroking her hair and comforting her softly, thinking of his own lost daughter. "Shhh," he said. "Everything's gonna be fine. It'll all be okay."

The waitress came by with more coffee, but when she saw them, she quietly left them alone.

Laura Ann cried and cried until she could cry no more.

Norris bundled her into the old Buick. She was too exhausted to ask where they were going. She just leaned against the seat and blankly watched the blocks slip by. It had started to rain harder, and the drops hitting the windshield hypnotized her. They turned right on Nichols Canyon and followed the twisting road upward. Finally they stopped in front of a small, neat wood frame house. Norris helped her into the house and led her to a bedroom.

"You can sleep here tonight," he said, depositing her on the bed.

She was too tired and numb even to reply. She laid her head down on the pillow and fell instantly asleep.

Norris pulled a blanket over the sleeping girl and left the room, quietly closing the door behind him. He sat down in his worn armchair in the living room and looked out over the sprawling skyline of Los Angeles. He could imagine the night people in the city below, going stealthily about their business under the protection of darkness. His anger rose like sour bile as he thought about what Marcus had put Laura Ann through, how he had almost destroyed her. Los Angeles was full of Marcuses and Laura Anns, users and victims, the one preying on the other. He thought about his own daughter and silently prayed that wherever she was, she was safe.

Laura Ann awoke the next morning and looked around at the walls covered with pink striped wallpaper that matched the flowered chintz bedspread and curtains and realized that this was a girl's bedroom. There were books and posters and toiletries scattered around the room.

She got up and wandered into the living room and looked out a window at the canyon below. The rain from the night before had washed away the brown smog, and the city lay with dazzling clarity before her as far as she could see. To her left was downtown, the buildings like so many clumps of geometric mushrooms. To her right rose the black twin towers of Century City. On the uppermost part of the horizon, Santa Catalina Island hovered like a faint cloud.

Norris came up behind her. "Come have some breakfast. Then we're going to get your things from

278

Marcus's apartment."

"What if he's there?" she asked fearfully.

"So what if he is?" Norris dismissed her question, walking into the kitchen.

They ate a breakfast of hot cereal, orange juice, and coffee. As they ate, Norris explained to her that she could stay with him and sleep in the back bedroom temporarily, and he would help her find a job and get situated.

"Whose bedroom is that?" she asked.

"My daughter's," he answered shortly.

"Where is she?" Laura Ann persisted.

"She moved away," he replied, and by his tone, Laura Ann knew she should drop the subject.

Together, they did the breakfast dishes, and then it was time to go. Her apprehension grew in direct proportion to their proximity to Marcus's apartment. By the time they pulled up in front of the building, her folded hands were white-knuckled with fear. Only Norris's reassurances and her anger at Marcus pushed her onward.

"Keep calm," he said, patting her hand. "I'm right here. He's not going to try a thing in front of me."

From an apartment window across the street, Che Che watched Norris and Laura Ann pull up to the curb and pause in the car, talking. She threw on a silk robe and hurried down to the street. Laura Ann and Norris were just getting out of the car when she reached them.

"Well, look who it is," she sneered, looking at Laura Ann. "Ms. Precious. Looks like you got yourself a little dark meat. Marcus has been looking all over for you, and he ain't happy."

Norris stopped in his tracks and took a long, slow look at the frowsy over-the-hill hooker. "Looks like you'd better take that prune face of yours and go back in your apartment and forget you ever saw us," he said matter-of-factly.

Laura Ann started giggling in spite of her fear, and

Che Che glared at both of them. She pulled her robe tighter around herself and turned and stomped off. "Yeah," she called over her shoulder. "Well, wait 'til Marcus finds out. Then we'll see who has the last laugh."

She stormed back into her apartment, slamming the door behind her. She'd fix that pussy, Laura Ann, good. Marcus had stopped by earlier, looking for Laura Ann, and he had mentioned he was going to the lounge on Los Angeles Street. Che Che called information and dialed the number she was given. "Is Marcus there?" she asked the bartender when he answered.

"Just a minute. Yo, Marcus," she heard him call.

"Yeah," Marcus said a few seconds later into the phone.

"Marcus, honey, this is Che Che," she said in her sultriest voice.

"Yeah," he repeated, waiting for her to continue.

"Laura Ann and some black dude just showed up at your apartment. I thought you'd want to know."

"Thanks, Che Che. I owe you one."

"I'm sure we can work something out, lover," she purred.

Marcus hit the disconnect button. "That's what you think, cunt," he said arrogantly to the empty line. Then he grabbed his jacket and left the lounge.

Laura Ann and Norris climbed the steps and walked down the dark hallway. She had never really noticed how shabby and dingy it looked with its dirty and threadbare orange-and-gold hall carpeting. The air smelled musty, with an overlay of frying onions from someone's apartment, and the Thompson Twins wailed on a stereo from behind a closed door.

At the end of the hallway, Laura Ann slipped her key into the lock of Marcus's apartment door. She took a deep breath and turned the key.

"Marcus? Marcus?" she called as she opened the door. There was no answer. "I guess he's not here," she said with relief, closing the door behind them.

"All the better," Norris growled. "Get your things together and let's get you out of here."

She went into the bedroom. The bed was rumpled and unmade, so she knew Marcus had slept there last night. She pulled her suitcases from under the bed. It was the first time in over nine months that she had seen them, and so much had happened in those nine-plus months. She pictured her arrival at the bus terminal, how she had dragged the two suitcases, one of which had been fastened with masking tape by a porter because the lock had been broken during the trip.

"There you go, little lady," he had said. "That's a good job even if I do say so myself. That should get you all the way to the promised land and back again."

"The promised land," she said, bitterly, out loud to herself. That's exactly what she had thought Los Angeles was when she had walked through those revolving terminal doors. She had felt that the whole city was holding its breath, just waiting for Laura Ann Gilmore to arrive.

She reached down to lift one of the suitcases onto the bed and noticed it was caught on something under the bed. She had to get down on her hands and knees to untangle it. It was a decorative chain on a wallet. She inspected the wallet closer. It was *her* wallet, she thought in confusion, the one that had been stolen the first day she arrived; but how could that be?

She sat down on the side of the bed to recall the incidents of that day. She had been struggling to get her suitcases to the curb, trying to be especially careful with the broken one. She had caught out of the corner of her eye a flash of blue across the street as a teenage black boy walked out of a doorway and cut across the street a short way down from her. A few moments later, she had felt a tug and turned just in time to see a dark figure

281

in blue dart around a corner. She put the two incidents together. A figure in blue coming out of the doorway of the bar, and the same blue flash running around the corner with her wallet. Then she remembered looking up and seeing Marcus running out of the bar and across the street toward her, the late afternoon sun catching the golden threads of his hair. Bathed in the sunlight, he had looked just like a knight coming to her rescue. Marcus had come out of the same doorway as the boy in blue. Maybe it was just a coincidence.

But then another incident came to her mind. She and Marcus had been sitting in their booth at the same neighborhood bar when a black teenager walked by them.

"Hi, Mr. Fent, Laura Ann," he had said as he passed.

"'Lo, Snake." Marcus had nodded.

"How did he know my name?" she had asked.

"Oh, he probably heard me mention you," Marcus had said, casually dismissing the question.

There had been something about that boy, she had thought at the time. Something, but she couldn't place what. Now all of a sudden it clicked. He had been wearing the same unusual shade of blue, the same shirt she'd seen rounding the corner on her first day in Los Angeles. It couldn't be, she thought. If all of that was true, it would mean Marcus had manipulated her from the beginning. Other sequences, like frames of film, floated through her mind: Flash and the photography studio; Marcus and Flash talking about her as if in a dream.

"How are you doing, Laura Ann?" Norris asked, coming into the bedroom and startling her.

"Not very good," she answered and told him of her suspicions. "Do you think things could have happened that way?" she questioned him closely.

"Of course. It happens every day. It's one of the oldest cons in the book."

"Oh, my God," she said numbly, sitting back on the

282

bed. "I can't believe what a fool I've been."

"You're not the first, and you won't be the last," Norris said. "But you'd better step on it. Let's get out of here."

Laura Ann pushed the thoughts from her mind and jumped up to start cramming clothes from the closet and drawers into the suitcases. She didn't have much, so she was finished in almost no time. She wobbled into the living room under the weight of the luggage.

"Here," Norris said, starting for the cases. "Let me have those."

At that instant, they both heard the scratch of a key in the lock, and the door swung open. Marcus's face registered a look of triumphant rage.

"Son of a bitch," he swore. "Where do you think you're going, cunt?"

Laura Ann froze in her steps as Marcus started across the room toward her, his face twisted in anger.

But before he could reach her, Norris stepped between them. "Chill out," he said, blocking Marcus's way.

Marcus raised his arm. "Get out of my way, pop," he snarled at Norris.

In one smooth motion that belied his age, Norris ducked and twisted his body, grabbing Marcus's upraised arm at the same time. He twisted it around and slammed Marcus, face first, against the wall. There was the sickening crunch of bone fracturing, and Marcus screamed with pain as blood gushed through a split on the bridge of his nose.

"You broke my nose," he yelled.

"I said chill out, dude," Norris repeated between gritted teeth. "The lady doesn't want to live here anymore and she's leaving. Now."

"Laura Ann—" Marcus started to say, and Norris jerked his twisted arm behind his back another notch. Marcus groaned in pain.

"She's got nothing more to say to you and you've got nothing say to her. Am I right, asshole?" Marcus's arm went up another inch.

283

"Laura Ann," Norris said, still holding Marcus, "you pick up your suitcases and get out the door."

"Laura Ann—" Marcus gasped and twisted his head around, trying to see her.

She was rooted to the floor. The mere sound of Marcus's voice was enough to strike terror into her heart, and now, seeing him humiliated by Norris, she knew he was raging inside. God help her if he ever found her. She had no doubt that he would make her pay for this.

"Say what, boy?" Norris calmly slammed Marcus's face back against the wall, leaving a bloody smudge. "You're a slow learner, aren't you?"

"Go on, Laura Ann," Norris repeated. "Do as I say. This boy is not going to hurt you."

Laura Ann came to her senses, picked up her luggage and staggered slowly through the open front door.

Norris gave Marcus an unexpected shove, causing Marcus to lose his footing and tumble to the floor.

"You forget you ever met Laura Ann Gilmore, *boy*," Norris said, pointing a finger at Marcus for emphasis. Then he turned and walked out the door, slamming it behind him.

Laura Ann was waiting in the hallway. He picked up her suitcases and started down the hall with her. Laura Ann could feel eyes upon them as the tenants, drawn by the sounds of a fight, peered through the peepholes in their doors. As they rounded the corner and started down the stairway, they heard a door open, and Marcus began screaming after them.

"I'll get you, bitch. Wherever you go, I'll find you! You'll never get away from me. Never!"

She glanced back over her shoulder and shuddered at the sight she saw. Marcus was standing in the hallway, holding his nose with one hand and blood streaming between his fingers. His clothes were blood-splattered, and his golden eyes captured her in a deadly stare. She shivered with fear and relief.

Chapter Eleven

"I did it," Kabrina exclaimed to Helena and Jaimie when she reached Helena's apartment with her belongings. Although she tried to say the words with nonchalance, her quavering voice gave her away.

Helena threw her arms around Kabrina and gave her a reassuring hug. "Good for you. You did the right thing."

Even Jaimie was touched by what Kabrina had gone through. "Yes," he said. "The sooner you packed your things and got out of there, the better."

He looked at the two serious faces before him and decided he'd better try to lighten things up. "And think about it, Kabrina," he said with a straight face. "That fairy could have worn out *all* your underwear dancing around like that night after night. It would have cost you a fortune to replace them."

The two women looked at Jaimie in disbelief, then realized he was joking. The three of them burst into laughter and the somber mood was broken.

"Yes," Helena continued, taking the joke one step further. "And you might have even learned some new dance steps."

"That's true," Kabrina answered, smiling as she dropped down onto the couch beside them, her sense of humor returning. "It could have been my big chance."

She shook her head with mock regret. "I don't know how I could have ever been taken in by him," she said seriously. "It's not like I haven't been around. I've been to parties where people have been doing coke. It just never entered my mind that Noel could be doing it, too. He's a doctor, for God sakes!"

"It's hard to be objective about someone you're emotionally involved with," Helena said sympathetically.

"You're right," Kabrina agreed. "I kept thinking that it was something I was doing to cause his bad moods." She remembered how hard she had tried to do everything just right when Noel was in one of his moods, and how nothing had seemed to help. It was as if he walked around with a black cloud over his head. If she even looked at him in a questioning manner, he would fly into a rage.

"Assholes who do drugs are masters at disguising it," Jaimie said knowingly. "I'll guarantee that he's been doing it for a while, too; that's the course things take. In the beginning it puts them in a good mood all the time, and then, as time goes by, they start having the severe mood swings, so they snort more and more to try to bring back the high."

"Well, you were lucky to find out when you did," Helena added. "Things could have gone that way for months before you realized what was happening. Thank goodness you were strong enough to leave when you did."

"Can you imagine if he had been high when he operated on me?" Kabrina said incredulously, the thought making her wince. Her face was her career, and it could have been over forever with one stroke of a scalpel.

"Yeah." Jaimie shook his head. "You might have ended up with a banana nose in the middle of your face."

The two women looked at him. "Jaimie," they

squealed in unison.

"I don't know how many calls come in for models with banana noses," Jaimie continued with a straight face.

The two women burst out laughing.

"Just ignore him, Kabrina," Helena smiled. "Let's put your things in Nicky's room. He won't be back from Seattle for a couple of more weeks."

They carried her suitcases into the bedroom, and Helena opened the closet and pushed Nicky's clothes to one side to make room for Kabrina's things. Just looking at Nicky's things made Helena lonely for her little boy. She was counting the days until he was back with her.

"I can't tell you how much I appreciate your letting me stay here," Kabrina said, breaking into Helena's thoughts. "I don't know where I would have gone."

Visions of her father's house in Nichols Canyon came to her mind, but Kabrina firmly shut them out. "I know I'll be able to find an apartment in a week or so."

"Don't worry about it," Helena said kindly. "That's what friends are for."

Kabrina thought about Helena's words as she hung up her clothes. Friends; it had been a long time since she'd truly had a girlfriend. She'd had plenty of acquaintances. Roberto had been a friend, but he had been a guy and she had never confided in him as she would with a girlfriend. In Europe and New York she'd kept a wall around herself. She had had no desire to open herself up to anyone until she met Noel. And look what had happened. Life was strange, she mused to herself. It had taken her full circle back to Los Angeles before she could open herself up again to love and friendships.

"I'd better go and say goodbye to Jaimie," Helena said, interrupting Kabrina's thoughts.

"I'll go, too," Kabrina said.

They went back into the living room, where Jaimie

was pacing impatiently.

"Jaimie, thank you so much for all your help." Kabrina gave him a big hug. "I don't know what I would have done without you and Helena."

"Don't be silly," Jaimie said modestly. "It was nothing. I'm glad we could help."

Helena nodded in agreement.

"You just relax, honey," he said, patting Kabrina's arm paternally. "Everything will be fine now."

"I'll walk you out to your car, Jaimie." Helena put her arm around his shoulders.

They walked out to Jaimie's Rolls.

"You are so sweet," Helena said, affectionately hugging Jaimie when they reached the car. "And you're so nice to my friends. It makes me love you all the more."

"Well, what could we do? We couldn't throw the poor kid out on the street. That asshole plastic surgeon should be strung up by his balls.

"See what I mean, Helena?" he continued, never one to pass up an opportunity to plug himself. "You are so lucky, it's beyond belief. You could be out there dating jerks like that; instead you've got me."

"You're right, Jaimie," Helena agreed patiently. She had heard this story so many times before.

"Now," he said, deciding it was time to maneuver himself into a position of strength. "How soon before she moves out? She's cramping our sex life."

"Jaimie, she just got here!"

"Well, how long do you think it will take her to find a place?" he persisted. "Why don't you help her? After I leave, the two of you should go out and drive up and down the streets, looking for vacant apartments."

"Do you mind if she has a chance to unpack?" Helena said dryly.

"I know," he went on, totally ignoring what Helena had just said. "She can look for apartments every afternoon while we fuck!"

"Jaimie," she cried angrily. "Stop it!"

"I was just trying to be helpful," he defended himself, for the first time noticing Helena's irritation. "You don't have to get angry. You know, sometimes I think you don't appreciate me," he said, using a ploy that usually worked with Helena. "I try to make you happy and that's the thanks I get. It's not easy for me, you know—"

"I do appreciate you," Helena said firmly. "Good-bye, Jaimie; see you tomorrow."

She was beginning to catch on to his manipulations, and her words caught him off guard.

"Oh," he stammered. "Yeah, well, see you tomorrow. Think about what I've said," he said gruffly as he drove off.

Helena nodded and waved at the disappearing car. "What a character," she muttered.

Helena went back inside to see how Kabrina was doing. Kabrina had already unpacked most of her things, and Helena sat down on the bed to keep her company.

"I imagine you find Los Angeles very different from New York and Europe," she said, combining some of Nicky's things in his nightstand so Kabrina could put some of her clothes in a drawer.

"Yes, it is different," Kabrina agreed. "But I grew up in L.A., you know, so I'm used to it."

"I didn't know you were from here," Helena said. "Do you have family here, too?"

"Well," she said slowly, "my mother died when I was very young, and my father and I had a falling-out when I told him I wanted to become a model."

"Really?"

"Yes," Kabrina answered. "He's a vice cop and he wanted me to go to college. He had an idea in his head that modeling was the same as hooking. I tried to tell him differently, but he wouldn't listen."

"You're kidding," Helena said incredulously.

"Ninety-five percent of the hookers in Los Angeles tell people they're models. He's around prostitutes and pimps day in and day out, so you can imagine what he thought when I told him I was going to model instead of going to college."

"Couldn't you convince him otherwise?"

"Not a chance," Kabrina continued. "I felt he should have realized that he raised a daughter who would never even think of being a hooker. I finally took my college money and went to New York. I tried to call him and let him know that I was okay, but he refused the call."

"How long ago was that?" Helena asked.

"Seven years," Kabrina answered. "I have to say—even though he doesn't realize it—I made it as a model because of him. I was determined to prove that he was wrong. I was going to make him eat his words."

"And you've done it," Helena added for her. "Did you let him know that you're back in Los Angeles?"

"No," Kabrina said slowly. "After I made it, I realized I really didn't care what he thought. When I needed him, he wasn't there, and now I don't need him."

Kabrina said the words in a cavalier manner, but Helena could tell that that wasn't how she felt deep inside.

"Oh, I don't know," she said carefully. "As a parent, we always try to do what we think's best for our kids, but we're only human. Our actions are colored by our experiences, and sometimes we make mistakes. Don't be too hard on him. You know, if you gave your father another chance, I'd be willing to bet he would love to hear from you."

Kabrina weighed Helena's words. "Maybe," she said slowly. She wondered how different her life would have been had she and her father mended their differences. She wondered how he was, what he was doing. Would he be proud if he knew how successful she was? She was a big-time model, but she had no one to share her success with.

Helena thought about her own words, and they made her miss Nicky even more. She thought about the difficulty she had had in the past year, trying to juggle her time between her son and Jaimie and modeling. It had not been easy and she vowed to work harder to devote more time to Nicky. She understood how hard it was for him to start over and leave his friends and family behind, but she also hoped he understood that it was something that had to be done. She couldn't continue to live with her ex-husband's selfishness and indifference for the rest of her life. She thought about the times she had begged him to go to a marriage counselor with her. Such utter selfishness, her mind raced on, suddenly making her think of Jaimie and his actions. Suddenly she realized how selfish Jaimie was, too. She thought of the look on Nicky's little face when Jaimie sometimes made up reasons to get him out of the apartment, and she wished Nicky were there right now, so she could hold him, reassure him that he was loved and wanted. The women sat quietly, each immersed in her own melancholy thoughts.

Kabrina was the first to break the silence. "Are you going on that interview for Chanel tomorrow?" she asked.

"Yes. And you?" Helena answered, quickly brushing away a tear that had trickled down her cheek before Kabrina could see it.

"Yeah. Carol, at the agency, told me that the marketing director from Paris was going to be there," Kabrina said. "I'm wondering if it's Daphine Jonquelle. She was the marketing director when I did their press show, two years ago in Paris."

"You did Chanel's press shows in Paris?" Helena asked enviously.

"Yes," Kabrina said offhandedly.

"Well, you shouldn't have any problem with the

interview tomorrow," Helena mused.

"I don't know. Who knows if she'll remember me, even if she is there."

The next morning, the two women tried to dress as close as possible to the current Chanel styles for the interview. They both wore black—Helena in a black short skirt, black opaque hose, and a white silk blouse, Kabrina in a basic black Chanel dress that she had bought in Paris and black opaque hose. Both of them wore the traditional Chanel gold chains around their necks and gold button earrings.

"We might as well ride together," Helena said. "We're going to the same place."

"I'll bet that they called every agency in town," Kabrina grumbled.

"Probably," Helena agreed.

Kabrina was right. When they arrived at the boutique on Rodeo Drive, the store was packed with models overflowing onto the sidewalk outside.

"There have to be a hundred and fifty models here," Helena said. "What a cattle call."

"Come on." Kabrina made her way through the crowd. "I've got an idea."

She squeezed through the line of models to the back of the store. There, along the back wall, a path had been cleared and the manager of the boutique was having each model walk. This was the hardest kind of interview. Not only did a model have to walk before a group of people scrutinizing her every movement, but she also had to walk with all of her peers looking on. It was extremely hard on a model's self-confidence. A lot of the models couldn't take it and left before it was their turn. When she reached the front of the line, Kabrina looked around and finally spotted the woman she was looking for.

"Daphine, Daphine," she called, waving.

A short, dark-haired, middle-aged woman looked around at the sound of her name and spotted Kabrina waving at her. She broke into a big smile. "Kabrina," she exclaimed, hurrying over to them. "I didn't know you were in Los Angeles." She spoke in heavily accented English.

"I've been here for about three months now."

"Of course you'll do our show for us." It was a definite statement.

"I'd love to," Kabrina said enthusiastically. "This is my girlfriend, Helena Sinclair, Daphine. We work together all the time."

Helena held out her hand. "It's very nice to meet you."

"And nice to meet you, too, Helena," replied Daphine. "We'll have you do the show, too. One minute, please," she said, holding up a finger. "I'll be right back." She walked over to the group of people watching the models walk.

Kabrina elbowed Helena and smiled.

Daphine said something to the others and pointed to Kabrina and Helena. Then she walked back to them. "It's all set," she said. "I told them I want both of you in the show."

"Wonderful," Kabrina exclaimed. "Thank you so much, Daphine."

"Yes, thank you," Helena agreed. "It was very sweet of you to do that."

"It's nothing," Daphine replied, shrugging her shoulders. "Leave the card with me with your agencies' telephone numbers on it and we'll let them know that you're booked."

The women pulled out a composite from each of their portfolios and gave them to Daphine.

"À bientôt, Daphine," Kabrina said.

"Goodbye," Helena added politely.

"Ciao, girls." Daphine dismissed them and returned to her interviews.

"Kabrina," Helena exclaimed when they reached the street, "thank you so much!"

"Thank *you,*" she replied. "It's the least I could do for a friend."

"Let's go get a cup of coffee before we go home," Helena suggested.

"Okay. How about Il Fornio's?"

They walked over to the little Italian pastry shop two blocks over and sat down at one of the little natural wood tables and ordered cappuccinos.

"You know," Kabrina said as they waited for their orders, "I saw Susan waiting in line. I wonder if she ever had a talk with Pam about the earring."

"Oh, I forgot to tell you," Helena said. "She had a little talk all right. It was closer to World War Three, from what I understand."

"What happened?"

"The way Susan explained it to me was that she ran into Pam at the agency the day after the Pagnini fur show. Pam was wearing the one earring, European-style."

"Uh-oh," Kabrina said.

"Uh-oh is right," Helena continued. "When Susan saw that earring, she went crazy! She ripped it out of Pam's ear!"

"Oh, my God," Kabrina exclaimed. "Then what happened?"

"I think Susan was ready to kill her, but Catherine came between them and held Susan back. It seems that Susan's boyfriend, Trace, had been sneaking around with Pam for the past two months. Neither of them had the nerve to tell Susan."

"I'm not surprised that Susan wanted to kill Pam; I know she was ready to kill me," Kabrina said.

The waitress brought their cappuccinos to them. Kabrina added extra sugar to hers and stirred it thoughtfully. "I guess I'm not the only one with boyfriend problems," she said ruefully.

"Guess not," Helena agreed. "Can you see Catherine trying to hold Susan back at the agency?"

The vision of the wizened, tough-talking little Catherine trying to separate two furious models twice her size brought smiles to the two women's faces.

"Actually, Catherine's so tough," Helena said "that she could probably take care of both of them."

"You're probably right, from what I've heard," Kabrina agreed. Unlike Catherine Beck, Carol, her own agent, was a joy to be around. She always had a positive, bubbly attitude. "So what finally happened?"

"Susan kicked Trace out. She told him to go live with Pam, and he did."

"Good for Susan," Kabrina said enthusiastically.

"Oops, I forget the time." Helena checked her watch. "Jaimie is meeting me at the apartment at noon."

"He was so sweet to me yesterday," Kabrina said. Personally, she suspected that Jaimie was a little less than thrilled to have her staying with Helena. Being a married man, limited to when he was able to spend time with Helena, and, from what Kabrina saw, Jaimie was passionately in love with Helena, he was very possessive of Helena and watched her every move. It would drive her nuts to have someone that possessive of her, Kabrina mused to herself, but to each her own.

"I'm going to start my apartment hunting today," Kabrina said, drinking the last of her cappuccino. "I picked up a *Beverly Hills Review* earlier, and after I go through it, I'm going to hit the streets."

By the time they reached the apartment, Jaimie was already there. He had let himself in with his key and was sitting on the couch drinking a cup of coffee.

"Where have you two been?" he said with just the slightest note of irritation in his voice.

Helena gave him a quick kiss on the lips and sat down next to him. "We had an interview at the Chanel Boutique on Rodeo."

"Did you get the job?" he asked, mildly interested.

"It looks like it, thanks to Kabrina," Helena said,

telling him about their interview.

"That was very nice of you, Kabrina," Jaimie said politely.

Kabrina shrugged. "It was nothing."

"Are you two ready for lunch?" Jaimie asked, changing the subject. "I'm starved. Where do you want to go?"

"I'm afraid I'm going to spend the next few hours going through the ads to find an apartment," Kabrina answered.

"Oh, come to lunch with us," Helena urged her. "You can look through the ads after lunch."

"Yes," Jaimie agreed gallantly. "You can't hunt for apartments on an empty stomach."

It was his plan that they would all have lunch together so Helena wouldn't feel that she was being a poor hostess. During lunch they could scan the rental ads, and he would personally make sure that Kabrina had more than enough apartments to look at so she would be occupied for the entire afternoon. Then he and Helena could make love without interruption.

"Are you sure?" Kabrina asked, not wanting to intrude on their privacy any more than she already had.

"Jaimie's right," Helena insisted. "You need to eat."

"I'll tell you what," he said, as if the idea had just occurred to him. "Bring the paper with you to lunch and we'll go over the ads together and mark the ones that sound like a possibility. Then after lunch you can go look at them."

"That's the perfect solution," Helena agreed.

"All right," Kabrina conceded, thinking that since Jaimie had insisted this strongly about her accompanying them he must really not mind if she came along.

They ate lunch at a crowded little deli on South Fairfax Avenue. It had the best corned beef in Los Angeles, Jaimie told them. Throughout lunch, they circled apartment ads, and even if they only sounded like a slim possibility, Jaimie insisted that Kabrina take a look.

"Poor Kabrina will be out 'til midnight looking at all these apartments you've marked, Jaimie," Helena protested, beginning to think that was Jaimie's idea. She hoped Kabrina didn't notice.

"You can't leave any stones unturned when it comes to apartment hunting," Jaimie said to the girls.

"Jaimie's right," Kabrina agreed. "It's not easy finding just the right apartment."

After lunch the three of them went back to Helena's apartment and Kabrina left to apartment hunt. As soon as she was out the door, Jaimie started for Helena's bedroom.

"I'm tired; let's take a nap."

It was his usual routine. "A nap" meant that he wanted to make love. Although Helena enjoyed making love with him, it had all become so routine. Every day, the same thing, the same way; he never asked if she was in the mood. He always desired her, and he just assumed that she felt the same way.

Helena did care very, very much for Jaimie; but more and more, she viewed their relationship as a dead-end situation. She knew Jaimie was happy with the way things were. He had told her over and over again that she should be satisfied with their situation too. And on some level, she was. Being with him had opened a whole new world for Helena, giving her a taste of luxury that she now wanted for herself and for her son. But at the same time, she realized that her situation with Jaimie would never change and that if she wanted all the finer things and a free man, she would have to make different choices. She would never become rich as a runway model—at least not as wealthy as she wanted to be. In fact, just the opposite was true. As time passed and she grew older, her bookings would eventually become fewer and fewer and she would have to find another career. That reality was in the back of the minds of all the models she knew. They just didn't talk about it a lot. No one enjoyed facing the fact that she was growing older, even if she was getting better. But unlike the other models, Helena had already thought about it and had discarded dozens of career choices. But the one idea that stuck in her mind was writing. She had always felt she had a flair for it, and it was something that she could do and still remain independent. As the days passed, the idea of writing was growing stronger and stronger within her. Jaimie's voice jolted her from her reverie.

"Helena," he called impatiently from the bedroom. "What's keeping you?"

"You know, Jaimie," she said thoughtfully as she walked into the bedroom, "I've been thinking."

"Hurry up and get undressed," he said from under the covers. "What were you thinking about?"

"I was thinking about writing. Maybe I'll try my hand at it."

"That's nice." He took off his watch, only half listening.

"Yes, I could take some extension classes at UCLA," she went on.

"That's a good idea," Jaimie said casually. Then he realized that those classes might cut into his time with Helena. "You mean at night, right?" he asked sharply.

"Well, I'm not sure whether the classes I want are at night or during the day," Helena responded honestly. "It would only be for an hour or so during the day, anyway."

"Absolutely not," he shouted. "I hardly get to see you during the day as it is. I forbid you to take a class during the day. Take it at night."

"You forbid me!" she said, furious at his presumptuousness. "Who do you think you are to forbid me to do anything? Besides, at night I'd have to leave Nicky alone. During the day he would be in school."

"He's old enough to stay alone," Jaimie retorted, growing impatient. She was wasting their afternoon with her silly talk.

"I know he's old enough. That's not the point. The point is that I don't want to leave him alone. I want to spend as much time as possible with him!" Sometimes Jaimie was so selfish that he was unbearable.

"Just get into bed," he said angrily. "I'm going to have to leave pretty soon and we won't have any time together at all!" He didn't say "to make love," but the words hung in the air between them all the same.

"Is that all you ever think about?" She was in no mood to make love now. She had wanted to have a serious talk about her future, about what she was going to do with her life after her modeling career ended.

"No, it's not," Jaimie shot back. "But if you truly loved me, keeping me happy would be uppermost in your mind. You would want to make love anytime I wanted to."

It made him feel insecure and not in control when Helena balked at making love. In his book, making love solved all their problems. Over the months, he had fallen deeper and deeper in love with Helena, but lately she seemed to have become more independent, and he felt threatened. He wanted her completely at his beck and call.

"I do love you," she tried to explain, "but I need to think of my future, too."

"I'm your future," he insisted. "Now get into bed and we'll talk about it."

Helena slowly undressed and slipped beneath the covers. "I think I can write, Jaimie," she said, lying back on the pillows.

Jaimie looked at her glossy, dark hair spread out on the soft peach of the pillow, the soft rise and fall of her breasts beneath the sheets, and he imagined the silky feel of her skin. He felt himself growing hard. He wanted her so much, just like the first time.

"We'll talk about it later," he said huskily, leaning over and cupping her breast in his hand. He manipu-

299

lated the nipple between his thumb and index finger. "I have other things to discuss with you now."

"But Jaimie—"

"Shush," he whispered, pushing his lips down on hers, his tongue searching out hers.

She gave up. She knew she wouldn't get any further now. She'd have to plan a better time when they were both dressed and Jaimie was satisfied.

Jaimie ran his hands over her body. She never ceased to excite him. He'd never met a woman who excited him as much as she did. Helena nibbled on his throat and ran her tongue around his nipples. He guided her head down toward his cock, anticipating the feel of her warm lips on it. When he could stand it no longer, he pulled her to him, crushing her in an embrace, holding her to him as if he would never let her go. And his mind whispered, I'll never let you go, Helena, never.

"You love me, don't you?" he whispered softly in her ear.

She nodded silently.

"Then tell me," he whispered urgently. "I want to hear you say it!"

"I love you, Jaimie."

His cock found its way between her satiny thighs, and the two of them moved together in sync, faster and faster until they came in a wave of passion that lingered on and carried them off into a cloud of satisfied exhaustion.

I want her with me always, Jaimie thought to himself as he drifted off to sleep. Always. Always. The words vibrated in his dreams.

Kabrina returned home late that afternoon, just as Jaimie was getting into his car.

"I found an apartment," she called to them in excitement.

"That's great," Helena cried, happy for her friend.

"Yes, it really is." Jaimie let the car engine idle. This was easier than I anticipated, he thought to himself. "Where is it?"

"It's just a few blocks away. It's a one bedroom and it's furnished," Kabrina rattled on. "The manager said that I could slowly replace the furniture with my own if I want to."

"When will it be ready?" Jaimie asked. With a little luck, he thought, she could move tomorrow. He didn't like sharing Helena with Kabrina.

"Oh, that's the only catch," she replied. "I hope you won't mind, Helena, but it won't be available for two more weeks. I tried to get the manager to make it sooner, but the present tenants won't be out for a week and a half; then he has to clean it."

"Two weeks," Jaimie stammered. He couldn't believe it. "Did you offer him money to get it ready sooner?"

"Two weeks is just fine," Helena said firmly. Sometimes Jaimie was so embarrassing. Poor Kabrina was doing the best she could. "It wouldn't do any good to offer him money if the current tenants aren't moving for a while."

"Well sometimes—" he persisted.

Helena shot him an exasperated look. "Jaimie," she said emphatically.

"I was just trying to be helpful," he said innocently. "I just figured Kabrina was eager to get into her own apartment."

"Oh, I am," Kabrina said. "He told me he'd let me know if it was ready sooner."

Jaimie shot Helena a "see, I told you so" look.

"Well, I've got to go," he told them, shifting the car into gear. "I've got one of those boring black-tie affairs tonight at the Beverly Glen Country Club." He poked his head through the window and kissed Helena on the forehead. "You behave yourself, baby. Here." He peeled off two 100-dollar bills from the huge wad he

301

always carried with him. "You girls go out someplace nice for dinner and celebrate Kabrina's new apartment. Make sure you don't bring any change back with you."

"Thank you, Jaimie," Helena said, "but you don't have to do that." She knew he was feeling guilty about going out with his wife and was trying to make it up to her.

"I know I don't," he said affectionately, shoving the money at her. "Just take it!"

That night Helena and Kabrina went to The Palms for dinner. Its casual atmosphere, sawdust floors, and walls covered with celebrity caricatures belied its prices and its status. On any given night, any number of the celebrities whose images covered the walls could be found dining there. Tonight, Helena spotted Robert Wagner and Shecky Green in two booths in a corner and David Letterman across the room.

There were no menus or prices and the waiters rattled off what was available, with gigantic fresh lobster as the specialty. "If you have to ask the price, then you can't afford it," was the motto at The Palms. They ordered lobsters, tomato salads, and wine, with cheesecake for dessert. When the waiter came with the check, Helena found that Jaimie's two hundred dollars just about covered it. She paid the tab and they left the restaurant. Earlier they had discussed going to Le Dome or Nikki Blair's on Sunset Boulevard for a nightcap, but after the enormous dinner they were both too tired. Instead, they drove home and settled for a cup of herb tea in the living room before retiring for the evening.

The next day, Jaimie arrived about noon to take them to lunch.

"You know, I haven't heard from Nicky in over a week," Helena said, thoughtfully. She, Jaimie and Kabrina were sitting in the living room, trying to decide

302

where to go for lunch.

"He is supposed to come back next week to get ready for school. It's very strange that neither he nor Kyle has called me," she continued.

"He's probably just caught up in kid stuff," Jaimie said offhandedly.

"You know how kids and their attention spans are," Kabrina agreed. "They're easily distracted."

"You're probably right," she agreed hesitantly.

In the past week, she had left several messages on her ex-husband's answering machine but he hadn't returned her calls. She hoped that Jaimie and Kabrina were right, but the fact that her calls weren't returned left her with an uneasy feeling in the pit of her stomach. Two months had gone by since Nicky had left for Seattle, and Helena missed him terribly. At the beginning of the summer, Nicky had talked to her every few days, faithfully; but in the three weeks since she had returned from France, the calls had dwindled. He had sounded a little distracted on the telephone recently, but Helena had assumed he just had his mind on other things.

It wasn't easy being a single parent without the security of a nine-to-five job, but modeling allowed her a more flexible schedule and more time to spend with her son.

She loved her little boy so much, and she eagerly awaited his return. Even the glamour of her weeks in the South of France hadn't made up for her loneliness, and not a day had gone by that she didn't wish he were there, sharing the wonderful experience of Europe. Sometimes it had been difficult trying to balance her relationship with Jaimie and motherhood, but she did her best and she hoped that Nicky realized that he always came first with her.

Her love for him was so intense and strong. Before Nicky had been born, Helena couldn't imagine loving anyone enough to lay down her life for him. But with her son, if the situation ever arose, she wouldn't have a second's hesitation. She knew she would kill, without thinking twice, anyone who threatened her child's life. Even on a day-to-day basis, her heart ached when he came home from school troubled. If she could have her way, her child would never know pain, or sorrow or unhappiness of any kind. She loved him with the fierceness of a lioness.

Helena did her best to instill moral values and social graces and temper them with the golden rule. She tried to build his character and expose him to and protect him from the world all at the same time. Sometimes, she thought, it was like juggling five things at once while molding a lump of wet clay. There was no sure way to guarantee success, and much of the time she felt as if she were flying by the seat of her pants. But she was doing the best that she could.

"I think I'll try to reach Nicky right now," Helena said slowly. It was late Saturday afternoon and she had no idea if Nicky would be at home or not; but at least she would have a good chance of connecting with Kyle.

She dialed the number and the phone rang and rang. It was strange, she mused to herself; that phone number had belonged to her for years, and now, after less than a year, it didn't even seem familiar. Her life had gone through so many, many changes in the past months. She was just about to hang up when, after ten or so rings, someone picked up the telephone.

"Hello? Hello," she said. On the other end of the line there was dead silence, although Helena could sense someone was listening. "Hello, is someone there?"

No one replied, and there was an abrupt buzz as whoever it was on the other end of the line hung up the phone.

"What's the matter?" Jaimie asked, noticing the puzzled look on her face.

"I don't know," she said in confusion. "Whoever picked up the phone hung up on me. They didn't say

304

anything, they just hung up."

"Call again," Kabrina urged. "Maybe it was just a bad connection."

"It's so strange," she said in a troubled voice. Whether it was a mother's intuition or a sixth sense, Helena wasn't sure; but suddenly she was filled with dread.

Her fingers shook as she redialed. Again, it rang and rang. Finally, someone on the other end picked up.

On a hunch, Helena said, "Nicky? Nicky, honey, is that you?" Her voice cracked a bit on the words.

At first there was silence; then she heard a small, tight voice. "Yes, Mommy," he replied quietly.

"Hi, honey, how are you?" she exclaimed. "Did you pick up the telephone when I called a moment ago?"

He paused for a few seconds before answering, and for a moment Helena thought he was no longer on the line.

"Yes," he said hesitantly.

"Why did you hang up?" she asked. "And I've called several times and left messages on Daddy's answering machine, but no one's called back. I need to know when you're coming back. Are you all right?"

Her words released a damn of pent-up emotions inside Nicky and the words tumbled out. "I'm never coming down there again! I hate it. I don't have any friends and I miss Daddy and Grandpa and Grandma," he screamed at her. "And I hate you! You ruined everything! Daddy and I were happy until you wrecked our family," he cried, slamming the receiver down.

She quietly replaced the receiver. Jaimie and Kabrina had noted the stricken look on Helena's face and had been able to make out the sound of Nicky's angry voice.

"What is it, Helena?" Kabrina asked, touching her arm. "What's happened?"

Instead of answering her, she redialed Kyle's number. I've got to talk to him, she thought wildly.

There must be some mistake. This time the telephone was answered almost immediately by her ex-husband.

"Kyle," she cried. "I just talked to Nicky."

"I know," he said calmly. "I was standing right here."

"I don't understand. He told me he hated me!"

"What's to understand?" Kyle said coolly. "He pretty much told it the way it is. You wrecked our family. We were happy until you decided to go Hollywood!"

"That's not true," she cried in desperation. "We weren't happy! I didn't leave you to go Hollywood. I left you because we weren't a family anymore!"

She thought of the many nights Kyle had left them alone. She thought about how she had covered up for him, and now her good deeds had come back to haunt her. It was costing her her child.

"I liked things the way they were; it was right for me," Kyle said emotionlessly. He had liked having Helena supporting the family; that way he was able to do what he wanted, when he wanted. She had been the goose that laid the golden egg, and she had left, taking their son away from him; he was going to pay her back. "And it was right for Nicky, too. He's not coming back."

"I'll fight you to get him back. He's in my custody," Helena said hotly.

"Go ahead. I've already spoken to my attorney and you haven't a prayer," he crowed. "Point one: I'm a dentist, you're a part-time model in sin city, Los Angeles. I think I've got a pretty good case for getting him back."

"But the only reason you're a dentist is because I put you through college and dental school," Helena reminded him, with vehemence in her voice.

"So what?" he sneered. "It doesn't matter. Point two: Seattle is a healthier environment than Los Angeles is. Los Angeles has one of the highest crime rates in the country. And point three: Nicky refuses to live with you. He wants to stay here with his friends and his

306

family and with *me!*"

"But I'm his mother," Helena cried. He was scaring her with his tactics.

"I'm his father and you haven't a chance," he said confidently. "I also understand you have a married boyfriend. Any court in the country would reverse the custody decree, especially with Nicky begging to stay with me!"

Helena was speechless as she felt her world collapsing around her. She was losing her son.

"Now, you behave yourself, and I'll give you custody of Nicky during the summer and on holidays. I might even talk to him and try to convince him that his mother isn't quite as horrible as he thinks she is."

"Why are you doing this?" Helena cried. "You never wanted the responsibility of a child full-time."

"My parents want him around," Kyle said casually. "After all, he's their only grandchild. He'll stay with them during the week and go to school nearby. In exchange, they'll make sure I have no financial worries. I'll work when I feel like it—and play when I feel like it."

Helena was silent. All the pieces were in place now.

"Well, my darling ex-wife," he said cockily. "I'm going to let you mull things over for a while. After you think about what I've said, I'm sure you'll see things my way."

She heard a click and the line went dead. I can't handle this, she thought numbly. This is too much for me to take.

"Nicky doesn't want to come back to live with me," she whispered, her heart breaking.

Her eyes stung with hot tears and she tried to take a deep breath, but she couldn't. It was if someone had punched her in the stomach. She gasped and tried again to gulp air into her lungs. The room began to spin. Jaimie saw the color drain from her face.

"Put your head between your knees," he ordered,

shoving her head down.

His voice sounds so far away, Helena thought in a curiously detached way. Then both Jaimie and Kabrina faded away and the room turned black.

When she came to, her head was in Jaimie's lap and Kabrina was holding a cold cloth to the back of her neck.

"Helena, Helena," Jaimie said, softly patting her cheeks.

For a minute, she couldn't remember what had happened. Why did Jaimie and Kabrina look so scared? she thought in confusion.

Slowly things came back to her. She remembered the telephone call and Nicky's accusations, and she remembered her ex-husband's confident threats. Tears filled her eyes and spilled down her cheeks. She felt more pain in her heart than she thought she could bear. The child that she loved more than life itself hated her. She had tried so hard to shelter him and to preserve his image of his father. Now her noble efforts were her undoing. She struggled to speak, and her words came out in huge rasping sobs.

"N-Nicky hates me," she sobbed. "He said I ruined everything; I wrecked our family. Jaimie, he doesn't understand how it really was," she cried hysterically. "I tried so hard to protect him from the truth. We weren't a family. Kyle never cared about Nicky and me; he only cared about himself and now he's taken my baby!"

Jaimie held Helena close and stroked her head. "Everything's going to be all right. It'll all be fine," he crooned to her.

"But it's not the truth," she protested. "Oh, Jaimie, Jaimie, what am I going to do? My baby hates me!"

Oh, please, God, she prayed to herself, let it all be a horrible nightmare. Let it be anything, but don't let my son hate me. Don't let Kyle take him from me. It's more than I can stand. She had always tried to create a wholesome image of his father. The nights he was out

308

partying, Helena covered up by telling Nicky he was studying or at meetings. She was careful never to say anything negative about him to Nicky. She had tried to be a pillar of strength. I can handle it, she had told herself, if I'm blamed for the breakup of my marriage. Deep in the innermost recesses of her heart, she knew she was doing the right thing for her son and herself. It had just never entered her mind that the blame would come from Nicky. She had believed their relationship was stronger than that.

"How could Nicky say those things?" she cried over and over. "I thought he understood."

"He's a child," Kabrina said gently, speaking for the first time. "Children can't be expected to think like adults. Children don't want their lives changed all around, even if it is in their best interests," she went on.

"I couldn't stay in that nightmare of a marriage! I couldn't," Helena cried. "In the long run, it would have been more detrimental for Nicky if I had!"

"You know that and I know that, but we're adults and we can see all points of view," Kabrina explained. "Children only see one point of view—theirs. And what Nicky sees is that his calm life was turned upside down. You made him leave his friends and family and move down here and start all over with strangers. He's angry and frustrated and unsure of things, and he has to blame someone. His dad is still in Seattle, his friends are still in Seattle. To him, you're the cause of all his problems."

Helena's heart ached with pain that was almost physical. Her whole world seemed ripped apart. How could she continue without the love of her child, without her child with her? It was too much for her. She understood what Kabrina was saying on an intellectual level, but on an emotional level it was unbearable.

Why couldn't he understand? she cried over and over again. Jaimie stroked her and tried to soothe her, but she was unreachable. She cried until she could cry no more, until her throat was raw and her voice gone. Finally, she lay with her head on Jaimie's shoulder, exhausted, numb. He spoke quietly to her as he would a child. Then took her by the hand and led her to her bed, where she lay down and stared at the ceiling. Salty tears continued to etch trails from the corners of her eyes down her cheeks, but she was quiet. He and Kabrina tiptoed from the bedroom.

"Do you think we should call a doctor?" Kabrina asked. She had never seen Helena like this; she had always been so together and in control of her life. She was worried that Helena could be having a nervous breakdown.

"No," he replied. "She'll be all right."

"Are you sure?"

"Positive," he said firmly. "I know my girl. She'll be fine. Let her sleep. You're right, you know, about Nicky. Let her rest for now; tomorrow we'll get everything straightened out.

"I've got to go," he said. "We're expecting company for dinner."

He went back into Helena's bedroom to say goodbye. She was lying on the bed staring at the ceiling. He sat down on the edge of the bed and stroked her hair. "I have to leave now, sweetie," he said gently. "I'll call you later tonight. Things will work out; trust me. Nicky's just a little confused. He's surrounded by not just Kyle's family, but your family, too. Maybe you and Kyle can work it out so that you'll have joint custody. It might be better for Nicky, too. Think about it, baby."

Helena didn't answer him. She just stared at the ceiling. Jaimie kissed her on her forehead and stood up.

"I'll call and check on her later," he told Kabrina as he went out the door.

Jaimie mulled over the afternoon's events on his way

home. He felt so powerless. He knew how much Nicky meant to Helena and he didn't know how to help her. Guiltily he thought about the times he had wished Nicky lived with his father. He was a nice enough little kid, as far as kids went, but it always seemed like he showed up at the most inopportune times. But he had never wanted to see Helena in such pain; he loved her too much. He wished there were something he could do to ease her pain, even if it meant having Nicky back all the time. Maybe things could be worked out to everyone's satisfaction, he mused, just as he had told Helena: joint custody. Yes, he thought, that would work out best for everyone concerned.

In her bedroom, Helena fell into an exhausted and troubled sleep. Kabrina checked on her several times throughout the evening, and her heart went out to Helena. She was such a good person, and she had stood by Kabrina throughout her troubles with Noel. Now it was Kabrina's turn; she wouldn't let Helena down.

Helena made it through the next few days in a fog. Kabrina and Jaimie were with her constantly, and they worked diligently to cheer her up. Jaimie had given the situation hours of thought, and he was convinced that the best solution was joint custody, with Nicky going to school in Seattle. That way, he told himself, I'll have Helena all to myself for nine months of the year. I always spend the summers in Europe, so while I'm gone, she can see Nicky. She won't be apt to meet anyone while I'm gone, either, because her son will occupy all her time.

"Look," he told her again one afternoon. "Kyle's right. Careerwise and in terms of stability, a dentist looks a lot better than a model. You know the kind of reputation models have. And Nicky *wants* to be in Seattle, not in Los Angeles. Even if you could convince a court to let you keep custody of Nicky, he would fight you every step of the way, even if being with you was the best thing for him," he reasoned. "Let him live with his father; it's what he wants."

Helena couldn't answer him; she was sobbing too hard.

"I have to agree with Jaimie," Kabrina told her, thinking of how her own father had reacted to modeling. "Let him stay up there for now; in time he'll mature and he'll want to come back. Trust me. Don't force him right now."

Helena was so confused; she didn't know what to do. The things Kabrina and Jaimie were telling her made sense, but how could she continue without her son— her son who told her he hated her?

During the next few days, she tried to calm down and weigh the pros and cons logically. She told herself that Seattle was a better place for a boy to grow up in. After all, she thought, Kyle could take him hunting and fishing, do all the things a father and son should share. All she could offer was fashion shows and a big city. In the end, fearful of further rejection by Nicky, she gave in with an aching heart.

"I'll speak to Nicky," her ex-husband condescendingly told her. "Maybe in time, he'll want to talk to you. I'll do my best to help you. It's more than you did for me!" he added snidely.

Helena bit her tongue to keep from calling him a liar and tried to calm down. Let him talk, she told herself. Don't provoke him. In time, I'll win Nicky back; I know I will.

During the several days following her conversation with Kyle, she began to think more and more about a career change. She racked her brain for a career that would afford her the luxury of working at home so that she would be there for Nicky, and one that would never end, as modeling eventually had to. At the same time, it had to be something she would enjoy, because she realized that regardless of whether Nicky returned, she had to be happy in whatever career she chose. At this point, her career was all she had left.

She kept returning to thoughts of writing. She had loved telling Nicky stories, and she had always had a flair for writing short stories in school. Perhaps this was a viable avenue to explore.

Chapter Twelve

The confrontation with Marcus left Laura Ann completely unnerved. During the drive back to Norris's house, she couldn't stop shivering. The look of hatred on Marcus's face was forever etched in her memory.

"What am I going to do?" she said to Norris over and over again in the car. "What if he finds me?"

"He's not going to find you," Norris firmly told her. "And what you're going to do is start a new life. Los Angeles is a big city; you can live here for years and not run into anyone you know."

"I don't know," she said dubiously. "I'm so afraid of him. I wish I had some blow to help me through the next couple of days," she said more to herself than to Norris; but he heard.

He hit the brakes and the old car screeched to a halt, almost sending her crashing against the dashboard. Norris grabbed her by the shoulders and squeezed them so hard that it brought tears to her eyes.

"Look," he said furiously. "I didn't help you out of one nightmare so you could start another. If you're too weak to stand on your own two feet, then get out of my car right now and go back to Marcus."

He grabbed the door handle on her side and jerked it upward so the door flew open. His actions were so abrupt that Laura Ann almost fell out onto the pavement.

"Get out," he told her angrily. "I thought you were strong enough to handle a second chance, but it looks like I was wrong. Go back to Marcus. He'll give you all the coke you want and kick the shit out of you for good measure, too."

"No," she cried fearfully. "Please, I didn't mean it. I really don't want any blow; I do want a second chance."

"I don't think so," Norris spat out, ignoring her pleas. "I should have known. Once a snorter, always a snorter; you're a waste of my time."

"Norris," she begged, pulling the car door closed. "I swear to you I'm off the stuff for good. I've been cutting back the past few weeks and I've hardly had any! I'm straight, I swear!"

He silently glared at her.

"I want this second chance," she pleaded. "Not just for me, but for you. I won't let you down, I promise. I'll never go back to that life. Never!"

He studied her for a few minutes. "Okay," he said, and he slowly shifted the car into gear and pulled away from the curb. "But if you ever touch a drug of any kind again, I'll throw you out so fast, you won't know what hit you!"

"I promise I won't, Norris," she cried earnestly.

They drove the rest of the way in silence, both immersed in their own thoughts.

Laura Ann thought back over the nightmare of the past ten months, a living hell she thought she would never escape. She silently promised that she would never do drugs again. Norris had put himself on the line for her and she wouldn't disappoint him. It didn't matter that she might never become a model. The only thing that did matter was that she was away from Marcus and she would never have to see him again.

Norris was pensive too. He was still angry and afraid that Laura Ann wasn't strong enough to withstand the hypnotic pull of coke. He'd seen it happen hundreds of times before. He knew that all his encouragement and all his threats wouldn't keep her away from the snow. Even the drug rehabilitation programs he'd recommended when he was a cop and dealing with drug addicts couldn't keep her off drugs if she didn't have the desire to quit. She had to make that decision on her own and stay clean for herself, not for him or anyone else. He didn't know if she was capable of doing it but all he could do was wait and watch.

The following days were a recovery period for Laura Ann. She stayed at Norris's and slept in his daughter's bedroom. She went to bed early and slept late and worked to exorcise the demons she had been living with.

Her friendship with Norris deepened. He was like a stern but caring father. They talked superficially about what she had been through, but much of the past ten months she kept locked away in her mind; she was too ashamed to talk about it.

Laura Ann was curious about Norris's daughter, but each time she brought up the subject, he changed it. Sometimes she saw a misty, paternal look in his eyes when he looked at her, and Laura Ann wondered if she reminded him of his daughter. He told her stories of when he was on the police force and about his wife who had died years earlier, but the subject of his daughter always drew silence. Laura Ann's preoccupation with her own problems kept her from pursuing the subject too strenuously.

Even though she had been off drugs for several weeks, she still felt their seductive pull whenever she thought about them or even saw a television commercial about Coke. Norris was a pillar of strength, though, and as the days passed, the pull lessened.

Norris watched a transformation occur in Laura Ann. Gradually, her skin lost its pasty pallor and color returned to her cheeks. The look of fear in her eyes dimmed, and sometimes his worn-out cop jokes brought a faint smile to her lips. Occasionally he thought he could see a look of hunger and wanting in her eyes, and he knew she was fighting her desire for coke; but after that first day, she never mentioned it again.

She gathered a new strength from within and started to hold her head up instead of hanging it self-consciously. Norris tried to help by giving her guidance and a crash course in self-esteem.

"Forget about looking to other people for approval," he told her over and over again. "You have to believe in yourself. You have to truly like yourself."

"I do like myself," Laura Ann protested. "It's just that there's so many people in Los Angeles who are better than I am."

"See, that's exactly what I'm talking about," Norris patiently tried to explain. "You are very special. No one else has exactly the same looks, talent, and personality you have. That makes you unique, and you have to believe that you are unique."

"Do you really think so?" she asked, looking to him for approval.

"It doesn't matter what I think," he exploded, pacing about the room in frustration. "I told you. It only matters what *you* think about yourself. You have to believe that you're special; then others will believe it, too."

"Oh," she said in a tiny voice, watching him apprehensively. The memories of Marcus's rages and beatings still haunted her.

"I want you to make a list of all your positive qualities and all of your negative qualities," he said in a gentler tone of voice. He had seen the fear in her eyes and vowed that he would not be so hard on her. "Then we'll go over them, one by one." He handed her a pencil and paper and patted her on the shoulder reassuringly.

He had no formal training in counseling, only his cop's street smarts, but he felt if he could instill a little

317

bit of self-esteem and confidence in her she would blossom and develop on her own.

God knows, he thought to himself, these are the same things I said to my own daughter. Wherever she is, I hope that she has remembered them. It made him sad to think about Kabrina, and he tried to put her out of his mind.

Day after day, Norris worked with Laura Ann, and gradually she grew stronger. Norris began to see a marked change in her, and after a few weeks, he felt it was time for her to try standing on her own two feet.

"I've talked to Sam, a friend of mine, who owns the Sunrise Coffee Shop on Sunset Boulevard," Norris said to her one day. "He needs a waitress and I told him about you."

"Really?" She was feeling good about herself and she was ready to strike out on her own.

"Yes. I told him that you'd stop by this afternoon and talk to him."

"Great," she replied, excited by the prospect of getting on with her life.

Norris didn't offer to drive her to her appointment. Instead, he threw her his car keys and gave her directions to the coffee shop. He watched closely to see her reaction to going on her own and was pleased to see she had no apprehensions.

When she returned, late in the afternoon, she was ecstatic.

"Sam hired me on the spot," she exclaimed as she burst through the front door. "I start tomorrow."

"That's great, Laura Ann," he said, grinning at her zeal.

"And that's not the best part," she bubbled on. "One of the other waitresses, Wendy, was looking for a roommate, and Sam introduced me to her. I'm going to move in this weekend. And best of all, the apartment is only a few blocks from the coffee shop, so I won't need to buy a car! Wendy said that if I ever needed one, I

318

could borrow hers. Isn't it great!"

"It certainly is," he agreed.

He looked at the young woman standing before him. The change in her over the past two weeks had been phenomenal. Her youth had returned with the color in her cheeks. He was happy with her progress and glad that she was standing on her own two feet, but he would miss having her around. In so many ways she reminded him of Kabrina, and he had forgotten the joy of having a youngster in his house again. He vowed silently to try to contact Kabrina in New York.

Laura Ann started her new job. For the few days she had left before moving in with Wendy, Norris drove her to work and picked her up at the end of the day. He met Wendy, and to his relief, she seemed like a nice, down-to-earth person. She would be a good influence on Laura Ann, he told himself. At the end of each day, Laura Ann would entertain him on the way home with stories of her day on the job.

When it came time for Laura Ann to move in with Wendy, Norris drove her, with her suitcases, to Wendy's apartment, above Sunset Boulevard.

"I don't know how to ever thank you," Laura Ann said as he pulled up in front of the apartment. "Without you, I would never have made it."

"Yes, you would have," he replied. "You're the one who did it. You always had the strength within you; I just showed you how to use it."

"I'll always remember what you've done for me," she said, tears coming to her eyes.

"Hey," Norris protested gruffly. "You act like you're never going to see me again. Don't forget you invited me to dinner tomorrow night!"

"I didn't forget." Laura Ann smiled through her tears. "Eight o'clock, okay? I just wanted you to know how much I appreciate what you've done for me and how much I care for you. You're like a father to me."

"Go on, get out of here," he said fondly, ruffling the

top of her head.

She gave him a quick hug and jumped out of the car, hauling her worn suitcases behind her. Norris watched her ring Wendy's bell to be buzzed in. As she pulled open the doors to the building, she turned around and blew him a quick kiss.

"See you tomorrow night," she called.

He waved back as she disappeared inside the building. Then he pulled a big white handkerchief from his pocket and blew his nose.

"Kids," he muttered to himself, already counting the hours until dinner the next night.

"La-la, I just put a deuce at your station," Dottie, the hostess at the Sunrise, called.

"Got it," Laura Ann answered briskly. She picked up three orders from under the heat lamp and lined them up on one arm, grabbing a coffee pot with the other hand. She maneuvered deftly through the counter area and down the aisle to the back booths in the cheery coffee shop. She set the coffee pot down on the edge of the formica table and slid the three orders in front of her customers.

"Eggs scrambled, eggs over easy, and French toast," she announced. "Anything else I can get you?"

The customers shook their heads in unison.

"Okay," she said, refilling their cups. "Enjoy!"

She continued on to the next table and poured two cups of coffee for the elderly couple sitting there.

"Morning. You folks decided what you want?" she smiled.

"Yes, we have," the little gray-haired man replied. "I'll have fried eggs, sunny side up, sausage and pancakes. My wife would like orange juice and rye toast with no butter. She's watching her figure," he added, grinning.

"Just one of those things we girls have to do to keep

the men interested," Laura Ann answered, winking conspiratorially at the plump, grandmotherly woman.

"After all these years, it had better be more than my figure that keeps him interested," the older woman chuckled.

Laura Ann laughed and returned to the kitchen. "Eggs up, squealers, and a side of 'cakes. One O.J. and dry rye," she called professionally to Sam in the kitchen.

She had been working at the coffee shop for two months now, and with each passing day, her life with Marcus had faded further and further from her mind. She felt good about herself and her life again. Sure, she sometimes told herself, she wasn't a glamorous model, strutting on a runway or posing in front of a camera, but she did have a good job and she was earning an honest living. The people she worked with were nice, and she had almost stopped looking over her shoulder, waiting for Marcus to appear. No one in the coffee shop knew about her former life. She was just another farm girl who had come to the big city with a dream. At first she had daydreamed a lot, and Wendy had begun calling her La-La, after Los Angeles's nickname of La-La Land. Laura Ann didn't mind and the name stuck.

Norris came by almost every day to have lunch and to chat, and like a proud parent he positively glowed at the changes he saw in Laura Ann.

Laura Ann was just picking up her order for the old man and woman when Wendy hurried up to her.

"La-la, guess what," she exclaimed.

"Rob Lowe just called and asked you for a date tonight," she quipped, balancing both orders on one arm and picking up the coffee pot with the other hand.

"Yeah, and he's got a friend for you," Wendy shot back without hesitation.

"Sorry, I'm busy tonight," Laura Ann said airily. "I have to wash my hair."

The two young women started giggling.

"No, seriously," Wendy said. "You know Mrs. Kreshland, who owns that fancy shop on the corner of Sunset Plaza Drive?"

"The woman with silver hair that always comes in for decaf and bagels at the counter?" Laura Ann asked.

"Yeah, that's her. Well, anyway," Wendy continued, "she asked me if I would be interested in making a little extra money, working as a dresser for this fashion show she's having Monday night."

"Hey, that's great," Laura Ann said enthusiastically.

"She said she could use another girl. You interested?" Wendy added.

"Sure," Laura Ann said casually, and she hurried off to deliver her customers' orders before they got cold.

Inside, her heart jumped at the thought. Even though it wouldn't be her on the runway, it would be exciting to be backstage and watch all those beautiful models work.

"It's all set then, I'll tell her," Wendy called.

By the time Monday arrived, Laura Ann could hardly contain herself. The day seemed to drag by. Norris came by and smiled to himself at her childish excitement. He watched her bounce from one table to another taking orders and serving food.

At last the shift was over, and Laura Ann and Wendy walked back to their apartment to change before the fashion show. Laura Ann dressed with extra care, changing her outfit several times before deciding on the one she would wear.

"We're only going to dress some models," Wendy explained, watching her change outfits over and over, "not sit in the audience, for God's sake."

"I know," Laura Ann said. "I just want to look good."

She finally chose a pale blue print blouse and a pair of tan cotton slacks and loafers. She applied her makeup with extra care and even curled her long blond hair.

322

"Thank goodness Mrs. Kreshland didn't ask you to be in the show," Wendy joked. "You would have had a nervous breakdown getting ready."

Laura Ann gave her a withering look, but Wendy's words stuck in her mind. That would be a dream come true, she thought wistfully. She imagined herself floating down the runway with the audience cheering her on.

"Fat chance," she said under her breath.

"What?" Wendy asked, not catching her words.

"Oh, nothing," she replied. "I think it's time to go."

They stood breathlessly at the driveway entrance of the Beverly Wilshire Hotel. It was straight out of *Lifestyles of the Rich and Famous*. Lacy black wrought-iron gates rising thirty feet high and covered with miniature Italian white lights guarded the cobblestone entrance. Chauffeured limousines, Rolls Royces and Mercedes slowly pulled in and out, discharging their glittering passengers. Valets liveried in red and black scurried to help disembarking guests. Gentlemen in tuxes, strutting like proud penguins, escorted some of the most glamorous women in the world.

If the men shone like polished leather, thought Laura Ann in awe, then the women sparkled like jewels in comparison. Directly in front of them, a woman stepped from the back of a black Rolls Royce. Her dress was a mass of solid silver sequins and bugle beads, and she radiated like a diamond. Another woman slid from the back of a white limo. She was an amethyst in royal purple taffeta. Two others, dressed in satin the color of rubies and emeralds, greeted a friend in jet black. The procession continued, each arriving guest more lavish than the last, and each one wearing a king's ransom in jewels.

"My God," Laura Ann breathed. "I didn't know people like this really existed outside novels!" For a small-town girl from Iowa, it was almost intimidating.

"Come on," Wendy said, taking her hand. "We'll be late."

They made their way through the crowds to one of the glass double doors.

"May I help you?" a doorman asked, blocking their way.

"We're dressers for the models," Wendy told him importantly.

"The Grand Ballroom is down the hall to the left," he sniffed, pointing the way.

They followed the white marble walkway, lined with mirrors, through two gigantic ivory-and-gold double doors. Before them, the Grand Ballroom seemed to stretch for miles and miles. Table after table set with white linen, creamy china, polished silver, and candles sat on a carpet of rich red. Down through the middle of the room ran a snow white runway about four feet off the ground. It was edged in white lights, and spotlights from six different angles cut through the dimly lit room, illuminating it.

They picked their way through the field of tables to get backstage, where the glamour stopped. The tiny room was edged on three sides by rack after rack of clothes. The fourth wall was lined with mirrors and lights. Models in various stages of undress and makeup crowded together in front of the mirrors. Laura Ann immediately recognized the exotic black model she had seen in the window of Lina Lee's on Rodeo and then again at the William Halsey Hallowell Agency, months before. Kabrina, she heard another model call her. Scattered around the floor by the racks, were models' bags filled with makeup, spare underwear, and pair after pair of shoes.

Laura Ann tuned in to snatches of conversation. Two of the models nearest to her at the mirrors were planning their routines.

"Let's snake it down and back," one said, and Laura Ann wondered what she meant. Beyond them, three other models huddled together, gossiping.

"My agent told me she wanted my hair short, but I think long hair is coming back," the one on the left said.

"Honey, that woman is living in the dark ages. Don't you dare cut your hair," the model in the middle advised.

The third model nodded solemnly in agreement.

Laura Ann and Wendy spotted Mrs. Kreshland in the corner, laying out jewelry on a table, and hurried over to report in.

"Hello, Mrs. Kreshland," Wendy said. "You remember Laura Ann from the coffee shop, don't you?"

"Yes, of course," Mrs. Kreshland said distractedly. "You're just in time. Let me assign you to your models." She glanced around the room to see which models still needed dressers.

"Wendy, you help Cragen," she said, pointing to a tall, lithe blonde. "And you, Laura Ann, you help Helena."

She indicated a model sitting on the floor with her back to them, pulling shoes out of a huge leather satchel.

"Helena," she called, "here's your dresser."

The model looked over her shoulder, and Laura Ann gave a start of recognition. It was the same gorgeous creature she had passed at the Catherine Beck Agency months before. There was no mistaking her flawless features.

Gorgeous was not an adequate description, Laura Ann thought to herself. This woman was breathtaking. She was dressed completely in deep purple silk and suede, and the color made her translucent skin glow. Her dark hair was pulled back into a simple chignon, making her luminous eyes and high cheekbones stand out more. When she smiled, her whole face lit up.

"Hi, what's your name?" she asked Laura Ann.

"Laura Ann," she answered, awestruck. She couldn't help but compare herself with the beautiful creature—

but there was no comparison.

"I'm Helena. It's nice to meet you." She smiled warmly. "Have you ever dressed before?"

Laura Ann shook her head.

"Okay. Then let me explain everything to you," Helena said in a businesslike tone. She stood up and marked off a group of outfits on the rack. "The clothes are lined up left to right. This is my first," she said, pointing to the first dress on the left. "And this is my last." She indicated the last dress on the right.

"It will be easier for you if you unbutton everything before the show," Helena continued. "Have the change off the hanger and ready to go before I come back from the stage. Hand me my clothes just like you'd dress yourself; blouses, then skirts, then jackets. You'll have to help me button things and make sure I don't have any tags showing. Okay?"

Laura Ann nodded timidly, so impressed with meeting Helena, she was tongue-tied.

"Oh, and let me show you what shoes and hose I'm going to need," Helena said, lining up her shoes beneath each outfit and going over their sequence with Laura Ann.

"Do you have any pockets?"

"Yes," Laura Ann replied, puzzled.

"Great," Helena said. "Here's the jewelry I'll be wearing with some of the outfits. Just put it all in your pockets so we'll know where to find it. The rest I'll get from Mrs. Kreshland. Do you have any questions?"

"No," Laura Ann answered, having recovered from her awe and now feeling excited by the prospect of the show. It was all so glamorous and Helena seemed so friendly.

"We'll be moving so fast that you'll get a workout," Helena smiled. "Things only look slow and relaxed out on the runway; backstage, they're crazy!"

"Ten minutes, first change, everyone," Mrs. Kreshland called.

326

"Pam's not here yet," Cragen said.

"What! We're missing a model," Mrs. Kreshland cried. "Has anyone talked to her today?"

All the models shook their heads.

"God! What are we going to do?" Mrs. Kreshland exclaimed. "I can't divide up her changes because you're all in specific groups, and I can't just leave them out. It'll ruin the whole show. Damn that girl! Wait 'til I get ahold of her agent."

She gazed wildly around the room as if she were waiting for someone to come up with a solution; then her eyes rested on Laura Ann. "You," she said, pointing to Laura Ann. "Turn around!"

Laura Ann was so dumbfounded that she did as she was told without a word.

"What size do you wear?" Mrs. Kreshland demanded.

"A size six," she replied, not understanding what Mrs. Kreshland was getting at.

"You're going to model," Mrs. Kreshland exclaimed. "Someone give her some lipstick and eye shadow and put her in Pam's first change. What size shoes do you wear?"

"Nine."

"Cragen, Gayanne, Suzanne," Mrs. Kreshland said, "you girls must have enough extra shoes between you that Laura Ann can wear for her changes."

The models quickly checked Pam's changes, went through their bags and came up with the needed shoes.

"Come on, Laura Ann," Helena said, taking her hand and leading her to Pam's rack of clothes. "Get into that first change. I'll get you some lipstick and eye shadow."

"I can dress both Laura Ann and Cragen," Wendy volunteered.

"But I've never modeled in a show before," Laura Ann protested, finally finding her voice.

"Don't worry about it," Helena said, pulling a gray

327

tweed skirt off the hanger. "I'll talk you through it. You'll do fine."

Laura Ann quickly put on the tweed skirt and matching peplum jacket that Helena held out to her. Her pulse racing wildly and her stomach twisting in knots, she did as she was told. She put on the red lipstick Helena gave her and brushed charcoal shadow on her eyelids.

"Pull your hair back," Helena told her. "It's a cleaner line with the clothes. Here's a rubber band."

She pulled her hair back into a ponytail, and Helena twisted it and secured it into a chignon.

"Now listen carefully to me," Helena said. "The first change, we're going to walk out and make a picture. That is, pose in front of the audience for a few seconds. Then I'm going to work the runway first."

"What'll I do?" Laura Ann asked, her voice quavering.

"Nothing. You just stand there and smile and watch me. When I get to the end of the runway, you start," Helena explained. "All you have to do is follow me and do exactly as I do."

"But what if I trip?" she wailed, thinking of the worst possible situation.

Helena took her by the shoulders and looked her straight in the eyes, trying to instill some confidence in her. "You won't," she said firmly. "And even if you do, just smile and pretend it was planned. Remember, the audience doesn't know the difference. Anything you do out there is okay. You're in control. Got it?"

"I-I guess so," she said, not at all convinced.

"Line up, everyone," Mrs. Kreshland called. "Helena, Pam—I mean, Laura Ann—Kabrina, Cragen, Anita, Susan, Linda, Misha, Pat, Suzanne, Julie, and Gayanne," she called, going down the lineup order. "And smile, everyone; have a good time!"

Have a good time, Laura Ann thought to herself. She must be kidding. What have I gotten myself into? It

328

was always so easy in her fantasies; she was always so in control. Now here she was in real life, her big opportunity, and she was quaking in her shoes. She wished she were anywhere but where she was. All of a sudden, the music started. Please, God, Laura Ann prayed, just let me make it through this without making a fool out of myself.

"Come on," Helena whispered. "That's our cue." She stepped through the red velvet curtains, and after a beat, Laura Ann followed.

On the pitch black stage, Laura Ann could barely make out Helena's shadowy form as she struck a pose on center stage. Standing next to Helena, Laura Ann thought the runway looked endless.

"Pose," Helena whispered as the dim lights started to come up. "Smile," Helena said through her teeth.

Laura Ann stood there, rooted to the floor. The spotlights hit them, blinding her. Helena started down the long ramp. Laura Ann's heart pounded so hard in her ears that she could barely hear the music. This was nothing like what she had expected. She looked out at the sea of people and imagined that they were all focusing on her, waiting for her to make a mistake. She was positive everyone knew she was an imposter. She felt the heat creep up her neck, and she knew her face was flushed bright red. Nervous perspiration beaded on her upper lip, and droplets trickled down between her breasts and under her arms.

She watched Helena gracefully turn halfway down the runway. When she hit the end, she smoothly slid off the jacket she was wearing and flipped it inside out in one movement to show that it was reversible. The audience murmured with approval at the showy move. Laura Ann stood watching, unconsciously holding her breath. As Helena turned and started back up the runway, she smiled reassuringly at Laura Ann and gave her a slight nod.

Laura Ann, frozen to the spot, wanted to move, but

her feet wouldn't budge. As Helena passed her, she turned and addressed the audience one last time. At the same time, she gave Laura Ann an imperceptible little shove and whispered, "Go!"

It was enough to break the spell. Laura Ann took a breath and started down the runway, which still seemed to extend forever. She thought she would never reach the end. The audience was silent and she was sure that they would start booing her at any moment. When she reached the end, she slowly turned around and started the long trek back. She tried to keep smiling, but her lips started quivering and she had to press them tight together. All of a sudden, her arms felt heavy and awkward. She put one on her hip, as she had seen Helena do, but it felt clumsy, so she let it drop to her side.

She had been looking down at the runway as she walked, too nervous to look up, and when she did glance up, she saw to her horror that another model was coming down the runway toward her. It was the black model, Kabrina. Laura Ann panicked. The runway seemed far too narrow to accommodate the two of them, and she knew she should move to one side so that Kabrina could pass her. But she was glued to her course down the center of the ramp. Kabrina caught her eye and nodded her head slightly, indicating that Laura Ann should move to one side. Laura Ann wanted to move, but her legs woodenly continued on straight ahead.

As they drew abreast of each other, Kabrina whispered to her, "Move over!"

She tried, but she could only follow her feet, and they were determined to take the path down the center. Kabrina turned sideways and tried to slip by Laura Ann, but she lost her balance and took a step backward into thin air. The audience gasped as Kabrina teetered for a moment, then dropped with a plop onto the soft lap of an overweight man sitting directly below her.

Laura Ann didn't see what happened after that; she just rushed up the remainder of the ramp and off through the curtains.

Mrs. Kreshland was directing people backstage and hadn't seen what had happened. When Laura Ann stumbled backstage, Mrs. Kreshland pushed her toward her rack.

"Quick, dear, get into your next change," she exclaimed, pointing to Wendy, who was holding her next change.

"But, Mrs. Kreshland, I can't go back out there," she cried in embarrassment. "I—"

"Nonsense," Mrs. Kreshland interrupted. "You haven't time to talk. Get dressed!"

"But you didn't see what happened," Laura Ann insisted, trying to explain.

"Laura Ann," Mrs. Kreshland said sternly, motioning for Wendy to start undressing Laura Ann, "I don't want to hear about anything. We have a show to do! I'm sure you were just fine. Now go."

Laura Ann looked around her and realized that no one had seen what had happened. The others were too busy concentrating on their own responsibilities. Wendy had stripped off Laura Ann's clothes and held out the next change for her to put on.

"Hurry up, La-la," Wendy urged, holding out a pair of menswear trousers for Laura Ann to step into. "I'm sure you were great!"

She started to put them on as she heard her name being called again for lineup.

At that instant, Kabrina came tearing through the side doors. After landing on the man in the audience, she had been unable to climb back on the runway, so instead she had to walk through the audience to the side entrance. The audience had applauded her as she gathered together the little poise she had left and, holding her head high, made her way through the audience to the exit. She couldn't remember being

331

more embarrassed, and she was furious.

Laura Ann had her back to Kabrina and was stepping into the trousers when Kabrina grabbed her by the arm and whirled her around. Laura Ann, caught with one foot in the trouser leg, lost her balance and fell heavily against a clothes rack.

"What the fuck were you doing out there?" Kabrina shouted at her.

"I-I'm so sorry," Laura Ann stuttered. "I tried to move to one side, but I couldn't—"

"I told you to get over! Can't you understand English?" Kabrina hissed, beside herself with anger and humiliation.

She took an involuntary step toward Laura Ann, and Laura Ann cringed against the rack of clothes. At the same time, Kabrina felt a hand on her arm.

"Calm down, Kabrina; we've got a show to do," Helena said, at the same time strategically placing herself between the two girls.

"But that bitch knocked me off the runway," Kabrina protested.

"Talk to her about it later or you'll never make your change," Helena advised Kabrina calmly.

"I intend to," Kabrina exclaimed.

She turned to Laura Ann and glared at her. "You'd better not get anywhere near me for the rest of this show!" She turned back to her rack and started pulling off her clothes.

"Oh, thank you," Laura Ann whispered gratefully to Helena, while keeping one eye on Kabrina. "It was really an accident—"

"Hurry up, we're on," Helena interrupted, giving Laura Ann a quick smile. "And stay away from Kabrina."

Wendy buttoned up Laura Ann's blouse and cinched an ornate belt around her waist; then Helena pulled her over to the stage entrance.

"Stay to the right; pass on the right, *always,*" Helena

332

explained to her firmly as she clipped on a gold earring. "Don't go down the middle of the ramp! You understand?"

She looked at Laura Ann sharply to see if her words were sinking in. Laura Ann nodded.

"Go," Mrs. Kreshland whispered to Helena.

"Remember," Helena said over her shoulder. "Stay to the right." And she disappeared through the curtains.

"Go pose," Mrs. Kreshland said to Laura Ann after a moment's pause.

Laura Ann took a pose at the top of the runway and watched Helena glide down the runway and execute a graceful turn at the end. As she started back, she motioned with her eyes for Laura Ann to start walking. As she made her way down the ramp, she stayed as far over on the right edge as possible. Maybe it was her imagination, but she thought she could hear the audience murmuring, and in the far back of the room, someone snickered. She hung her head in embarrassment, but she kept walking. As she turned and walked back up the runway, she saw Kabrina waiting at the top of the stage. She kept to the right, but Kabrina waited until she was completely off the ramp before starting down. She refused to acknowledge Laura Ann; instead she stared stoically straight ahead.

Laura Ann stepped through the curtains and dashed over to her rack, where Wendy was waiting with her next change. She quickly put on a blue plaid suit with a matching hat and purse and hurried back to Mrs. Kreshland.

"You're going to open the next sequence, Laura Ann," Mrs. Kreshland told her after referring to her lineup sheet.

Petrified, she turned to Helena, who was waiting to go on. "Do I have to go out there by myself?" she asked, her eyes wide with fear.

"You'll be fine," Helena said. "Mrs. Kreshland will

tell you when to go. Just pose until the lights and music come up before you start walking."

Then she stepped through the curtains and was gone.

Runway modeling wasn't anything like she had imagined in her fantasies; it was scary and her stomach churned nauseously. She didn't have time to contemplate anything because in what seemed like seconds, Mrs. Kreshland gave her a little push through the curtains.

Laura Ann stumbled onto the stage. In the dark, she found her way to the top of the stage and posed, just as the lights and music started coming up. She tried to smile bravely, but her upper lip stuck to her gums and she was afraid it looked like she was sneering.

Walk, she told herself. Stay to the right; once down and once back. Her feet took one step after another and her confidence grew. Hey, she thought, I'm doing it! I'm really modeling! She felt a surge of accomplishment as she did a stiff little turn at the end and walked back. At the top of the runway, she turned and addressed the audience as she had seen Helena do earlier. Then she stepped through the velvet curtains backstage.

"I saw you that time," Mrs. Kreshland exclaimed, patting her shoulder. "You did fine, just fine, dear."

"Thank you," Laura Ann replied as she hurried back to her rack of clothing.

The dressing room was starting to resemble a sauna from the heat of several dozen bodies working together at top speed. Trickles of perspiration rolled down Laura Ann's back, but she was so engrossed in changing that she didn't notice.

"It was easier this time, Wendy," she exclaimed.

"See, I told you," Wendy said, buttoning up the blouse and tucking the tags up into the sleeve.

Helena overheard Laura Ann and smiled. "You're doing great," she said encouragingly. "Just pretend you know what you're doing."

This time when Laura Ann walked through the heavy curtains, she took Helena's advice. She pretended she was a top model, just as she had dreamed so many times before. She stepped into the spotlight and held her head high. She hesitated a moment, posing, before starting down the runway. This time she was really here, really on a runway, not under a faceless john's sweaty body. Her heart was beating at triple speed and adrenaline coursed through her body; it was a heady feeling. I can do it. I *am* a model, she thought. Me. Laura Ann Gilmore. And she walked a little straighter and held her head a little higher.

By the time Laura Ann was on the runway in her last change, she had collected enough confidence to try a little turn at the end of the runway, the way the other models did. She felt like she was ready for it, but unfortunately, her feet weren't. They caught in the long silk taffeta evening skirt, and she tripped a little. It was enough to take her confidence down a peg or two, and she confined herself to just walking straight back and off.

Backstage, all the models lined up for the finale. Laura Ann was standing in line waiting when she heard a voice behind her.

"You and I are going to have a little talk after the show," Kabrina said ominously.

Startled, Laura Ann quickly turned around. Kabrina's lips were set in a hard line, and her amber eyes shot a challenge to Laura Ann.

"I—I really am sorry. I didn't do it on purpose," Laura Ann said apologetically. "I tried to move over, but I just froze."

"Everyone go," Mrs. Kreshland said as the music crescendoed and hit a throbbing beat.

Laura Ann turned just in time to see the model in front of her disappear through the curtains, and she hurriedly followed.

The lights were up and the audience gave the models

a standing ovation. The sound of applause roared in Laura Ann's ears, and she knew she was hooked. She had been terrified, but in her heart she knew she wanted to model more than anything else. The models made a horseshoe down the runway in the final changes and then walked back through the curtains.

Once they were all backstage, the models broke into their own round of applause. They were high from the excitement of the show.

Wendy ran over and hugged her. "La-la, you looked terrific," she exclaimed. "I peeked out and saw the finale. You acted like a real pro!"

"Really?" she asked tentatively. "Did I really look all right?"

"All right? You looked gorgeous!" Wendy said excitedly, throwing her arm around Laura Ann. "Really!"

"Oh, Laura Ann," Mrs. Kreshland called, picking her way through the piles of clothes and shoes on the floor toward her. "I want to thank you for helping us out in a pinch."

"Oh, that's okay," she replied, her face shining. "I really liked it!"

"You looked very good in the clothes," Mrs. Kreshland said thoughtfully. "You know, I've got another show coming up next week, on Tuesday. Would you like to do it?"

"Oh, Mrs. Kreshland, I'd love to."

"Well, you can, and I'll pay you the regular rate, provided you can get some of the other models to give you a few pointers on makeup and walking to polish you up some," Mrs. Kreshland replied, smiling at Laura Ann's enthusiasm. "You call the store tomorrow and I'll give you the details." And she hurried off to begin packing up.

"Oh, my God," Laura Ann squealed to Wendy. "Did you hear that? She wants to use me for a show next week!"

The two of them jumped up and down, hugging each other. Laura Ann quickly started pulling off the evening skirt and blouse to put on her own clothes.

Helena had overheard Mrs. Kreshland's conversation, and an idea came to her, but before she could act on it she saw Kabrina approach Laura Ann.

"I want to talk to you," Kabrina said angrily.

Laura Ann, putting on her socks and loafers, glanced up, and a look of fear crossed her face.

Helena quickly stepped between the two women once again. "Kabrina," she said, "I've got to talk to you, right now." She grabbed Kabrina's arm and steered her away from Laura Ann and over to a corner of the room. "Give the kid a break," she said quietly to Kabrina.

"Helena, that idiot made me a laughingstock in front of five thousand people," Kabrina protested, her eyes flashing.

"Yes, but it was an accident; this isn't Europe. She's never been on a runway before and she just froze," Helena reasoned. "Remember how it was when you first started?"

A vision of herself in Roberto's studio floated before Kabrina's eyes. "I remember—but I didn't knock anyone off a runway. Mrs. Kreshland probably thinks it was all my fault and I'm the klutz. She'll always remember me as the one who fell off the runway."

"I don't even think Mrs. Kreshland knows it happened," Helena said soothingly. "Besides, if we explain it to her before she hears it from someone else, we can smooth it over so it won't be a big deal."

"I don't know," Kabrina said dubiously. "I'd just better not ever have to see that girl again."

"Well, I've got news for you," Helena told her. "Mrs. Kreshland just booked her for her next show."

"Oh, no," Kabrina wailed. "Tell me you're kidding me!"

"Nope," Helena continued. "Which brings me to my

idea. I've got it all worked out. We explain it all to Mrs. Kreshland and offer to help Laura Ann."

"You can't be serious about helping that moron," Kabrina exclaimed darkly.

"Yes I am. You know how Mrs. Kreshland is once she gets something in her head. She likes Laura Ann and nothing is going to change her mind, so we might as well make the best of it," Helena continued. "On the one hand, it will impress Mrs. Kreshland that we want to help and on the other hand, if we teach Laura Ann to walk, she won't be knocking models off the runway."

"But Helena," Kabrina said, still not convinced, "it just doesn't seem fair that Laura Ann or whatever her name is comes out smelling like a rose."

"Come on, Kabrina," Helena said, looking over in Laura Ann's direction. "Did you see the look on her face? That girl is petrified of you. I thought she was going to disappear into the floor when you walked up to her. Besides," she continued, appealing to Kabrina's vanity, "you have the best walk of any of us. You're the one to teach her."

"Okay," Kabrina said grudgingly. "But she'd better be a fast learner. I don't want to make a career out of teaching her."

"Let's go talk to Mrs. K.," Helena said, dragging Kabrina over toward Mrs. Kreshland before she could change her mind.

"Oh, Mrs. K.," Helena called.

"Yes, Helena," Mrs. Kreshland said, turning away from her packing. "What is it?"

"Kabrina and I were thinking," Helena began, "that considering what happened to Kabrina and Laura Ann in the first sequence, it might be a good idea if we got together with Laura Ann and worked with her a bit."

"What happened in the first sequence?" Mrs. Kreshland asked, puzzled.

"Well, she froze a bit and didn't leave room for

Kabrina to pass, and Kabrina was knocked off the runway," Helena finished.

"Oh, my dear!" Mrs. Kreshland turned to Kabrina. "Are you hurt?"

"Only my pride," Kabrina said dryly. "Let's just say I provided the audience with a little extra entertainment this evening."

"These kinds of things happen to all of us at least once," Helena said, playing down the incident and smoothing things over. "It's part of the business. We'll all laugh about it in a week or two. So, anyway, we thought that perhaps we could give Laura Ann a little help so that it doesn't happen again."

"By all means," Mrs. Kreshland agreed. "I've booked Laura Ann for a show next week, provided she gets some help. You girls are so sweet. Imagine, after all that's happened, you want to help her get started. I always knew I booked the nicest girls in town for my shows!"

"Thank you, Mrs. Kreshland," Helena and Kabrina said in unison, looking at each other.

"We'd better go catch Laura Ann before she leaves," Kabrina said, looking around for Laura Ann.

"See?" Helena said as they hurried over to Laura Ann, who was making her way to the door. "I knew this was the right thing to do."

"Laura Ann," Kabrina called.

She turned around at the sound of her name. When she saw Kabrina coming toward her, her smile faded and a look of fear crossed her face.

"Kabrina," she began nervously, "I apologize, I don't know what came over me out there."

"Laura Ann, it's all right," Helena said, elbowing Kabrina.

"Yes, these things sometimes happen," Kabrina agreed, still upset.

"In a few weeks we'll all laugh about it," Helena

went on.

Kabrina looked at Helena. Don't get carried away, Helena, she thought to herself, it wasn't that funny to me.

"We were thinking," Helena said. "How would you like us to work with you a bit? We'll give you some pointers. We understand Mrs. K. has booked you for the next show."

"Would you?" Laura Ann exclaimed, her face lighting up. "I would really, really appreciate it!"

"Sure," Kabrina said resignedly. "Why not? We can meet at my apartment—say, Thursday evening about seven?"

"Thursday would be great," Laura Ann said. "I get off work at the coffee shop at five."

"Thursday night is fine for me too," Helena said.

"Okay." Kabrina took a pencil and a piece of paper out of her bag. "I'll write down the address."

Kabrina handed Laura Ann the slip of paper.

"See you guys on Thursday! Thank you so much, this is the happiest day of my entire life," Laura Ann exclaimed; then she and Wendy bounced out the door.

Kabrina watched Laura Ann disappear. "I wouldn't hold my breath waiting for that girl to become a model," she said dubiously to Helena.

"Nonsense," Helena replied optimistically. "With a little help, she'll be fine. Think positive."

"I'm going to remember those words next time some amateur knocks you off the runway," Kabrina retorted dryly.

Helena laughed and went back to her rack to organize her belongings.

Kabrina shoved her shoes and hose back into her model's bags thinking about Laura Ann and the look of happiness on her face when they told her they would help her. She remembered her own days of disappointment, walking the streets of Manhattan, trying to

340

convince someone in the fashion business to give her a chance. Only Roberto had been willing to give her that first break. Now maybe it was her turn to do someone else a favor, to help another young woman get that first break. The thought made her glow inside, and for the first time since falling off the runway, she felt like smiling.

When they reached Wendy's car, Laura Ann let out a whoop of joy. "Wendy," she exclaimed, hugging her friend, "do you realize this is my dream come true?"

"Let's go celebrate," Wendy said excitedly. "We'll get some champagne at the Vendome liquor store and have a toast!"

They stopped on the way home and picked up a bottle. As they entered their apartment, the telephone was ringing. Laura Ann ran to pick it up.

"Norris," she squealed into the receiver. "You will never guess what happened." She proceeded to tell him the whole story—how she came to model, the episode with Kabrina, her upcoming booking, and her meeting Thursday night with Kabrina and Helena—but never mentioned the other models by name.

"Laura Ann," he said after she told him everything, "that's wonderful. See, I told you that you could become a real model if you wanted to bad enough."

"Oh, Norris," she said with a catch in her voice. "I'm so happy. None of this would have ever happened if it wasn't for you."

"You always had the ability and the looks, Laura Ann," he told her modestly. "You just needed to believe in yourself. I'll stop by the coffee shop tomorrow and say hi," he told her, changing the subject. "Good night and congratulations."

"Thank you! Bye." She hung up.

On the other end of the line, Norris thoughtfully

replaced the receiver. Somewhere out there was his own daughter. Why hadn't he encouraged her as he had Laura Ann, he admonished himself sadly. Why did he drive her away? He wondered where she was; was she still in New York, or was she in some far corner of the world? All he could do was hope that she was happy.

Chapter Thirteen

Helena rapped sharply on the door of Kabrina's new apartment. It was the first time that she had been there since she had helped Kabrina move in the week before. It was a cozy little apartment that faced a flower-filled courtyard in the middle of the building. Although it came furnished with basic, uninteresting pieces, Helena could see that with a touch of Kabrina's chic Eastern style, it would become a wonderful apartment.

She was about fifteen minutes early for their appointment. "I thought I'd get here a little early so we could discuss where to begin with Laura Ann," she said when Kabrina answered the door.

"Well, we don't have to worry about teaching her self-preservation, if the way she bumped me off the runway is any indication," Kabrina quipped. "Come on in. Would you like a diet cola or some herb tea while we're waiting?"

"Diet cola's fine," Helena answered.

Kabrina poured them each a drink and they sat down in the living room.

"I think since she's booked for the show on Tuesday," Helena said thoughtfully, "we should teach her the basics of walking, showing clothes, and how to put herself together."

"That sounds like the way to go," Kabrina agreed.

"Then, a little later, we can teach her some of the ins and outs of working with a camera. I don't know, but I have a feeling she's going to be a real challenge," she added.

"Look at it this way," Helena told her with a grin. "It's your good deed for the week."

"Thanks," Kabrina responded, sipping her soda.

Just then, the doorbell rang, and Kabrina answered it.

"Hi, Laura Ann," she said, holding the door open for her. "Come on in."

She had seen a flicker of apprehension cross Laura Ann's face when she opened the door, and it melted any lingering grudges she had against Laura Ann.

"Hi, Kabrina," she exclaimed, a little timidly. She had stood with bated breath, waiting for the door to open, waiting to read the expression on Kabrina's face and listen for any threatening inflections in her voice. To her relief, Kabrina seemed genuinely friendly and pleased to see her.

Kabrina led the way into her living room. "Have a seat," she said casually. "Can I get you a soda or some herb tea?"

"Hi, Helena," Laura Ann said enthusiastically when she saw Helena. Helena had been awfully nice to her, and she was very glad to see her again. Even though Kabrina's welcome had been warm, she was still a little nervous and seeing Helena had a calming effect on her. "Soda's great," she answered in the same breath.

Kabrina brought her a diet soda, and the women began to map out a course of action.

"Laura Ann," Helena said, "we've decided that the best way to start is to get you ready for the show on Tuesday. Then, after the show's over, we'll work on other things, like polishing you, photography, things like that."

"I don't know how to ever thank you," she exclaimed. "You'll never know how much this means

344

to me, never."

Her youthful enthusiasm touched Kabrina and reminded her of herself, years before.

"Don't worry," she said, tongue in cheek. "It'll be thanks enough just to see you work the runway without knocking someone off it."

Laura Ann's face fell a bit, but she bravely smiled at the joke.

"Okay," Helena said briskly. "Time to work. Laura Ann, stand up and walk across the room for us."

Laura Ann stood and walked across the room and back. She felt a little self-conscious with the two glamorous models staring at her like an insect under a microscope, but at the same time she was so excited that it didn't matter. She was going to be a real model.

"Good," Helena said to Kabrina. "Her posture is good. That will save us some time."

"Now watch." Kabrina stood, facing Laura Ann. "See, it's almost like a dancer. Stomach in, butt tucked under. Lift your rib cage and shoulders, that's right."

She nodded approvingly as Laura Ann imitated her posture.

"Now square your shoulders, Laura Ann," Helena coaxed her. "Yes, that's right. See how you seem even taller. Just that little bit gives you a presence."

"Head up, Laura Ann," Kabrina continued. "You have to project a presence and a confident manner on the runway. You can't do it by hanging your head."

"Okay." Laura Ann nodded, trying to do everything the women told her. Stomach in, butt under, rib cage up, shoulders squared, head regal. There was so much to remember.

"Now walk casually," Kabrina commanded.

"Walk casually? You've got to be kidding," she said in mock desperation.

Her words broke the ice and the three women started laughing.

"It becomes second nature. Eventually you'll forget

345

all the steps involved," Helena laughed.

"Does it really become second nature?" she asked dubiously.

"Positively," Helena answered.

"Now try walking across the room and back," Kabrina ordered.

They watched Laura Ann walk back and forth across the room.

"That's it," Kabrina said. "That's right. Keep going until we tell you to stop. You need to establish the feel firmly in your mind. Square your shoulders. Keep your head up."

After Laura Ann had worked the room about ten times, they told her she could stop.

"Now," Helena said. "We'll work on your walk. When you walk, opposite shoulders and legs work together. That is, left shoulder and right leg and right shoulder and left leg. Let your arms hang naturally from your shoulders; don't stiffen them and they will swing naturally when you walk."

She demonstrated what she meant to Laura Ann, who watched with open admiration at the way Helena glided across the floor.

"Now you try it," Helena said.

She did her best to imitate Helena, but she couldn't help feeling clumsy. She blushed and hung her head.

"That's right," Helena said encouragingly. "Keep your palms facing inward. Good. Head up!"

"You're doing great, Laura Ann," Kabrina said when they let Laura Ann take a break.

"Are you sure?" Laura Ann asked doubtfully.

"Of course," Helena said, agreeing with Kabrina. "Now, the next thing to remember is, when you walk, you roll your foot, from your heel to the ball of your foot to your toe. Feel each step roll. Feel the control in your leg. That way, you won't clomp when you walk and your stride will be graceful and smooth. And put one foot in front of the other, just like you're walking

346

an invisible line."

"Listen to what she says," Kabrina told Laura Ann. "Helena has one of the smoothest, most graceful glides of any model I've seen."

"Well, let's not get carried away," Helena said, embarrassed at the compliment.

"It's just the truth," Kabrina insisted. "Now you try it, Laura Ann. Don't forget, roll off the ball of your foot."

Laura Ann followed their instructions, walking back and forth in the room until she thought she would drop.

"I never thought there was so much to modeling," she finally said, breathlessly. "I'm using leg muscles that I didn't even know I had."

"You've only just scratched the surface," Kabrina said. "Take a break, and we'll go on to turns."

The women sat back and chatted for a few minutes. For Laura Ann, it was like a dream come true. Not only did she have an opportunity to talk with two real models, but they were actually teaching *her* to be one too. Hardly able to contain her happiness, she had a million and one questions to ask, but she was afraid she might sound silly. Her curiosity finally overcame her shyness, however, and she asked how they got started, when and where and every other related question she could think of. They laughed at her enthusiasm.

"I just can't believe I'm really here, having two of the top models in Los Angeles helping me," she bubbled. She thought of the long months and all that she had been through. How different her life would have been had she met Kabrina and Helena instead of Marcus when she first arrived in Los Angeles, but of course she didn't tell them. Some things were best left unsaid, she thought.

"Well, we wouldn't be here teaching you if you didn't have the potential," Kabrina said.

"Do you really believe I have potential?" she asked,

347

her eyes shining.

"Of course we do, but it's more important what you think of yourself," Kabrina said. "You have to think that you're special and that you can model. If you have faith in yourself, others will have too."

Laura Ann looked at Kabrina in amazement. "I can't believe you're saying that," she said, thinking of Norris. "I have a good friend, a sort of mentor really, who told me the same thing! He's told me that all along, but it's just now sinking in!"

"Well, he's right," Kabrina said firmly. "My father used to tell me the same thing. You have to believe in yourself." She had no idea that she and Laura Ann were talking about the same person. "Who knows what I would have been doing today if I didn't have faith in myself," she said, thinking about the strength it took for her to follow her own dream of modeling seven years ago, even against her father's disapproval.

Their words took Helena back to the dark morning she'd left Seattle for her new life in Los Angeles with no encouragement save a belief in herself and the dream in her heart. Even now, in the face of all that had happened with Nicky, she firmly believed she had done the right thing.

For a few moments, no one spoke. They sat silently thinking about the course each of their lives had taken. It was in those few quiet minutes that a bond of friendship formed among them. They were three women from very different walks of life who had had many diverse experiences, but they shared a common bond: a dream and love of modeling and a belief in themselves. Helena was the first to break the silence.

"Come on, guys," she said, standing up. "Time's wasting. Okay, Laura Ann, you've had your break; now it's back to the salt mine."

Laura Ann giggled and stood up. "I wish I had discovered this salt mine earlier," she exclaimed happily.

They worked on Laura Ann's walk for another hour, teaching her how to do various turns and how to show clothes so that everyone in the audience would want them, by emphasizing a pocket or a skirt. There was so much to learn that they couldn't possibly teach Laura Ann in one evening, so they made plans to meet again the next night and continue.

By the time Laura Ann was ready to leave, her head was swimming with modeling techniques. She and Helena left together.

"Don't forget to practice between now and tomorrow night," Helena called to her as she got into her car.

"I won't forget." She waved good-bye. "And thank you again!"

"You're welcome."

It had been a good evening, and for the first time since her conversation with Nicky, Helena had been able to forget her heartache for a few hours. She smiled at Laura Ann's enthusiasm, and she was happy to help her.

The evening had been beneficial for Kabrina, too. In the past few weeks since she and Helena had become fast friends, and now with her developing friendship with Laura Ann, her outlook on life had changed. Even the shocking end to her relationship with Noel couldn't dampen her new attitude. She had kept such a thick wall around herself for so long that she had forgotten how much she missed having close friends to confide in. Just laughing and being frivolous with girlfriends left her in a buoyant mood, and helping Laura Ann get started gave her a warm glow inside. The thought came to her that maybe Laura Ann was helping her more than she was helping Laura Ann.

Laura Ann was on top of the world. She could hardly wait to tell Wendy and Norris about her evening. *Thank you, God,* she prayed. *I'm so happy!* She fairly danced around the room when she arrived home. Norris called in the middle of her conversation with Wendy, and she had to start her story all over again. She told him every detail of the evening, except the names of the models that were helping her. Somehow, it just didn't seem important to mention their names, so Norris had no idea that one of the "good samaritans" was his own daughter, Kabrina.

Laura Ann moved through the next day in exuberant spirits. Always known for her cheerful nature, she was beyond cheerful.

"You must have a new boyfriend," Sam asked her drolly. "Something's making you mighty sparkly."

She laughed, but kept her good news to herself. There would be time enough to tell people after she really did a show, like a real model.

After work, she rushed home to practice before her next lesson with Helena and Kabrina. She tried to remember every single thing they had told her, and she practiced over and over until it was time to go.

At Kabrina's apartment, the three women reviewed the lessons from the night before. Laura Ann walked for Kabrina and Helena, and they worked to smooth her stride and her turns.

"Keep your head up when you turn," Kabrina instructed Laura Ann. "If you look down, you'll lose your balance. Keep your head high and your weight in your back leg as you go into your turn!"

Over and over again, Laura Ann turned until she was dizzy. She did half turns and full turns, one-and-a-half turns and Double Diors.

"Let me sit down for a minute," she finally exclaimed, dizzy and exhausted.

"Okay," Kabrina said. "But only for a minute. You've got much more to learn. In the meantime, I'll make us some tea."

She hurried into her little kitchen and popped three mugs with spearmint tea bags into the microwave oven. In less than two minutes, she was carrying them into the living room.

"You know, I don't even miss the mansion in Bel Air," she said, referring to Noel's house.

"Goes to show you that all that glitters isn't gold," Helena said, quoting the old adage.

"You mean you used to live in a mansion in Bel Air?" Laura Ann said in awe.

"Well, I did until I learned it wasn't worth the price I had to pay," Kabrina said, then briefly outlined the story of her relationship with Noel. "So you see," she finished flippantly, "by the time he finished dancing around in my lingerie with that transsexual and I found out he was into drugs I decided it was time for me to find other living accommodations."

Laura Ann was silent for a few minutes. Kabrina's story reminded her all too much of her own recent experiences. Out on the streets, transsexuals were not all that uncommon. In fact, she had met several. And she knew all too well the lure of drugs.

"I feel sorry for your doctor friend," she said quietly. "His life must be such a horror, having to lie and cover up all the time and not having the strength to leave drugs alone. It's like being caught in a whirlpool and sucked down, faster and faster with no escape." Her voice drifted off. "No one to turn to."

Kabrina and Helena looked at her curiously.

"You almost sound like you're talking from firsthand experience," Helena said.

"No," she replied quickly. "I—I just imagined that's how it would be."

"You're very street smart for someone so young," Kabrina mused. She thought about the desperation and fear on Noel's face that last time she had seen him, and for the first time, she softened and felt compassion toward him. "Yes, I think you're right. It must have been like a whirlpool pulling him down. Let's hope he finds a lifeline within himself, 'cause it sure ain't gonna be me," she finished pragmatically.

"Back to work, girls," Helena said, breaking the

mood. "It's time to teach you how to do your hair and makeup."

"That will have to be your jurisdiction, Helena," Kabrina smiled. "I'm afraid my experience with hair and makeup won't help Laura Ann unless she wants to look like a brownie pie."

They all laughed and then Helena showed Laura Ann how to do her hair and makeup.

"The important thing is to show the clothes to their best advantage," she explained. "So you can't wear your hair down, or it will cover up the neckline of the clothes."

She pulled out hairpins and a brush and showed Laura Ann how to style her hair into a chic chignon.

"Look what a difference it makes already," Kabrina exclaimed, holding up a hand mirror. "You have great cheekbones under all that hair!"

Then Helena gave her lessons on applying makeup for the runway. "You have to remember that the spotlights will wash everything out, so you have to apply extra heavy makeup." With a few deft strokes, she showed Laura Ann how to bring out her bone structure and emphasize her big blue eyes.

"See what a difference a little makeup makes? It will look great under stage lights. Of course, in natural light you'd look like a hooker," she laughed.

Laura Ann winced at the words, but still managed to laugh with Kabrina and Helena. She had no intention of telling anyone about her past. It would be forgotten forever.

Time passed very quickly and before the women realized it, the clock was striking midnight.

"I'm sorry," Helena said, yawning. "I've got to go. I've got an early morning booking and I have to get my sleep."

"Me, too," Laura Ann agreed. "I have to work all day at the coffee shop. Saturday is always a busy day."

"Hey, look," Kabrina said, "I've got an idea. I have to run errands all morning, too. Why don't Helena and I meet you at the coffee shop at lunchtime, and maybe you can take a break and we'll all have coffee together!"

"Sounds fine to me," Helena agreed. "Jaimie has some family thing tomorrow, so I won't be seeing him."

"Sure," Laura Ann said. "I'll wait until you guys come before I take a break.

Helena and Kabrina arrived at the Sunset Boulevard coffee shop at the same time. The hostess showed them to a booth in the back. Laura Ann was just finishing up two tables when they got there, and she motioned to them that she would be there as soon as she could. They saw Wendy bustling back and forth, and she gave them a cheery wave, too.

A few minutes later, Laura Ann joined them, carrying three steaming cups of coffee, and plopped down next to Kabrina. She handed them the coffee and tucked a stray wisp of hair behind her ear.

"Whew," she said, taking a deep breath. "This is the first break I've had since I got here five hours ago. All of Los Angeles must go out for breakfast and lunch on Saturdays!"

"I don't know how you do it," Helena marveled. "I know I couldn't keep up a pace like you do for five hours."

"You get used to it after a while," Laura Ann answered. "How was your booking this morning?"

"Oh, it was fine," Helena replied. "It was just a little breakfast show at Neiman Marcus in Beverly Hills. It was in their Club Room. The fashion coordinator there is so nice. After you've gotten a few shows under your belt, you should go see her."

Laura Ann could hardly imagine herself really working for a prestigious store like Neiman Marcus.

But then, she thought to herself, I couldn't imagine ever being able to work as a model, either. So who knows . . .

"I practiced a little with my hair and makeup before coming to work this morning," she told them proudly.

"Good for you," Kabrina said encouragingly. "I think we should have one more run-through before the show."

"I think so, too," Helena agreed as she sipped her coffee.

"Do you think we could?" Laura Ann asked. "I was hoping we could, but I didn't want you to think I was taking advantage of you both."

"No, you're not. In fact, the better you are, the better the reflection on Helena and me," Kabrina explained.

"How about Monday night?" Helena checked her appointment book. "That way you'll be fresh for Tuesday's show."

"Monday night's fine," Laura Ann confirmed. "What about you, Kabrina?"

"No problem," Kabrina confirmed.

"Good," Helena said. "Why don't you both come to my apartment this time? Laura Ann, I'll write down the address for you."

"Terrific. I'd better get back to work," she said, pocketing Helena's address. "I was hoping that a friend of mine was going to stop by. I wanted both of you to meet him, but I guess he got caught up doing something."

Norris had said that he might stop by, and Laura Ann was eager to have him meet her new friends.

"Next time," Kabrina said, collecting her purse and rising.

They gave Laura Ann a quick hug, waved to Wendy, who was still rushing back and forth from tables to kitchen, and left the coffee shop.

"How are things going with Jaimie?" Kabrina asked as they were walking to their cars.

"Oh," Helena said, shrugging her shoulders, "about the same. You know, I really care for him, but he's driving me crazy with his possessiveness. He listens to my telephone conversations and reads my mail; he even plays back the messages on my answering machine. You wouldn't believe it!"

"Oh, yes, I would," said Kabrina rolling her eyes. "You forget I lived with you for two weeks. The man is crazy in love with you."

Helena blushed at Kabrina's words and tried to think of something clever to say, but she couldn't think of anything. Jaimie had been so sweet and supportive about Nicky that Helena felt guilty even complaining about his claustrophobic attentiveness and selfishness. The truth was that the closer Jaimie was getting to her, the farther she was backing away. The time was coming when she was going to have to make the difficult decision to break up with him, but she wasn't ready to do it yet.

Helena waved good-bye to her as Kabrina jumped into her Porsche, and an old Buick pulled into the parking lot and waited patiently for Kabrina to back out.

Norris drummed his fingers on the steering wheel in time to the radio as he watched a sleek white Porsche 944 pull out of its space. He admired its streamlined body and thought a girl was driving it, but it was impossible to tell for sure through the darkly tinted glass. A very pretty white girl was just getting into a midnight blue BMW convertible, and she waved gaily at the Porsche.

Kabrina zipped out, and with a honk of her horn and a final wave, she disappeared down Sunset Boulevard. Helena also pulled out of the parking lot. Behind her, the old Buick took the space left by Kabrina, and Norris got out of the car and went into the coffee shop.

"Oh, you just missed my friends," Laura Ann cried when she saw him. She hurried to a window and looked

355

out to see if they were still there, but both women had already left.

"I'll just have to meet them another time, I guess," Norris said casually. "In the meantime, I think a little apple pie à la mode and coffee might hit the spot."

Helena pulled off to the side of Sunset and took the top down on her Beemer. It was a glorious day, the perfect day to sit and relax and formulate some ideas about writing. Jaimie had plans with Donna, and she wouldn't see him until Monday. Lately he had occupied so much of her time that it was becoming a full-time job just to entertain him. It seemed like she never had any time to herself anymore. She turned down Doheny and then rounded the corner onto her street. As she pulled up in front of her fourplex, she noticed with irritation Jaimie's white Rolls Royce. Jaimie was standing on the sidewalk in front of the apartment building, pacing.

"Where have you been?" he demanded as she stepped out of her car.

"I had a booking." She tried to conceal her irritation. He always seemed to be giving her the third degree.

"That was this morning," he persisted. "What have you been doing all afternoon?"

"I met Kabrina and Laura Ann for coffee. I thought you were spending the day with Donna," she said, still trying to control her anger.

"I was able to get away for a few hours, and I've been standing around here twiddling my thumbs for the past half hour," he said peevishly. "You should have come straight home. You know I always like to know where I can reach you at all times."

"Jaimie," Helena said, punctuating his name with irritation, "I had no idea you were coming over, and I made plans of my own."

"Open the door," he grumbled, tossing aside her

356

explanations. "I left my key at home."

Exasperated and angry, Helena unlocked her front door without a comment. Once he was inside, Jaimie pulled her to him. "I know what you want," he said huskily.

She was in no mood for lovemaking and what she wanted was a little time to herself.

"Would you like some coffee?" she asked him, playing for time. "It's such a lazy day that I thought I'd just relax and try to make a start on my writing."

"Writing!" he exploded. "I take all the chances, I break my neck to get over here so I can spend a few hours with you, and you want to write! Do it on your own time, when I'm not here!"

"This was my own time," she retorted coldly, unable to hide her anger any longer. "You said you wouldn't see me today."

"Well, my plans got changed. I would have thought you'd want to see me any chance you got," he sputtered, looking hurt. Guilt always worked, he thought to himself. She'd fall right into line. He was so positive of that that he was shocked when Helena didn't.

"I'm sorry," she said firmly. "Of course I always want to see you, but I really want to write this afternoon."

"You'd rather write than fuck?" he asked incredulously.

"Jaimie," she patiently explained, "I'm not in the mood. I want to write." It was the first time she had ever refused him.

"You should always be in the mood," he scolded her as one would a child, pacing around the apartment and waving his arms in the air. "My even touching your shoulder, or, or . . . your nose, should put you in the mood!"

"Well, I'm not," she said flatly. She also wasn't in the mood to be tactful any longer.

"Well, maybe I should just leave then," he said,

watching her closely to see her reaction. He was sure that threat would bring her begging for forgiveness. It was beyond his comprehension that Helena would not want to make love or be with him. He knew he wanted to spend every second of the day with her; of course she had to feel the same way.

"I think that's probably a good idea," she agreed. Although he made her feel guilty, she was now more determined to spend the afternoon the way she had planned. "I'll see you on Monday." She gave him a hug and a kiss.

Jaimie didn't respond; he couldn't believe what he was hearing. Now he had painted himself into a corner and he had no choice but to leave. He quickly turned on his heel and started for the door. "I'll give you one last chance to change your mind," he said as he opened the door. "You know you'll miss me as soon as I'm gone. You always have fun with me." He looked at her hopefully.

Helena almost caved in. She did always have fun with Jaimie, and she knew his feelings were hurt. But no, her mind was made up. "See you on Monday, Jaimie," she said firmly.

He scowled and slammed the door behind him. Stubborn brat, he thought. *Now* what was he going to do with his afternoon? He couldn't go home, because Donna would be suspicious; he had told her that he had a meeting that would last all afternoon. Then an idea came to him. He'd go girl hunting. That would fix Helena. He'd show her that she wasn't irreplaceable. In Beverly Hills, pretty girls were a dime a dozen. He started up Burton Way and turned left on Canon Drive. Sure enough, everywhere he looked there were gorgeous women; but somehow he discovered that he really wasn't in the mood. It took a certain zing to get the old patter going to pick up a girl, and he just didn't feel zingy. He decided to stop at the Brighton Way Café and have a cup of coffee. Perhaps some of his friends were there. After a cup of coffee, maybe he'd feel more like the old hunter on the prowl.

Helena watched him drive off, feeling both relieved and sad at the same time—relieved because now she had the freedom to spend the afternoon any way she wanted, and sad because she knew that the time for her and Jaimie to go their separate ways was slowly drawing near. She wished that things could be different—that he was free, or that his money didn't mean so much to him that he was unwilling to lose half in a divorce, or that she was the kind of person that could be satisfied with half a relationship. All of these things crossed her mind, along with her ultimate wish: for Nicky to be here with her and happy.

"It doesn't look like any of those wishes are coming true," she said sadly out loud. She sat down at her dining room table and began to jot down some ideas to take her mind off the unhappiness in her personal life.

Then Jaimie called. "I wasn't going to call you," he said after Helena said hello, "but I figured you were probably missing me and you were sorry you were so mean to me."

She felt a rush of affection for Jaimie. He was such a character and he was adorable—sometimes. Other times, he was the most frustrating person she had ever met. He had the unique ability to test the limits of her anger and then turn around and win her back with his boyish charm. "You're right," she said. "I am missing you."

"Good, I knew you were," he said, feeling macho and in control again. "I can stop by for about five minutes on the way home. We won't be able to do anything but talk, though, because I have to be home promptly at five."

"Okay." That was fine with her, because she didn't have any intention of doing anything but talk.

"See you soon, baby," he said, hanging up.

All the way to Helena's apartment, Jaimie debated

with himself whether to make up a story about what he did all afternoon to punish her or just to let it go. He finally decided to wait and see how she acted. If she was happy to see him, then maybe he wouldn't try to make her jealous. If the truth were known, all he did was mope around the Brighton Way Coffee Shop and count off the minutes until a decent amount of time had passed so he could call her.

She greeted him with a warm hug. She was glad to see him. She had gotten some writing accomplished, but at the same time, she was a little lonely. Then she started thinking about Nicky and all that had happened. She missed him terribly. There had to be a way to regain his love.

"Jaimie," she asked after they had settled back on the couch in her living room. "What shall I do about Nicky? Do you think that if I call him, he'll talk to me?"

"Kyle told you that he'd have a talk with him," he said. "Why don't you give him a call? I don't believe he really hates you. He's just upset by the divorce and he needed to strike back at someone. You're the one who moved away and took him away from everything familiar to him, so that's why you're getting the brunt of things. If Kyle had been the one to move, Nicky would have blamed him. Now that you've given him a little time to think and calm down, he'll talk."

Helena was eager to talk to her little boy, but at the same time she dreaded it. What if Jaimie was wrong? What if Nicky screamed that he hated her again? She didn't think she could take it a second time. She picked up the phone and put it down again over and over trying to get up the nerve to dial Seattle.

"What if he won't talk?" she asked fearfully.

"Then you try again another time," he said. "Helena you never give up and you never stop trying in life. The moment you do, you're dead."

In the end, Jaimie grabbed the phone and dialed the number. "Here," he said, handing her the phone when he heard it ringing. "Now talk! Nothing heavy, though. Just light stuff."

She said a silent prayer while the phone rang. Just as she was going to hang up, someone finally answered.

"Hello?"

Helena's heart skipped a beat. "Hi, pumpkin," she said. There was a lump in her throat and she swallowed hard. "How are you?"

There was a brief pause before Nicky answered her. It was like an eternity to Helena. Would it be a repeat of her last conversation with him?

"Fine, Mommy," he finally answered.

She took a deep breath. So far, so good, she thought. She asked him what he'd been doing—had he been seeing his friends, had he been to the Woodland Park Zoo, where she used to take him, was he ready for school—every question she could think of except the one she really wanted to ask: Did he love her? But she took Jaimie's advice and kept the conversation light. She wanted to stay on the phone forever, to keep the sound of his voice captured in the receiver and imprinted forever in her heart. But finally, in the background, she heard her ex-husband's voice asking Nicky who he was talking to.

"Mommy," she heard Nicky answer.

"Let me talk to Mommy," she heard Kyle say.

No, no, she wanted to cry out. Just let me talk to Nicky a little longer. But instead, she calmly asked her son to put his daddy on.

"See?" Kyle said. "I told you that I'd talk to him for you. Just take things easy and everything will be all right."

She hated the condescending tone in his voice. But she didn't want to chance offending him for fear he would poison Nicky against her even more.

"Gotta go now," he was saying. "Why don't you call back in a week or so."

Helena heard a click before she had a chance to

answer, and she slammed the receiver back in its cradle.

"Stay calm," Jaimie said soothingly. "Things are going just right. You had a nice conversation with Nicky. Next time you'll have an even better one. One step at a time, baby."

"I know you're right," she confessed. "But it's just so hard. There's so much I want to tell him. It just isn't fair."

"Who said life was fair?" he said. "There's nothing fair about life. You have to make your own breaks in this world. Don't forget that!"

"I know," she agreed, taking a deep breath.

"Look, I gotta go." He stood. "Give me a kiss and I'll see you on Monday."

She kissed him. "Thanks for coming back and cheering me up," she said sincerely.

Jaimie melted as he looked at her. He was so crazy about her. He tweaked her chin. "Chin up, princess. Everything is going to be fine."

"I know," she sighed and gave him a little smile. It was times like these that she couldn't imagine her life without Jaimie; and yet . . .

Helena spent Monday with Jaimie. He was extra sweet and did his best to put her in a cheerful mood, but her situation with Nicky, coupled with her slowly evolving decision to break up with Jaimie, kept her in a subdued mood.

She was still depressed when Kabrina and Laura Ann arrived that night at her apartment, but she hid her feelings from them. The three of them reviewed everything they had taught Laura Ann up to that point. Although her movements weren't as smooth as Helena's or as stylistic as Kabrina's, they were passable. She had practiced on her hair and makeup over the weekend, and there was a dramatic improvement in her look.

"What you eventually need to invest in," Kabrina said, "are shoes and jewelry."

"Kabrina's right," Helena agreed. "For the show on Tuesday, we'll share our shoes with you, but for the future you'll need to purchase a whole basic wardrobe of various types of pumps and flats, daytime and evening shoes. You'll also need a selection of earrings," she continued. She went into her bedroom and returned with a fishing tackle box.

Laura Ann wondered what she was doing with a tackle box—it was incongruous with her impressions of Helena—but she didn't say anything.

Helena opened the box, which turned out to be filled with earrings, each pair arranged in its own little compartment.

"I've found that it's easier for me to keep my earrings in this tackle box," Helena explained. "Other models keep their jewelry in jewelry rolls or whatever."

"Yes," confirmed Kabrina. "I keep mine in a jewelry roll. It's whatever you feel most comfortable with. When I modeled in Europe and New York, we hardly ever had to bring our own jewelry or shoes," Kabrina added. "They were always furnished for us."

"I wish things were like that here," Helena said. "I spend a fortune each season on shoes and accessories! Which reminds me: Laura Ann, what you do need for tomorrow is a selection of pantyhose: nude, black, sheer, black opaque, white sheer, white opaque, taupe, and bone. And you also need a half slip."

"I didn't realize models had to bring so many things of their own to bookings," Laura Ann marveled.

"I know," Helena agreed. "Most people think models just show up and walk. There's a lot more involved."

"You have to develop your own fashion sense and keep up with current fashion trends, too," Kabrina added. "I can't tell you the number of people who come up to me and ask me fashion questions, like what will be in style next season or what should they wear with a particular outfit. People just take it for granted that

363

models know everything there is to know about fashion."

"They'll be in for a rude awakening if they ask me," Laura Ann giggled. "I'm lucky if I can put the right T-shirt with the right pair of jeans."

"Don't kid yourself," Kabrina smiled. "You pick up fashion information almost by osmosis. Just being around fashionable people and doing fashion shows, you automatically begin to develop a fashion sense."

"That's another thing," Helena pointed out. "Start subscribing to at least one fashion magazine and read it faithfully each month. That way you'll keep on top of what's happening in the fashion world."

They chatted on for another forty-five minutes, until Laura Ann got up. "I have to leave," she said, stifling a yawn. "I have to work the morning shift, then run out and buy pantyhose before the show."

She gave Kabrina and Helena each a hug. "I can't begin to tell you how much it means to me to have the two of you take the time to work with me. You both are so warm and down-to-earth. I never thought about models being so friendly. I always had the impression they were sort of cool and aloof."

"Don't even give it a second thought," Kabrina smiled. "Call it an act of self-preservation."

Laura Ann blushed and hung her head. She knew Kabrina was teasing her about the runway incident, but now that she knew her better, she knew that Kabrina had truly forgiven her.

"See you tomorrow," she said, gathering up her jacket.

Helena walked her to the door. "Just remember what you've learned and you'll do great. Kabrina and I will be there, too, to give you any help you need."

"Thanks again," Laura Ann smiled as Helena shut the door behind her.

Helena walked back into the living room, where Kabrina was getting ready to leave.

"Well, what do you think?" Kabrina asked. "You think she's going to be all right?"

"Yeah," Helena nodded. "I think with a little more polishing she'll be just fine."

"She's a nice girl," Kabrina mused. "Street smart, too. I'll bet she didn't learn that in Iowa."

"Who knows?" Helena shrugged. "Los Angeles is one of those cities where you grow up real fast or you don't grow up at all."

"Speaking of growing up," Kabrina said, "have you heard from Nicky?"

Helena's expression clouded over. "As a matter of fact, I have. I talked to him briefly on Saturday," she said quietly. "Not a long conversation or anything important; but it was a start."

"How was he?" Kabrina didn't want to push or bring up sad memories for Helena, but Helena was her closest friend and she cared about her.

"Guarded. But at least he didn't tell me he hated me again," she answered ruefully.

"See, things are looking up already," Kabrina quipped, trying to lighten Helena's mood. Then she changed the subject. "What about your writing? Did you work on it Saturday afternoon, like you planned?"

"I did a little, but Jaimie showed up and I didn't get too much done."

"I thought you said he had some family thing to attend."

"He did," Helena explained. "But he told Donna he had an important meeting to go to and just left."

"Doesn't that woman ever become suspicious?" Kabrina wondered. "Jaimie spends more time with you than he does at his own home."

"I don't know," Helena answered. "The two of them have lived with Jaimie's promiscuity for a long time; maybe they've just adjusted to it over the years. Maybe Donna fools around, too."

"I would if I were her," Kabrina said definitely.

"I would, too," she agreed slowly. "You know, Kabrina, I've been thinking that it may be time for me to move on, too."

Kabrina looked at Helena curiously. "You're thinking of breaking up with Jaimie?"

She nodded. "His situation is never going to change. He's never going to leave Donna, and I don't want to be someone's mistress for the rest of my life. I have my own future to think about. He loves me now, but what happens when he meets someone younger and prettier than me? You know, Donna looks an awful lot like me, Kabrina," she continued. "I will have devoted all my time to him and I'll have nothing to show for my life.

"I'm not insecure about getting older, either; that's not the point. The point is that I left one situation in Seattle that was wrong for me and now I'm involved in another. I came down here because I believed in myself and to follow a dream. So far, it's cost me my son, but I still believe in my heart that I did the right thing. Happiness and strength come from within. Other people can't make us happy or give us strength. I couldn't have stayed in Seattle, even if it meant having Nicky with me, any more than I can stay with Jaimie and neglect my dreams.

"Does any of this make sense to you, or does it just sound like I'm rambling on?"

"It makes perfect sense to me," Kabrina answered. "You forget, I left my father and the only life I'd ever known to model, and I've never regretted it either. I had a belief in myself, too. I've always felt that you have one life to live and you have an obligation to yourself to make the most out of it."

"Who said life was fun?" Helena demanded jokingly, breaking the somber mood.

"Not me," Kabrina smiled as she picked up her purse and walked to the door. "Even though I keep trying to convince myself that it is!"

*   *   *

366

Mrs. Kreshland's fashion show went relatively smoothly the next day. Mrs. Kreshland had put together the lineup so that Laura Ann was between Helena and Kabrina for most of the segments. Only once did she have to work the runway alone. She shook uncontrollably, but she remembered what Kabrina and Helena had taught her and made it down the runway and back again without any mishaps. She even managed a full turn at the end of the runway, though she forgot to keep her head high and lost her balance a little in the middle of the turn.

Kabrina and Helena talked her through each segment when they doubled with her and reminded her of all the little things they had shown her, like emphasizing a waistline, using her pockets, and addressing the audience before leaving the runway. All in all, Laura Ann did a good job. Such a good job, in fact, that Mrs. Kreshland booked her for another show.

After the show, as the three women were leaving, Mel Stephens—Mr. Mel, as he liked to be called, the fashion director from Sak's Fifth Avenue—came up to them and introduced himself. Tall and thin, he was impeccably dressed and sported a neatly trimmed salt-and-pepper beard, which he had an unconscious habit of stroking.

"What agency are you with?" he asked Laura Ann.

"Well—" she stammered, unsure of how to answer. She was afraid that if she told him she wasn't with an agency that he'd immediately dismiss her.

"Laura Ann's new in town, Mr. Mel," Kabrina broke in. "She hasn't signed with an agency yet."

"Do you have a composite with your home phone number on it?" he persisted, stroking his beard.

"Her new composites are at the printer," Helena said glibly. "But why don't you just write down your phone number, Laura Ann, and then you can call when your photos are ready."

"That would do just fine," Mel said. "I've got some

367

shows coming up that I'd like to book you for."

"Thank you," Laura Ann answered. She was excited by his words, but she managed to keep her poise. She wrote down her phone number and gave it to Mr. Mel.

"See? You've got your start!" Helena exclaimed after Mr. Mel walked off.

"I can't believe it," Laura Ann cried happily.

"Well, believe it," Kabrina said, holding the door for the other two. "Obviously we have to get a few pictures together, and then we will set up appointments for you with our agents."

They walked down the street and paused next to Laura Ann's car to continue the conversation.

"I've got a friend, Dakota DeForest, who owes me a favor," Helena said, adjusting her bags on her shoulders. "I'll bet I can get him to take some pictures of you for just the cost of the film."

"That's perfect," Kabrina exclaimed.

Laura Ann was silent, remembering Flash's studio in East Los Angeles, where her nightmares began. It had only been a little over a year ago, but it seemed like a lifetime.

"Is something wrong?" Helena asked, noticing the look on Laura Ann's face.

She hesitated a minute. "No, that would be great," she answered. "I really don't know how to thank both of you, that's all." Her life of a year ago no longer existed, so there was no need to be afraid. She was a different person now and her new life was just beginning.

"I'll call him when I get home and let you know what he says," Helena said enthusiastically.

"In the meantime, Laura Ann," Kabrina instructed her, "I want you to get four or five fashion magazines and go through them. Look at the way the models pose—their expressions, body movements, makeup and hair. Then I want you to practice their expressions and body poses in the mirror. Really look at your face,

368

get to know which angles are best for you. You got that?"

Laura Ann nodded intently.

"Then sometime in the next few days, I'll work with you on photography," she finished, "so you'll be ready when Helena sets up your photo shoot."

"That would be terrific," Laura Ann exclaimed, getting into Wendy's car, which she had borrowed. "Do you really think an agency would take me?" she asked shyly.

"With the right pictures, sure," Helena answered without hesitation. "We'll vouch for you, too; that will help. I'll call you and let you know what Dakota says."

"And we'll get together soon to practice," Kabrina promised.

"Bye," Laura Ann called as she pulled out of her parking space.

"You know," Kabrina said, "I really like her. She's a nice girl."

"Yes, she is," Helena said.

The two women walked down the street to where they had parked their cars. As they started to walk across the lot, a man jumped out of a silver Jaguar and accidentally bumped Helena, knocking one of her bags off her shoulder onto the ground.

"I'm sorry! Are you all right?" he apologized, bending to retrieve her bag without really looking at her. He picked up the bag and handed it to Helena, looking at her for the first time.

"Helena?" he asked in surprise. "Helena Sinclair, how are you!"

She looked up at the man in surprise and then gave him a smile.

"Richard, hi," she said. "I'm fine, thanks. It's so good to see you."

"It's good to see you, too. You look as beautiful as ever." He grinned, looking at her appreciatively.

"And you're as charming as ever," she tossed back at

369

him. "This is my friend, Kabrina Hunter. Kabrina, Richard Rosenfeld."

"It's nice to meet you, Kabrina," he said, politely holding out his hands, but his eyes were fixed on Helena.

They stood there silently looking at each other, and Kabrina could feel the electricity between them, almost feeling like an intruder.

Finally Richard spoke. "So how have you been?" he asked again, mesmerized by Helena.

"Fine, fine," she said, smiling.

They've already covered that ground, Kabrina thought to herself. Time to come up with some new material, guys. And Richard did.

"Ah, how's our friend Jaimie Cramer?" he asked, suddenly remembering his last meeting in France with Jaimie.

"Ah, well, he's fine," Helena admitted. "Look, Richard, I'm sorry I didn't explain to you that I was seeing Jaimie. It wasn't right and I'm sorry."

"That's all right," he said. He'd had a couple of months to cool off, and he had forgotten how attracted he'd been to Helena. "I'm a big boy. So," he continued, deciding how to handle the situation. He wanted to take Helena out again, but if she was still seriously involved with Jaimie Cramer, there was no use wasting his time. Besides, he didn't believe in sneaking behind someone's back. "If your situation changes with Jaimie, why don't you give me a call?"

"Okay," she said, still smiling at him. She had forgotten how handsome she had thought he was.

"Let me give you a business card." He rummaged through his pockets. "Here, it has both my office and my home numbers on it. Call anytime."

"I will," she promised, taking his card and dropping it in her purse, then holding out her hand. "It was really good to see you again."

"Yes," he said, taking her hand in his. He really

didn't want to let it go. It was soft and warm, with long, graceful fingers and carefully manicured nails.

"Bye," she said, walking off.

Kabrina followed her. "It was nice meeting you, Richard," she called over her shoulder.

"You too," he answered, walking off in the other direction.

"Who was that?" Kabrina exclaimed when they were out of earshot.

"Someone I met in France this summer," Helena said with forced casualness.

"Well, I hate to be cruel, but why would you keep dating a married man when you've got someone like that dying to go out with you?" Kabrina asked in blunt astonishment. "I mean, Jaimie's nice and he has been very supportive of me; but good God, Helena, he's married and he always will be. His kind always is!"

"Richard wasn't all that interested in me," Helena said, brushing off Kabrina's remarks. "Do you think?"

"Helena, the man was mesmerized by you," Kabrina exclaimed in exasperation. "I'm lucky he even noticed that there was someone else with you!"

"Oh, Kabrina, he was not," Helena argued. If only it were true, she thought to herself.

"Well, all I can say is that you'd better not lose that card," Kabrina said as they reached Helena's car.

"Oh, I won't." She hugged Kabrina goodbye. "Talk to you later."

"Bye."

Helena's thoughts drifted back to the dates she had had with Richard in the south of France. There had been a definite attraction even then. She remembered how disappointed she was when Jaimie told her he had spoken to Richard and told him she was his girlfriend. No, she thought, she wouldn't lose his card a second time.

When she pulled up in front of her apartment house, she saw that Jaimie was already there. He had let

371

himself in with his key and was sitting on her couch drinking a club soda.

"Where have you been?" he demanded angrily.

"I told you yesterday that I had a booking today," she said, dropping her bags on the floor. She resented being under his thumb all the time.

"Yes, but the show should have been over earlier," he complained. "What took you so long?"

"Jaimie, I can't predict exactly how long a show will last. What would you like me to do, walk out in the middle of it?" she said facetiously.

"What I think you should do is to only take bookings that don't interfere with the time I spend with you," he grumbled.

"I can't do that!" Helena exploded. "This is my livelihood! How do you expect me to support myself?"

"I told you; *I'm* your livelihood. I'll give you money not to work."

She was furious. They'd had this conversation over and over again, and she wasn't about to allow him to support her. Then she'd be at his beck and call twenty-four hours a day.

"I don't even want to discuss it," she told him, beside herself with anger. "And another thing: I'm going to write tomorrow afternoon, so I won't be able to see you."

Jaimie hit the ceiling. He was so angry he couldn't think straight. "You're *what?*"

"I'm writing tomorrow afternoon," she said, her mind made up.

"You'll write at night, not during *my* time." His eyes flashed in anger, but he saw the stubborn set of her jaw and it was like a challenge. He decided to take another tack. "It's too bad that we don't place the same importance on our relationship," he sniffed with injured pride. "I always arrange my schedule around my afternoons with you. Nothing keeps me from being with you. Even if I have an important meeting, I make

372

sure it doesn't interfere with you. That's because I love you and you're the most important person in the world to me."

"Jaimie, I love you too, and you're very important to me too," she protested, thinking how he always made her feel like she was in the wrong. At the same time, she thought about Jaimie's wife, and she was torn between her anger and her need to prove she cared about him.

"It's so difficult for me," he continued with a martyred whine. "I have to go home each night to a situation that I don't want any part of. I have to pretend while all the while my heart longs to be with you. Donna begs me to sleep with her, but I can't do it. All I can think about is you. I know she must wonder"—he dropped his eyes to the floor in a gesture of hopeless unrequited love—"but I can't help myself; I only want you."

"I'm sorry, Jaimie," she sighed in defeat.

It felt good to be in control again, Jaimie thought. There's no way she was going to control this relationship. He kept his eyes cast down at the floor. Now he'd reel her in slowly. Then he happened to glance at her purse and he noticed a business card sticking out of one corner.

"What's this?" he said curiously, grabbing the card and reading it. "Richard Rosenfeld," he boomed, forgetting his plan and his tone. "Oh, and how's ole Richard these days?"

"I just ran into him in the parking lot this afternoon."

"Oh, really," he said jealously. "And he just happened to give you his business card."

Helena nodded. "Yes."

"And did he just happen to ask about me or just happen to ask if you'd like to go out?" he continued sarcastically. "Or maybe, if you'd just happen to like to fuck!" He threw his hands into the air dramatically, and the business card fluttered, unnoticed, to the carpet.

373

Helena couldn't help but smile at his antics. "I told him I was still seeing you."

"Oh, that was big of you," he sneered, but she knew he was joking. "Why don't you throw the dog a bone. I'm like your dog, you know, waiting around wagging my tail hoping you'll give me a little pat on the head."

"Jaimie, stop that," she laughed.

"Come on," he said, heading toward the bedroom. Timing was everything, he thought to himself. "I want a little pat on the head." Arguing with Helena always made him want her more.

"Okay, okay," she said, giving in.

As she followed him to the bedroom, Helena bent down and surreptitiously picked up Richard's business card and pocketed it.

Chapter Fourteen

Kabrina met with Laura Ann at the apartment she shared with Wendy above Sunset Boulevard. Compact and a bit shabby, it was nonetheless comfortable and homey, reminding Kabrina of the little cottage she had grown up in, high atop Nichols Canyon.

Laura Ann had done her homework well. She had purchased all the current issues of the top fashion magazines—*Harper's Bazaar, Vogue,* and *Glamour*—and several others, and diligently studied the many pages of photography models. Now Kabrina reviewed them all with her.

"Naturalness is the key," Kabrina told her. "Everything is loose and relaxed. It's almost like a graceful ballet with the camera. Pose and click, pose and click. There's no need for big, abrupt movements; little movements will show up on the contact sheets. Sometimes the perfect shot is only a minute movement away. If you've made some grand gesture change, that perfect shot is lost forever."

They worked with angles and lighting, Kabrina showing Laura Ann how the right lighting on her face would bring out her bone structure or hide lines and flaws. She demonstrated how to pose with exaggerated style to get that casual magazine-model look.

"Eek," Laura Ann exclaimed, trying to imitate

375

Kabrina's sleek movements. "I feel like my body is being bent like a pretzel. How can you hold poses like this?"

"It just takes practice," Kabrina answered.

"Models make it look so easy in the magazines," Laura Ann declared. "And it's really so hard."

"It's all part of the business," Kabrina pulled out her own portfolio to show Laura Ann. It was filled with pictures and impressive tearsheets from all over the world. Kabrina had so many different looks that she was like a chameleon. In some pictures she was wholesome and kicky, in others sporty, in others fashionable and sophisticated, and in still others seductive and flirty.

"Now watch me," Kabrina instructed, and struck a series of poses and facial expressions. "You have to focus on the camera, just like it's a real person, so your personality comes across on the film."

Kabrina's words reminded Laura Ann of another photo session eons ago, and she involuntarily shivered and blocked the memory.

"The personality you project has a lot to do with the image you're trying to get across on film: seductive happy, sophisticated, serious, or a hundred other moods and nuances," Kabrina continued. "A lot of it i just practice."

Laura Ann practiced over and over again, faithfull searching through the fashion magazines, imitating, i her bathroom mirror, the expressions and poses of th models she found. She worked hard to decide whic angles were her best, which smile was the most natura and which look was the most seductive, or pouty . . . o whatever. She tried to make as many expressions a she could possibly think of.

Helena worked with Laura Ann at her apartment too. Together they practiced with Laura Ann's look changing it from sporty to glamourous to couture

376

Laura Ann thumbed through Helena's portfolio and was speechless at the many ways Helena could change the way she looked.

"In some pictures, you look like you're eighteen years old and straight off the farm," she said in amazement, "while in others, you look like you belong in a palace."

"It's all makeup," Helena said matter-of-factly.

Helena taught her how to shadow and highlight her face for black-and-white pictures. "Use shadowing to make things recede and highlighting to bring bones forward. See?" She demonstrated on Laura Ann's face by highlighting her cheekbones and shading them underneath to make them more prominent. Then she shaded the sides of Laura Ann's nose and highlighted the length of it with a narrow line to make it look thinner. "The camera only sees things in two dimensions, so we add the depth with shading and highlights."

Laura Ann marveled at the results. With a few deft strokes of makeup, she was transformed from a wholesome-looking teenager into a glamorous young woman.

"Amazing," she breathed in awe. "Absolutely amazing!"

"Well," Helena said after they had gone over makeup thoroughly, "I think you're ready to do some testing."

"Am I really?" Laura Ann exclaimed excitedly.

"I think so. In fact, I've already talked with Dakota and he said that he had Sunday afternoon free. How is Sunday for you?"

"I'm scheduled to work at the coffee shop," Laura Ann said thoughtfully, "but I think I can get Wendy to switch with me. Wendy!" she called into the other room. Wendy poked her head in the door. "Would it be possible for me to switch with you on Sunday so I could do some testing?"

"Sure," Wendy agreed, "on one condition: that you teach me how to apply makeup after Helena teaches you."

"It's a deal." She smiled happily, then turned to Helena. "We're on!"

"Okay," Helena said. "Now comes the hard part. I want you to put together four looks for the shooting on Sunday: a sporty casual look, a high fashion look, a glamorous evening look, and a bathing suit or leotard look. Use your fashion magazines for reference on how to put your outfits together."

Laura Ann's face dropped. "I can put together a sporty look and I have a terrific new bathing suit, but I don't have anything that's high fashion or evening," she mumbled, looking at the floor. "I'm a waitress. We wear a uniform, and when I'm not working, I just wear casual clothes."

"Let me see," Helena said thoughtfully. "Do you have any credit cards?"

Laura Ann shook her head. "Nope."

Helena hesitated a moment, formulating a plan in her mind. "Well, I do," she decided, slowly. "I'll tell you what. We'll go out and charge two outfits on one of my cards; you'll wear them for the shooting and then we'll return them afterward."

"You'd do that for me?" Laura Ann asked, wide-eyed. She couldn't believe how supportive Helena was.

"Sure. All the models do that for a shooting. It's no big deal. The question is, when can we go? Time is running out."

"I could go tomorrow evening," Laura Ann said.

"Tomorrow's okay for me too. Why don't I meet you at the center elevators in the Beverly Center at six-thirty?" Helena directed Laura Ann briskly.

They met at the appointed time, and Helena took Laura Ann on a whirlwind tour of the Beverly Center. She knew exactly which stores carried the kinds of clothes that Laura Ann needed, and in no time they had selected the appropriate outfits.

One ensemble began with a tweed pantsuit with a crop top in shades of gray flecked with black, teal, and fuchsia. Helena paired it with a thin turtleneck sweater, black opaque hose, and black high-heeled pumps. Finally she added a black, fuchsia, and teal print challis scarf on one shoulder.

"Wear your hair back from your face, either in a long braid or a chignon, with this outfit," she instructed Laura Ann. "This will be your couture look."

For Laura Ann's evening look, Helena pulled a black velvet long-sleeved backless cocktail dress that had a glitter-encrusted short tulle skirt.

"I have the perfect pair of earrings that you can borrow to wear with this dress," Helena said as the clerk wrapped the dress. "It's a good contrast to the pantsuit. It's short, so it will show off your legs. Wear black sheer hose and basic black evening pumps, and, oh, I have just the right little evening gloves to match it. *Voilà*—we're finished!"

The walked back to the red elevators in the center of the mall.

"I'll see you Sunday at Dakota's," Helena said, pressing the elevator button.

"I don't know how I can ever repay you and Kabrina for all your help. Laura Ann's eyes filled with tears at their kindness and she hugged Helena. "You'll never know how much all of this means to me."

She thought of Marcus and the "dues" she had paid to get to this point in her life. If she had only believed in herself sooner instead of looking to Marcus for support.

"Don't even think twice about it," Helena said, brushing aside the compliment. "You'd do the same thing for me."

"Oh, I would, Helena," Laura Ann agreed. "If there

is anything I can ever do for you or Kabrina, please let me know!"

"I will," Helena called over her shoulder as she stepped into the elevator.

During the next few days, Helena's relationship with Jaimie continued to unravel. He refused to let her have any time to herself, and he complained unendingly about her bookings. When she told him she was going to spend more time writing, he stormed out of the apartment, only to return minutes later to continue to browbeat her for wanting to use some of "his" time to pursue her new career. The constant conflict was beginning to take its toll on Helena, and every day brought a new blowup. There was no middle ground with him; his way was the only way, and sadly, she knew that her time with Jaimie was nearing an end.

As her relationship with Jaimie dwindled, her relationship with Nicky grew. She made daily calls to him, slowly bringing him out of his shell and developing a new relationship with him. She gently explained her love for him and why she had had to move to California; and she carefully avoided placing blame on anyone. Her heart soared each time she heard the sound of his little voice, and each day brought the promise that someday their now tenuous relationship would be firm and everlasting.

As for Kabrina, the rest of the week raced by. She was modeling almost nonstop. Accounts clamored to use her. It was good therapy, because it kept her mind off any lingering residue of depression over her breakup with Noel. She had been giving more and more thought to Laura Ann's words about Kabrina's father, and a desire to see him began to gnaw at her.

One cool, bright Sunday morning Laura Ann turned

Wendy's car onto South Main Street. Down the length of the street, the Santa Ana winds were blowing the last crisped leaves from the scraggly maples that lined the street. The trees stood as monuments to a long since defeated councilman's contribution to urban renewal. Laura Ann pulled into a space on the street behind Helena, just as the latter was stepping from her car. It was 10:00 A.M., the time that the three women had decided on for the shooting at Dakota DeForest's studio in downtown Los Angeles. As Laura Ann stepped from her car, she glanced up at the building and had an unsettling memory of Flash's studio. She quickly looked around, half expecting to see faces from the past lurking in the shade of the doorway. No ghosts appeared to haunt her, however, so she brushed off the feeling of apprehension and hurried to join Helena, who was waiting for her on the steps.

The studio was a converted office, and it resembled Flash's studio in that it was also whitewashed from floor to ceiling with the windows covered over. There was no bed, however; camera and lighting equipment was scattered throughout the room, and rolls of backdrop papers hung from the ceiling at the far end.

Dakota, a relaxed, slow-talking man, was in his mid-twenties, with a thatch of thick, unruly dark hair and a ready smile that lit up his whole face. He was born in a little town near Bismarck, North Dakota; hence his nickname. He and Laura Ann took an instant liking to each other. It was important that there be a rapport between photographer and model if the pictures were to turn out well.

Kabrina had talked to Angela, a friend who was a makeup artist, into volunteering her services in exchange for prints from the shooting. All in all a positive mood and a spirit of gaiety permeated the set. Angela was a petite young woman with quick, birdlike movements, and within an hour she had Laura Ann ready for her first shot.

381

Helena and Kabrina helped Laura Ann get ready, and when it was time to shoot they gave her suggestions; ultimately, however, it was the chemistry between Laura Ann and the camera. Dakota was gentle and patient, and he had the talent to wait for the perfect expression to evolve, instead of rushing the shot.

After a couple of hours, Helena and Kabrina excused themselves. They could see that Laura Ann and Dakota were working well together and there really was no need for them to stay. The hours flew by, and before Laura Ann knew it, it was late afternoon and her shooting was over.

"I should have the contacts ready for you to see on Wednesday," Dakota told her as he snapped his lens cover in place and switched off the umbrella lights, "if you want to come by."

"I'm so excited, I can't wait," she exclaimed.

"I know I got some great shots," Dakota said, equally enthusiastic. "You're going to be real happy with the contacts."

Laura Ann left the studio on winged feet. She started to drive home, but on a whim she changed her mind and pulled over to a telephone. She dialed Norris, so she could share her wonderful day with him, but he wasn't home. She left a happy message asking him to call her as soon as he picked up his messages. Then she jumped back in her car and drove to her apartment. Wendy was still working, so Laura Ann had no one to share the glorious events of the day with.

The next morning, Helena leaned over again and looked at the clock on her nightstand. The watery gray dawn seeped through the cracks in the vertical blinds enough to illuminate the clock's face. The hands pointed to 5:45 A.M., twenty-three minutes later than the last time she had looked. She rolled over on her back and gave up trying to sleep. She had finally

382

made her decision.

She was ending her relationship with Jaimie. Half of her was excited about the prospect of moving on to a new challenge in life. It was an opportunity to broaden her horizons and prove she could be successful without Jaimie's help. The other half longed for the comfort and the security of his wealth and status. Jaimie had always told her that the successful make their own rules in life. But as of late, Helena realized that the values instilled in her as a child had ultimately won out over Jaimie's pat philosophy.

It wasn't as if her decision would be a shock to him. There had been a tenseness between them for weeks as he had become increasingly jealous of her time. She knew he must sense her discomfort. And whether or not he sympathized with her reasons, she was beginning to feel like the proverbial bird in the golden cage. She could have anything she wanted and yet there was no future.

Time after time, she tried to explain to him how she felt, but it became clear that he wasn't listening. He merely repeated the same empty rhetoric: She had to wait until the time was right. She couldn't push fate. But time told her not to wait. Whenever Jaimie promised her that they would always be together, it sounded wonderful and romantic; but she couldn't help wondering when she'd be traded in for a younger mistress. If she waited too long, it would be too late for her to follow her own dreams.

As it was, each day was dedicated to entertaining Jaimie. Like clockwork, unless she had a booking, each day consisted of lunch, then Jaimie making his business calls with Helena looking on; then the two of them taking a nap and making love. And then it was time for Jaimie to go home to his wife.

She had to start thinking like a winner. And yet, still nagging in the corner of her heart, she had doubts. What if Jaimie was the one love of her life? What if she

383

was ending her one true love? No, this couldn't be the love she was looking for. It had to end.

"Book out. We're going to Oklahoma tomorrow for the rest of the week," Jaimie shouted as he breezed through her front door six hours later.

"But I have shows the rest of this week. I can't cancel them," she said, taken completely by surprise.

"You'll do what I say, and when I say it," he said angrily.

"But Jaimie, I'll lose my accounts," she protested in dismay, for a minute forgetting her decision. "You know how those fashion coordinators are: out of sight, out of mind."

"Bullshit. What's more important, me or your shows?" he argued vigorously. He was getting tired of her mutinies over the past weeks, and today he was going to nip it in the bud instead of spending the day discussing his decisions.

"You are, of course," she replied. His overbearing manner made her hesitate for a moment. "But I can't lose my accounts. I won't work."

"Good. Then you'll have more time for me. I told you before I'll take care of your expenses," he insisted, tossing her own ideas back at her. "Besides, then you can start writing, like you want. Forget about modeling!"

"Jaimie, we've gone over and over this before. You know I can't forget about modeling yet," she patiently explained.

"I don't understand why not," he said sulkily, refusing to understand.

"Because I'd have no independence. Furthermore, I don't want to depend on you for my and my son's financial well-being. I'd be at your beck and call twenty-four hours a day. My life literally would no longer be my own. And in truth, I think you'd even see

384

to it I'd never have time to write. You couldn't even tolerate competing with that, or with anything that takes my time!

"And," she said almost matter-of-factly, while we're at it, I want to talk to you about something."

"After you call the agency and book out," he repeated again. "You know you'll have a great time. We always do."

"Jaimie, I can't go." She took a deep breath for strength. "Anyway, I think we need a break from each other."

"Well, I suppose I could postpone it for a couple of days," he grumbled peevishly, ignoring the last part of her statement. He walked into the kitchen, leaving her to follow behind him.

"I'm not happy with our relationship," she said in a firm voice that even surprised her.

"It's always modeling, modeling, modeling," he repeated. "Is that coffee fresh?" He poured himself a cup of coffee. "I'm the last on your list. I always suck hind tit."

"There's no future to it. We should each go our own way," Helena continued, refusing to be baited by him.

"I'm your future!" Jaimie shouted, finally listening to what she was saying. He slammed the cup down so hard that the coffee spilled over its sides onto the counter. "How many times have I told you that? Make me happy and you'll be happy."

"I've tried—"

"You're making a big mistake if you don't believe that! Who else in this world is more on your side?" He spoke with intimidating belligerence, but inside he was fearful. There was a calm determination about her he'd never seen in her before.

"I know you are, but I've got to make my own way," she said, trying to keep calm. "The time is right for me to prepare for a career change to writing."

"I told you to," he exclaimed angrily, walking back

385

into the living room, leaving her to follow him again. It was an obvious psychological ploy to shake her from her stance. "But no, you have to take every two-bit modeling job that comes along. I can give you the luxury you need so you can stop modeling and get on with your writing. Any of your girlfriends would give their eyeteeth to be in your position."

"Sure," she said sarcastically.

"Don't kid yourself, Helena," he exploded and whirled to face her. "I thought I taught you to think logically and deal in reality."

"You did, and I *am* dealing in reality," Helena told him, refusing to be swayed by his rhetoric. "The reality is I have to be successful in my own right. And I want a relationship with a man I don't have to share with a wife."

"You don't share me," he declared, repeating the words that had always worked in the past. "You always come first. You're always with me whether I'm here or not. Just relax. Let the future happen. You can't push it."

"I've laid back long enough. It's time for me to make a move," she said, her voice rising and the blood pounding in her temples. "Before it's too late."

"You're stupid! I'm telling you, you're making a big, big mistake if you think you can push me into making a decision," he threatened her, suddenly realizing how serious the situation was. "I've told you before, I've worked too long and too hard to give my wife half of everything."

"Jaimie, I'm not trying to push you into anything," Helena told him almost sympathetically. She could see that he really didn't understand her motives. He thought this was just a power play. He didn't realize it was the end of their relationship.

"I refuse to give up the empire I've built!" he ranted on, still not listening, pacing back and forth in his agitation. He had to make Helena understand that he wouldn't be pushed into giving up everything in a messy divorce. "I won't start over, not for you, not for anyone!"

"I'm not asking you to." She paused and then added, "I've just finally realized, it's time to leave you."

"You've met someone else. That's it, isn't it?" he blurted out, grasping wildly at straws. The question hung unanswered between them.

Helena read the anguish and fear behind his angry face. She swallowed back tears. It tore at her to see this strong man she had loved and idolized crumble. She wanted to take him into her arms and promise him that everything would be all right, but she found the strength not to.

"No," she barely whispered. "No, Jaimie. There's no one else."

"I tell you," he responded desperately, "it's only a matter of time until we can really be together. Please—" he added almost under his breath, his voice cracking with emotion.

"I can't stay with you." She opened her eyes wide to keep the tears from spilling over her lashes. "I'm sorry, Jaimie. I have to do this for myself."

"But I love you," he insisted in disbelief. Their months together flashed before his eyes: their first meeting, the chase, the conquest . . . his growing love for her. He stared at her, stunned. This couldn't be happening, he thought, and all pretenses dropped from his demeanor.

"I know. I love you too," she breathed softly. She wished she could turn time back to yesterday, but the words had already been spoken. Now there was no turning back from her future.

"You'll be back," he said, and his voice caught on the last word. His eyes teared, but more with determination than sadness.

Without another word, he turned and walked out of the apartment. Helena watched through the window, her heart aching to call him back, but she forced herself not to.

"Dakota said the contacts would be ready by five-thirty," Laura Ann said excitedly over the phone to Kabrina.

"Then you've got to fight that traffic from downtown," Kabrina replied.

"Plus I've got to change," Laura Ann continued, mentally marking off the time. "But I can be at Prego's by seven-thirty. How does that sound?"

"Perfect," Kabrina responded. "We can have an early dinner and go over your contact sheets. I can hardly wait to see them! I'll bring my loop."

"What's a loop?"

"It's a small magnifying glass. That way we can look at your pictures in detail," Kabrina explained.

"Oh," Laura Ann said, "I understand. I can hardly wait, too! My first professional modeling pictures. See you!"

The clock on the Union Insurance Building on the corner of 13th and South Main read 5:20 as Laura Ann turned onto South Main Street. There was no available parking on the street, so she pulled Wendy's Honda into a small parking lot that was hidden in the shadows between two towering office buildings. Its sign advertised parking: $1.50/each 20 minutes, $8.00/all day.

"How long you gonna be, miss?" the Mexican parking attendant asked.

"Until five-forty-five at the latest," Laura Ann replied, grabbing her bag and jumping from the car.

"I close at six. If you're not here, your car will be locked up 'til tomorrow."

"I'll be back in time," she assured him over her shoulder.

There was a lightness in her walk, a confidence. She had worked hard this past month—during the day it

388

the coffee shop and at night and in her spare time—striving to put a modeling career together. It was a dream come true. Now, with the contact sheets she was about to pick up, she was beginning to feel like a real model. More than that, she believed in herself for perhaps the first time in her life. Maybe fairy tales did come true. She smiled to herself. She was so deep in her own thoughts that she almost collided with a young black man who was sauntering down the street.

"Excuse me!" she exclaimed, not giving him a second glance as she turned into Dakota's building.

The young man, however, gave the beautiful young woman a second glance—and a third one, too. In fact, he abruptly changed his course of direction and peered into the lobby of the building she had just entered, in time to see her disappear into the elevator. She looked different, radiant and healthy—not at all like the gaunt girl with the fear-ridden eyes he remembered—but it was Laura Ann just the same. He smiled to himself and leaned back in a doorway to wait.

At five-forty-five, Laura Ann emerged from the building as the late afternoon shadows melted into pools of twilight. A thick fog from the ocean had rolled over the beaches and crept silently inland. Wispy tendrils curled their way as far as downtown Los Angeles and muted the sounds of traffic moving through the canyons of the business district. Laura Ann shivered as the cool night air hit her face. She adjusted her shoulder bag to her other shoulder and clutched the manila envelope holding her contact sheets. The contacts were good—in fact, they were great—and she smiled to herself in anticipation of showing them to Kabrina. She sidestepped a bag lady who was slowly wheeling all her wordly possessions down the street in a supermarket shopping cart.

"You got any spare change, miss?" the ragged old lady asked hopefully, turning a grimy face up to Laura Ann.

389

She started to say "No," but the old woman's flat, worn gaze held hers. Instead, she stopped and dug through her purse until she found her wallet. She emptied all her change out and handed it to the old woman.

"Thank you, miss," the bag lady said, holding out a greasy, blackened palm. "I was once young and pretty, too," she cackled and wandered on, bobbing her head to herself.

Laura Ann looked after the retreating figure, then continued walking. She rounded the corner and started to cross an alley that bordered the back of the parking lot. Ahead of her, the lot was almost deserted and the waiting attendant paced back and forth, his back to Laura Ann and the alley.

A sharp noise behind her caused her to jump and whirl around. A crumpled Coors can, caught in an updraft of wind, toppled end over end down the dark alley and lodged in a doorway. She exhaled deeply with relief and turned back toward the parking lot.

As she started to turn, she thought she saw something moving in the gray shadows. Before she could identify the movement, an arm reached out and wrapped itself around her waist, jerking her back into the blackness of the alley. Simultaneously, another arm snaked around her throat, cutting off a scream before it could leave her lips. The manila envelope slipped unnoticed from her grasp and dropped to the pavement.

She fought violently, but the arms seemed to be everywhere, pinning her, crushing the air from her lungs. Lashing out with her fingers and nails, she tried to find somewhere to grab her attacker, but all she connected with was empty air. As she twisted, one of her heels broke off and fell next to the curb. Jerked backward by her attacker, she lost her footing and fell against him. Her struggles became more feeble, a bright spots popped and burned behind her eyes. H imprisoned her, and she finally gave herself up to the darkness. *Why?* was the final thought in her suffocating brain before she gave in to unconsciousness.

A short distance away, the Mexican attendant snapped and unsnapped his key box impatiently. Then he pulled out the last set of keys from the key box and pocketed them. He snapped the chain across the entrance to the lot. As he walked away, the moon rose over the one remaining car in the lot. The clock on its dashboard registered 6:12 P.M.

Laura Ann opened one eye a crack, and the bright light she saw through her lashes blinded her. Quickly closing her eye again, she swallowed, her throat raw and bruised. She inhaled sharply, the mere effort sending a spasm of pain through her chest. She lay there for several minutes, not moving, concentrating on relaxing her body from the pain and collecting her thoughts.

She opened both eyes, blinked, and looked around her. Nothing looked familiar, and she closed her eyes again, trying to retrace the events of the afternoon. She remembered leaving Dakota's studio with her contact sheets and noticing how dark it had gotten, the old bag lady as she passed, and the sound of the beer can tumbling about in the wind, but that was all. Between then and this moment was nothing. And where was she now? She was lying on a bed or sofa of some sort. She could feel the rough fibers of nubby fabric pressing against the skin on her arms and legs.

She took a mental account of her body without moving: feet, legs, torso, arms, hands. There didn't seem to be any damage. Nothing was broken, and she wasn't restrained in any way that she could tell.

The shock of lights had made her eyes water, and now a salty tear found its way to a corner of her eye and wound a path down the soft curve of her cheek.

391

"Ah, my 'little jewel,' I see you're finally awake," she heard a voice above her say. It was a smooth, quiet voice, but it conjured up a hundred ugly, loud memories. A shiver of fear shot through her as she realized it was a voice she had hoped never to hear again. It was the voice that called to her a thousand times from her worst nightmares. Slowly, she opened her eyes and looked directly into Marcus's pale yellow eyes. They glittered like marbles in the bright room. He stroked her forehead gently, and she started to sit up.

"Hold it," Marcus said, pushing her firmly back; his voice, edged in sugar, cut like a knife in the quiet room. "You've had quite a scare. Snake thought he was doing me a favor by grabbing you. He didn't know I had forgiven you for leaving me a long time ago. It wasn't easy, you know," he continued quietly. "I was hurt. I loved you. You hurt me!"

Her heart raced and her pulse throbbed in her bruised throat. "You didn't love me. You were only interested in money—" she croaked through her aching throat.

"Oh, you're so wrong, baby. I only wanted us to have enough to go away together ... so we could have a future, just the two of us. Just like we planned." He held out a glass of brandy. "Here, drink this. It'll relax you."

"I'm not thirsty."

"Drink it, I said." There was no sugar in his tone this time.

She wavered a moment but then took a gulp of the brandy. It had a bitter undertaste. "Marcus, you used me and you beat me. That's not love," she accused him boldly.

"Baby, baby, I hit you because I loved you. Can't you see that?" he whined, holding his hands up in a gesture of helpless submission. "You made me do it. It was all your fault, you know. I only did it for your own good when you were bad. You needed it. You know I still

392

love you and I forgive you."

Marcus continued, his voice pulling at her, entangling her in the past. "Who took care of you when you first got off that bus? Who covered for you when you murdered that man?"

"But I didn't murder anyone," she told him defiantly, her eyes blazing. "Norris said that no one died in that fire."

"We didn't know that then, honey. But I was still willing to cover for you, even if it meant the slammer . . . just to protect my baby," he went on soothingly, his voice caressing her with its poisoned words. "I'm the only one who really cares for you."

"It wasn't like that, Marcus," she insisted, trying to push his hands away and escape.

But he held her firmly against the couch, pinching her chin in between his fingers and forcing her to look at him. "Oh, but it was, baby," Marcus hissed between gritted teeth. He forced the glass between her lips and poured more brandy down her throat.

He twisted and turned the truth. With every word he uttered, her strength seemed to ebb. She was petrified, but she was determined to escape.

"I told Snake I'd kill him if he ever put another finger on you, baby," he whispered.

He refilled the glass and forced more brandy down her throat. She choked and tried to spit it out, but he just smiled and forced more into her mouth. She couldn't seem to get her mind clear. She knew she was in dangerous circumstances, but how was she going to get away from him this time?

"Let me go," she cried, and her voice echoed faintly in her head. Her arms and legs felt warm and rubbery and her head was spinning. He had definitely spiked the brandy.

"Don't worry, you can leave any time you want. I'm not going to hurt you," he commented, stroking her hair. "I just want you to feel good. I slipped a coupla

393

'ludes in your drink just to relax you. Just like old times."

"Oh, God, no," she exclaimed in despair.

His voice sounded disengaged from his body, and he seemed to be speaking to her through a long tunnel. She heard the sounds, but her head was filled with cotton and the words hit and bounded off without their meaning sinking in. Her body felt loose and disjointed. With the last of her ebbing strength, she pushed Marcus away and tried to run, but her legs collapsed and she fell to the floor in a heap. He was on her in a flash, jerking her back onto the couch by the collar of her jacket.

The hypnotic force of the quaaludes was overwhelming, pulling her back in time as if she had never left Marcus. Thoughts of modeling and the faces of her new friends—Norris, Wendy, Helena, and Kabrina—faded. Ony Marcus was there with her. She reached up and touched his cheek, as if to confirm that he wasn't a dream, then pulled her hand away.

"Hey, baby," he said, huskily. "I see the 'ludes are working. Feels so good, huh? Don't Marcus always take care of his investments?"

"Marcus," she slurred, "please, please let me go. I'll do anything—"

"I know you will, sugar," he said, grinning. "Snake! Get the fuck in here!"

Snake appeared at the door. "Yeah, Mr. Fent?"

"See," he said over his shoulder, "didn't I tell you? I can do anything I feel like with any bitch. Look at this one! You got everything set up like I told you?"

"Yeah," Snake answered, his eyes narrowing as he saw Laura Ann lying helplessly on the couch.

"Good." He leaned over and picked her up. She moaned and threw a limp hand over his shoulder. "Hold on, cunt, 'cuz you're gonna have the greatest high of your life." Marcus chuckled. "And so am I." He carried her into the next room and deposited her on

394

the bed.

No, no, her mind screamed, but she was helpless to control her limbs. They wobbled like a puppet's, and this time Marcus was pulling the strings.

"Marcus, Marcus," she begged him out loud. It was as if her mind and body were separate; she struggled to control her body, but it was impossible.

Marcus reached down and slowly unbuttoned her blouse and slipped it off. She moaned as he pressed his mouth against hers, searching hungrily for her tongue. Behind his back came the soft whir of a camera. Marcus unsnapped her skirt and tossed it on the floor. The camera moved in closer as he produced a knife from nowhere and slipped it under the strap of her bra and sliced slowly through the elastic band. Then he peeled it off her in one motion.

He's going to rape me, she thought, feeling like a dispassionate observer, watching from a distance but not really involved. Her body seemed to belong to someone else.

"Laura Ann, baby," he whispered. "I got one little favor for you to do. Then you can go for good. You'd help Marcus, wouldn't you?"

Her mind was now completely under the hypnotic trance of the drug. Gone was the fresh beginning she had established for herself and her dreams of a new career. Her mind was filled with one all-encompassing thought: Get the rape over with and get out. She nodded drunkenly.

They moved together in a dance of passion as ancient as time itself—his passion for revenge and her passion for survival—one mind, one desire, one body, both of them straining to complete the act. Behind them, the camera lens caught the twisting arms and legs . . . Marcus with his back always to the camera, Laura Ann always in full view. The film rolled on, capturing each movement, each gasp, and each shudder on its celluloid strips. Marcus's voice seemed to be everywhere, stroking and urging, haunting her like no nightmare ever could.

"C'mon, baby," he whispered, "This is your big chance. Go with it. Show me what you can do. That's it, feel me! Feel me." He popped an amyl nitrate under her nose and at the same time shoved his hard cock deep inside her. "Sniff it!" he commanded, pushing her head down to the amy.

She obediently inhaled the popper deeply, the strong odor instantly exploding in her brain in a profusion of fireworks; then she felt herself tumbling over and over into blackness. She felt that familiar sensation building inside of her, her muscles straining, tightening. Her breath started to come in gasps. Her body was hot and flushed and she was deaf to Marcus's sugary words. All she could hear was the loud throb of her own heartbeat in her ears as her whole body vibrated from the drug. The blood rushed to her brain, bringing long waves of heat washing over and over her. Her body strained upward against Marcus, and she shook involuntarily.

.Abruptly, a blow to her abdomen hurled her flat against the bed, knocking the breath from her lungs. She felt a searing in her stomach and she gasped, trying to force air into her empty lungs. Instead of diminishing, the pressure in her abdomen grew. The searing sensation in her stomach changed from hot, to white-hot, to numbness, and she felt no pain.

The force of the blow swept away the thick film of drugs from her brain, and her eyes flew open. She stared into the icy eyes above her. They were dilated and held no lust, no passion. With one hand, Marcus held her down on the bed, the other hand pressed against her stomach.

"No one ever leaves me, cunt," he stated calmly "Ever!" To emphasize the word, he jerked his fist upward.

Dazed, Laura Ann looked dumbly at his arm. His muscles bulged and his veins stood out as he strained

396

each knuckle blanched tight and white, his fist clenched around the handle of something that was against her naked abdomen.

She heard a ripping sound as Marcus's fist moved slowly upward, leaving a ragged, bloody gash in its wake. Wet, pink entrails squeezed through the ugly rip and slid onto the dingy, bloody sheets. Her hands fluttered impotently down to her stomach trying to stop their flow. Instantly, as the realization of what had happened hit her, her conscious mind mercifully snapped into shock.

There was a gasp behind them and the camera fell to the floor with a loud crash. It lay there, its motor still cranking the film, capturing the floor of the room for posterity.

"Pick it up, God damn it!" Marcus screamed, his eyes never leaving Laura Ann's face. "Keep it on her! You're missing the whole snuff scene!"

Snake, gagging loudly, reached down and picked up the camera. Marcus hadn't told him about this, but nevertheless, he aimed it at Laura Ann's face. Even Snake couldn't take the bloody scene. He turned his head and threw up.

The room swirled around her and faded, and her mind slipped back to a time long past. It was night, and a thunderstorm had rolled across the flat farmlands of Iowa. Ribbons of lightning sliced through the blackness, illuminating the bleak landscape. A six-year-old Laura Ann awoke from her nightmare with a scream. "Daddy!" she cried in terror to the man above her, and the adult Laura Ann gave up her dreams and her life.

It was 9:00 P.M. at Prego's in Beverly Hills and the trendy restaurant was packed. The fragrance of fresh baking pizza wafted from wood ovens and permeated the restaurant, commingling with the smell of cigarettes and exotic perfume. Wealthy patrons were crammed in

397

the small bar area.

Kabrina checked her watch for the fifteenth time in twenty minutes.

The man sitting next to her at the bar checked her out and tried to start a conversation for the third time. "My nutritionist tells me that the yeast in white wine inhibits sexual drive, so I've switched to straight vodka," he said to her with a knowledgeable leer. "What about you?"

"Please," Kabrina said, "give me a break!"

She stood up abruptly and marched through the crowd to the pay telephone upstairs. She dialed Laura Ann's number, and Wendy answered.

"Hi, Wendy, this is Kabrina Hunter. Is Laura Ann there?"

"Hi, Kabrina," Wendy answered. "I haven't seen her since this morning."

"She was supposed to meet me for dinner at seven-thirty but she hasn't shown up," Kabrina explained, starting to be concerned. "If you hear from her, would you tell her I waited at Prego's for an hour and a half? Ask her to call me at home."

"Sure," Wendy said in a worried tone of voice. "I can't imagine where she is. It's not like her."

"I know it isn't. Thanks, Wendy," Kabrina responded. "Bye."

She walked through the restaurant and out the door to the valet. As she handed her ticket to him, she heard a voice behind her.

"I live right around the corner. I don't suppose you'd like to stop by for a little drink?"

Kabrina looked over her shoulder. It was the player from the bar.

"You're right, I wouldn't!" she said, giving him a long, withering look. She quickly slid into her Porsche and pulled out into the traffic.

Waiting for Laura Ann had left Kabrina depressed. She still hadn't adjusted completely to being alone afte

398

Noel. It wasn't that she missed him; it was that she missed the companionship and the closeness of another person. He was someone to go home to instead of an empty apartment, someone to tell the day's events to. She had once enjoyed being alone. Then she had met Noel and had opened herself up and trusted him. She had made him privy to her innermost thoughts and feelings. That was something she had not allowed herself to do for years—not since the break with her father.

Whenever she was alone now, she thought about her father. She wondered where he was. Once, several months after she moved to New York, he had left a message with her agent, asking her to call. It had surprised her. She didn't think he even knew what city she was in. She was shooting in Europe at the time, and when she returned, her pride kept her from returning the call. She supposed he was still somewhere in Los Angeles. She wondered if he was still patrolling a beat. Maybe he's working that big street in the sky, she thought sarcastically, but the thought put a lump in her throat.

On impulse, she maneuvered through the traffic and pulled up to a telephone booth next to the 76 Union Station on Little Santa Monica Boulevard. She thumbed through the phone directory. There it was, N. E. Hunter. She exhaled with relief. Then, drawn on, Kabrina dialed the number. The phone rang and rang and the answering machine clicked on. Kabrina wasn't sure if she should leave a message or hang up. Hesitating for a moment, she decided to break the connection and quietly dropped the receiver on the hook.

Later that night a figure lounged in a doorway. He could have been mistaken for any other shadow except for the constant staccato of sniffs from his cocaine-congested nose. The skin under his nostrils was irritated and peeled back to reveal an angry reddish brown color.

Snake had been casing the Lucky Liquor Locker for almost three-quarters of an hour. In that time, he'd seen five people enter and leave the store: three workmen, a chunky Mexican broad, and a street rat with a bottle of Thunderbird. As the bum reached the sidewalk in front of the store, his bottle slipped from his fuzzy fingers and splattered on the sidewalk. The old man dropped to his knees and picked through the broken pieces of bottle in a vain effort to save any of the wine. He pressed his palms to the ground, soaking his fingers with wine and slurping at them noisily. When he had finished he shuffled on, muttering to himself. From his vantage point, Snake giggled nervously at the bum's predicament.

After the old man tottered on, Snake walked nonchalantly to the entrance of the liquor store. His eyes darting everywhere but focusing nowhere, he was ever ready to turn and flee if anything seemed wrong. But the way was safe. As he entered the store, he pulled a Beretta from the pocket of his windbreaker.

"Yo," he said to the clerk, motioning with the gun. "Gimme yer money!"

The clerk made a furtive movement as if to pull something from beneath the counter.

"Asshole!" Snake screeched. "I said gimme the fuckin' money and keep yer fuckin' hands on the register where I can see 'em." He jiggled the gun in his hand, nervously chicken-stepping from one foot to the other.

"Okay, sure," the clerk said, quickly scooping up the bills from the cash register and handing them to Snake.

"Get down on the floor, now," Snake hissed, and the clerk dropped to the floor.

Snake stuffed the money in his windbreaker, his nose running freely now as he wiped it along the length of his jacket.

"You make a peep in the next ten minutes and I'll blow your fuckin' head off," he threatened.

Snake bolted from the store at a dead run. His second stride propelled him directly into the puddle of wine left by the wino. His foot slid on the broken glass and flew out from under him. He scrambled, trying to catch himself, and instead fell headfirst onto the pavement. The wad of paper dollars escaped from his jacket and fluttered above his prone body. The gun flew from his hand and spun along the sidewalk, landing in the gutter. He lay there for a few moments, stunned. Then he slowly pulled himself to his hands and knees.

"Hold it right there, punk," a voice said behind him, and a hand caught the back of his collar and dragged him to his feet.

Snake looked over his shoulder. To his horror, it was the two cops who walked the neighborhood beat.

"Well, well, well. Look who it is, Tom," the one holding him said. "Our old buddy Snake."

"Yeah," his partner said. "And he's in his usual position: on his belly."

At that instant, the liquor-store clerk ran from the store. "He robbed me! He robbed me!" he cried.

"Sounds like you've had a busy day, lizard-breath," the first cop said, shaking Snake by his collar. "Tom, you wanna get a statement while I read this scumbag his rights?"

Chapter Fifteen

When Laura Ann failed to return that night and hadn't shown up by the following morning, Wendy was more than a little worried. By noon, she was beside herself. She called all the hospitals in the area and checked with the police for traffic accidents, but found no sign of Laura Ann. Finally, on the edge of panic, she called Norris. He offered to fill out a missing-person report and poke around the precinct to see what strings he could pull to get some action on the report.

Norris had been retired for several years, and yet when he walked through the doors, it was as if he had been there only a shift ago. The time-streaked walls were still a dirty beige. The dusty fluorescent tube lights still hummed overhead, one or two flickering occasionally, and the air was still tinged with the stale smell of sweat and cigarettes. There was a strong sense of people on the edge.

Laura Ann was like a daughter to him, and he anxiously scribbled out a missing-person report. Then he poured himself a cup of coffee and restlessly drifted through the precinct greeting old friends. Out of habit, he found himself in the roll call room as the 3 P.M. shift was getting briefed. He slouched against the doorway, only half listening to the sergeant and soaking up the memories.

"A local dopehead made a run at the Figueroa Street Liquor Locker last night. The perp tripped on his own feet as he was leaving the scene." As the sergeant continued, a round of snickers circled the room. "Tom and Nick caught him and he came up ranting and raving about some broad he'd seen killed. He even told us they'd left her in a dumpster down in Compton.

"Well," the sergeant continued, "we contacted the Compton police and sure enough they found a female stiff in a dumpster. The coke-poke dropped a name for a walkout, and now we got an APB out on one Marcus Fent, small-time pimp."

At the name Fent, Norris jerked to attention. "Did you get a name on the dead girl?" Norris interrupted.

The sergeant looked over the heads at Norris. "Look who it is: the Hunter. You slummin', Norris?"

Norris shrugged and grinned.

"No, no name yet. Heard there was a phone number in a pocket, but it's still being run down. So far, she's just another Jane Doe, down at the city morgue."

An alarm sounded in Norris's head and he skipped the rest of the briefing. He turned and limped quickly out of the precinct and back to his car, filled with dread.

Kabrina stopped at a pay phone and picked up her phone messages from her answering machine. Today there was an unusual message: Detective Frank Hollis had called and left his number, saying it was important to get in touch with him. Curious, she dialed the number immediately.

"Detective Hollis," a deep, rough voice answered.

"This is Kabrina Hunter. You left a message for me."

"Yes, Ms. Hunter. Thanks for calling me back. Do you know a girl, say eighteen to twenty-three, about five foot eight, a hundred and twenty pounds, blond, blue eyes?"

"Detective Hollis, I'm a model and that description fits half the models in Los Angeles," Kabrina said flippantly. "Why?"

"Well, this one's posing in the city morgue," Detective Hollis shot back at her. "We found her in a dumpster. She had no ID, but your name and phone number, along with seven-thirty P.M., were written on a scrap of paper found in her pocket."

Kabrina's stomach turned over and she swallowed hard. "Does she have real long, blond hair?" she questioned, wanting to block out his reply.

"Yeah, below her shoulders."

"Oh, my God!" Kabrina moaned. "It sounds like Laura Ann!"

"Ms. Hunter," Detective Hollis pressed on, "we'd like you to come down here and see if you can positively identify the body."

"I'll be right down. What's the address?"

"The municipal building on First and Hill. Go down to the basement. There are signs to direct you. I'll be waiting."

Kabrina pushed open the door of the telephone booth with shaking hands. Even the warm California sunshine couldn't warm the cold feeling that engulfed her.

She didn't remember the drive to the municipal building. Only memories of Laura Ann and Helena and herself played before her eyes, especially their first meeting and the runway incident. Laura Ann's insecurities and shyness had been replaced with confidence the more Kabrina and Helena had worked with her. Laura Ann had just begun to discover herself and her dreams.

"Please, Lord," she prayed silently, "don't let it be true."

Kabrina parked the car and hurried up the wide, flat stairs. The government offices were closed for the day, so the lobby was empty. Her footsteps echoed on the marble floors as she made her way down the escalator to the lower level. "City Morgue," the sign pointed with an arrow.

The dim hallway was deserted, with sterile green walls that seemed confining, almost stifling to Kabrina. She followed the arrows that wound around the mazelike hallways. It was eerie. There were no sounds except for the occasional drumming beat of a typewriter that emanated from behind closed doors on either side. Kabrina shivered, longing for the open sunlight. Only the fear of what she would find in the morgue moved her forward. Abruptly, a door opened and a tall, beefy man in a rumpled tan suit appeared. Kabrina jumped with surprise.

"I thought I heard footsteps," he said, peering sharply at her, giving her the once-over with a practiced eye.

"You startled me! I'm looking for the city morgue." Kabrina marveled that her voice projected a calm she didn't feel.

"You got it. Are you Ms. Hunter, by any chance?" he asked, holding out his hand.

"Yes, I am," she replied, shaking his hand. "And are you Detective Hollis?"

"Yeah, Frank Hollis." He held the door open for her to enter. "Come on in."

In the large, windowless room cold overhead lights lit every corner and blanched out all warmth. Along two walls were floor-to-ceiling stainless steel cabinets, and the thick smell of death lay in the air.

They look like giant filing cabinets, Kabrina thought absently to herself, staring at the cold metal cabinets where dead bodies were filed.

"Like I said on the phone," Detective Hollis said, "this woman had no identification on her, only your phone number."

"Where was she found?" She glanced nervously around the room, wanting to look anywhere but at those huge filing cabinets.

"In a dumpster in Compton," he explained, leaning casually against one of the cabinets. He was chewing peppermint gum and Kabrina could smell its sweet, sickening odor when he spoke. "Someone had killed her and then dumped her there."

"H-how was she killed?" Her voice began to shake.

"She was knifed. Some sicko ripped her from her abdomen to her breastbone. It ain't pretty, but we gotta get a positive ID on her," he explained, unemotionally. "It's the only way we'll have a shot at catching the murderer. You understand?"

Kabrina shuddered and stood her ground. "Okay." She nodded.

Visions of Roberto came to her mind. She remembered her last minutes with him. He had been lucid in the end, whispering quietly, his chest moving faintly up and down with the last efforts of breathing. And then he was gone. She'd had to deal with his death, and now another friend might be dead, too.

Detective Hollis pulled the handle on one of the cabinet drawers and it slid open quietly on well-oiled bearings, revealing a sheet-covered form.

How odd, the sheet's green. In the movies, the sheet is always white, Kabrina mused absentmindedly.

He lifted back the sheet to reveal the body beneath it.

Laura Ann lay on the table in such a peaceful repose that for an instant, Kabrina wanted to shake her awake. Her skin was as smooth and translucent as marble, and her long golden hair swirled around her face and shoulders. A look of peace was on her face. Kabrina, without thinking, touched a smooth cheek. It was as cold as the marble it resembled.

"Do you know her?" Detective Hollis asked.

Kabrina nodded, bursting into tears. "It's Laura Ann Gilmore," she sobbed hysterically. "Oh God, oh God! Why?" Her knees buckled and the floor raced up to catch her as she started to slide downward.

Detective Hollis pulled her against his huge shoulder

and clumsily patted her back. "I'm sorry, Ms. Hunter. C'mon," he said gently. "Let's sit you down and get you a glass of water."

He helped Kabrina into the reception room and sat her down on a chair.

She slumped in the chair, sobbing. "Why?" Kabrina cried, over and over. "Why would anyone hurt Laura Ann? She was so sweet. She would never hurt a soul!"

"We don't know," Detective Hollis said as he poured a glass of water from the water cooler and handed it to her. "We were hoping you could tell us."

Kabrina was unable to answer, but she shook her head, sobbing.

Norris opened the back entrance to the morgue. Here was another place that never changed. The smell of alcohol and death clutched at him, bringing back familiar memories. The room was empty, but one of the drawers was open and the body sheet pulled back from the figure on the table. Curious, Norris walked over and looked down.

His heart leaped and a cold shock hit him from his body to his fingertips. He stood looking down for several minutes at Laura Ann's still, young face. Memory after memory hit him. He remembered the first time he'd seen her, and her show of bravado; the pain and terror of Marcus's secret hold on her; and finally her blossoming strength and determination as she'd carved out a new life for herself. They were such heavy burdens for the shoulders of one so young, and now just at the peak of her life she was gone.

Filled with overwhelming grief, Norris took her still hand. "You depended on me and I've failed you, too," he said quietly, his voice breaking with emotion. "I promised . . . I promised you that everything would be fine and you believed me. Forgive me, Laura Ann."

He slumped down on a nearby chair and rested his head on the cold metal table. As he struggled to control his emotions, he gradually became aware of the sound of crying coming from the next room. Curious, he raised his head. A woman was crying and he could hear the murmur of a man's voice as he tried to comfort her.

He crossed the room and opened the door to the next office. A chicly dressed young black woman sat huddled in a straight-backed chair in the corner. A man stood over her, awkwardly patting her shoulder. Even in her sorrow, there was a familiar grace about her. At the sound of the door opening, the man looked up.

"Can I help you?" Detective Hollis said.

"I'm Norris Hunter, LAPD retired, and I've come by to identify the Jane Doe you've got in there."

At the sound of his voice, Kabrina looked up through tear-blinded eyes. "Daddy?"

"Lord, Kabrina," he exclaimed in amazement.

It had been seven years since he'd seen his daughter, yet it was like only yesterday. The wall between them fell away with the moment, and he felt the pain of Laura Ann's death and the joy of his reunion with his only child at the same time.

In three strides, he was across the room and had picked her up before she could rise from her chair. He folded his arms around her and rocked her like a baby.

"Oh, Daddy," she sobbed and threw her arms around his neck. "My girlfriend was found murdered. She was so young. I don't understand."

"I know, Kabrina. I know all about Laura Ann," he said gently.

"You knew Laura Ann?" she asked in surprise, and then suddenly she realized what he meant by the way he said it. "*You* were the 'older man' that she said helped her."

"Yes," Norris admitted sadly. "I tried to help her. But I guess I didn't succeed."

"But you did," Kabrina exclaimed, wiping away her tears. "She always said she had a guardian angel watching over her! It was you! I can't believe it, Dad.

You were the reason she began believing in herself. She told me!"

"I loved her like another daughter, Kabrina," he said quietly.

"And she was my friend," she said, burying her head in his shoulder. "She was my friend, Daddy."

"I know, baby," he answered, stroking her head. "Detective Hollis," Norris said, his police demeanor returning. "Give me a few minutes with my daughter. Then I think I can put this case together for you, complete with the murderer—one Marcus Fent."

The detective nodded. "I've got some papers to fill out down the hall. I'll be back in about fifteen minutes."

"I appreciate that," Norris replied.

He wondered how it was possible to be so happy and so sad at the same time. It had taken the death of one child he loved to bring back the other.

"What are you doing in Los Angeles?" he asked Kabrina, still holding her tightly, as if he were afraid she might disappear.

Kabrina briefly explained to him and then looked at him in confusion. "But how do you happen to know Laura Ann?"

When Norris explained, Kabrina was shocked. "Helena and I had no inkling of her past life, none whatsoever," she exclaimed. "We just assumed that she had been working as a waitress all this time."

"She was a good girl, Kabrina," Norris reassured her. "She just got trapped and couldn't get out by herself. There was something about her," he went on, "that reminded me of you. Maybe helping her was my way of making up for failing you."

"Daddy, you never failed me! I know that now. You were only trying to protect me, based on what your experiences were. Laura Ann and Helena helped me to see that!"

At the mention of Helena's name, Kabrina remembered her booking. "Oh, no," she cried shakily, drying her eyes and looking at her watch. "I forgot, I have a fashion show to do!"

"You can't do a fashion show in your condition," he said. She was shaking and her eyes were swollen.

"I have to," she said, trying to pull her emotions together. "It's too late for them to replace me."

As if this alone were not enough to bear, she suddenly thought of Helena again. "How can I ever tell Helena?" she said quietly. "The three of us were the best of friends."

"I can't answer that, baby," he replied. "When the time comes, the right words will come."

"I have to leave now," she said, although she didn't want to. She wished she could stay in the protection of his arms forever, but she knew she couldn't. "I'll be home tonight, Dad," she smiled, hugging him through her tears.

From his usual spot, at the bar across the street, Marcus had an unobstructed view of the bus depot. It was time for a fresh fish and he was ready to throw out the hook. Having learned the virtue of patience, he was willing to stake out the bus terminal entrance for as long as it took to pick just the right girl. He had given Snake orders to show up for the purse scam in case he spotted the right prey, but Snake hadn't shown up for their game.

"Little asshole," Marcus said under his breath as he belted down the last of his Jack Daniels. "Wait'll I get ahold of him. I'll teach him to follow orders."

A crowd of people spilled out of the terminal's revolving doors, and his eyes narrowed as he singled out the shape of a young girl from the group. She had a suitcase in each hand and struggled to lift them. There was a fresh fish all right.

"Marcus Fent?" a voice above him said.

Marcus was so intent on the young girl that he had neglected to see the two men enter the bar and walk over to his table.

"Yeah, what's it to you," he sneered arrogantly, his eyes still following the girl across the street.

"Detective Hollis, LAPD," the taller of the two responded. "You're under arrest for the murder of Laura Ann Gilmore."

Marcus sprang with the grace of a panther. In one movement, he backhanded the other officer, knocked him to the floor, and leaped over him. In a step, he was at the door. He crouched, pulled a small handgun from the waist of his pants, and fired wildly at the two detectives. "Fuck you!" Marcus screamed, whirling around and running for the street.

Detective Hollis threw himself to the floor, tipping over a table for cover. "Hold it, Fent!" he shouted, returning the fire.

Hollis's bullet struck Marcus in the back and its momentum propelled him forward. He staggered and fell in the middle of the street, but crawled onward.

The young girl, frozen by the sound of gunfire, watched in horror as Marcus slowly inched himself toward her. As he reached her he collapsed, stretching his hand out to clutch her foot. The girl screamed in revulsion and kicked his hand away.

Hollis ran across the street and rolled Marcus over. Pink foam frothed from his lips.

"I told that bitch, Laura Ann, that I'd get her," Marcus choked. "And I did." Bright red blood poured from his lips as his lungs collapsed.

Hollis stood up. "Call the garbage collector and tell him to pick up this piece of shit," he called to his partner.

411

Epilogue

Helena returned to her apartment in Beverly Hills. After the show, at the Beverly Hilton Hotel where Kabrina had told her the shocking news of Laura Ann's death, she and Kabrina had talked at length. Kabrina had told her Laura Ann's whole story, and Helena had been stunned by the news.

She dropped her model's bags on the floor near the door and lay down on the couch to digest the tragedy she had learned of today, and to review the events of the past month.

So much had happened in the month since she had met Laura Ann. Her whole life had turned upside down. Not only had she made and lost a dear friend, but she had lost her son and was only now slowly reestablishing her relationship with him. She had ended her love affair with Jaimie and was on the threshold of embarking on a new life. Her modeling career had never been better, her writing was a new and exciting challenge, and perhaps, she mused, thinking of Richard's business card, she might try her hand again with a new romance. As it did for Kabrina, the heartbreaking end to Laura Ann's life signaled a new beginning for Helena, too.

The idea for a story slowly came to her. She turned it over and over in her mind, and it grew and blossomed.

Finally, she roused herself from the couch and sat down at her typewriter.

SATIN SMILES, SILKEN LIES
by Helena Sinclair

"A brown haze hung over the promised land . . ."